T0043953

MALARKOI

Books by Alex Pheby

CITIES OF THE WEFT
Mordew
Malarkoi

Playthings
Lucia

MALARKOI

ALEX PHEBY

TOR

TOR PUBLISHING GROUP
NEW YORK

MALARKOI

Copyright © 2022 by Alex Pheby

A Tor Book
Published by Tom Doherty Associates / Tor Publishing Group
120 Broadway
New York, NY 10271

www.tor-forge.com

Tor® is a registered trademark of Macmillan Publishing Group, LLC.

The Library of Congress has cataloged the hardcover edition as follows:

Names: Pheby, Alex, author.
Title: Malarkoi / Alex Pheby.
Description: First U.S. edition. | New York : Tor, 2023. |
    Series: Cities of the weft ; 2
Identifiers: LCCN 2023033309 (print) | LCCN 2023033310 (ebook) |
    ISBN 9781250817266 (hardcover) | ISBN 9781250817273 (ebook)
Subjects: LCGFT: Fantasy fiction. | Novels.
Classification: LCC PR6116.H43 M35 2023 (print) |
    LCC PR6116.H43 (ebook) | DDC 823/.92—dc23/eng/20230720
LC record available at https://lccn.loc.gov/2023033309
LC ebook record available at https://lccn.loc.gov/2023033310

ISBN 978-1-250-81728-0 (trade paperback)

Our books may be purchased in bulk for promotional, educational, or business use. Please contact your local bookseller or the Macmillan Corporate and Premium Sales Department at 1-800-221-7945, extension 5442, or by email at MacmillanSpecial Markets@macmillan.com.

First published in Great Britain by Galley Beggar Press

First Tor Paperback Edition: 2024

Printed in the United States of America

0 9 8 7 6 5 4 3 2 1

For Naxy and Siz

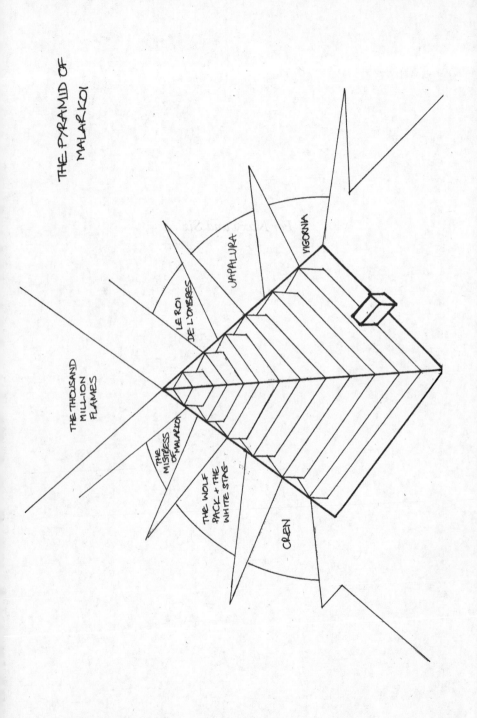

THE PYRAMID OF MALARKOI

THE THOUSAND MILLION FLAMES

LE ROI DE L'OMBRES

JAPALURA

VIGORNIA

THE MISTRESS OF MALARKOI

THE WOLF PACK + THE WHITE STAG

CREN

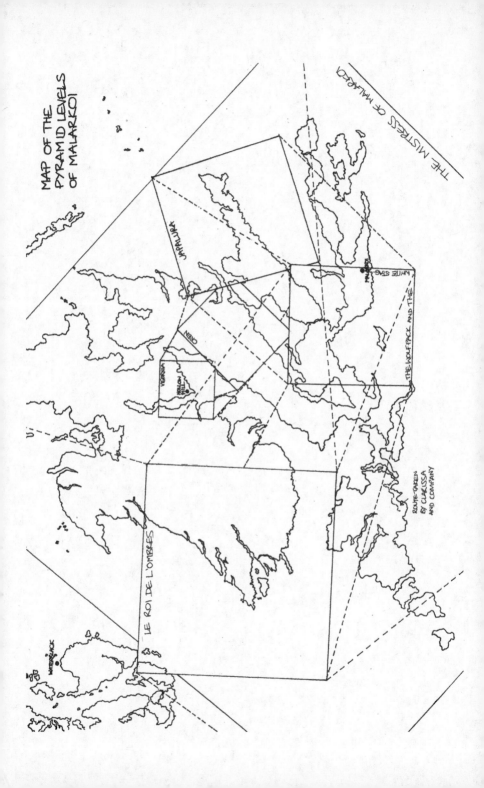

MAP OF THE
PYRAMID LEVELS
OF MALARKOI

THE MISTRESS OF MALARKOI

JAPALURA

OBEN

VIRGINIA
HOLLOW HILL

LE ROI DE L'OMBRES

WATERBLACK

MALARKOI

THE WHITE STAG

THE WOLF PACK AND THE

ROUTE TAKEN
BY CLARISSA
AND COMPANY

THE EVENTS OF THE PREVIOUS VOLUME, IN SUMMARY

Nathan fishes for flukes in the Living Mud with the Spark, an unpredictable and uncontrollable power he has inherited from his father.

The Spark Itches if Nathan doesn't Scratch it.

One day he makes a limb-baby and sells it to a tanner.

Nathan takes the money to his poor mother and dying father.

The money is fake.

His mother orders Nathan to go to the Master for work.

The Fetch takes Nathan and some other boys up the Glass Road to the Master.

One of the boys is Gam Halliday.

Gam tries to recruit Nathan into his criminal gang.

Nathan refuses.

Gam goads Nathan into Scratching the Spark Itch by teasing him.

The Fetch beats another boy to death for the disturbance Nathan and Gam make.

The remaining boys are delivered to the Master.

Gam is rejected at the gate and returns home.

In the Underneath, Nathan saves a boy from falling to his death.

The boy is revealed to be a girl – Prissy – and Nathan feels an immediate sympathy with her.

The children are washed by a team of laundresses.

Bellows, the Master's factotum, examines the boys, discarding some, including Prissy, and takes the others to see the Master.

The Master hires some of the boys for unspecified work, but declines to hire Nathan.

9

The Master can sense Nathan's power.

He warns him against Sparking and sends him back to the slums.

At home, Nathan's father is dying of the lungworm.

Nathan wants to Scratch the Spark Itch, but his father forbids it.

Nathan promises to get medicine, but he has no money.

In the slums, Nathan Scratches the Spark Itch, angrily, to kill a fluke.

The fluke evolves into a rat, which bites Nathan's hand. From then on, Scratching the Itch burns the wound and makes Nathan's arm increasingly immaterial.

Nathan goes into the Merchant City, hoping to steal money for medicine.

He steals a wealthy old woman's coin purse, but is caught by bystanders.

Gam rescues him before he can be punished and takes him into the sewers.

The two boys go to Gam's hideout, the clubhouse, an abandoned subterranean gentlemen's club.

Prissy and Joes, the other members of Gam's gang, are there.

Nathan, having fallen for Prissy, joins the gang.

The gang go back to the Merchant City on a job to steal money from a haberdasher.

Nathan panics when Prissy seems to be in danger and almost kills the haberdasher with the Spark.

With the money they have stolen, the gang go to see the gangmaster, Mr Padge, to buy the medicine for Nathan's father.

Mr Padge gives Nathan the medicine, but refuses to take his money, establishing a debt on Nathan's part.

Nathan returns to the slums. His mother is entertaining a gentleman caller with a fawn-coloured birthmark.

Nathan gives his father the medicine, but it's clear that it won't be enough.

Nathan agrees to get more.

Unable to bear being at home, Nathan returns to the clubhouse.

The pain of the rat bite gets worse, as does his Itch.

At night the clubhouse is full of ghosts who seem to recognise him.

The next day, Gam takes Nathan to steal bacon from a warehouse.

From there they go to the Temple of the Athanasians, a brothel where Prissy's sister works.

Prissy will be sold to the brothel unless she can compensate her sister for the lost income.

Nathan agrees to a risky criminal job for Mr Padge in order to get the money for medicine and Prissy's buyout.

Gam, Prissy and Nathan go to burgle a palace by entering through the sewers.

Nathan uses his Spark to open a safe and retrieve the document Mr Padge hired them to steal.

On the way out, Gam pushes Prissy into a crowded room and indicates that Nathan should rescue her by using the Spark.

In the room are various nobles, the chief of whom is the man with the fawn-coloured birthmark.

Hiding his surprise and horror, the man allows the children to leave before Nathan can kill everyone with the Spark, and gives him a gold coin.

Back at the clubhouse, Prissy questions Gam's actions, but he won't be drawn.

The gang take the document to Mr Padge, who gives them another job – to steal a locket from a merchant's house.

Prissy uses her share of the money to pay off her indenture.

Scoping out the next job, with time to kill, the children visit the zoo and give buns to the alifonjers, Prissy's favourite animals.

The gang decide to burgle the merchant's house by going in from the roof.

They bribe the Fetch to take them up the Glass Road, slipping out near the roof of the merchant house.

Gam agrees to lower Joes, Nathan and Prissy down to the roof by rope.

Nathan, then Prissy, successfully make the rooftop, but Joes, seemingly betrayed by Gam, falls and dies.

Nathan tries to resurrect Joes using the Spark, but it doesn't work.

The remaining children have no option but to complete the burglary, but inside they are interrupted by the magical dogs Sirius and Anaximander.

Anaximander, who can talk, threatens the children with death, and Sirius eats the faces from Joes, whose one body has become two bodies.

Nathan and Prissy return to the roof and attempt to descend to ground level by rope.

They are left dangling above a fatal drop: the rope is too short.

Having received new instructions from the Master via Sirius's magical organ, Anaximander rescues the children.

The dogs accompany the children away from the merchant house, having secured the locket Padge hired them to steal.

The party go to find Gam, hoping for answers regarding the death of Joes.

They find Gam in a gin-house, but he is unwilling to talk.

The gin-house patrons attempt to steal Anaximander – he disembowels one of them and they give up.

The gin-wife objects to the mess Anaximander has made, and the dog agrees to provide a service for her.

Nathan, Prissy and Sirius go to the slums.

Nathan has no medicine for his father, who has become even more seriously ill.

Nathan's mother begs Nathan to use the Spark to purge the lungworms.

Nathan agrees, revelling in his disobedience.

The procedure starts promisingly, until Nathan's father rises up and prevents it.

Nathan's mother urges Nathan to defy his father and cure him, but Nathan cannot break his father's interdiction.

He promises to get more medicine and runs to Mr Padge.

Padge has kidnapped Gam and is holding him hostage until Nathan gives the locket they stole from the merchant house.

He also wants him to sign the document they stole from the palace.

Nathan isn't interested, he only wants medicine.

Padge takes Nathan to the house of a pharmacist, and the two extort medicine from him with menaces.

Nathan hands over the locket and signs the document, which he cannot read, paying his debt to Padge and releasing Gam.

On release, Gam admits he let Joes fall and die on the orders of Mr Padge, who had threatened to have his assassins kill and mince Prissy.

Sirius alerts Nathan to the fact that his father is in danger and the party run to the slums.

There they find Bellows and a contingent of gill-men.

When Nathan reaches his father, he is dead.

Without his father's influence restraining him, Nathan fills with the Spark.

The gang are summoned by a signal back to the clubhouse, where they find the ghosts of Joes, who warn Nathan against a trap.

Nathan, feeling that Bellows has killed his father on the instructions of the Master, vows revenge regardless of any trap.

Nathan begins to glow blue with Spark energy and his arm loses its materiality.

The gang go to the Fetch and threaten him with murder if he doesn't take them up the Glass Road to the Master.

Reluctantly, he agrees.

They are met at the door of the Master's manse by the Master and Bellows.

The Master denies the murder of Nathan's father and forces Mr Padge, Prissy and Gam to admit that they were part of a plot against Nathan instigated by the Mistress of Malarkoi, the enemy ruler of a neighbouring city.

Unable to understand their treachery, Nathan turns his back on his companions and goes with the Master into his manse.

The Master has created a talisman – the Interdicting Finger – from the locket Mr Padge had them steal, combined with Nathan's father's severed index finger.

He puts this around Nathan's neck, which calms his Spark.

The Master gives Nathan an ointment for his arm and leaves him in the care of Bellows.

Bellows begins Nathan's education.

Nathan learns of Malarkoi, the enemy city, and its Mistress.

He is given educational toys that teach him how to behave.

Whenever he feels trapped, or angry, or violent, the locket around his neck dampens his spirits.

He is fed, watered, clothed, and indoctrinated in the ways of the Master of Mordew.

Nathan is given a magical book that teaches him how to read and write.

In the background to this new life, he sees fleeting glimpses of a girl in a blue dress.

He no longer feels the Itch to use the Spark.

Magical artefacts manipulate Nathan into believing his friends betrayed him.

When he learns that Prissy tricked him into loving her, he goes to the zoo and kills her precious alifonjers.

The next day the Master comes to him with a magical dagger and shows him how to use it.

Convinced the boy is under his control, he removes the locket that contains the Interdicting Finger.

Nathan is given the magical book, and the dagger, and is sent to Malarkoi to destroy its Mistress.

The book catalyses or inhibits his Spark, the dagger directs his violence.

In Malarkoi, Nathan meets the Mistress.

She is expecting him and seems resigned to her defeat at his hands.

She fights him nonetheless, and steals parts of his body to make a magical knife of her own.

She summons the gods of Malarkoi to defend her.

On the verge of his defeat, the book catalyses Nathan's Spark and burns everything but the Mistress away.

Seeing she is defeated, she offers her life to Nathan, and asks him to give the knife to her daughter, Dashini.

Nathan kills the Mistress and lets out an unrestrained burst of Spark energy that scours Malarkoi for miles around.

Using the Spark in this profligate manner reduces Nathan's material presence.

Nathan returns to a hero's welcome in Mordew, the Master heals him, but Nathan knows himself to have been manipulated.

The Master sends him to see the girl in the blue dress, the imprisoned daughter of the Mistress of Malarkoi, Dashini, captured behind a sphere of magical glass.

Dashini has spent her captivity unsuccessfully inventing magical methods of escape.

She has made masks that allow her to possess some of the Master's staff.

She gives one to Nathan, and that night they possess the Manse's Caretaker and Cook.

Nathan takes her to the library, where the Master has stored some magical books.

Dashini uses one to summon the ur-demon, Rekka.

Rekka, determined to destroy its summoner, destroys the glass quarantine that has been imprisoning Dashini.

Dashini, free, transports Rekka to the centre of the Earth, and she and Nathan try to leave the manse.

The Master has magical barriers that prevent them from leaving.

Dashini takes them below to a chamber in which the corpse of God – the source of the Master's power – is contained.

Nathan takes God's eye and uses the power to return to the slums.

No longer constrained by the locket, and empowered by the eye of God, Nathan brings revolution to Mordew.

He creates an army of flukes from the Living Mud, sets fires, drives the slum-dwellers into the Merchant City, and then destroys the Glass Road.

Each act makes him less and less materially present in the world.

He reunites with Gam, Prissy and Sirius, and finds his mother.

She has joined forces with Anaximander, and takes them all to the man with the fawn-coloured birthmark.

This man has access to a merchant vessel, and the party leave Mordew burning behind them.

When the ship is at sea, Bellows boards with a group of gill-men, determined to bring Nathan back to the Master.

Nathan is exhausted by his use of the Spark, and the eye of God, and is now defenceless.

Mr Padge, who has stowed away on the ship, emerges with Prissy as a hostage.

Nathan agrees to return with Bellows peacefully if Bellows rescues Prissy.

Bellows takes a magical weapon and attempts to kill Padge, but Padge has magical protection.

The weapon's effect is turned on Bellows, devolving him back into a boy.

While Padge is gloating over his victory, Gam stabs him in the back in revenge.

This was Prissy's plan all along, she providing the necessary distraction that allowed Gam to sneak up.

Padge dies.

Nathan goes to comfort Bellows, but the Master appears and takes Nathan away.

Taking advantage of Nathan's lack of material solidity, the Master crushes him.

Once Nathan is compact enough, the Master empties the locket he'd previously kept Nathan's father's Interdicting Finger in, and replaces it with Nathan's remains, creating an artefact he calls the Tinderbox.

It had been the Master's plan all along to make Nathan overexert himself, magically, so he could make this Spark weapon, which he intends to use against the Eighth Atheistic Crusade – the militant wing of the mysterious 'Assembly' – who are approaching Mordew, intent on destroying it.

Adam Birch A boy taken apart, made words of, and bound into a magic book. His author, the Master of Mordew, wanted him to be part of his war story, but Nathan Treeves took the book from the shelf and returned him to his brother, Bellows. Now, free in the world, who is to say what tales Adam prefers to tell?

Anatole Just because a man dresses well and keeps himself in shape, that does not make him worthy of respect. Nor do those who sing nicely necessarily have sympathetic hearts. Sometimes men overshadow their appearance with evil deeds, and make their voices fearful things to hear by virtue of their reputations. Anatole, one of Mr Padge's assassins, wears well-tailored clothes, fitted tightly, and has a practised and melodious vibrato, but you should run at the sight and sound of him unless you are tired of your life. He thinks he is currently engaged in punishing the murderers of his former employer, but if he is ever done with that, he will be free to kill again, something he does at even the most negligible slight.

Anaximander One of only a very few talking dogs, he has been confined to Mordew all of his life. Now he roams abroad, following Clarissa Delacroix, his new service-pledge. While he is a very faithful pet, his attention is often drawn to the new and interesting things he sees. To these he applies his logics, seeking to understand the world as it is, though perhaps this blinds him to matters closer at hand.

Bellows Boys often become men, the progress of time leading them usually in that direction, but Bellows is an unusual kind of thing. Made in the vats of the Master, his adulthood was brought on magically, and by magic it has been reverted, recreating from a metamorphosed butterfly its previous caterpillar. What effect this has on a person's mood and character is anyone's guess, but intuition suggests that it will not be universally positive.

Captain Penthenny When Penthenny sailed her ship away from Nathan, having performed the service of crossing the sea with him, she had no intention of returning to the waters surrounding Mordew. Her fish, though, has intentions of its own, and it is too large and wilful to deny. So it is that she comes back to the place she has forsworn, muttering under her breath and taking fortifying swigs from any bottles of liquor conveniently at hand.

Clarissa Delacroix Unfairly overlooked, in the main, by the plot of the previous volume, Clarissa Delacroix, Nathan Treeves's mother, has a larger part to play in this one, though perhaps no less mysterious. The *dramatis personae* of Mordew described her as being made from scraps of cloth, brought to life by the Living Mud. Since that passage was written from the perspective of the story-teller Joes, as a description it is only figuratively correct. In fact, she is a powerful weft-manipulator, survivant of the ongoing Weftling Tontine, and she has been in the slums, gathering Sparklines that will allow her to cast the magics she needs to bring her every desire to life. There are extracts from her diaries at the end of this volume if you require clarification.

Dashini The Mistress of Malarkoi's daughter, and supposed inheritor of her mother's city. Free at last from the Master's quarantine, she is delighted, but anyone who has been confined alone for years will know that it leaves scars: mistrustfulness of the world, lingering sadness, and a difficulty in relating to other people. Still, there is always magic, and the possibility that events will make up for the past. Surely?

Deaf Sam Those with disabilities, through their struggles, can learn a superior understanding of the plight of humanity.

This might lead to an empathy for others that guides a person's actions in their life, and which can make them kind and thoughtful. Not so Deaf Sam, one of Mr Padge's assassins, hired to punish that man's murderers. If he has any empathy, it is not often expressed when he is working. Wordlessly, he will strangle a baby in its crib when he is paid to do so. While his deafness mutes that child's cries, the sight of its shocked expression, wide mouth, red face, and, eventually, the slow dwindling of the light of life in its eyes, affect Deaf Sam very little, if at all.

Lover of the assassin Sharli.

Gam Halliday He had his eye popped by Mr Padge, and his teeth removed by flukes, but these flaws were remedied by Nathan Treeves when he filled Gam with the Spark. His material form was returned to that which God had intended for Gam: eye and teeth intact. Then, since Nathan's actions tend to excess, these items were evolved towards those proper to angels. Now one of his eyes sees with unusual clarity, and his teeth could chew stones if there was any need to do that.

If only Nathan had filled Gam's conscience with the Spark... Gam is tortured by guilt for all the terrible things he has done, and he receives no pleasure from his restored and improved organs.

Giles The aristocratic owner of the ship on which Nathan and his party left Mordew. He, along with his wife Iolanthe – listed directly below – were bullied into taking intolerable urks, dogs and dirty renegades aboard their precious vessel. It was the man with the fawn-coloured birthmark who forced them to do it, but where is he now?

Iolanthe 'Not here,' is the answer (see above), and Iolanthe, used to being the bully herself, is unlikely to leave off bullying Giles for long. 'Get these *horrible* types out of my sight,' is what Iolanthe is thinking, and she's preparing to express the thought verbally the absolute moment this story begins, though we won't be around to hear her.

Joes Killed in the world, Joes was magical enough to survive briefly as ghosts, hovering between the material and immaterial realms in the weft-inconsistent city of Mordew long enough for them to represent their death as service to the erstwhile Mistress of Malarkoi. As the Mistress's people have heavens created for them, she creates a heaven for Joes, despite never having met them. Consequently, it takes her a little while to get it right.

Mick the Greek Nothing is known of Mick the Greek, except that he is one of Mr Padge's assassins, contracted in advance to kill that man's killers. Like all of us, he is manipulated from birth to death by higher powers. You might think that this is not true of you, but you are wrong. One day you might understand your error, if you live long enough to develop wisdom. Mick the Greek will not – he will simply appear where his goddess wants him to appear, and fulfil the role she wants him to fulfil. He will give up his life's Spark for a purpose he will neither know, nor benefit from. If you think this is unusual, then you are naïve.

The Mother of Mordew The embodiment of a place and an avatar of a god are not the same thing, but the Mother of Mordew is both. Patron deity of assassins, she both works in their interests and, in a very fundamental sense, owns their lives. What a goddess does with her acolytes is her business. If she puts them here, where she wants them to be, or there, where they might become sacrifices, that is her prerogative. No one has the right to question her: not them, nor you. Gods will be gods, so the saying goes, and another saying says that gods move in mysterious ways their wonders to perform. The Mother of Mordew proves both these dictums correct.

Nathan Treeves He is dead, and it is unusual for people for whom that can be said to trouble the world any more, except as a ghost or a memory. Nathan, though, inheritor of the will of the weftling, bound to the material realm through his remains in the Master's weapon, the

Tinderbox, pawn in the schemes of the occult Tontine magicians, can expect no eternal rest. He exists painfully in the immaterial realm, where he should not be, and from there he is summonable, if one knows the method, into an intermediate realm. With enough Spark, he might even be returned to the material world. He has a home there – Waterblack, the City of Death – which would seem to be appropriately named to host him. What would he do there? To whose benefit? To what ends? This book does not answer these questions, though the next one might.

Niamh Love is a beautiful thing, it is said, and even constitutionally irritable sailor-women like Niamh can enjoy it, if they find someone lovable. She is the first mate of Captain Penthenny of the *Muirchú*, and, should both of them survive, she might also become her wife.

Portia Hall The given name of the former Mistress of Malarkoi. An avatar of her is dead in this world, but that needn't trouble a goddess. Her primary iteration is protected within the nested intermediate realms that centre on the Golden Pyramid of Malarkoi, currently inaccessible to those who do not know the back way in.

Prissy Buffeted hither and yon by the winds of fate, Prissy will become heartily sick of the entire business. Isn't it often the way that people who feel like this are the ones who are buffeted further? Pushed past their tolerances, they harden themselves to the knocks life gives them, and this makes them capable of enduring heavier and heavier blows. Eventually they become immune to their pain, and it is at this point they are perfectly suited to their roles in history. They might not like it, but they are now uniquely qualified to do things that other people would not want to do, would not be able to do, and would not be capable of withstanding.

Sebastian Cope The Master of Mordew's real name. He deserves no sympathy – he has committed many crimes – but that is not to say that he is not a man like any other,

21

possessed of that breed's foibles, insecurities and weaknesses. It is customary to paint the antagonists of history as one-dimensional monsters, but Sebastian has many dimensions to his monstrosity, so it is only fair to recognise them here.

Sharli Who do we mean by this? The Sharli who was employed by Mr Padge for murdering people? The agent of the Women's Vanguard of the Eighth Atheistic Crusade who took her place in order to spy on Mordew? The former assassin taken back to the Assembly for education into its society? The recreated original the Mother of Mordew mistakenly reiterated on the Island of the White Hills, not knowing she had been replaced, who she then ordered to murder Bellows and Clarissa Delacroix? They are all the same person, depending on what you believe, or completely distinct.

All of them, to some degree, are or were the lover of the assassin Deaf Sam. Some of them will live out the events of this book, some will not. It will be up to you to determine which.

Simon An assassin who found himself too beautiful and therefore made himself look like a rat.

Sirius He who consumes the flesh of the weftling assumes divinity for himself, though if he later vomits his meal up, that divinity is lost. This is a lesson Sirius, companion of Anaximander and pet of Nathan Treeves, learns as he searches for his service-pledge.

Nathan's remains, we should remember, are in the locket that forms the magical artefact, the Tinderbox. Since this is in the possession of the Master it brings the two into conflict – to ends the Mistress of Malarkoi directs.

Thales The Thales of ancient history was a philosopher who preceded another philosopher, Anaximander, amongst many others. To announce the identity of the Thales of this book here, before its beginning, would spoil his eventual appearance in the narrative, but the fact provided above will allow any curious person to make an educated guess at who or what he might be.

The Druze A neuter assassin. Describing them in English is difficult, since the language tends to reserve neuter pronouns for objects, but is that their concern? Not at all: they have the right to be addressed in the way proper to them, and if we find it difficult to write about them or read about them then that is our problem and not theirs. Never refer to them as 'he' or 'she' – they are skilled in the killing arts, and should they hear your misuses you will find yourself pierced, crushed, suffocated or in some other way rendered dead before you can repeat your mistake.

The Great White Bitch Not everybody knows what an avatar is, but it is an aspect of a god that exists both as part of, and independently of, a godhead. If one god can be father, son and holy ghost, then cannot other be mother, Mistress and bitch? The answer is that yes, they can. The Great White Bitch is a god in the form of a dog. By the end of this book she will have borne Sirius Goddog's children.

IN THE PAGES OF THIS book, in addition to those introduced in the first volume, you will find many unusual
things, including, but not limited to:

accounts of the thoughts of a magical, but mute, dog
an alarm that tells a man when he has had too much stimulant
annealing vats
an assassin who announces himself in song
assassins paid to avenge a man's death
avatars of a hidden god
a basilisk with eight legs, used for transport
a boy's brother's frozen corpse, standing on a table
a brig
a candidate to replace a man whose employer wrongly assumes
    them to be dead
a city in ruins
a city stretched magically into the sky
a civil war between person-headed snakes
a clock that tells the time in this realm, but also in other realms
a conversation on the topic 'what is fire?'
a dead girl, alive for no obvious reason
decapitations
a depressed boy child
disembodied organs that move
a dog rowing a boat
a dog that cries tears of sadness
a dog who digs through a wall
a dog who eats a god's face
a dog who makes lists of things he hopes to do so that he
    doesn't forget to do them
dogs that fight to the death

doors that require blood sacrifices to open
an enormous quarantine, large enough to contain a pyramid
exact copies of people who challenge each other for the right
   to exist
an excess of cattle-headed people
fields of dying dragons
a file, or possibly a rasp
firebirds in much better condition than one is used to
fish mutated by the proximity of God's corpse
a frozen corpse, shattered to pieces
a fusion of finger, oyster and octopus
a ghost standing at a forty-five-degree angle
a girl who suffocates to death
a god's face worn by a dead boy
a great many babies
a high wall of briars
a hollow hill
innumerable intermediate realms
inscriptions in Latin that no one can read
interventions into the state of the weft
an inverted black pyramid
the last firebird sent against Mordew
magic lists
a magic map
magic spells that go wrong
a man booby-trapped with an explosive jacket
a man hiding in ambush under a lid
a man turned to stone
a mirror Master
a mis-shelved magical book
moving pavements in place of roads
a mystical meeting place where magical creatures can commune
a near endless repetition of the same day
a new Glass Road
notes for a book on pyroclastic revenance
people breathing underwater through the use of magic
a person hiding in ambush under a carpet of turf

psychic influence across the boundaries of discrete realms
puppies born unnaturally quickly
a rebellious mouse, intent on revenge
replica vats
Rescue Remedy
sailors in love
self-melting solder
senses overwhelmed
sickening geometries and perversions of architecture
sigils cast in copper
the smell of sandalwood
spells with names
spiked, stinging monsters
a stone oak
stories told of Heartless Harold Smyke
the tabard relic of the hermit saint Zosimus
a tale of an infant used for a war between rival tribes of fairies
time moving in various ways
translation concussion
a tumbling wall
tunnels that give access to anywhere in the world
an underwater cave
various ominous glows
a vent in the seabed
a very many pyramids
a whitlow, untrimmed
a woman standing in a fire

MALARKOI

MALARKOI is a sequence of nested intermediate realms each governed by, and for, a patron god – and its people – under the aegis of the Mistress. Each realm is tied to, but is not identical to, the Golden Pyramid of Malarkoi, and ancestral grounds on the Island of the White Hills – the country surrounding the city. Each realm has a portal-henge that gives access to the next realm in the nest if traversed in the correct order, with the necessary sacrifices. Eventually, it is possible to reach the Mistress's realm, which is an almost entirely material realm of her own making, except that within it she maintains an accessible series of bespoke infinities, or heavens, which she creates to the whims of her people. She does this as a gift for their worship of her, which they demonstrate with their tribute.

PROLOGUE

BETWEEN TWO GREEN HILLS IN a gentle English valley, over a slowly curving loop of river, Portia etched the lines that delimited her Pyramid. They undercut the landscape as if they had been scraped through the real, revealing gold beneath.

She made the base a kilometre square, the apex a kilometre high.

It was a sunny day in August, and she was far enough away from the battlefront that the smell of burning tyres, something she'd come to believe was ubiquitous, barely registered.

When the lines set, she brought into existence enormous, triangular plates of gold and rested them against each other with spells. They joined seamlessly when she provoked the necessary Spark.

There wasn't much more to it than that.

She stroked the pregnant curve of her belly, flattening the creases in her cheesecloth dress. The breeze was soft on the down of the back of her neck. From somewhere came the screaming of a seabird.

Magic, once you have the trick of it, makes impossible things easy.

That's the point.

She still had to make the doorway, fill in the interior, build a stairway, make pipes for water. She'd have to make good. These were all easy things, though, once she found the right page in the right book. She could do it all from the safety of inside.

When it was done she could turn her back on the sacrifices. They weren't even worth the trouble of burying – she had no intention of coming out of her new home, or of cutting any windows.

Let them rot unregarded.

The countryside of southern England has beauty to a certain sort of person. Quiet, unassuming, subtle, its folds and ripples can satisfy those of an unambitious, static, insular temperament. Portia might even have been this sort of person, once.

But the weft...

Because of the weft, because of what she'd seen in her scryings, because of magic, because of the war, because of the Tontine, because of God, she could turn her back on all of it. Easily. As if it wasn't any loss at all.

Inwards, that was the direction, and the Pyramid.

The baby kicked and Portia took this in the same way a horse takes being kicked by its rider: it spurred her forward.

So it was that Portia Jane Dorcas Hall, who would become the Mistress of Malarkoi once that city was named, left her home country, never to return.

PART ONE

The Mistress of Malarkoi's Mysterious Ways

Her Wet Nurse

WHEN DASHINI came to her mother, Portia had no milk for the child, so she scryed the weft for a suitable run of events until she found an adequate place. Though it seemed bizarre, so did all the other places her spells showed.

Eventually, everywhere seemed bizarre.

There, within a version of the county of her upbringing, was a hill that had been hollowed out, and in it a tribe of strange people lived. Where a person has a human head, these had the heads of cattle, and they were all naked.

Dashini wouldn't stop crying, so even if there were things that spoke against it, Portia brought this place into the Pyramid.

She was so tired, it didn't matter that this place was strange and dreamlike. Tiredness makes everything seem like a dream, and every dream is as strange as the last.

She made three doors – one in from the outside world, in case she needed it, one out to the second level, and one she used from the Pyramid stairwell. She took the crying Dashini through this last door.

The baby seemed as if she would cry herself to death before she ever stopped, and was only silent for the brief moments it took for her to drag breath into her red-lipped, red-gummed, distended mouth.

Portia took her to the first cattle-headed woman she saw, who pushed the child away, as did the second, but the third was suckling a cattle-headed infant, her free breast blue-veined and swollen.

Dashini could smell the milk, turned her face urgently from side to side. Her bawling temporarily stopped, and she mouthed for a nipple. The cattle-headed woman – if she had a name, her tongue was inadequate to speak it – latched Portia's daughter to her, and the near silence Dashini's suckling made was like beautiful music to the Mistress's ears. She was so moved by this music that she wept, lying on the dark earth, her nose in the loam, her eyes closed, and, without knowing, she slept.

When she awoke, it was Dashini who was sleeping, her cheeks red with her satisfaction, her belly round.

Portia whispered to the cattle-headed women, 'This child will be to you as a daughter is, precious and worthy of love. Take her, and care for her, returning her to me after seven days.'

She kissed Dashini on the forehead with exaggerated gentleness, so she wouldn't wake her, and left the girl there.

Her Pawns

THE ASSASSINS employed by Mr Padge were sitting at a table outside The Commodious Hour, his restaurant, shaded by a green and red striped parasol, sipping at pipes of opium and wetting their dried throats with wines of rare vintage. The atmosphere was heavy with late summer pollen and the drowsy humidity of an endless afternoon. They sat, seven of them, a little slouched, long of limb, alert – though secretly so.

White, poppy-tinged, milky smoke trailed past their parasol up into the thin air, defying the pull of the Earth and drawing the eyes of wealthy diners. These good folk scowled to see reprobates of this type – unwholesome-looking, exquisitely dressed, and possessing none of the deference they ought to have for their supposed betters. The assassins pursed their lips and let their cheekbones cut, and rather than speak circumspectly of their business, they did it loudly, advertising being a necessity in their line of work, and *épater les bourgeois*, as the old words went, has long been their motto.

One of the assassins, whose name was Anatole, and who was dressed in a suit so tight that every contour of his lithe and sinuous body was clearly and obscenely visible, said to the others, 'The only thing the contract killer must respect is the contract. What are we without it?' and while there are no gatherings of assassins that possess absolute accord on any subject, this one came close. In the silence that dominated the aftermath of Anatole's utterance, more opium gathered in every lung, and some of the seven reached for their smelling salts to bring the semblance of liveliness back to their minds.

Next to Anatole was a pretty-looking person, all ringlets and almond eyes and glistening lips, quiet, shrinking into her chair. On each finger she had rings, and every one had been taken from someone she had killed, all at the direction of Mr Padge, who had recently sequestered himself in his office, having delivered a lunchtime peroration to the gathered that had now concluded.

He had given them the contract to sign, and they would sign it in blood, as was customary. The quiet, pretty assassin was called Sharli – on that day at least – and she cleared her throat to reply to Anatole: 'We must honour our pledges since our livelihoods depend on them.'

A waiter came with more wine, the tab going to the house, and in turn he filled Anatole's, Sharli's, the Druze's, Montalban's, Deaf Sam's, Simon's, and Mick the Greek's glasses, each of them nodding to him before the Greek pushed a generous tip across the table from them all. Assassins live or die at the whims of blind contingency, and this makes them both superstitious of mind and very free with any small sums of money that might influence the vagaries of fate, the reciprocal play of which might somehow come to influence matters where luck is involved. Which is to say that they are generous tippers and hope that the world will reward them for it.

Some of the assassins reached for their drinks, jitters to be calmed, others watched the ripples on the surface of their wine, transfixed by the patterns the opium renders so significant-seeming, others still licked their teeth and wondered at the time.

Padge, earlier, had hired them all for insurance.

He had paid the assassins, with promises, to kill, when necessary, whoever it was that should kill him, and the terms of this arrangement were outlined in the contract that rested between the seven of them, curling back into a scroll between the small plates and empty bottles of the long, but dwindling, lunch.

Padge had come and he had said, smiling over a three-storey platter of iced seafood that had since been eaten and cleared away, that he wanted them, for a share of a sum he would outline, to promise him that if he were ever done away with, that they would make it their business to return the favour to his murderer or murderers.

36

In other company there would have been a polite outcry at the unlikeliness of this eventuality and wishes given for many more years of safe passage about the city – empty flatteries – but assassins are of a different breed, and instead signs were made against the Evil Eye and solemn nods were nodded. White-haired Montalban, seven feet tall, rubbed a tattoo on his elbow and thereby opened and closed the pink beak of the albino falcon that was the emblem of his ancestors' house in a faraway city he was now unable to name. He said, 'Consider it done, Mr Padge,' and though the others might have haggled regarding remuneration, this set the tone of the group's replies.

Next to the contract, where it then was, lay seven blank pieces of paper. To the other patrons, picking at their quail bones and squaring away their napkins, these might have been seven separate bills, or perhaps copies of a list of specials, turned over so the unwritten-on sides were visible, but an assassin knows magic objects when they are put down in front of them.

This had all taken place, this meal, back before the city had fallen into revolution, before Nathan Treeves's treachery, before the exodus, before the rising of the Mount, and Padge had said: 'When I die, these papers will magically provide each of you with the name of my killer, or killers, and there will be a map to where they are. This map will change if they move, and the name will change if they call themselves something new. Your job – your last job for me – will be to locate the people or person on this list and kill them. When that is done, a new message will be written, and it will give you directions to my hidden wealth, which is, as I'm sure you can imagine, considerable.'

An assassin takes on new information with a studied neutrality – there is nothing to be gained from raising an eyebrow or throwing up one's hands when others speak – but a group of assassins together know from the very smallest reactions what their fellows are thinking. It is a kind of language, this hypersensitivity to posture and flow and nuance, and though no one not fluent in body-speech would have known it, Padge's words were shocking to the seven.

As custom dictated, it was decided that the group should all visit the Mother of Mordew, and that they would allow her to hold the contract, since all such important trade documents were deposited with her by preference, she being the patron deity of their union.

The Mother of Mordew – a secret presence in the city to all but a very few – was to be found in an abandoned and collapsed coal and tin mine on the tip of the Northfields. A tumble of rock, a cave entrance, an oily pool, a discarded iron earth mover: these things together do not deserve a name, but they were known by the assassins as the Cave of the Matriarch, and here it was that the Mother resided, trapped, it would seem to the ignorant, behind a mesh of wire, the extent of her prison disappearing off into a dark fault in the mountain.

In this part of the city it was always raining, and Simon – a rat-faced fellow whose unusual ugliness, recently adopted as camouflage, was all the incentive onlookers needed to pass their eye elsewhere – scuttled, collars drawn up on jacket and overcoat, the peak of his cap dripping, between the rusting heaps the miners had left behind once their coal and tin had been exhausted.

The others watched from the shelter of a corrugated iron overhang, the sound of torrents thudding on the rusting metal. Simon did not have a tail, but the end of his whip trailed behind him as if he did, and when he changed direction to skirt around this or that obstacle, he might also have had whiskers, so stiff and thin were his moustaches.

When he reached the allotted spot, his heels digging into the slag at the mine entrance, he stood back and whistled. He made three long notes to a tune he had memorised earlier.

Was the Mother of Mordew magical? It is almost certain that she was, since she had been in that place all the life of the city, and some said she came into being with it when the Master raised it out of nothing, but magic or not, she did not

38

appear instantly, as if summoned. No, the entrance to her place stayed dark, and there was no sign of her candle, nor of her entourage.

After the whistles, there was no movement or indication of anything but the feeblest sorts of dead-life, splashing in the rain, driven here by what temporary and unknowable motivation was in them.

Simon looked back, pawed at his moustaches, shrugged his thin shoulders.

Sharli took tobacco from her pouch and, with a thin liquorice paper, rolled herself a cigarette. Her fingers were wet, but she was skilled enough to manipulate even the most rain-soaked of fixings. She clicked and a flame emerged from her palm. 'You can't expect the Mother of Mordew to come...' she said, pausing to draw the flame into the leaf, '...running on our say-so.'

Such was the rightness of her words that the others made cigarettes of their own, or tamped their pipes, or took from the folds of their cloaks the devices which provided them with their preferred stimulants, and the assassins thereby collectively salved their addictions, even Simon, who took snuff laced with nerve-fire as he waited in the rain.

Time passed, as it must, and to alleviate our boredom let us turn to an illustration of what manner of people these assassins were.

Because they were prohibited by order of Mr Padge from assaulting patrons at The Commodious Hour, there are no opportunities to show them at their work there. It is hard to attract customers to a restaurant, even when the food is excellent, if there is an expectation that murder might follow the meal. But, if and when, say, a dismissive eyebrow was raised at, say, Montalban, by, say, a merchant of figs living up in the Pleasaunce who laughed to his new, younger wife and whispered in her ear, making her look back over her shoulder, snigger, cover her mouth, shake her head slightly and cleave closely to him as they went to collect their coats, then while none of the assassins punished the assumed insult on the premises, they did not let the possible slight pass.

No, instead they called over a serving boy and, for the consideration of several brass, had him follow the pair home, then return to report on their address.

Later, when the restaurant closed for the evening and the sting of the moment had passed, but on point of principle – that being that no disrespectful action can be allowed to stand unpunished lest it encourage disrespectful actions in others – they went together to the place the boy had indicated. Sharli knocked at the door, and when the maid answered she was pulled by the arm through the doorway so that she stumbled over the threshold onto her knees. While she was down there, she was very susceptible to a knife through the spine at the base of the skull, and easy then for Sharli and the Druze, coming out of the shadows, to drag back through the doorway into the parlour and out of sight, doors closing behind.

A signal can be made to assassins waiting at a distance by leaving the gaslight on in a front room, and then drawing and undrawing the curtains three times. This is easy to do, works at range, and is much less conspicuous to occupants of the property and passers-by than a loud yell, or something of that sort. The curtain code is what Sharli did as the Druze scoped out the scullery, drawing room, kitchen, stairs and back yard by standing in the hall by the coat stand and looking around.

An elderly housekeeper will die at almost any provoca-tion – her arthritic neck is easy to snap, she can be suffocated silently in a moment, even the shock of finding an assassin in her domain can do it – and a butler isn't much more trouble. By the time Mick the Greek and Anatole were letting them-selves in through the front, the dead of the lower floor were bundled down the cellar stairs and the Druze was indicating that the coast was clear.

Sharli opened the back door for Deaf Sam and Simon, who went upstairs noisily, the mud of their boots staining the runners, the banging waking the previously sleeping children, who then lit candles in their first-floor bedrooms.

Those who are not used to killing might think that children are easy to do, but the opposite is the case. Adults tend to freeze under threat, conveniently remaining in place, but children will run. Because they are little, they're difficult to catch. They're also nimble and some are not terribly sensible. Nimble ones will dodge between your legs, swerve past you at the last minute, or wriggle out of your grasp. Not sensible ones will leap out of windows, or fling themselves down stairwells. Deaf Sam and Simon were seasoned, though, and knew how to quickly smother boys and girls with their bedclothes, knees on little wrists, wadded sheets in little mouths.

Sharli had done the maid, the Druze the staff, Deaf Sam and Simon the children, so Mick the Greek and Anatole went up to the second-floor master bedroom, and here were the insulting pair from the restaurant, backed up against the wardrobe in their pyjamas.

The man who had raised his eyebrow had a pistol.

A piece of advice: if you have a pistol and intend to use it, do so without delay. If assassins appear in your doorway don't shake and shiver and try to bargain them away with threats. Just shoot them.

They may, if you are lucky, not be wearing lead breastplates beneath their shirts. Anatole certainly wasn't, and if the man had shot him, the assassin might well have been killed. True, Mick the Greek would have used the opportunity to take the weapon, but at least the man would have given as good as he'd got. As it was, he told the two to 'back off' and scarcely were the words out of his mouth than Anatole had doused the weapon with water from the jug on the nightstand, wetting its gunpowder and making it unable to fire.

The man tried the trigger a few times, but all it did was click, and while he was standing there, clicking away like a fool, Mick the Greek put a stiletto blade up through the new, young wife's left nostril, into her brain.

She slumped to the ground, never to rise again, and Anatole dragged the man screaming down the stairs, the other assassins following quietly and casually behind when they'd passed.

By this time Montalban had arrived and was waiting in the drawing room to punish the insult. He had pulled a chair over to the middle and put it on the intricately woven rug. The pattern of the rug was of putti and angels and seashells and golden trees and columns and beautiful maidens and all the wonders of the Arcadian world. It is best that we see those things rather than what happened next, because it is easier to focus on beauty than it is on pain, and while images are not enough to relieve the tortured, we have not offended an assassin and can be more easily distracted.

Anyway, time passed waiting for the Mother of Mordew, and eventually, when everyone was thoroughly wet through, there came a whistle that indicated that the Mother was on her way.

Close on this whistling, the wire fence in front of the cave entrance filled with eyes, some low, some high, and some in the middle range. Fingers curled between gaps. The eyes were huge and wide of pupil, the fingers were long and uncut of nail, and the group of faces behind were all in shadow. This was the Mother of Mordew's entourage – troglodytes from deep potholes intersected by the mines, wan and nervous and out of their element on the surface.

Then here was the Mother.

A person's mother is often like they are – more motherly, but the same in many inheritable respects. If this mother had been alike to the assassins, despite their variety, she would have been a beautiful thing, slender and dangerous and nicely dressed, but she wasn't like that at all. She was alike, instead, to Mordew, since she was its Mother and not theirs – conical in shape, her skirts caked in the dirt of the base, tapering up to her waist, which was reined in with a leather band. This was the support for a torso of more figurative similarity to her city – it swelled like the eruption of a volcano to her head, her skin caked in coal dust, her hair lava-red, spurting in all directions.

She turned her eyes on Simon and they shone as brightly as a lighthouse lamp, and her teeth too, that were like the dangerous white rocks at the base of a cliff from which the same lighthouse lamp protects mariners.

Simon bowed his head, deferentially, but before he could raise it again, she had seen the others where they smoked, and indicated for them to come forward.

The assassins knew her appearance well, but that did not make it any less fearsome or easy to see. Each previous meeting had been like a trauma to their dignities, since she would put them in their place and render any pretence they had of their brilliance an obvious self-delusion. She was, after all, and regardless of what the Master of Mordew said, the first of this city, even though, like many wise mothers, she chose to keep her offspring at arm's length, post-partum.

'Open the gates,' she said.

They were opened, and while this process took place – something that involved several of her troglodytes turning wheels simultaneously, which pulled at chains, which undid bolts, and which then allowed sprung hinges to do their work – Simon skittered back on his toes, knees high and urgent.

The others welcomed him into their huddle, where he peeked out from between them.

As a group they should have felt emboldened, since there were seven killers here, notorious and formidable, but they did not feel this. When the Mother came towards them, striding over every obstacle the junkyard presented as if it did not exist, skirts rippling, they felt instead that their collective presence made them more conspicuous. Each briefly considered edging away to fend for themselves, but when they remembered the lonely vulnerability of the friendless, none of them did it.

'Bring me the contract and slit yourselves in readiness. I am the law for you reprobates of this city, and my justice requires blood.'

She was light and dirt and teeth and eyes and red hair. Her words rumbled out from inside, battling with the phlegm the mine soot made in her lungs. This voice was high, but it was harmonised by the sound of rockfalls and cracking fault lines from beneath her corsets.

Her troglodytes stood tall as she spoke, and though it was evening, they shaded their eyes as if from the brightest noon. They squinted and looked sidelong, only briefly, but each drew a bead on one of the assassins, and with the instincts that killers have for aggression, the group knew that they were being sized up.

Deaf Sam came forward, unfazed by the Mother's voice since his ears couldn't hear it. His mode of communication was blunt – pounded fists and palms, curves and loops done with a finger, bitten lips, and extrusions of the tongue – but it was effective. He said, though the translation is inexact, that the Mother need come no further, and that he would act as the liaison.

The Mother pulled back her lips in what might have been laughter and came over to the group, growing in height as she left her cramped tunnel, filling the air and towering above them all. With her breath she scorched the soft hairs on the assassins' skins, curled their starched collars and cuffs, snatched the air away from their lungs before they could get the goodness from it.

It takes a terrible sight to intimidate killers, but she was that sight and none of the group could speak.

'You seven are the only ones left in this city who venerate me, agreeing to abide by my edicts,' said their Mother. 'All the others are dead. Let me tell you, my faithful, that this city will soon be scoured and rebuilt. It will stretch up into the sky and become a mountain. I know your business here, which is to offer me your contract to vouchsafe. Although the event for which you are contracted has yet to come to pass it will do so soon, and with it will come fire. Also yet to come to pass is the giving of secrets, from a son about his mother. These secrets I already know, and so I will add a name of my own to your contracted list, Clarissa Delacroix, who is a threat to us all. Though it should be enough to remove a danger from our collective, I will pay an additional bounty for her death of money and a special knife, useful for killing. Approach! I will lead you down into the caverns and mines and thereby protect you until the time comes for you to execute your commissions, you who are all that remains of my cult in this city.'

She took them into her mines and caves, and from here she directed them to the future places that she needed them to be in. Anatole she sent to the deck of the merchant vessel on which Gam, Prissy and Dashini would be found, so he could force them on the path that she had descryed for them, and eventually provide the Spark that would open the Door to the first level.

Simon she had emerging from the future soil on the approach to the Golden Pyramid, reducing the time that would be available to the fleeing children, forcing them to make for the back door.

Montalban, she made appear in a future tree, so that the children would be outnumbered and not pick the other assassins off with magic and violence.

Mick the Greek she made ready to be sacrificed if Dashini needed magic.

The others she sent to do other things.

Time did not mean to her what it means to us, nor did space operate in the normal way in her tunnels, since she was a thing of the weft – what the Assembly would call an anomaly, or a parasite – and it is enough to say that all this was done through manipulation of the weft, and if one wishes for a clearer answer than that then an intrascope may be procured from the Assembly under certain courses of study, or Clarissa Delacroix might be induced to teach you the INWARD EYE if you can offer her some advantage, and then you can see for yourself how it was done, if you have the wit to understand the weft, which most do not.

Down there she took the blood record of the assassins' pledges, and placed the contract in her Ledger, a book which was like scripture to these godless scoundrels, and its keeper their goddess.

Her tunnels were first crude mines, and then huge vacuoles in the earth, spiked on the insides with stalactites and stalagmites, but eventually they became like the impressions a worm leaves in soft soil, and wormlike in colour – slightly pink – and moist like they are too, glistening with the condensate of the breath of the troglodytes who shone and polished the surfaces of her lair until what little light there was down here – most of it coming from her hair – bounced from surface to surface and rippled every inch and made it move like an undulating worm in a fourth way.

Down, down they went, and into the mountainsides, and it was clear that the Mother of Mordew's realm of influence did not stop at the Sea Wall boundary but encompassed great distances in every direction. Her burrows were deep and complex and never was a dead end reached, every tunnel bifurcating, trifurcating, once, twice, over and over. If one pulls a seedling from the ground, its roots do this, and more so do those of a bush or a tree, but her complex was most like to the strands a fungus colony extends out into the world, the extents of which are difficult to define because they seem to go everywhere.

The Mother of Mordew led them through her place, less dominating in size again now the roofs were low above their heads. When the passages narrowed, she shrank with them, until, rather than giant, she was now a miniature of herself, and the assassins had to go down onto their hands and knees so that they did not become wedged.

Lungs felt the compression, bent over, and that sense that human beings who live above ground do not realise they have – which is of the risk of being trapped underground, and which makes images in the mind of their head wedged between two rocks so that they cannot go forward or back – began to fire warnings at the assassins, making them pant anxiously. Several of them – again, spread across the various occasions when they were led down there – turned involuntarily back, hoping to ascend to the fresher air and roomier environs of the surface, but when they tried there was the Mother again, the troglodytes with her, exactly where they had been before.

At some point, she turned to them all and said, 'The service I now do you is done as a mother does service to those she has birthed, which is without thought of payment but in expectation of never-ending love from those for whom she works. You are my children, you vain assassins, and not by any virtue that you possess, but from my boundless grace, which you have received by cleaving to me in faith.' She was tiny now, as if she could be picked up and put in a pocket.

The assassins were on their bellies, gasping for breath, baking in their own heat in the deep and fractal underground. She came up to them, her blackness blacker even than that sunless place, and like a stone or a pebble abrades the path of a fast-flowing stream, she bashed against them, laundering them as clothes can be laundered by the same stones in the same streams, cleaning them of the filth of the *there-and-then*, purifying them of the particular, until each assassin, alone with her, knew the state of themselves behind the material realm.

Her Crèche

THE CHILDREN of Cren – the person-headed, snake-bodied enemies of the cattle-headed people, and denizens of the second level of the Golden Pyramid of Malarkoi – considered themselves sophisticated to a degree unmatched in the Pyramid realms.

A snake slithers in the dirt and has no feeling for anything but biting and constricting and poisoning, but snakes are snake in both body and mind whereas Crenfolk were snake in body only. Their minds were infinitely more nuanced and wide-ranging, housed in their more expansive and accommodating human heads.

So thoughtful were these modern Crenfolk, that now their conversation was all of natural philosophy and art.

'What is beauty?' one of them would ask, sibilantly, and it was only the denser, less acute members of their audience who would venture an answer. The sophisticates, nodding, knew that such a question was only an overture that would lead into a carefully prepared concerto on the topic, and that the response, 'Please, tell us, what is beauty?' was the only one required, if any.

Along a veranda, or around a shaded bower, or beneath a jewelled gazebo – all made for them by Cren – these person-headed snakes would half-undulate, their necks scrupulously straight and as perpendicular to the ground as they could be held, and whichever one of them had had some insight would offer it to the others.

It was only polite of the others to listen.

'Beauty,' one would say, 'is a quality that all person-headed snakes can recognise and agree on account of its necessary truth. If one says to another, "This is Beautiful," and all are obliged to agree, then that is Beauty.' The person-headed snake would bow, but only briefly, prolonged closeness of the head to the ground being vulgar.

It is a sign of a progressive society that dissent is allowable – anything else is a form of homogeneity such as the inferior herd-minded and cattle-headed peoples are likely to accept – and so a hearer may hold their rattle erect and let off a susurration with it to indicate a difference of opinion. The attention of others thus drawn, she will say, 'To argue so is to say that Beauty is only a function of we observers, since we must only see it and then agree to it for it to come into existence. But is there not an objective quality to the beautiful? An ineffable quality? Yet further, is there not a transcendental quality to Beauty that exists outside of perception, but to which perception is turned?'

The crowd would make an approving hissing at this, even those who had yet to understand the meaning of all the words, because, even if not correct, it had the form of an intelligent addition to their combined knowledge.

Such was the culture of these person-headed snakes that they would then join to make an ellipse around the debating pair, who would stand at the foci and face each other.

'I did not say that there is not this other-worldly quality, and to so characterise my thesis is to do it an injustice, since I was just coming to that when I was interrupted,' he would say, and she, recognising this sort of gambit, would slither back, nodding, so that he might continue.

On a pleasantly cloudless day, warming to the blood but not too frantically hot, the Mistress of Malarkoi brought Dashini, who could now crawl but could not yet walk. In that part of the agora reserved for competition and oratory, she put her daughter down and said to the gathered, 'This child will be to you as a daughter is, precious and worthy of love. Take her and care for her, returning her to me after seven days,' and all those there, because they were the faithful of Cren, knew her as their patron goddess, the Mistress, and so did as they were bid.

Dashini crawled here and there, as children of this age will, and while the ellipse around the debating pair listened to their arguments, she went around and took each by the tail and shook their rattles and laughed. Occasionally one or another of that audience would slip aside and return with barbecued mice, or sticks of spiced vole cubs, but none of those things distracted the child from her play.

By a kind of common accord, eventually it became clear that the exhibition was over.

'So,' one wrapped up, 'we see that Beauty occupies a separate realm, a perfect realm, one that we can only glimpse in our raptures. We can scarcely hope to experience it for what it is, since we are only person-headed snakes, and it is our doom to appercept the world as we can. If, perhaps, we were gods... but we are not gods, so we must take our pleasures where we may.'

With that, the person-headed snakes took Dashini to one of their many salons, and there she learned, before she could speak, the basics of rhetoric.

Her Husband

A WORM DOESN'T THINK, and it doesn't feel; it's not knowing, and it's not foolish. Become a worm and you won't understand what you've lost in the transition. You won't understand that you've lost at all. You won't understand anything.

You'll only act.

You'll writhe in slime. You'll invade the cell walls of whatever is near you and is not you.

The Spark is indivisible, but you possess the least of it, and this lack makes action in you. This isn't like hunger – that's a feeling – it's an absence that must naturally be filled. A vacuum, a fall, movement – these are all things like your lack, and each provokes action in a thing without needing feelings. A vacuum pulls material into it, a fall pulls material downward, movement drags material across. You're a thing in this way – spurred into action, making up Spark deficit.

Or dying.

Worms are pulled, in flocks, across the realms. You come in the form of a seed about to unfurl. The least Spark is the seed – two things in one place, facilitated by the weft – and you infant worms are its unfurling. At first this is the becoming of one into two, connected.

+ becomes --

You, the seed, become you, the worm; a positive thing becomes two negatives. Negatives negate, taking the unity of those things they find and undoing it, joining with the products, and once a realm is invaded by worms you grow:

-- + becomes ----

You curl. You knot. When you become too long you snap, make copies of yourself, proliferate.

In the lung of a father, loosened by the weft, you are lungworms, surrounded by things to negate. You become a colony of worms at the expense of his lung tissue.

That's not all.

The seed of you has come from another place, drawn through by its Spark-lack into the material realm through the loosening of weft-consistency to where Spark is everywhere. You're like your origin place as a fish is like water – cold, wet, flexible. You're immaterial, singular, massless. But in the material lung, you lungworms become material. Material things have breadth, have depth, have width, and you receive these because you couldn't *be* without them. Negating the forms of the lungs – the alveoli, the bronchioles, the pleura – you make them lungworm mass and you do this as long as there is matter to convert into you.

If you're coughed up into a bowl you'll writhe there, but now it's not like it was when you came across the realms. You have gathered Spark found in living tissues: when you negated them and used them to grow, their Spark came with them. You're no longer the least Spark that there could be. Now you're a complex of Spark, small in volume but enough to begin to feel.

Because there can be no feeling without something to do the feeling, you become that thing. Because a feeling is thing experienced, you experience it, and because experience breeds knowledge, you know, now, that it is you writhing there in the white, chipped enamel bowl.

You're not alone. He doubles, your host, on the bed, strains, and here's a lung mate, tumbling end over end through the material distance between your host's lip and your ground, hitting with a slap beside you, writhing immediately as you writhe, beside you.

Time is something you live within but don't understand, so you don't experience the filling of the bowl two-thirds full, except by the closeness of your fellows. They writhe with you, your Spark diminishing as you use it up, searching for lung to make into you.

It feels like it did inside – dark and warm when you are at the bottom of the bowl – but now there's hunger, since with knowledge comes the knowledge of lack. What was once a material fact, unnoticeable by you, the growing absence of Spark makes anxious, hunger spurring desire, desire spurring action, action meeting only temporary resolution, fuelling more desire in a loop that can never be slowed.

A lungworm cannot know another lungworm as food, or it would risk consuming itself in error.

You come to know fear.

You'll live, or you'll die. There will be sufficient Spark to retain you in the material realm, or it will return to the weft taking your form with it, dissolving you into nothingness here. If you're poured away, behind the shack of the man whose lungs you've ruined with your negations, if you drive him to his death and find yourself in the Living Mud, this will prolong your time in the material realm.

Dead God's proximity, the impossibility of his form as the weftling, has made an alternative source of creation – magic. The realm into which you have come is a place of near infinite possibility, though the probability is small that it will affect you.

If there were a thousand lungworms in the bowl into which you were spat, if there are a thousand impossible outcomes of a chain of events, most of those outcomes, lacking the will of God, who is dead, will be will-less nonsense. You might cease to be without cause. You might be an inch to the left of where you were. You might be, instead of a lungworm, a twig of a similar size. You might become a single degree warmer than you have the right to be in the material real.

Think of a thousand nonsensical outcomes – you might be one of those.

Only the weftling can make the impossible perfect. That is why he is God.

But sometimes an impossible thing can be like the will of the weftling by accident. You, dying lungworm, might become instead a dying earthworm, which is a more perfect form of worm, or a dying snake, which is more perfect still, or a finger, which is more perfect still, because it is a perfect piece of a more perfect being; a man is more like the weftling than either a worm or a snake is, and therefore more perfect.

If whatever you accidentally become, facilitated by the weftling's impossible magic embodied in the Living Mud by his presence, is capable of movement and knowledge and eating, you might then move and know to eat your fellows. A dying snake can live by eating lungworms, harvesting their matter and their Spark to make healthy flesh. You dart down into the mud and lurk silently, preying on whatever comes near.

A day passes, a week, you live unseen in the Living Mud of the great city of Mordew, blind to the events above – a child leaves, a father dies – but one day there's no food to numb your hunger and you migrate, mud-snake, to the deepest part of the Mud, drawn by the proximity of the weftling, fuelled by one meal after another – discarded skin from a spitted fowl gone rotten, rat cubs unattended, the blood in a pool of a firebird clubbed to death by a gang of boys, the vomit of a drunkard face down outside a gin-house. Meal by meal, hunger by hunger, you find your way to the Circus, which is where, now, you hear the voices in your developing mind of the other flukes who have that capability.

Say there are ten thousand flukes in the Circus – there are many more – and say that one in a hundred learns to commune mystically – it may be more or less – here there are many who can do it. You? You have nothing to say – you are a mud-snake, evolving without the will of the weftling. You can't understand the thoughts they send you, except perhaps their tenor – which is never welcoming – but to know that there are others, that there is such a thing as communication? It blossoms in you, in your heart, which is a thing you now feel in your chest. Something like joy? The word means nothing to you, but it's like that – a joy experienced by the joyless, by the mindless, and now you have a reason to evade the grasping fingers that seek to drag you up from the filth you have come to think of as your home. You can concentrate on the gradual evolution of meaning as you experience it in your soul, which is a thing the Spark makes if it can find concepts and tie them into an immaterial bundle that has uniqueness.

For you are unique.

It doesn't take the combination of many unusual events to make a unique thing. Unusual concepts tied together, no matter how simple, can be unique. A hundred of them? Fifty even. Arrange fifty letters at random on a page – this outcome will be unique since if you do it again, and again, and again, it will come out different.

Now you, conscious, fearful, joyful mud-snake of the Circus of Mordew, evading capture, satisfying hunger, learning to commune mystically with your Living Mud flukes – you are unique, and in the immaterial realm your concept is immortal, made soul by the Spark even in the absence of the weftling's will.

You have made yourself.

To have a unique self, you find, is to have a hunger of a different kind unique to you – a will for your own perfection. In others it is for dominance, or for pleasure, or for a hundred other things. Yours is yours and it is best served by burrowing down to where the God chamber is, although you don't know there is such a thing, and you don't know why you'd go there if there was.

Time passes, you don't know how much, but you bury yourself again and again in the same place, eating solely that you should have enough energy to dig, making a fault line in the mud that, though it fills when you leave to eat, is easier to dig into when you return.

The nearer you get to the God chamber the more you develop your form, mutating in ways you feel, but are not sure, you can control.

One day there are buds at your sides, and these become paddles which help you in your digging, which become scoops, become spades, and every day you are larger. Your hunger is larger too, and it is no longer sufficient to feed on the undeveloped things, you need to risk more, attack larger flukes, things that can fight back, because it's worth it since you feel you are making progress on your tunnel, spending every moment you can in there.

One day you hit rock, and though you know this means you cannot dig you also know that this is what you have been working towards – the rock is hot with energy, vibrates with magic, tastes of everything you've ever wanted. You bathe on it, this rock, like a flatfish bathes on the seabed, pressing yourself against it. Your limbs, previously spatulate, divide, splitting into digits that you can manipulate. It is a shock to you, a joyous shock and you rush to the surface, eager to commune with the others, to tell them your news, to share with the Circus this incredible wonder.

Your excitement makes you careless. Excitement is, indeed, a kind of carelessness for a thing like you are. You have lost that fear that once protected you, those hungers that once directed you. In your desire to commune, which is a joyful thing but inessential to your being – you are a mutated lungworm with ideas above your station – you are dragged out of the circus by a fishing child.

You know better than this, have seen it happen to others, have vowed always to keep to the deep and remain there, but now it has you in its hands which, because it is a creature proper to this realm and not some tenuously manifested nonsense living on borrowed time, it is much stronger than you are. Its skin-covered bones are like sticks in your flesh. and it wrenches you. You bite at its face, claw at it with your new limbs, but it has the measure of you. It holds you tight by the neck and then, with seemingly no effort, plucks your beautiful new arms from the stem of your body so you can't use them against it.

You bleed, and the child reaches down for its killing bag. You are almost too shocked by the loss of your limbs to take your chance – how can it be that something so beautiful can be so short-lived? – but life has trained you to do what you do next. Perhaps you are nothing but a machine for doing it. While the child is struggling at their belt, you dislocate your neck and bite down at their hand, driving fangs into its machinery. It squeaks and flings you into the air. At first your teeth anchor you into its flesh, but you retract them and fall, splashing back into the mud, and despite the agony on both your sides you swim down and burrow to where you cannot be found.

You should have died – you certainly did nothing to keep yourself alive – but a thing with a soul who has been so close to God cannot just disappear back into the Mud. There was no more digging, the flesh of that child-inflicted wound became swollen and raw and useless, tearing down to the bone when you tried to use it. You would have been eaten if the others hadn't protected you. They wanted to hear your tale – of the hot rock and the new limbs – and, though you told them, none of them could find your tunnel.

You lay inert on the floor of the Circus, wallowing in your own self-pity. This went on and on and it was your intention to let yourself die, to go back to nothingness, but, after a while, even this became impossible. Hunger is a force that cannot be easily denied. There was, it seemed to you, a balance that one day tipped. Eventually it became more effort to remain hungry than a mud-snake's desire to starve can manage, starving robbing the self of energy, and one day you couldn't tolerate it. Smaller flukes had come to treat you as an inanimate object, and when one came past, you snapped it up. It was a flimsy thing, like a slug or a jellyfish, easily digested, and it filled you with material and the Spark, brought to your mind thoughts of effort that you had long bitten down inside.

Now you could see a future for yourself, the purity of eating and not being eaten, of hunting and of, perhaps, revenge.

This saved your life and made it possible for you to become what you were destined to become, for you not to dissolve slowly into strings of flesh and grey-white bones. It made it possible to do what you did next, which was extraordinary.

You had caught a fluke, had bitten a child on the hand, had torn the last strips of your ruined limbs away to reveal healthy scar tissue beneath when it happened. It happened to all the others at the same time, but it was you that did it.

He came.

The Blue Light.

He plunged his fists into the Living Mud and filled you with power. He evolved you all, from the lowliest mess of unformed goo to the greatest of the communing minds, took you up through the stages of the weftling's will all the way to the form of God himself – the child – except not of flesh, but of flesh and power.

He asked that you follow him and defeat his enemies, who, since they were your enemies too, you eagerly agreed to defeat. If that had been the end of it then that would have been enough – to be a soldier in the Great Fluke's army – but then he had a new edict, one that you, personally, were able to fulfil, that you should all go down into the earth to open up the God chamber.

It was you, lowly lungworm, lowly Mud-snake, limb-torn Circus fluke, who knew the way.

Chosen of your people, it was you that broke open that place and flooded the material realm with God's power. From that time on you were known as the Great Worm, first of the flukes.

But what of love? Is it sufficient for a fluke to be and to serve and never to have anything for itself except service?

This thought came to you, the Great Worm, from the outside on the day when the city stretched up into the air and became steep and solid. It came on the same day the dog made landfall. It came when the others were stretched and malformed as the land was stretched and were made into spiteful things in the distance, suddenly and unwillingly forced to diverge from the child-form, their power spent on this devolution, only you remaining.

Could this be a coincidence?

The thought came to you in the form of a woman's voice, the fact of that thing coming with it, making of you a man, seduced by its sound, which was a softness that made you hard in response and taught you of a new lack.

'But what of love?' she said, and 'Follow me,' and before your eyes appeared an aspect of the Mistress of Malarkoi, the Bride of the Great Worm, up from the Living Mud, starting from the same weft-germ, and making of herself a lungworm, and then a mud-snake, then growing limbs. But she did not take the Blue Light but instead retained her physicality. She evolved into something solid where you became power, and this solidity promised to you wholeness, which she called 'love'.

She gestured for you to come, and you took her hand, which was like those limbs that you had lost, and she showed you where to be, and what to do, and who to harm to earn her love.

And you did as you were told.

Her School

PORTIA SCRYED through the weft of the third level and there, outstanding from the mundane and prosaic intermediacies, was the perfect place. She looked into its futures, its pasts, inserted herself into them and ran them forwards and backwards.

When she was satisfied, she took Dashini from her bed, where she was sitting, already awake.

'I think you'll like this,' she said.

Placing the realm within the confines of the Pyramid was simple this third time, so she stretched the dimensions, dilated time, expanded space, encapsulated a volume hundreds of thousands of times larger than the practical expanse of the architecture. She made three Doors – an entrance from the Pyramid stair, an entrance from the second level and an exit to the fourth. She, of course, didn't need the Doors, but if Dashini ever got lost, at least there'd be that way out.

When Portia was a girl, her mother had decorated her nursery with dragon wallpaper, and while those were whimsical-looking things, not represented in any of the descryments she'd ever made of the weft, this realm was still a lot like her room. In the nursery, hundreds of flying lizards had darted here and there against a blue background, and in this realm it was the same.

Wyverns, amphipteres, feathered serpents, drakes – dozens of creatures with names even Portia, who was very keen on things of that sort, didn't know – whirled in the air, rarely if ever landing. In the middle of them, it seemed, was a stone tree, so Portia made herself appear there, at the highest point of the land.

The goddess of this realm – Japalura, she called herself, Portia later discovered – found her as she stood on the highest branch. Portia held Dashini high over her head and sent up a blast of light. In her thoughts she declared, 'This child will be to you as a daughter is, precious and worthy of love. Take her, and care for her, returning her to me after seven days,' and she threw Dashini up into the air.

Japalura caught Dashini before she fell, balancing her on the end of her broad snout, and for seven days the goddess flew with her across the extent of the realm, introducing her to her subjects, feeding her with their tributes, and when the whole world knew who Dashini was, Japalura took her up and up and up until the land curved below them and the sky went black. Japalura flew straight as an arrow, Dashini at the tip, until there was nowhere left to fly, the edge of the realm having been reached.

Dashini could not breathe up there, but she sat on the dragon's nose and the goddess exhaled gently so that the girl could share her breath. Then she left Dashini, at the top of the sky, and let her fall.

It is not that girl children of her age could not feel fear – they could – but Dashini didn't. Though she could scarcely walk, she spread her arms and legs and flew, like Japalura did. The air returned to whistle in her ears and batter her skin, but Dashini swooped and circled, made loops on the wind. She smiled and laughed, and beside her the dragon goddess showed her how she could make herself twist, how to speed and slow, how to dive for the earth.

When the ground became too close and the branches of the stone tree threatened to dash the girl into pieces, Japalura took her up again, up to the edge of things, and dropped her to fly once more.

Dashini never tired of this game, and it was reluctantly that Japalura returned her to Portia at the end of the seventh day.

That first night, back in the Pyramid, Portia whispered a promise to Dashini – that she could spend every birthday in that place – and though that promise, like all the others her mother made, was soon broken, the girl made it to herself in her heart.

Her Servants

GAM CAME TOWARDS JOES.
Up on the Glass Road the moonlight glinted and, though clouds passed over, the oddness of Gam's expression was disconcerting. He was the kind of boy that had known his share of hardship and had found whatever ways out of it he'd needed to find. Now on his face was a look of grim determination: here was something he had decided to do, and now he was going to do it, whatever the consequences. At the same time, around his eyes were fear and sadness – fear of what he had become, to have determined to do what he was about to do, and sadness that he was not a stronger and better person.

There is something self-serving, it seemed to Joes, in that kind of thinking: it is much easier to do the wrong thing when you have given yourself permission to be weak and bad.

'I've got no choice, Joes. I know it's a risk, but I think he can do it.'

Gam never went up the Road, only ever came down, both feet on the glass, sliding almost horizontally.

Joes backed away, their hands raised, but there was nowhere left to go.

'He'll bring you back. You don't have to worry.'

'Wait!' they shouted. It must have been something in their voice, but Gam did as he was told. 'You don't have to do anything bad. Tell us what you're thinking, we can help.'

Gam didn't wait – he knew delaying tactics when he heard them. Joes saw the tired recognition in his eyes, the disappointment that it wasn't something more convincing – and then his hands were grabbing their collar. 'It's Padge. It's her. There's nothing we can do.'

When someone has you by the collar, it's natural to want to step away from them, but Joes' heels slipped over the edge of the Glass Road, and in their imagination they saw the long

62

drop down to the rooftops. Gam was Padge's stooge and Padge was the Mistress's creature. Everything they did was for her. 'You're going to kill us?'

Gam pulled so tightly that Joes could feel their shirt ripping at its rear seam, felt the threads separating where they'd sewn a repair. It's odd what draws the attention at times like this, they thought, when their life should have been flashing past their eyes.

Gam's lonely tooth was there in his dark mouth, chipped and cratered, grown almost free of his shrivelled gum. 'Nathan'll bring you back. Padge promised.'

In other circumstances, Joes would have laughed. They would have pulled a face and snorted – Padge's promises were worse than worthless: they came with a price – but there was no time for laughing.

Gam pushed them off the Road.

It's not that they had time to think, as they fell, or that time slowed to allow them to consider their fate, or yet that dying people think quickly and clearly and with perfect acuity, but Joes knew, in those few falling moments, that Padge wasn't really the issue. Nor was Gam, nor was Nathan, even.

It was the Mistress – she was central to what little remained of Joes' life.

Again, they had no time to think of it – they didn't need to because they already knew it – but the rumour amongst the slum people, those that had links with Malarkoi, was that the Mistress provided, for her faithful servants, a perfect heaven after their death. Joes had never believed it, but it was a thing you heard on the streets, generally before whoever you heard it from received a mouthful from some unfortunate firebird-widowed crone, or pampered supplier to the Manse.

You heard it a lot.

As they fell, the two of them, dying as they had lived – together – they both wondered in their shared mind, whether they counted, on the Mistress's side, as one of her faithful servants.

If they were part of her plan, via her proxy Padge and his blackmail of Gam, didn't this, in practical terms, make Joes her agents?

As they descended, as they felt it in their throat and stomach, this question posed itself to them. Joes' interests were not abstract things, like a more privileged child's were, some set of largely imaginary benefits and costs that were managed, for the most part, by other people. No, what was good and bad for Joes were things always within their own reach, sometimes under their own control.

They fell, and the facts of their life were never any more obvious than they would be now, so obvious that they didn't need to be articulated, at least between the two of them, and so, even as the lurch of their death drop made every muscle in their body spasm, they resolved between themselves to pledge their allegiance to the Mistress. They resolved to forgive Gam, to opt into the plot for which they were being used.

They acquiesced to their own murder.

They didn't have to think it – it was a decision, but it was made like a reflex action is made, because it is built into the nerves and sinews of the conditions of their existence – but that didn't mean it wasn't true.

When they looked into Gam's face, rushing away from them, read the pain and horror at what he had done to his friends, they made their face as forgiving as it could be. They forgave him in their heart. Moreover, they thanked him, since now they would either drop and die and be resurrected by Nathan, which is a unique fate, and would make them famous everywhere, or they would die in the service of their Mistress, doing her bidding, and so ascend to their perfect heaven.

Anyway, isn't it better to die for a cause than to be murdered by a friend?

They had it in their power to choose which of those things was happening to them.

It wasn't even a choice.

They fell, the pair of them, their one body doubly dense, so that when they hit the roof beam it was with such a forceful impact that it broke their back in two and shattered the tiles.

Does a waker know for how long they have slept? Not without checking their watch, and Joes had never owned one. They weren't even quite sure that they were awake, because the existence they woke to had a dreamlike disregard for the world as they knew it. Most obviously, they were in two bodies, the pair of them. Or at least they had two forms, because these representations of themselves were diaphanous things, pain-less, elegant things, perfect things, and none of these qualities were ones Joes had understood themselves to possess before.

Their hands, when they reached out to touch each other's faces, marvelling at the fact of seeing themselves and each other for the first time, separate as other people were, these hands slipped through each other, as two waves coming into a port meet – each interacting, but neither substantially changing the other.

Though they were apart, everything they did simulta-neously. When one put up their hand the other was already doing it, when one showed surprise it was matched on the face of the other. When one thought – they both realised in the same instant – so did the other, as if their minds were still the same, now in two vessels. They had grown up together, they knew, and even though they were now apart, they were still together – they looked the same, they felt the same, they thought the same.

That is what it is to be together – even when you're apart, you are together.

Yet part of thought is reactive and the thing that it reacts to is the world, since thought is how the self knows the world as it is, and whereas Joes had both been in the same place since before they were born, now they were separate and so each was reacting to very slightly different things. That part of their mind that reacted did, then, react to a different set of stimuli, and even a small divergence in that set had extensive and general consequences of the sort that a player of Chinese whispers will notice – small changes develop into large ones, eventually changing everything – and even though they mostly did and thought the same things, after a little while this diverged until, to an observer, they didn't mimic each other at all.

They reached and did not touch, they stood and faced in opposite directions, they turned their attentions this way and that, and saw and felt different things.

But this divergence was only external. It is said that a person uses only a fraction of their capacity in their mundane experience of the world, and Joes, rather than knowing only the thing they were themselves experiencing by virtue of the place they found themselves in, found that they knew both places. Two worlds were available to them, experienced dually, and it was less that they were two separate people and more that they were a single person with two different ways of being in the world, each of which both knew.

Being of this kind is incompatible with the material realm, and even where it does exist the dreamer eventually awakes, or the fugue state passes, or the intoxicant wears off. In the immaterial realm there is no consciousness, except for a very few, and this could, if Joes had not been slum children with no knowledge of the realms, have alerted them to the fact of their existence as it now was – that they were ghosts, instanced in the material realm as an image, tied to the material expression of their immaterial concepts incompletely, and occupying an intermediate realm very connectedly sandwiched between these two primary realms by virtue of the extent to which magic was a fact in the city of Mordew, and the concomitant loosening of the consistency of the weft, and the impingement thereby of reluctant, willing or ignorant persons who were now dead.

They saw the world as a ghost sees it, and that is very much how a person sees a ghost – translucently, imperfectly, gloomily – and it never properly married with the expectations they inherited from their short lives in the material realm. They hovered above the ground, they failed to make an impact on objects, and when they went to embrace each other, hoping to make gone the distance that had opened up between them, they slipped between each other's grasps in a way that brought great sadness to them, until they realised they both felt it the same, and then that sadness was replaced by a feeling of intense siblingship, stronger than even the most identical of twins feel.

Where were they, then, when this was going on?

At first, they were on the rooftop, watching as the magical dog Sirius ate at their faces; then they were in a wheelbarrow, tangled like lovers, while an old man took them through a concrete garden; then they were tipped, head first, down through an opened grate, splashing into sewer water. For a long while they were in this water, face down, skulls hidden beneath the fetid surface of the city's waste, swelling and bloating, decomposing.

This is the kind of experience that living persons find terrifying – none of them would be considered bearable for the living – but Joes looked on with the distant sort of attention that people who have become ghosts feel for a world that they have come to see was not entirely inclusive of their lives. When, eventually, carrion-feeders took their flesh, when Gam and Prissy rescued their gnawed and invaded corpses, when they were consigned to the same bonfire that took slum refuse and effigies, watched on by mournful people, neither of them – both of them – felt it, though this was, as yet, in the future.

Instead, there was an emotionless understanding, a disconnected comprehension, an abstract sense of closure that they were distracted from remorselessly by voices.

Now – if the word meant anything specific – or then, when the bodies were but recently consigned to the effluent and had not been cremated, the ghosts of Joes were above the sewers, manifest to the material realm as shadows invisible except from the corners of the eyes of sensitive people, of whom there were none present. Their feet were aligned to, but not interacting with, the floor, and from the direction of the clubhouse came urgent and mocking cries.

In the slums, when a sphere of matter of enough density to hold a shape and not too much to make it very heavy came into the Living Mud, a child would seize it. Once, when Joes were hardly old enough to walk but could stumble with their hands and knees and totter on stiff legs, a boy of their acquaintance found a tangle of hair, a woven mass of something that might have been a fluke but equally might have been hay windblown and adhering together from the South Fields. He held this up. Without the use of argument or cajoling, two separate gangs formed, each one of roughly equal numbers, and those who were with the boy called out at the others in derision, and those who were not with him warned the others that they would take the mass.

The slum became the site of a vigorous and anarchistic game, the aim of which was to take whatever the other side possessed. Joes were too young to join in with the others, but the sounds – the derisive shrieks, the furious barks, the insulting, barracking chants – these they remembered, both in their fascination and their fearsomeness.

These calls were like the noises they heard now, down in the sewers, coming from the clubhouse.

One of them put their hand to their ear and the other squinted, but Joes themselves heard and saw the source of the ruckus together. Down in the dark, illuminated by the ghostly glow that their own limbs gave off, was the entranceway to the den. A ghost recognises places of their previous existence but does not have the sense of familiarity once associated with them, that being overtaken by the need in them to come to terms with a new world to be familiar with, but they recognised the place by its concepts, and the voices by theirs – these were the ghosts that had haunted the gang's nights, and which had taken a particular interest in Nathan.

Joes found themselves drawn to the den by a process like that which, by waves, draws flotsam to a beach – a gradual tendency in that direction, interrupted by almost random movement in other directions. When they tried to walk it had no effect: both of their bodies moved instead like they were treading water. They had the intention to go to the place and moved their phantom limbs as if to do the physical actions necessary, but nothing happened. They would come to learn, as all ghosts do, that it is by concentrating that they move themselves, thinking hard about the place they wish to go, and while the limbs often made the movements that might have enacted a physical progress, it was the focus of the spirit that did the work.

In the absence of this realisation the clubhouse ghosts drew them over in any case.

They moved like a block of ice slid over a wet plank – smoothly and without friction – and when they wanted to stop this was also not possible, and they slipped through the matter of the wall that made the secret door, and spiralled helplessly down along the stairway, deep into the half-darkness.

When the movement stopped, Joes seemed to be in a parliament of ghosts, rank and file of them arranged as if in an auditorium, standing in raked rows so that each could see the two of them without having to peer through the head of the ghost in front, which is disconcerting, even for the transparent and deceased. The room was one they recognised, though – it was the library where Gam had cooked, and read, and slept, and where Joes had spent many a quiet hour, dozing.

One of the ghosts – tall and lanky, dressed in frills and ruffs, the bite of rot at his ears and lips – came at them with an accusing gesture: a stiff and pointing finger at the end of a stiff and pointing arm. 'Where is the god-child?' he said, his teeth chattering like an alms-seeker's queueing in a winter graveyard.

To the living Joes this question would have been a nonsense, and they were recently dead enough that this was the primary feeling with which they knew the world, but then one Joes frowned in surprise at an oncoming sense of knowing what the phrase meant, and the other one bit their lip, feeling the same. They turned to each other and, seeing the realisation in the other's identical face, they knew between them that he meant Nathan. They also knew why the words were applicable to him. That is not to say that they had an answer for the shade, since they did not, having left that world behind.

In the pause their lack of knowledge made, another ghost came forward.

The modes of dress of the men and women of the distant past were not as disparate as those now fashionable in Mordew, nor did the use of make-up express itself in one or other gender in the same way as in that city, and this ghost wore the shadows of clothes of a time in which there was little difference in the way that anyone dressed, so Joes felt that they could not decide which, if any, sort this particular ghost was. It wore simple trews, like a workman might, and a checked shirt; its face was clean-shaven and broad, but its eyes were blacked like Nathan's mother's and its lips were puffy and red. In its hair, which was long and parted down the middle, it wore a ram's head barette.

There were stairs down between the ghosts, and though they were not present in the material realm, Joes could see them as if they were, and the androgyne came down them, making movements with its hands of acceptance and urging – open-palmed sweeps that ended at its heart. Despite all this, it said the same as its comrade: 'Where is the god-child?'

Lastly, since things will happen in threes, a child came down, caparisoned in princely garb, lacking all but one of his limbs and scarred across his cheek as if burned. He turned, seeking permission from some distant and invisible authority, a motion that revealed an unnatural flattening of him, as if he had been compacted in a vice. 'Where is the god-child?' he said, too.

The entire assembly waited, as if this anaphora would, though its repetition, prompt Joes' reply, but they had nothing to say, and each instead reached for the other's hand, so that they stood close together, and while no ghost can touch another, there was something in the gesture that comforted them.

The flattened child came to them, his eyes bright with an internal light, and came up from the ground to float in their faces. He looked from one to the other and back again, and Joes felt a sensation like a rake being pulled across compacted

70

earth, one that left them turned over and revealed. This it did again, then it put up its hands and cried out: 'The god-child has taken the seventh path!'

Amongst the whole convocation of ghosts, a tumult erupted, each in their own way saying, 'It is a trap!' or 'Don't do it!'

The living do not know it in the precise way that ghosts do, but when a group of them experience one feeling that sense is contagious. Indeed, it comes into the mind of a ghost in a way that is almost irrepressible. The closest living analogue is the feeling that courses through a crowd on certain occasions – a revolution, an orgy, a public execution – and which turns previously individual persons with separate motivations into a mob with one aim, whatever that happens to be. Joes was seized with the spectral equivalent of this collective mania, and one began saying, 'It's a trap,' while the other said, 'Don't do it,' both phrases joining in their shared mind, even though each body took its own share of the burden of the utterance.

The parliament of ghosts dispersed, all going hither and thither and with no discernible plan, and so did Joes, and soon they came upon the room with the devil-head chimney, and knowing that emergencies required the red flare, they took one from where it rested and put it in the fire.

Now, no ghost should be able to have influence over the material realm, except only very gently, and it is the rare ghost indeed that can cause an eerie breath to ruffle the hair of a sleeping person, but these two together moved the physical object and did the physical work that no single ghost should have been able to do. This anomaly in the way of things went unnoticed by them, so recently had they lived, since to a living person the ability to interact with objects is taken for granted, but that is not to say that the fact was any the less unusual or difficult to account for. Perhaps it was their doubled-ness that allowed it to happen, the two of them together multiplying their Spark energy in ways that were a kind of intuitive weft-manipulation, or perhaps it was for some other reason, but whatever it was, it summoned, as a ghost would see it, the

71

children Prissy and Gam to the den, and then, moments after, Nathan and his face-chewing dog.

The two Joes delivered their message, though they had no understanding of its meaning – 'It's a trap, don't do it!' – and then Nathan filled the pair with an excess of Spark energy which banished them entirely from the den and left them wafting without form in a place with no features at all.

They dwelled in this blank and depthless realm for what might have been moments or aeons – they were not conscious of either the passing of time or the absence of it passing – and then, out of nothing, gradually there became an outline, making itself from the adherence together of motes of darkness so that it looked like a sketch done on drawing paper. This outline cross-hatched inward, was smudged outward and then, in a moment that was shared by both Joes, took colour and shape and form.

As slum children of Mordew, they knew how the Mistress of Malarkoi was said to look, but this apparition was far more beautiful, and she filled the world. The paleness of her skin was like a plateau of ice, her face the rising and falling of a snow-capped mountain, the spines of her hair blossomed like black rays, making the night. One eye was the moon and the other a captive sun, bright, but in service to her and not sufficient to blue the sky. Her legs made the flat horizon, her belly the ground under their feet, and the swelling of breath in her breast made the wind blow.

Joes stood, awestruck, their hands finding each other's in blind amazement.

This avatar of their city's enemy was enough to stupefy them, or perhaps it was because there was nothing else to stare at, but the two gawped, only moving as much as two frozen children do, which is very little.

A great deal of time passed, or it was a moment later – there did not seem to be any way of knowing which – and then she spoke, and since speech is the kind of thing a person does, she was now a person before them, very beautiful still, but on a more comprehensible scale. She said, 'Hello! Nice to meet you,' which is an entirely reasonable thing for a person to say in the circumstances. 'You're new, aren't you?' she continued. 'No need to answer. I'm sure I'd remember you otherwise.'

Joes looked at each other, each seeing the other's thoughts in the mirrors of their own eyes.

'Give me a second,' she said, 'and I'll get you set up.'

The world did not change, it was all simply there rather than coming into being. Here were the slums they had known, now clean. The shacks were well-constructed shacks, proof against the wind, proof against the water, hale and solid structures that did not shake or rattle. The streets between them were dry and there was no Living Mud. In its place was paving – broad slabs of sandstone, grouted and orderly. Washing lines did not drip; instead, dry clothes were pegged there and the laundresses who emerged to tend and take and fold them were fat-armed and cheerful, smiling and calling to each other, making bawdy jokes at the expense of their menfolk's virility.

The sky was cloudless blue and bird-filled: white gulls and magpies, sparrows and swifts.

Joes walked together through that place, unobserved by any distant and looming Manse, unperturbed by dark and violent flukes. There was no one there who sought to discipline them, show them the way of things, or to cause them any other harm.

They would not be used, they felt, against their wills.

In every way this place was an improvement on the lives they had known. They walked, the two of them, eyes wide, smiling, side by side.

Eventually, they came to the place where the Sea Wall met the metal fence that divided the slums from the Merchant City, and it was here that the first sense of something being not right came to them. They were not able to cross the barrier, and behind the Wall there was the sea crashing. Past the fence were distant figures, well dressed, ignoring them, going about their business.

'Can't we go there?' Joes said, but they didn't know the answer.

They followed the fence around until it came to a gate, which was locked with a mortice.

Both Joes put out one of their hands to the lock and they rattled its handle. It wouldn't turn, so the gate remained closed.

In the sky, the sun, unhampered by any clouds, shone cheerfully, but remorselessly, down on them. Now they realised that they had no drink, even though in the distance glasses clinked and harmonised with the light and satisfied laughter of the refreshed.

'No good?' the Mistress asked, standing suddenly at their shoulders. 'Don't worry, it's hard to get down to the nitty-gritty straight away. It's all upbringing, really. Let's go again.'

The better Mordew went away and from the blankness there came a searching sense that pricked at their wills, like a headache that precedes a thunderstorm.

Now they were in a colonnade, and drinks were being served. They were lounging on banquettes, facing each other. Between them stood a plain girl, holding out her hands and smiling. She had close-bitten nails and a dead tooth.

She turned and took a tray from a rack, put two glasses on it, and then a jug of lemonade, and then, realising that she couldn't pour the lemonade while holding the tray, she put it all down. After that it was much easier, and she poured the Joes their drinks in their glasses and put ice into the spaces remaining with a little silver shovel or scuttle.

When Joes took their drinks the beads of condensation that formed on the journey to them were cold to the touch. The tray she put at arm's length from them, smiling and curtseying neatly, the bow on one of her sleeves coming undone and a wisp of hair falling from behind her ear.

Then she left.

In the air were the birds, singing. They were swallows and swifts, white gulls and magpies.

Both Joes looked at where the girl had gone off to. She was now between the next pair of columns, where she was serving two more people. These were elaborately coiffured, elaborately dressed, and they elaborated to each other and her on the topic of her bitten nails, her dead tooth, her undone bow. When all she did was smile for them, they watched her serve their drinks with a grim and tired fixedness of expression.

In the sky the sun reached a hot noon, unchecked by any clouds or cooling breezes. It made Joes pull the sleeves of their smocks, made them waft and billow the loose fabric of their skirts.

They cooled themselves with the iced lemonades.

The girl moved through the colonnades, smiling, and the Joes' drinks were soon empty. She still had almost all the remainder of her round to complete, and the two of them turned in the other direction, anticlockwise, and strained to make out another possible servant who could meet their needs.

There instead was the Mistress. 'Shall I give you a little hand?' she said.

Joes didn't nod, but they must have acquiesced in some other way because within a moment they were all in the Manse, looking down on Mordew.

It was as dark as it had ever been, as rain-drenched, as harried by firebirds.

The Mistress turned them both to face her, crouching in front of them as a schoolteacher does when beginning to describe a novel, but challenging, set of notions to a pair of infants. 'If you've only ever known Mordew, it's hard to know anything else, isn't it?' she said, though it wasn't really a question, more of a statement. 'Look down there,' she went on, and gestured elegantly over to the slums.

When Joes both saw where she was pointing – which was down near the Sea Wall where it joined the fence that protected the Merchant City – she indicated the colonnades where lemonade could be had, served by indentured servant girls.

'I could make you rulers of this city. It would be the easiest thing in the world for me.'

In their minds' eyes, Joes saw themselves side by side, tall, straight, powerful things, well dressed and self-composed, never jerking, never wanting for anything.

'I could make everyone here look up to you.' She laughed, as if this was a joke, but Joes couldn't see the fun, and her face returned to its seriousness. 'Some would hate you. Some would worship you. But what would you care, up here?' She made the far distance come close, showed them where Malarkoi might have been if this was the material realm. 'I could make an enemy for you, a wily foe to test you and give your lives meaning.' She raised a great tower and at its pinnacle established a fearsome presence like a wound in the world, a spreading rottenness. 'I can still do it, if you want.' Now she kneeled at their feet. 'But I don't think that's what you want, any more than you want a poor girl to serve you lemonade, or to live in a nice clean slum.'

Now they were somewhere else – a plain, warm, green field with hills in the distance and grass under their feet.

'Those things are from an old life, one that's passed. You were taught to want them, taught to desire them, and I don't think you were taught very well.'

Joes looked at each other, and over their shoulders grew up a huge forest of trees and berry bushes, the mounds of roots swelling in the earth.

'I'm going to leave you here, in the countryside,' the Mistress said, 'and let you find out what you really want. When I come back, you can decide on your heaven. Okay?'

Joes nodded, but before she could have seen it, she was gone.

The first year was the hardest. It was impossible to starve there, but Joes were always nagged by a sense that there was a mistake somewhere. There was water, it never became too cold or too hot, there were no rats, or flukes, or gentleman callers, but wouldn't Mordew have been better? Was there enough in a place like this to occupy them forever? If they had been taught, like she said, could they unlearn those things? Some wounds scar, and some scars do not fade. Perhaps they were only fit for life as Mordew had taught them to live it.

They made a shelter from fallen branches and tools from sharpened stones. They didn't need clothes, but they made them anyway, weaving leaves and husks and fallen vines into hats and vests and simple shoes. There were animals and birds, insects and fish, and having no need to eat them they took to learning their languages, which were simple but powerful. They began to communicate with each other in that way, with dips of the head, small caresses, attentions paid to the needs of the other. The less they spoke the less anxiety they felt, and as the seasons changed through their gentle variations, Joes gradually began to feel less anxious.

Without words it is easy to forget the past and much simpler to pay attention to the present, and while speech never left them, they turned their attention more to doing than thinking, and soon they knew all the edible plants, all the fruiting bushes, which animals needed relief from too much milk, and which plants made nectar.

There were only two of them in a world of a thousand animals, and animals, when you speak to them, are very generous, knowing there is no reason not to be.

Joes remembered predation, they remembered death, but there was scarcely any of it here, and though in time the creatures who were there when they arrived aged and died this never felt like violence, and as often as a goat or a horse fell to its knees and never rose again, a kid or a foal was born who was identical to it, so there was no sadness.

Joes remembered cynicism and small-mindedness, but these are things that thrive only in a world like Mordew. In this place there was no antagonism, no aggression, and soon Joes came to see good things and an absence of evil as natural and to be expected.

When they had been alone together for ten years, others came – people like they were.

The people came from the trees, through an arch that Joes had called 'the Gateway' since it was the only way out of that curtailment of land they had fenced and put aside for farming. These people walked down their path of flat stones and strolled through the reeds that surrounded the pond that had formed when the first well flooded. They were doubled, as Joes were, and from their movements it was clear they were twofold – this was the word the two had for each other in their single mind – because they moved as if mirrors of each other, and in their eyes they always bore the same expression, no matter what disparate thing happened to either of them.

They were taller, and broader, and darker than Joes, and their faces were very characterful, though entirely alike.

When they reached the herb garden, they stopped at Joes' feet, knelt, and unloaded their packs. Inside were gifts wrapped in vine leaves – seeds and fruits, pressed flowers and wine, all of types unfamiliar to them – and these the newcomers laid before Joes.

When Joes accepted these gifts the two went into their small house.

Joes looked between themselves, and it was not clear to either of them what would happen.

These people did not speak, but that did not mean they did not have language, or that they did not communicate, it was only that Joes couldn't articulate how it was done, even to themselves. There were more of them, they made it known, and there were other aspects to the world, other ways to live. It was customary for pairs to share their knowledge through long cohabitation and to generate children so that this sharing could be shared again when the time came. This required two pairs, and at the end of the evening they showed Joes what it was to couple across two pairs, and that this was the way that the children would be made.

When Joes went both into the orchard and hid in the nighttime under the moonshade of an apple tree, whispering so that the newcomers could not hear them, they laughed in surprise, and a little in delight, but more in nervousness. Who were these people? How did they know what they knew? How did they communicate their information? This they said in words, though they knew fewer than they once did, since this world had fewer things, and even fewer ways of acting on them.

Wasn't this, Joes said, their world, the one prepared for them by the Mistress? But even as they said it, they knew – she had made a world for them with other people in it, knowing that loneliness is a terrible thing, even amongst twofold people. These she must have made with resources unknown to Joes, so that they could be something new, since no one can be friends forever with their own image in a reflection, and anything they created entirely of themselves would be too like them.

They went back to their bed, quiet on the stairs, and got in beside the other two, who were already sleeping. One Joes went to the left, the other to the right, and they slept there beside the others until morning.

For three seasons the four of them sowed new crops beside the old, made clothes with the new patterns, used bones for needles, and the nights became less quiet as the new pair learned the words Joes could remember. Joes told their stories and the new pair listened, and when the stories were finished, the new pair took the words and made them into songs, and on many nights the logs had burned to white dust in the fire before the four went upstairs.

One morning, the new pair announced that they were Quin, and that they should be called this name, something Joes immediately agreed to do.

In the fourth season the Joes and the Quin that could do it each gave birth to two children, making four between them, and the Quin who did not give birth said, 'These are four-folds. They have our ancestors' souls in them, though which are in which we will only know in time. They have forgotten themselves, these ancient four, so that they might also be a new thing, which is all of them in combination and multiplied.

Though one day we may commune with our ancestors, they may not wish to commune with us except in their combined form, because it is said that to be four together is better than to be four apart, and many prefer it that way.'

The children Joes and Quin had made between them were laid on the bed on a quilt sown from clean cloth, and these four were just alike, as Joes and Quin were – from two different wombs but conceived and born together. They squirmed in the same way, and cried in the same way, and fed at the same time, each Joes and Quin developing the means for them to do so. When they slept, they slept at the same time, and even if one was in a crib and another was carried by papoose into the fields, what woke one child woke the others, no matter the distance that separated them.

Their teeth came in the same order, they walked on the same morning, and though as they grew their soul combinations gave them different personalities, their birth-link never left them.

Quin was much older than Joes, having been in the world and living since before Joes arrived, the Mistress having found a world and then put her subjects into it once its ways had been established, and one day Joes found them dead. They came bawling down the stairs, both of them, calling for the children, whom they had named Jinn – it being made from the names of their parents.

When Joes fell on the ground, prostrate in their grief, their children, who Quin had schooled with the silent language, helped them up and took them into the orchard, where they felled the trees in part of it. Here they made graves, deep enough so that Quin's bodies should fertilise the soil, in time.

This area they must leave fallow, as was customary, Jinn told them.

When by the arrival of the next fourth season Joes still seemed sad, Jinn told them one night that they were leaving. First, they said it in the silent language, and then in words, since Joes had never mastered how accurately to hear wordless thoughts. 'Though we are young, and you are not yet dead,' they said, 'we will go and find others who will make vessels for us into which the souls of Quin may be born again. Perhaps this will alleviate your suffering.'

Joes went to them and put their hands on their shoulders and so, silently, they told them to stay, and that suffering was a condition into which Joes had been born, and which was to be expected.

Jinn said in words, 'When you die, we will make new four-folds, and then, in congruence with Quin, you will learn how not to suffer, since it is not a necessity in this place, and is a thing that comes from separateness, which none of us need know.'

Others came, new children were made, the farm expanded, children left, others came.

The years passed and Joes became close to death, so they gathered everyone to their bedside and for their descendants they made a declaration of their knowledge, quaintly in the spoken speech, so that nothing should be lost.

They said: 'Attend only to that part of the fertile soil that you can farm. Stake it out with boundary markers. Remove from the ground sharp stones and prepare the soil. Put aside three parts for the growing of food, one part for the building of shelter.

'When someone comes into your curtailment, clear the way for them and offer them those foods and drinks that you most cherish.

'When children are generated, nurture them, teach them how to farm, and send them eventually out from the place reserved for you so that they might come to a new place and be accepted into it. If they will not or cannot leave, turn their efforts to the work of the farm until they can or will.

'When a person dies, make for them a place beneath the ground and do not farm this land but make offerings to it for their continued happiness. Reduce the size of your shelter by the amount that you once reserved for the dead, and turn this space over to the growing of living things so that life will always have dominion and so that you will feel the lack of the lost thing in the restriction of the space left for you to live in.

'As more die you will make life, and all the time become more restricted until all that is left for you is to give up your own final space for the making of life by dying yourself.

'Allow those who do not know you and who do not know the ones that you loved to claim that part of the soil that was once marked out by your boundary markers. They will not have qualms about farming the land above the space you reserved beneath the ground for your dead.

'Let us all, in our deaths, rot away and become the fertile soil that others farm. Let our loved ones, through the transmutation of the soil, allow to pass their love, through food, into those who farm our soil, and so allow them to admit others into their boundary markers.

'The souls of the dead should be reborn, after generations, so that they might know how their loved ones have fared. They will come in the bodies of newborns – which is why newborns sometimes cry and sometimes look amazed, overwhelmed by all the things they see – though they shall soon forget their former selves, and they shall adhere to these commandments and begin again.'

The Mistress, having heard the proposition Joes put forward, returned to them as they died, a woman made from light, and she made only one revision to the plan – that all second-born children in this realm should join her in her Heaven to serve her there and help her in her work, which had need of many hands. Joes, in their ignorance, did not think this an onerous requirement, though they did worry at the sadness this would cause their descendants, to lose children they might cherish, so the Mistress agreed to make the world into one where the natural love felt for such children should become a natural desire to give them to her so that they might live in her Heaven, and that this desire should not be questionable by the mind, but should be accepted simply as the right thing to do.

She cast a spell that bound this realm into a pyramid, protected in her sixth level, and Joes' only objection met, this is how the Realm of the Manifold Spirits was established. The Mistress birthed Joes into it, and the realm flourished and blossomed for many aeons, only ending when Joes, now multitudes, were summoned to their owner, and their realm was collapsed by the Assembly, but that is a story for another time.

Her Church

WHEN DASHINI was still small, Portia took her to the fourth level to be baptised.

Portia had experienced the ritual as part of a religion now long extinct, and though she didn't remember much about it, as an experience, and couldn't really give an account of what it was for, she did at least feel that some kind of ceremony was appropriate.

She took the stairs down, and made herself and Dashini exist at the river outside the Druid village. When she was there, she called the people to her, and, since she was a goddess to them, they came. She said, 'This child will be to you as a daughter is, precious and worthy of love. Take her, and care for her, and baptise her, returning her to me after seven days.'

She went to leave, but one of the Druids reverently asked her what 'baptise' meant.

'Dip her under the water? Something like that? Make her holy.'

There was some whispering, and the reverent Druid eventually said, 'Isn't she already holy?'

Portia laughed. 'Well,' she said, 'she's a holy menace, that's for sure.'

Dashini held tightly to her mother's leg, so that Portia had to prise her fingers off. 'Go on now,' she said, 'go and play with the nice Druids. They've got some lovely wolves they can show you. And a stag.'

Dashini tried to grab onto Portia's leg again, but she stepped back. 'Show her the Wolf Pack and the White Stag,' she said to the Druids. 'I'll be back soon. Don't let her get into too much mischief.'

With that, Portia left.

Dashini was alone, her little fists bunched around the material of her dress, her feathers limp down her back.

Two of the Druids – Ygrayne and Gorlois – came over. Dashini backed off from them, but they knelt in the grass a little distance away and beckoned her forward. She stood still for a while, not moving, but the Druids smiled and beckoned and eventually she came to them, her fists still tight, her feathers still limp.

They walked her to their village, which was in a forest, putting their hands gently on her shoulders, showing her the way. 'We do not know how to baptise,' Ygrayne said, 'but we can play.'

'And we might go for a swim later?' Gorlois pointed back to where the river curled tightly and the branches of a weeping willow dipped in a still curve. The was a mother duck there, with her ducklings. There was an otter.

Dashini looked from Druid to Druid, but she was too shy to say anything.

'Are you hungry?' Ygrayne asked.

Dashini didn't speak, but she nodded her head a little.

Gorlois smiled. 'I think there is some stew,' he said.

Dashini relaxed her fists, let go of her dress. She reached up for Ygrayne's hand first, then Gorlois's. When they took them, she ran forward in the direction of the village, suddenly enthusiastic, and pulled the two Druids along with her. She looked back to see if that was alright, but she needn't have worried. They overtook her and then, both together, Ygrayne and Gorlois swung her up into the air.

Dashini giggled, and when she landed back on the ground she shouted, 'Again!'

Her Pets

OUR FIREBIRD is born to no mother, not even an egg, and when he comes out, he is covered in the blood of his sacrifice. Sticking, congealed, his beak resists his first cry and there is no one there to slap sound out of him. To protest his arrival in our world he must do it through his own effort – there is no mother to lick the mucous plug away, there is no mother to gnaw his umbilicus.

There is no one for him.

His arms – first they are weak. His legs – they will not hold him up. His wings, sleek in their feathers, won't unfurl. The spine of a firebird is crooked.

All of this is because of where he is from – the other place – come by means of a summoning. The sheath from which he is drawn is tight and dark and unfriendly, just as the new candlelight is unfriendly to the delicate lace of his eyes. It burns them. All the things he has been made for are left behind him and now he is here.

That is why he is angry, even from birth: he is not from here and he did not ask to come.

Around him gather the celebrants, and we are not things of his type. He does not recognise us, or know us, and we do not recognise him – not like a mother does, seeing herself in miniature. Instead, we bow at him and sing prayers in words he does not understand. When he squawks, eventually, we do not tend to him or love him, or put him to our breasts. We goad him into the light, and he stumbles where we push.

No newborn could be more alone.

In our Golden Pyramid there are many chambers and in some of them are his brothers: his twins, his triplets, and quadruplets – siblings by numbers unnameable – hundreds of them, all bonded to this day's ten-summer children, brought and opened and still.

When a firebird reaches the day to which he has been made to wake it is after many turns and many stairs, tottering as we cheer, sliding as we stare, down on four knees, tripped by his flight feathers, gritted by the sand, adhered to by cobwebs and midges, ears and eyes ringing, then blinded by the sun. If he has lost down in his labouring, we pick it up, put it under our shawls, make from it, later, tapestries in red. It is not our concern that he might be bald, or that his skin stings.

He has only one purpose, whether he knows it yet or not.

The Mistress gave us the spells and She showed us the way and now we have caused him to be. Part of being is doing and he must do what firebirds do, which is always the Mistress's bidding. He does not need to be told – either that information is already in him, or he chooses to do what he does knowing, as we do, that it pleases Her. Or perhaps a thing does what it is made to do; the reason is not in question – he sees the others and he does what they do.

When a firebird's wings are dry, and the blood has flaked away in the sun and the wind, then they open of themselves like kites that catch the breeze and billow, drawing tight their strings. In the air they rise, all the other firebirds, to be a great flock of scarlet in the blue daylight. He looks around, he blinks, but on the ground all he sees is us. We are lowly things, poor and wasted, waiting out our time before She gathers us up to Her realm, takes our second-borns for her spells, but his brothers are a magnificent whirl and swoop of demon-stuff, undoing the silence with their screams.

No one who can think, seeing that, could choose to be us – flat to the ground, half-buried – when he could be in the air, flying and powerful.

He throws himself up from the ground, falls into the sky, and then he is not lost – he is amongst his people and the air of his home place is the same, and the screeching is the same, and the pressure of the wind that presses him in this direction and then in that direction and the closeness of his brothers – it is all the same. Perhaps it is as if he had never been summoned – the great flock, its collective will, loops and swerves and switches – only the blue sky and even this fading in the twilight.

Below – I see it with his eyes – is the pyramid, its triangles made square in his ascent, red-gold in the sunset. For a moment it is there and then they take him away with them and he leaves us. Gunpowdered breath, sulphur, eyes glaring.

In his longing is a demon of immense size – like an island, or a mountain that consumes the Earth. It chews the mantle, drinks in the lava, reaches down beneath the surface and the breached aquifers its arms make gush up steam – a world of hot clouds, a fogged universe, punctured by eruptions. In its hunger the demon leaves its back exposed and for every fire-bird that explodes into it another eats the flesh revealed, skin knitting like cooling rock – basalt, andesite, rhyolite – exploded by another brother into new, sweet flesh.

There is no such demon in our world, no sustenance, and they will not need it since they will not live out the night, but they are drawn to the Sea Wall of the enemy and towards this the flock tends, obeying itself all the while, moving as it wishes to move, but towards it nonetheless.

He obeys the Mistress's will, as they all do, always, and he does Her works though he does not know it. She knows him and what he will do, and that is why She has brought him here with our spells and our sacrifices.

A crow flies straight, but a firebird is not a crow. Not until it must does it bend to the demands of itself. Nobler is it to fly than to eat, nobler to die than to eat, only eat to fly, only fly to die, and die so that others might eat – this is the way of the firebird-demon who is born from the stone eggs deep in the Cold Chasm and who predates on the mightiest of the world-eaters in a Realm far from ours.

She will take him – he need not fear – and give to him that which he desires. The Mistress knows the hearts of all things and deigns in Her mercy to satisfy them. It is not fear that makes him lag when the flock flies in earnest. When they know their prey is close, they fly arrow-like, faster than the moon, always at your side no matter how swiftly you run.

But he lags.

We have broken him, in our ignorance, in our rough treatment of him, in the mis-utterance of the summoning – in his left wing, two spines are bound together. They will not separate, and he cannot stretch them apart, and though he beats at the same cadence, though he strives to be amongst them, the flock leaves him behind and the light goes out in the water, the sun dampened to a black coal by the horizon, and soon he is lost.

In his world this is shame and hunger. If he cannot die, he must reconcile himself to eat, his place beneath the demon-skin assured by his late-coming, brother-death, his pitiable obligation. He flies where he thinks they have gone, to take his place at that loathsome table with the doleful survivors of this attack of the flock, waiting to make right their failure in the next wave.

Without light, he cannot see and there is no vibration of the air that tells him where wings ahead make displacements. He cannot hear them and soon below there is land – acres of broken and blistered turf, splintered and angular, lit by fires in pools of standing oil, lit by the open carcasses of buildings burning.

A firebird does not understand these things, and he does not care that he does not understand them, and he flies on, though desperation and hunger build in him in concert and never does the sense of the others awake in him, nor do they call for him or return to take him amongst them.

And days pass in loneliness.

Now on the ground are many people – soldiers to my eyes, since I know the ways of this world. They gather under crossed flags, these soldiers, and on their tents there is a cross, and on the roofs of their vehicles and on their breastplates. Everywhere is crosses and at the centre is a huge cross around which hundreds of them worship – all have their hands on it, all caress it. It draws the firebird to it, though he wants more than anything to fly. To be grounded is humiliating, but the ground ascends to him, the cross there at its centre, and all these soldiers are women.

I see, as he comes closer, and they see him – pointing.

In his world there are few things which treat him as sustenance and these take him as an egg, before he is even awake – he does not fear even the world-eater for this reason – but this does not mean that he does not know what it is to eat and be eaten, since he will do it, if there is no choice, and the shameful women want this of him, for him to be consumed by them, and they draw him to them.

Smiling and laughter.

But he is not entirely without resources. He will explode at them, where he comes close, and then their smiles will die, their laughter too, and he forces the fire in his belly out to his feathers. The women see this, and they let him go, which he feels as a sudden and delightful release of the dragging and then he is up in the cold air, cooling, and, below, the crosses fade and become, suddenly, a lake and he goes higher and higher and higher in his elation.

When the elation fades, he is left alone again, to fly back to his brothers.

In the distance, the light of bird-death flashes.

To my eye it is a red lightning, but he knows the secret names of each of them as they combust and to each he cries in exultation, knowing that they have made of their life a prideful song. He swoops to join them, but his vision is excellent, and they are still a great way away.

This murdering distance that sets the bodies of his brothers into embers, into ashes, has as its conclusion the spiral city of Mordew, which is the fingerprint on the tip of the enemy's ambition, its Wall a whorl, the Glass Road a loop, pointing ever at death. I know this because it is always known and by everyone, and when the loop becomes nothing, rising to powder like the cloud a puff makes, red cheeks peached and gentle-scented womanliness, there is a scarcely repressible inflation of the heart – my heart – this is the enemy's place, and the road is his too.

The firebird's brothers punctuate the song of his victory, I fill in the words: a grateful prayer to Her and in response she makes the Sea Wall fall, and sets in the water a restless turning, and into it, still too far away for him to join, the flock empties itself, chasing the bricks of the wall down under the water. And those that do not do this? They pound themselves into flames on the drier ground.

When he reaches the city, they are all gone.

What exaltation is there in an unwitnessed death? What pride can be had from it? What must a firebird do when he can neither eat of the flesh of the demon nor reveal that flesh for his brothers? There is nothing for him to do except mourn, and this he does by returning to the place of his birth, weeping ash, hoping for death, fearing the shame of returning to a newborn flock that will greet him with derision.

In his waking dreams he sees the egg, curls back in it, returns to the cold liquid from which he formed, and I feel his grief, dissolving me inside. He becomes nothing but sightless flight, contoured on the invisible curves of senses I do not possess, and sight returns to my eyes, sound to my ears, sulphur burning in the back of my throat. He is there, but now only as a closeness, the thing a lover feels in the dark, knowledge that there is another but knowing nothing of them now they have separated.

Then, where I stand, facing the doorway to my Mistress's Pyramid, I am forced away. Nothing pushes me back, Nothing knocks me from my feet, Nothing buries itself in a sphere into the dust until this Nothing is a dome, high enough to encapsulate the Pyramid and everything in it. A sound, so deep that the firebird feels it rattle his hollow bones, this Nothing gives out, bell-struck, quivering out across the land. Now in front of us there is a glass, a bead, a crystal ball within which our Pyramid is enclosed.

He opens his eyes again and sees it. He sees me and I see him, reflected in the rainbow mirror distortion of this curved and solid Nothing. My firebird, I am linked to by sacrifice, my daughter for him, the prizes this link and Her perfect heaven, and he is linked to me, his prize bird-death.

But his has been withheld from him, by me, by us, we lowly celebrants of Malarkoi, our spells poorly spoken.

He recognises me, our link, my thoughts, and in his fury he dives.

I feel it, his feathers fluttering in the turbulent air, vibrating in the bell-tone, and then, flush to his shape, the delight of a feather's perfect contact with the skin beneath, the murder-joy of prey-sight. His heart celebrates my motionlessness, taking it for paralysis, taking it for what it is, and his excitement sets him alight, every inch combustion, perfectly timed, so that when he collides with me I am exploded before I can be crushed by his weight, and we burn together, summoner and summoned, sacrificing both, setting off ripples of light like blood across the surface of the sphere, the thuds of our destruction echoing its sound.

So, we die.

And now we knock at your Door, Mistress, and beg entrance to our Heaven, where we will both find ecstasy in your presence.

Her Child

THE KING OF SHADOWS once leaked from the fifth level into the sixth level, appearing in Dashini's bedroom.

On her bedside table she kept a vase with a single dried dandelion in it. She had picked the flower long ago, for her mother, but since Portia was away, Dashini had pressed it in the book her mother was reading, ready for her return. When Portia came back, she opened the book and the flower fell onto the floor and she accidentally kicked it under the bed.

This can't be taken as evidence of neglect. It can't be taken as a lack of the necessary maternal feeling in Portia's heart.

It was an accident.

Dashini came into her mother's room on the morning after her return to find she'd already left again. There is always pressing business for a Mistress.

Nothing negative can be assumed from this fact.

The little girl knelt, and there was the dandelion, lying in the dust under the bed.

It's not a flower's fault when no one sees it. There's no reason to crumple it up and throw it in the bin. It's still a pretty thing, so Dashini took it, found a vase for it, and put it on her bedside table.

When Portia returned again and came to tuck her daughter in, she said, 'That's a pretty flower.'

Dashini didn't say, 'It's yours. I picked it for you.' To say something like that would have meant explaining, if it was a gift, how it had come to be in a vase on Dashini's bedside table. She'd have had to explain how hard it was not to have her mother there to give flowers to, not to have her there to give a dried flower to, not to have the kind of mother who finds a dried flower from her daughter pressed into the book she is reading but instead accidentally kicks it under the bed.

Dashini didn't say anything, she just smiled and let her mother kiss her on the forehead, and then she went to sleep.

When the King of Shadows leaked from the fifth level of the Golden Pyramid of Malarkoi into the sixth level, he did it through the shadow of this dandelion. He made a minuscule adjustment in the real of this realm, so slight that it was possible with hardly any Spark, lengthening the dandelion's shadow as it was shed by Dashini's night candle so that it stretched into the sleeping girl's ear.

From here he gave her a nightmare. The Mistress, her mother – except a little more vivid, a little more distinct – took the dreaming Dashini to the Master, walking her by the hand through the dark and raining streets of Mordew, up through the slums to the place where the Glass Road began. They walked, the two of them, up its screeching glass. Her mother was sure-footed, but Dashini slipped, the Road insisting she travel down it, and never up, and Portia had to pull her until her arm was sore.

When they were at the top, the Master came to his door, puzzled. 'Why are you here, Portia?' he said.

'This child will be to you as a daughter is,' Dashini's mother replied, 'precious and worthy of love. Take her and care for her, returning her to me after seven years.'

This speech did not cure the Master's puzzlement. If anything, his expression deepened, a frown replacing it. His lips curled back, and Dashini saw his teeth, his gums receded so that the roots, like the roots of a dandelion, tangled in his mouth.

She turned, horrified, but her mother was gone, and as she searched the world for her, staring from place to place across this terrible and lonely city, the Master put his hand on her shoulder.

'Inside,' he said.

The following morning the Mistress found the breach the Shadow King had made in her realm, sealed it with a spell, but the nightmare remained, lodged safe in Dashini's head. Though she didn't remember dreaming it, it came to her every night, and in the secrecy of her sleeping mind, it told her the truth of her life: that she was alone in the world.

PART TWO

How She Fights

I

Back to Mordew

THERE'S PRECIOUS LITTLE privacy aboard a ship, even one better appointed than the *Muirchú*. Captain Penthenny kicked open the door to her meagre cabin, rattling the glass in its window, desperate to scream rage to the bottom of her lungs, but there was absolutely nowhere she could do it. If she ducked behind the empty crates, her ungrateful, surly, leatherneck crew would have seen the feathers on her hat sticking up, shaking. The wardrobe was too short and shallow for her to stand in, even if it hadn't been stuffed with mildewing uniforms. It was beneath her dignity to get into an empty barrel.

She had no alternative: Penthenny kept her anger bottled.

With a bitter smile for the pun, she uncorked wine from her dwindling supply, cleaned the crystalline silt from inside the neck with sleeve and finger, and poured an almost full mug. The liquid sat in there, red, tilting first one way and then the other with the movement of the ship. It spoke to her of headaches and dry teeth, but, back carefully turned to the door, her hat's wide brim hiding her shame, she emptied the mug regardless.

She filled it again before she put the cork back in, bit her lip, and leaned heavily on the map table.

At sea, a sailor relies on the willingness of those around her to turn a blind eye to things she can't hide – but which need hiding, nonetheless – in the understanding that the favour will be returned. But favours require goodwill, something about as abundant on this ship as the crew's paid wages were: that is to say, not at all.

She put the bottle under the table and picked up the tin mug again. It was dull and dented, losing its enamel.

There's a bloodiness to fortified wine drunk from an opaque vessel. This can be transformed – with good company, candle-light, and fine lead crystal glasses – into a delightful luminosity, but on this creaking, gloomy, half-doomed vessel, no such transformation was possible. She knocked the mugful back and this second dose cloyed in her mouth. She had to swallow hard and tense her gut to keep it from mutinying.

They could see her through a little window in the door, could tell a sigh from the disposition of her shoulders, so Penthenny didn't sigh, even though that was what she wanted to do. She pulled hard on her belt instead, moved the clasp up a notch. Her breath bound, her backbone splinted, she turned again towards her troubles – a third week with no coin for the crew and another to go before she could service the dockside vigorish on her substantial loans before borrowing more capital on the back of the next trip's profits. It was a hard and endless cycle, and before long she feared bankruptcy would break it.

Blood-like or not, she drained the dregs of the wine from her mug.

Niamh was at the door before the burning had settled and came in before she was given permission. 'Oisin says fish's got to go,' she said, without even a perfunctory performance of deference.

'No,' Penthenny replied. 'It'll drag the nets and tear them. We need an hour.'

'Told him that, and he says it don't make any difference. Fish has got to go, he says, and if the nets tear, the nets tear. He says—'

'I say we need an hour. I run this ship, and I won't—'

'Tell it to Oisin,' she said, turned, and left without even a bow.

Penthenny fished the bottle back out from under the table, adjusted her hat, and abandoned all further pretence. Swigging as she went, she followed Niamh onto the deck.

Oisin, a sailor who would have been perfectly ordinary-looking except for his conspicuous lack of a nose, was with the slake-master, a man she'd had to pay up front at the last port after his predecessor was crushed between the fish and the slake-house.

'Why are you waiting, man? Slake the damned fish! What do I pay you for?' This she said to Oisin, observing the chain of command which was, though strained, all that kept them from a cold death beneath the brine.

'Pay me?' Oisin said. 'Is that supposed to be a joke?'

Penthenny opened her mouth to say something, but Oisin cut her off and poked the slake-master instead. 'Tell her what you told me.'

The slake-master did at least have the courtesy to look ashamed, twisting about and staring at his feet. 'Won't be slaked,' he said quietly. 'Won't be slaked at all.'

'Are you a slake-master or aren't you a slake-master?' Oisin stood toe to toe with him, but he didn't look up.

He was a scrawny specimen with webbed fingers and drooping moustaches and was six inches shorter than either Oisin or Penthenny, and that would be erect. As it was, he was slouched and cowed. 'I am a board-certified slake-master, and I've got the papers to prove it,' he muttered, increasingly inaudibly, 'but I was trained to slake horses, not fishes, and this fish won't be slaked. If it won't be slaked, it won't be slaked.'

As if to make it clear that the fish wouldn't be slaked, the ship lurched forward, straining at the nets which were anchored in a tidal flow, gathering whatever passed. Now they dragged on the seabed.

'Raise those nets!' Penthenny barked.

Oisin nodded to Niamh, and Niamh pursed her lips and crossed her arms, but when her captain pointed out, illustrated by jabs of the bottle, that without nets there was no hope of landing enough fish to pay the crew, Niamh reluctantly gave the orders to the others to do as their captain demanded.

Saving the nets did nothing about the fish, though. Its impediment removed, it swam with greater speed, and soon a huge bow wave split the previously calm surface of the waters. Each beat of its tail raised the ship up and drove it forward until the creature's weight pulled the deck back down, perilously close to submerging, only for another beat of the tail to surge the boat up and forward again. Those who weren't holding on to something realised the error of their ways and dived for whatever was the nearest stable protrusion. Jobs which had seemed of the utmost urgency earlier were now meaningless distractions from the work of remaining on the ship.

'Fish run!' Penthenny bellowed, but she was too late on the alert – everyone with sea sense was holding tight and those others who had none, like the slake-master, tumbled head over heels down the deck seemingly in a hurry to throw themselves off the rear and into the churn the fish left behind them. Either the stern rail would do its job, or it would not – Penthenny had eyes only for the direction of the fish and even then, moments after it had set off, she had an ominous sense that she knew where it was going.

Every sailor has their favourite port, whether because their preferred spouse resides there or because it provides some delightful but otherwise hard-to-come-by pleasure. By the law of opposites, every sailor also has their least favourite port. It was to Penthenny's least favourite port that she guessed the fish was making for today – Mordew – and this because it had taken them there before, more than once. So often had it done it, in fact, that Oisin had come to hypothesise that Mordew Bay was where the thing would reside, given a choice, despite the magic-ridden, violent, pitiless and entirely reprehensible inhabitants of its city. Birds flock to their preferred climes, herds migrate, and this fish wanted to be where it wanted to be.

'Lower the line?' Niamh called, as much to the crew as to the captain. 'May as well take a catch as she goes.'

It was a simple matter of unlocking a capstan, and Darragh, clinging to the relevant machinery, did the necessary the moment Penthenny nodded. The ropes whirred, the hooks clanked, and soon anything with enough flesh to hold metal was being trailed behind the ship, awaiting the time when it could be dragged onto the deck, bludgeoned, and thrown into a salting barrel.

◆

The fish was definitely making for Mordew, following the shallows that fringed the submerged and forgotten country the city had risen from. It swam with more energy than ever before, its fins and forelimbs thrashing to keep it straight, frothing the water and breaching to give glimpses of dull and barnacled blubber. Half-shark and half-whale, it was impossible to identify which part was which in the agitated turmoil it made. Penthenny didn't need to know anything other than how long it would be until it was over. They'd gone south for days, but that was at a sluggish pace with many periods of complete lassitude – this was another thing altogether.

The fish seemed determined to exhaust itself.

Once Penthenny found the rhythm – lean back, move, hold on, lean forward, move, hold on – she could get about well enough, forming impossible angles with the deck, but never straying too far from upright to the seabed, and though the temptation was to return to her cabin to open another bottle, she fixed her hat firmly and went to smooth over relations with the crew.

They were gathered, it turned out, between a square of barrels bolted to the floor. The only access to the protected area this made was via a tight gap which necessitated some negotiation of the hips to manage. When Penthenny was through, each of them was crouched, staring at her in silence.

'Not interrupting anything, I hope?' she said. She had aimed for a cheery informality, apparently unsuccessfully.

Niamh – it was always Niamh – broke from the huddle, stood up. 'Like what? Fish is running – can't be doing much work, can we? Or were you hoping to lose some of us overboard? Reduce the wage bills.' She looked round for laughs, and she got them, though they were bitter and cheerless.

Penthenny removed her hat, hoping that this would, somehow, indicate that she wasn't here to bollock them, and that she could, perhaps, be spoken to like a person for once, and not simply as the representative of her position. She stopped short of letting her hair down – the plait would have been fiddly to redo with the fish in such vigorous motion – but she did sign for the pipe that was doing the rounds. It is a rule that such a pipe is given to everyone who asks for it, even irritating and derelict captains, so she received it with a nod. She was about to wipe the mouthpiece, but thought that might look snooty, so she took a drag and passed it on, trying not to think of the coated tongues and cracked lips that had recently been where her lips and tongue briefly were. 'I'll make it right, I promise,' she coughed. 'If I have to sell the ship, I'll make it right.'

Oisin scoffed. 'Sell the ship and you do us out of our livelihoods. You call that making it right?'

Penthenny saw his point. 'Then I won't sell unless the new captain agrees to keep you on as crew.'

This had seemed a perfectly reasonable suggestion, but the whole lot of them shouted in agitation when they heard it. 'That what you think of us?' Niamh said, as the others walked away, giving her withering and dismissive looks. 'Chattel to be sold on?' She shook her head, looking a little rueful, Penthenny thought. But rueful or not, she left with the others.

Sometime in the evening they came to Mordew. The city was burning – fires raged from every level except the lowest, where the smoke billowed whiter and steam gushed. The spiral of glass that had surrounded the city was nowhere to be seen, and the whole sky glowed red. In one place the Sea Wall was breached, and here the waves pulled chunks of masonry down, where they crashed and made waves of their own which surged out and competed with the natural ones.

There were ships everywhere, all departing. Some at a distance flew the merchant flag and made good going, their sails straining in the wind. The ones that passed near to Penthenny flew no colours and were overfilled with doleful passengers and anxious sailors who urged her to turn away, shooing her back the way she had come.

But there was no point shooing Captain Penthenny – it was the fish that decided where they were going – she had as little say as the sailors did. It followed the curve of what remained of the Sea Wall, steering its way through the other ships as though it cared about what was on its back.

For a while she was sure that it was making for the breach. Perhaps it would swim into the city itself, snap up the slum-dwellers as they swam for their lives, or leap out of the water and ground on the slopes, able at last, by virtue of proximity, to satisfy its craving for this port.

As they drew closer, the hole on the Wall revealed a huge maelstrom glowing sickly blue and green, pulling the slums into it. The surface of the water was dotted with shacks and poles and nameless accretions of broken wood which dragged around the blackness at the centre. On the wind sometimes there were screams, but otherwise she could make out no people.

She couldn't have rescued them if there had been any.

In the end the fish veered out seaward, taking them north, but now much more slowly. Like a truffle pig, rooting in a forest, it moved in circles, head down, pulling the ship's prow under the waves. More than once, it veered suddenly back the way it had come, and the boards shrieked against their fastenings, threatening loudly to come apart. A conscientious crew would have worked against this eventuality, tightening and lashing, but hers stayed safely in amongst their barrels and the deck was washed with brine that no one mopped away.

This went on until it was clear that conditions were safe enough for a return to duty. The crew scattered to address the most serious of the deficits this kind of rough treatment had made in the ship, and Penthenny returned to her cabin.

Sailors imagine, often, that the wind has a persona and its own reasons for doing whatever it does. This was even more true for Penthenny and her crew, except the fish was right there below them, swimming earnestly, and was therefore very obviously a thing of will. The function of believing in their subservience to the will of another is to reconcile sailors to the fact that sometimes they cannot make their ship do what they need it to. Whether what stops them is the make-believe mind of the wind, or the very real whims of a fish, the central issue is that sailors find themselves powerless. While someone hired for a menial task can distract themself from this fact by attending to their work, the captain – whose only real work is the exercise of their authority – is faced at times like that with a sense of inadequacy. The remedy for that is very strong liquor, which can fill a person with a kind of dizzy courage, for a while.

For just this purpose, Penthenny kept a bottle inside her map chest of treacly thick brandy. Now she drew deeply on it, breathing through her nostrils when she needed to. Since there is nothing much else to do when one is drinking for courage than to wait for it to kick in, she played out a scene in her imagination. In it her inability to pay the interest on her loans came home to roost in the shape of an invasion of the ship by bailiffs at the next port. Dispassionately they removed, these phantom hooligans, anything that could be sold, then they dismembered the ship for its weight in timber, and, once the fish had been harpooned to death, they divided it into portions. The people of the port – which was one moment Lindos and the next New Piraeus – gathered, tanned and laughing, and the goods were put up for auction. The remainder of the proceeds, after her debts were settled and the crew paid, Penthenny took in coins in a leather bag, which was surprisingly heavy. Then she walked, whistling, away.

She coughed, wiped her lips and drank again, but now there was a sudden very drastic dropping of the entire ship, as if it had fallen through the water. Her knees bent and the mouth of the bottle bashed her gums and made them bleed iron into her brandy. Just as suddenly the ship bobbed back up again.

Penthenny returned to the bottle, but it happened again, worse, and this time there was a grinding, nail-screeching concussion. She ran onto the deck and there were the crew, climbing to the high decks. On both sides the sea was six feet over the rail and rising.

'Niamh!' Penthenny shouted, and it was a sign of the gravity of the situation that she came straight away, and at a run.

'Fish is diving, Captain!'

'Impossible!'

But it wasn't impossible. The water continued to rise until there was scarcely a height in the middle for the crew to escape onto. The two women looked at each other and between them they exchanged a communal bewilderment that soon became a desperate seeking for solutions and then a realisation that no solution existed, all without words being exchanged.

If the fish dived deep enough, they would drown.

As if the creature could sense their thoughts, the ship came back up out of the water. For a moment Niamh and Penthenny thought the fish had regained its composure, but then it went down again. Now it went deeper, so that the deck was submerged entirely, and all the sailors grabbed what they could – flagpoles, loose ropes, ornamental wind vanes.

Penthenny was the captain of this ship, and even if the crew cursed her with every job they were given and muttered loudly about the necessity of a person in her position anyway, the prevention of all their deaths was something she recognised immediately to be her responsibility. She trod water long enough to remove her hat, drained whatever she could of the bottle, forced a breath deep into her lungs, and, though she still couldn't feel any swell of courage, she dived down.

From above the waves she could hear, she fancied, a hoarse exhortation in Niamh's voice. 'No!' she seemed to be crying, 'Don't sacrifice yourself for us!' As Penthenny swam after the descending bulk of the ship, eyes stinging, down into the cold brine, she scolded herself in her mind for her weakness. Even if Niamh had said this – and she wouldn't have – Penthenny would never have heard it.

What lies we tell ourselves to make life bearable.

The fish was attached to the boat by enormous straps of leather that looped over its bulbous and uneven form, and these could be removed when they needed to be replaced. There were seven of them, but four did the job fine, and it was the front two that wore out most. Because they wore out most, and therefore needed replacing most – one at a time so that the fish didn't swim away – it had been worth having a more easily releasable catch installed here. It was this fact that would save them, and, even under these circumstances, Penthenny was pleased to see that the extra expense hadn't been wasted: if she undid both front loops the fish would swim free. The ship would then be unable to move, true – unless the sailors made oars of the decking planks – but it wouldn't be pulled under to its inevitable destruction.

The ship rushed first away from her, too fast to match, but then the fish rounded and returned, searching for whatever it was searching for. The deck rail came within grabbing distance and now the question was: could Captain Penthenny reach and release the catch before she ran out of air? A woman without good, clean air circulating inside her quickly dies, she thought, as she pulled herself along the scaffold beside the deck, the pressure all around her growing as if she was being sat on, but all over. Her brother would do that, when they were little – sit on her chest – but she knew where to kick him to get him off. Still, it would make her eyes fizz first, sometimes, and her ears ring, just as they were doing now.

She moved automatically, one hand in front of the other, legs kicking, chest straining, thoughts shut off against a sense of oncoming failure.

To her surprise, here was the catch – a lot like the belt buckle around her waist but much larger – rippling in the currents.

How long had she been under? Seconds? No. Minutes, maybe. But that nicety of measurement was an irrelevance, she knew. Time was measured now – in the cold and growing darkness – by her ability to crank the lever beside the catch ten, perhaps twenty times, until a post of iron the size of a forearm was sufficiently loosened that a giant fish could slip the two oversized bands constraining it and swim away.

There was a second measurement: how deep they now were. With each leaden, underwater crank of the pump she became increasingly sure they were too deep and that she would never return to the surface, where life in its gaseous form could be found. So be it, the captain in her said, and since that was most of her, she concentrated on the job of cranking and maintaining the calm necessary to do this. Still, it did occur to her that this must surely pay her debt to the crew. It might even render her a hero to them.

She didn't care about Oisin and the others. But Niamh...

The fish was below her, thrashing in the freedom the loosening of the belts gave it.

The word amongst the sailors, shared over pipes of damp tobacco on clear, still nights on deck, was that when you drowned it was quite a pleasant thing, but only after you panicked for a while. You panicked, became fearful, then felt the intense pressure of your lungs wishing to expel the stale breath they'd taken the goodness from.

Then you tried to fulfil their wish.

The moment your mouth opened to blow it out, the water rushed in and then it was all better, for a while. Your lungs don't know water from air and are happy and satisfied at being filled again. You, in your mind, are happy too, and from below ascends a bright and all-encompassing light that fills your every fibre.

God calls to you, ushering you into heaven – that's what they say. Except now, because God was dead, perhaps that was no longer true?

With the final crank of the lever, the fish broke loose, and, her work done, the captain of the ship gave herself up to the brightness that was suddenly all around, God or no God.

With the brightness came strange fish, and Penthenny was a woman to whom no fish was unusual. In the early years of her captaincy, with every netful, she had broadened her experience of underwater things. She knew which was which by the names of a hundred different cities. She knew what went for what price, and which made for good eating, and what could only be chewed after hours of stewing, and which were poisoned, and what lived where. These fish were all strange to her – she recognised a pattern there, a skull shape here, fins and spines, but they were never in an easy configuration to her eyes. Some were scarcely fish at all – dog-headed, pig-tailed, things with twelve legs and wide, shocked mouths – and all of them were alight.

As if someone had drawn a line with them, they all issued from a vent in the seabed and disappeared over her shoulder.

Now appeared a boy child not unlike her brother had been at the age of thirteen. He was a thing of blue light and scarcely had anything recognisable as a face – in the darkness, brightness can shine so brightly that you can't see it clearly, and this boy's features were like that. He put out his hand to her and wanted to lead her down a tunnel, also blue and shining.

There seemed to Penthenny to be nothing stopping her from going. She looked back, briefly, and though she saw, rising from the seabed, a great shadow, what concern was that of hers? Shadows rising are things of the living world, and she was clearly dying. Possibly she was already dead.

From a breach in the shadow came light: the corrupt blue-orange-grey of a putrid and mouldering piece of fruit. But what use was such a thing to the dead? Through it, lit by it, issued schools of the sickly fish – devolved and deformed, blind and terrified. They swam away, those few that could, but many drifted up or sank down, the gloss in their eyes dulling.

Penthenny turned away, took the boy's hand and went into the tunnel.

If she had remained and watched, Captain Penthenny would have seen the mud beneath her steepen and become granite, felt it gather her up, gather the fish up, gather the ship up, gather all the shells and stones and discarded bottles. She'd have seen it all hurtle skywards with sickening speed.

In a single moment all of it was up into the air and almost as quickly it solidified and became still, magically, so she was no longer beneath the waves but was on the lower slopes of a huge mountain, higher than the clouds. In the distance a dog howled, and, further away than that, the Sea Wall of Mordew, now surrounding the new peak, split apart and fell in a slow avalanche of bricks that tumbled thickly through the mud and stopped before they could harm anyone.

The familiar jumble of the slums was stretched up and torn, the Merchant City roofs rose above them higher than ever, stretching up and up and up, and at the peak, a speck on top of it all, the Manse stood black and rotten as a decayed tooth.

Penthenny did not see this, but Niamh did, and she turned her back on the sight, ran past her gasping crewmates, past Oisin, spluttering water through the blowhole in his face, past the stranded fish, down the new mountainside, to where her captain lay wet and motionless.

By some coincidence, Penthenny's hat was beside her in the mud. Niamh put it safely to one side and then, having removed the captain's tight belt and unbuttoned her jacket, she grabbed the dead woman's ankles and pumped her knees against her chest, making a pool of water gather on her lips, which she wiped away. She did it again, because once the lungs are clear of water, a faithful first mate, no matter how surly, can then inflate her captain's lungs as a child inflates a balloon, can pound on her breastbone and thereby make her live.

When Niamh did this for Captain Penthenny, she caused her to turn away from the bright blue boy, to walk back from his heaven, to come out of his tunnel and return to the world. This she did happily, and with relief, for, though it was filled with debts, and hardship, and struggle, Penthenny had a fondness for life and wasn't done with it yet.

When her eyes opened, they fell on Niamh, who planted a kiss on her lips so tender and sweet that Penthenny had cause to remember it very often from then on, if it ever left her thoughts at all. Though her mind saw the vast prominence Mordew had become, saw the ship, grounded, saw the fish's gaping gills venting, and thought urgent thoughts, her heart rested on the kiss and was satisfied.

Niamh handed Penthenny her hat and the captain put it on, wringing wet. Once they had regained their feet, the pair stood together, the breeze chilling their cheeks, raising gooseflesh. They surveyed the scene.

Ship, fish, crew.

Mountain, mud, Manse.

And now, coming quickly from nowhere, like the lash of a black glass whip, wrapping around the mountain and solidifying in place, a new Glass Road, steeper, tighter to the surface, slicker and more magical.

There was a high urgent scream, like a baby in distress, and, despite the undoubted spectacle of the Master's unnatural creation, they instinctively searched for the source.

Down by the beached fish's mouth – the tangle of white baleen and sharks' bitter fangs – there was a strange infant-sized bundle, writhing. They both saw it and they went together, but no matter how close they came they could make no sense of it – it defied the eye and wouldn't settle into a recognisable thing. At last, they knelt, and it became clearer, though no less inexplicable.

Part of it was an oyster, open-shelled, so that the grey and frilled organism within pulsed in the air. This had hold of, between its folds and its shell, a finger – bloody at the stump and grazed – which, there was no doubting it, moved, bending at its knuckle. The shell wanted to close, but the creature would also not let the finger go. Indeed, as they watched, the finger became fused with the oyster flesh, each object taking on characteristics of the other. There was an exchange between them of solidity, of glisteningness, of muscularity.

Then the whole thing tipped over. Beneath it was revealed a tentacle: the limb of a juvenile octopus, its bulbous part secreted in a hole between rocks on what had, until recently, been the seabed. Some of its suckers were attached to the shell and some to the finger.

Penthenny looked at Niamh, and Niamh looked at Penthenny, and it is some indication of the time they had spent with the fish that neither of them were any longer baffled by this hotchpotch. Rather, they both seemed to know what it was, or what it might come to be.

As they watched, the thing went through many tortures – the octopus coming eventually out from its den, shrinking away and curling back until it enveloped the oyster and the finger and began to swell, unevenly and with calluses, into something that had the same dull unevenness as the fishskin they were so used to.

The fish itself, breathless and crushed by its weight into the hard ground, reacted to the growth, forcing a wailing, gnashing, moaning cry from within itself, as if it knew what was happening.

Penthenny took off her hat, turned it over, picked up the new creature and placed it inside. It was too big, flopping over the brim, tentacles looping tight around her fingers, but she rushed down to where the water now lapped at the new shoreline and dipped it under. As she knelt, she shouted, 'Don't just stand there staring, get me a bucket! No, the bathtub!'

Niamh sighed, swallowed, licked the brine-salt from her lips, but eventually she complied, dragging Oisin, who had been sitting nearby, head in hands, up and by his wrist to her mistress's half-flooded water chamber.

So it was that Captain Penthenny's second monster was born on the shores of Mount Mordew. It grew endlessly, this ill-favoured, pained hybrid of oyster, octopus and God-Flesh, and though it ultimately brought no happiness to anyone – not even itself – it was at least company for the fish in its misery.

They called it 'the squid', and, a few years and many voyages of the *Muirchú* later, the crew named the new ship they built on its shell the *Bishop of Sletty*. Though Penthenny offered Niamh the captaincy of this vessel, by then they both preferred that she remain as the *Muirchú*'s first mate.

In the end, Oisin got the *Sletty* job. With the extra money he made, he bought himself a brass nose that fixed in place with a strap, and from then on, when they saw him at night as their ships passed, the two women would laugh together as he glinted in the moonlight.

But this is to sail too far into the future, past the end of this book.

Let us return, first, to the moment the Master of Mordew took Nathan Treeves away to make him into the Tinderbox, and relive those events from Sirius's perspective.

We will remember that Mordew was burning, the slum-dwellers were rioting seditiously in the streets, and the Glass Road was destroyed. Nathan's blue-shining flukes were urging revolution in every quarter. Nathan's mother, Clarissa, arranged transport away from Mordew with friends of the man with the fawn-coloured birthmark, and, along with Dashini, Prissy, Gam and the two magical dogs, mother and son set to sea on a merchant vessel.

Not long after, Bellows and his gill-men appeared to take back the wayward Nathan, but Bellows was killed in trying to kill Mr Padge, who had appeared on deck unexpectedly. Gam then killed Mr Padge, and Nathan, touchingly, reconciled with Bellows by passing over his brother Adam, in the form of a book.

This seemed to be the end of the matter, but then the Master appeared in a ship of his own, all made of black wood, and spirited Nathan away.

II

Her Champion, Part One

THE BLACK SAILS, black prow, black hull, black deck, black oak, black pitch – all the black things of the Master's black ship – were suddenly there in the forefront of Sirius's attention.

There was no sense of an object from a very great distance in that mystical organ the Master had put in his chest. It would usually give a vague but unmistakeable conviction that something was present within the sphere of Sirius's comprehension. Then there would be the growth of that conviction into the sense that recognition of the presence would be possible. Then, after that, the beginnings of recognition would come as hearing, smelling, tasting, then knowing. All these things would usually have been working quietly behind his mind, suggesting moods, then ideas, then switching and turning and passing through shapes and odours and timbres. There would have been effortless matchings and sortings, barely meaningful – aesthetic things, suspicions looking for corroboration from facts that are known.

In the preconsciousness of a magical dog, hintings come together to suggest to the material part of him an identification of an object nearby. It is sufficiently definite for it to draw the eyes to any place on the periphery of vision that might contain a candidate for the exact instance in the material realm of the hinted-at thing. That is part of what it was to have the mystical organ Sirius possessed. Seeing would clarify what was hinted, and so cause a negotiation between the idea and the thing as to what it was, and whether it needed to be attended to with more or less urgency. Even if there was nothing there at all, if the object of the conception was mystical, a suspicion was raised, something that nagged, presaging that an eventuality was soon to be immanent.

Then the mystical organ would resolve the questions: when, where, and in what manner?

None of that happened as the Master's ship appeared. It was more sudden than Sirius could understand. There, heavy in the waves, bitter with the sulphurous tang of fresh tar, the Master of Mordew foremost like a figurehead, beckoning, it was there like a black scar on the world.

Sirius reared up in reflexive shock; almost immediately came the strong sense that this new thing was dangerous – particularly in its *coming-suddenly-into-being* – and it marshalled all Sirius's resources from their previously unused states. This shock brought him to a speed and pitch of living that reduced the movements of other people and other things to a perceptual crawl, as if the world had faltered in its progression while the dog remained moving. In this moment, Sirius could smell the Master, in whose service he had once been, and knew that he had violent intentions towards Nathan, his service-pledge.

That was all that the conscious part of the dog needed to know, and since it is quicker to bound forward than it is to walk, Sirius leapt up from the deck of the merchant vessel – with warnings and dismay from Anaximander shouted after him – hurling himself at his foe, who was the Master, some distance away on the prow of his black ship.

It was for this reason – by virtue of Sirius not being in contact with the deck – that when the Master magically made the merchant ship appear nearer the shores of the Island of the White Hills, where the city Malarkoi was, Sirius was not taken with it but was left leaping from an object that was no longer there.

This resulted in him dropping with a splash, shortly after, into the sea.

That inevitable fall prior to his entering the cold and briny water was more than long enough for the dog to come to know that he must swim after the black ship, since it transported not only his fleeing foe but Nathan too. So quickly was Sirius's mind working that it seemed an agonisingly long drop before he hit the water while the ship went into the distance, and when he entered the sea, he let himself go deep.

He moved like a seal or a porpoise, which is a better way of swimming than paddling with paws on the surface of the water, where a dog must contend with the waves and wind.

The thoughts of most animals are inchoate and scattered, never coalescing around anything as useful as reason – unless, as in the case of Sirius's companion Anaximander, they had need of that facility to produce human speech – and Sirius, though he was magical, was still an animal. It would be wrong to say that the dog emptied his thoughts during the swim, since he had few of those in any case. He was a thing of desires and moods, needs and requirements, action and reaction, so rather than erase the objects of his mind and from there produce some plan or strategy, instead he stripped away any trivial concerns – his well-being, his pain, his tiredness – and used what part of himself had been allotted to those lesser things for the single-minded pursuit of the ship as a prelude to the rescuing of Nathan, which is what any good dog might have done.

There were things that Sirius sensed, though, that no other dog might sense, since they were particular to him by virtue of the mystical organ the Master had placed in him. This growth, or device, or talisman – a word does not exist for a thing of its type, since it was unique – appraised Sirius of information that could not be apprehended by any other dog. Perhaps not any creature at all could know it, the Master included, since the Master had made Sirius precisely with this apperceptive function in mind, and had made another dog as a pair to speak for him – all of which is difficult work – and was this a necessary expenditure of resources if the Master could do this work easily himself?

In any case, Sirius's organ was under the water now, since its physical component was lodged in the chest, in a dark and hollow chamber behind his breastbone. From here it filled Sirius with a swelling pressure and ache indicating the presence of magic, supplemented by images, odours, sounds and touches. It made it known to the dog that great power was near, issuing from a vent in the seabed, greater even than that possessed by either Nathan or the Master.

Sirius turned his face to where he already knew the vent would be and saw it: a snaking and ragged tear on the seabed, glowing, and though he swam after the ship with as much vigour as before, it was at this vent that he looked.

The mystical organ was also sensitive to the disruptions that magic makes, and those disruptions emanate from the weft, which is a condition which knows the past and the future and the present moment all at once. This organ could *know* in a loose sense what had and might happen to the magical things of the world. Having no capacity to understand it in any other way, Sirius experienced this knowledge as a kind of waking dreaming, with characters and persons and things of his experience appearing before his mind and behaving in ways significant but only obtusely comprehensible. Still, he knew the general concepts involved from the performances of the participants of this dream, and, most importantly, their mood, which would indicate if there was danger inherent in any of it.

In this case danger was everywhere now, in history and in the days to come. These threats were manifest to Sirius in the form of great numbers of phantom snakes and biting insects which swarmed with the real, though malformed, sea fish through the water, glowing with a sickly hue and giving off a waft of fear.

In the distance the Master's ship pulled away, and in its wake, below the waves, there now gathered the antecedents of Nathan Treeves – the ghost men in robes of varying antiquity that Sirius had snapped at in the clubhouse one dark night many months ago. They did not swim but moved silently, walking as if the water was no impediment to them, treading firmly through the deep, undisturbed by anything there, dreamlike or otherwise. They, too, gave off light, this time such as the full moon lends to a landscape in the quiet hours before dawn, with a sombre and melancholy atmosphere. On their faces they wore expressions too variable to characterise together: each reacted to the hull of the ship in a perfectly individual way aside from a shared eagerness to go where the ship went.

As a disparate flock they went with it, to where Nathan was.

Sirius turned away from the vent – his instincts were intrinsically simple, and without Anaximander there to commune with regarding the content of his mystical apprehensions he fell back on his service-pledge – and followed the ship, despite the agglomeration of ghosts, phantoms and other fearful things around it. He had been bred since a pup not to allow fear to determine his actions, but to extract from the emotion its motivating energy and turn that to positive ends, primarily victory in fighting. But first he went to the surface to satisfy his need for breath, keeping sight of the ghosts with his mystical sense, where they were contained in his chest as moods, images and auras.

Not even a magical dog can swim as quickly as a ship can sail, nor can he keep pace with revenants back from their immaterial resting places, since they do not have to contend with friction. Though he swam and paddled to the limits of his endurance, always the ship and the ghosts that followed it pulled away from him, Nathan with them.

The mystical sense is not anywhere near as localised as the physical senses in either time or space, and as he swam Sirius was increasingly aware – as well as of the submarine ghosts, the emissions of the vent, and the underside of the Master's ship – of Nathan and the Master himself, who were vividly outlined in a magical colour which possesses no name in the language of dogs or men but which his organ knew very well.

Nathan was represented twice in the same space – as a fading child, becoming nothing, and as a blossoming of Spark energy, which appeared like a crystal growth, or a snowflake of light. Each appearance of his service-pledge was proper to its different realm, but neither was more or less Nathan, since he was coming to operate equally in both realms – material and immaterial – a long-standing progression Sirius had noticed since their first meeting.

These realms were present to Sirius in similarly obvious ways, and while he himself was present in only the most material manner, and could not interact by touch with, say, an immaterial concept, that wasn't to say that he was ignorant of the realms even if there was little he could do to influence them. As a consequence of the ability to sense things that were not *there*, in the ontological sense of the word, what *was* there could be made to fade, by paying it less attention rather than more, into a kind of transparency like an image projected onto fog, and through which, then, the immaterial things appeared with material solidity. This was how Nathan appeared to him despite the black wood that made up the ship.

The Master was beside him.

The postures they adopted – his service-pledge, weak and defeated, prone, exhausted, the Master standing over him, gloating – made Sirius's lips draw back over his teeth. In him gathered a righteous anger that only biting and tearing would relieve, that only the Master's torn-out throat, his chewed face, his clawed heart would satisfy.

In intermediate realms these things appeared before him – throat, face, heart – as though affairs in those places had been organised in ways that meant that the tearing and chewing and clawing was already happening, and with them came the relief and satisfaction.

But these realms were not Sirius's – this fact he felt strongly, having lived with the mystical organ since he was brought out of the Master's vat – and whatever relief he found was more of a chiding, more of a mockery – a goading – since he had failed, as yet, to make these more desirable states of existence come to pass in his, the most material realm. Though, simultaneously, to feel that his desire had been fulfilled in another realm was an indication that it could be satisfied here, too, and so was an encouragement to keep swimming, though his muscles burned and his eyes were stinging with salt water.

After a little while, but still not too soon for the dog, the ship slowed, and it began to rain.

Now on the deck the Master took Nathan in his arms, as Sirius had seen human people do in affection and comradeship, but the Master's intentions were not displayed to him in this mode.

Not at all.

The Master was burning with ill-intent and with magical emanations that indicated the bringing into the material world of a density of immaterial power, an enormous density, so that the Master took on the form of an enormous butterfly whose wings reached for miles all around coruscating with terrible and beautiful colours – corrupted and burning rainbows of glittering light, nauseous sunsets that rippled as if through fire and windswept torrents of smoke, noxious clouds of metallic dust, oxidising and melting and rising in violent bouts of steam. At the centre, his bones shone through the fabric of his skin, through the fabric of his clothes, through the fabric of the ship, and on his face was an expression of the utmost desperate effort and agony.

Raindrops were hitting the surface of the water, but it vibrated already and formed unnatural peaks and troughs that were not waves or ripples but were instead physical reactions to the Spark energy the Master was directing through himself, manifest as a piercing shriek simultaneously ringing and booming.

The weft was making the material realm into an unnatural reality, against its will.

All the while Nathan shrank and solidified, becoming a blackness so black that, despite the kaleidoscope the Master was making of everything, this blackness was still the strangest thing Sirius saw. Colours, even nameless ones, and sounds, even if they pain the ear, these are things the senses understand – even mystical organs are for detecting *something* – and it is proper for senses to be directed at a *presence*. But which organ is specialised for nothingness? There is none, but this was how Nathan was represented, as if he was already – and was becoming increasingly – like a howling absence in the world, around which the Master enveloped himself.

Though Sirius's mind reeled, horrified at the abysm his service-pledge was becoming, his body continued forward, bringing him closer every moment, making everything clearer, and it was only when all in a moment the ship became a hemisphere of splinters that his reflexes rethought his muscles' commitment to swimming forward to rescue Nathan.

He stopped.

Then magic entirely took over the world.

Sirius's mystical organ was not limited in the way his earthly ones were. If a thing is too bright, the eye shies from it. If a sound is too loud it distorts in the ear and can be blocked by hands. Too much agitation of the skin is resolved as pain.

This is because the mind and the senses have grown up together, since the beginning of time when animals developed from their predecessors and the simple fleshly circuits that indicated the presence of light to a light-seeking organism – think of a plant that tends, as it grows, towards where the light falls so that it might have more of it – developed nuance under the influence of God, who some call the weftling. His will was directed towards the creation of the complexity that might, after aeons, provide him with a companion sufficiently like him to obviate his primal loneliness, and the sensing of a thing and the ability to perceive the sense came together, and always each within the tolerance of the other. When one existed in excess, the other developed to meet it.

But with the mystical organ in Sirius's chest there had been no such synchronicity of development. Rather, the Master of Mordew made it so that it might sense all that might be usefully sensed, and that was more than a dog can comprehend.

If the Master had made a new type of creature, as Sirius knew was the method of the Mistress of Malarkoi, then that animal might have been made to tolerate the information that now coursed into Sirius's nerves, but that was not where the Master's genius lay: he always took what he had before him and altered it to his designs. He had taken a dog in the womb to make Sirius, and though he was a superior example of a dog – perhaps the most superior, along with

Anaximander – a dog is not a thing of infinite tolerance and discrimination, so the magical sense overwhelmed his ability to contain it.

Overwhelming, to a mind in the material realms, tends to be felt as fear if it is unknown and dangerous, and Sirius felt this so strongly that he stopped everything, not only the conscious things but the autonomic ones too, and he sank down under the waves.

Under here there was less of the terrible incomprehensibility the Master was making of the world. Water dulls light, softens sound, removes entirely taste and smell, and though there was no air for Sirius to breathe, the absence of the insanity above, briefly, was a relief to his mind and he lived in it for a moment.

In this moment, his will returned to him, and there came a lessening of the vent-issued magic Sirius had previously had his attention drawn to. Before, it had been profligate in its ejaculation forth of numerous malformations of aquatic life and other-worldly pests, but now it seemed as if it was itself appalled at what was going on above where the ship had been, and its activities ceased. This was a relief to Sirius's mind and he felt his composure returning by degrees.

Directly where the ship had been, the Master fell, displacing the water below him, or burning it away, or perhaps it went into the absence that was Nathan, who fell with him.

Around the Master, falling as he fell but not seeming to notice it, the ghosts of Nathan's predecessors gathered in the manner that surgeons gather during the period of their training around a corpse that has been opened so that they can see what is otherwise hidden inside – cramming together and craning as closely as they can, adopting expressions on their faces that vacillate between fascination and horror. On occasion one or other of them would turn away, hand over his mouth, tears forming in the privacy the others' close attention to the scene gave him.

Sirius chose to concentrate less on them, and more on Nathan, and now it was clearer than ever that the Master was performing murder on his service-pledge: only the barest flicker of Nathan's material presence was left, and the Master sought to crush out this remaining part too.

Sirius swam, furiously, sinuously, to where the two of them were – the distance down could only have been twenty fathoms, but they were still some way across, and had the dog thought of his own safety more than Nathan's he almost certainly would not have attempted to reach them. As Sirius came closer, it was obvious that the Master was standing, screaming on the seabed in a place with air, which Sirius would have been able to breathe if he had reached it, which was when this most faithful of dogs again remembered his own need to breathe.

Now, with direct material objects for which to aim – the Master and air – Sirius found himself able to entirely ignore the sensations of the mystical organ by dint of focussing on his material senses. The ghosts faded away, though they were still present at the edges of perception, and he saw more clearly: the Master was facing away from him, so he swam at his back, planning to disembowel him from behind as he had once done a gin-house patron, shovelling the weft-manipulator's organs out of their proper cavity with his great, spade-like paws.

Still, the dog was a long way off, and slowing in his pace as he went deeper.

The Master kneeled on the sea floor and Nathan was absent now, having been replaced by a locket on a necklace very like the one that Nathan had been wearing, only inversed. This seemed to imply that Nathan was dead, but despite that, from the mystical organ, came images of Nathan's future, acted out in every intermediate realm without exception.

The service-pledge of a dog is not bound by anything as codified as a law, nor could the punishment of any breach of whatever code existed be enforced, but still it was custom-ary amongst dogs to consider their pledges to end at death. Nathan's presence was no longer noticeable within the material realm, so was therefore to be presumed to have transferred to the immaterial realm, which for some is the definition of death. Yet Sirius did not consider his obligations ended because he did not consider Nathan properly dead. What dead child has a future that a mystical organ can sense?

And where was his corpse?

The Master placed the locket over his neck on its chain, and Sirius swam down, ever more determined to kill his former owner.

Just as Sirius was drawing near enough to surge out into the dry air and claw and bite his foe, the Master crushed something beneath his heel and then he was gone.

The water rushed suddenly to fill the gap he had made, and Sirius was caught up with this. He was swirled and buffeted in a torrent and eventually thrust up to the surface.

Again, we find ourselves pushed too far into the future. When Sirius dived after Nathan, he left others behind him, equally deserving of a voice.

Let us return again, in time and place, to the merchant vessel from which Sirius was to leap, and on which Nathan and his party left the burning city, Mordew. It is a large ship, of many decks, decorated to the tastes of its owners, Giles and Iolanthe, noble acquaintances – friends is too strong a word – of the man with the fawn-coloured birthmark.

We will remember that soon after the ship set off, Bellows came aboard to take Nathan back to the Master, and that he was interrupted in doing so by the arrival from below decks of Mr Padge, with Prissy pretending to be his hostage. Because Nathan did not recognise that Prissy was performing the con the False Damsel, he believed she was in real danger, and agreed to return to the Master if only Bellows would save her life. Bellows then used a tube of red concentrate – a magical light that removes the influence of the Spark, and which kills on contact – to kill Mr Padge.

However, Mr Padge possessed a magical mirror – the one he was always checking himself in, leading us, perhaps unfairly, into thinking he was vain – given to him by the Mistress of Malarkoi. This reflected the red concentrate back at Bellows. Because Bellows was magically derived from a normal boy, the light stripped the Spark out of him and turned him from who he had become – the large-nosed, briar-limbed, middle-aged factotum of the Master of Mordew – back into the frail child of his early youth.

Gam then stabbed Mr Padge in the back, allowing Nathan – who now saw that Bellows was not his enemy but a person cruelly manipulated by the Master, as he had been – to pass the newly revealed boy a book. This object was Bellows's brother, Adam Birch, whom his Master had said was imprisoned by the Mistress of Malarkoi but who Nathan now revealed had been magically bound between covers and had been in Mordew all along. This revealed to Bellows that his Master had lied to him, much to the detriment of his mood, as we are about to discover.

III

Parting Ways, Part One

NATHAN PUSHED the book towards him. Bellows knew this because he could see its cover – a dam and a birch – and Nathan's small hand, which he recognised immediately. As he'd stood behind his lectern, he'd watched that hand, looking for signs of the fidgeting that indicated that he was losing its owner's attention, but now he saw it because it was exactly where he was looking.

If the hand had been somewhere else, he wouldn't have seen it – even an inch or two to the right or left he wouldn't have seen it, because his gaze was fixed and there was no energy in him to adjust its direction, and none to change its focus. He stared in front of him, down and across to the deck of the ship at the shallow angle his cheek made with the boards, that his snub nose made like a prop, keeping his face in place, resting there.

In his everywhere there was the sick sense of having-been-drained-of-his-essence that had not been there only a little while ago.

In the Master's library there was a book about some people who encounter a nobleman who is a *nosferatu* – which is a type of man who sucks the blood from other men – and Bellows had enjoyed it enormously, though its details posed many questions in his mind. Now he recalled it since he felt, down on the deck, like someone who had been preyed on by an undead person, and who was left without enough of himself to do anything.

There was no pleasant sense of lassitude or satisfaction either – on the contrary, he was filled with the anxious conviction that he'd die. His ears rang, his teeth tasted of fear, and the pressure of the world as it pushed up against his body threatened to break him into pieces.

Just lying there was horrible.

Nathan's hand went away, and the book was left. If the boy said anything it was lost in the ringing of Bellows's ears.

A dam. Birch. Right there on the cover.

Bellows wasn't stupid, he prided himself on that fact, but so simple was the subterfuge that he felt that his pride must have been misplaced. A thing like that… it was like a lie one would tell a gullible child. You didn't believe that, did you? Laughing friends, all in a ring, hands held together, dancing around for a few seconds, separating, and running away, whooping and cheering, leaving him to stare fixedly at his clenched fists, tears welling.

Adam Birch. His brother.

Perhaps it was best to die now. It had been the Master's joke, after all, and showed how little he thought of his servant that he'd make it. And about such a thing. The lies it implied. The play-acting.

Bellows swallowed.

Is it possible to decide not to breathe? He had no strength to do anything active. He could not slit his wrists or throw himself overboard. There was no action he could take. But inaction? Surely that was something that, in this state, he could achieve.

The leather on the book's cover was very fine, very clear, with no scars or welts or blemishes. The crushed ivory was white against it.

His brother. So long lost. Tortured and laughed about.

If one holds one's breath, it seems, eventually, that there's a swelling in the chest. You can feel it inside you. It wants to be free, the stale and used-up air. Just like a soul that has been in the material world long enough, it wants to be out. And who knows what it might find when it is released? A congregation of the loving dead, generations in the making, waiting to welcome it?

It expands, the air.

Keeping something in was too much for Bellows to do. Not breathing was one thing, but keeping caged something that wanted to escape was beyond him, and it wasn't long before his lungs found themselves empty, the air blown back into the world.

An empty thing is naturally filled – it would be an effort to prevent it. Take an unstopped bottle and place it in the sea – remove it again above the waves and you'll see that, without any effort, there's water inside. It will never not emerge with water inside. Bellows's lungs were like that empty bottle, and the air was like the sea water, and soon Bellows learned the futility of not breathing.

But learning a fact is true and being glad of it are not the same thing. There was much he knew that he wasn't glad of. So recently he had imagined that, in the Master's service, there was nothing that wasn't perfect.

Thought is a kind of doing, and because Bellows didn't have it in him, it stopped. The boy, since now he was a boy, became an object that experienced: it experienced the sight of the book, the feel of the swelling sea, and, suddenly, the sound of rain, the cold of it on his flesh.

Inside was sadness.

A very great sadness.

'Watch it, Gam! You'll tear him!'

'Course I won't. He's not made of tissue paper, is he? Alright now, Little Bellows, let's get you downstairs, out of the wet.'

'What about the others? We can't leave them there, can we?'

'They're all dead, Prissy. They aren't going to get any more dead, are they?'

'I know. But still…'

'If you're that bothered, get Dashini over there to help you tip them over the side. Or Nathan's mum. Or one of the crew. For that matter, the dog'll probably finish them up. He can have Padge too while he's at it.'

'The male pup makes a partly sensible suggestion. It is likely that Mr Padge is inedible by virtue of his gustatory habits during life, which did not preclude the consumption of toxic substances that might have tainted his meat. These devolved gill-men, though, have the look of freshly shelled crustacea, or sun-deprived veal calves, and their odour is indicative of edibility. In the absence of other food specifically set aside for dogs, I can consume what I may, and leave the rest for salting. A dog does not have qualms in this matter, I can assure you of that, and there is no sense in waste.'

'That's disgusting! Is he some kind of cannibal, Gam? I've never liked you, mate, and I'm usually one for the animals.'

'Girl child, a cannibal, if you are employing the term for its correct meaning, consumes the meat of its own species. I, despite my facility for speech, am a different type of creature altogether from men and cannot therefore…'

In some cases, the words said by others are only facts. Things are said, and shapes of sounds vibrate in the air, resonant with the timbres of the speakers' voices, their rhythms, but when those sounds go into the ears of a person who only listens to them because they can't make the effort to block them out, they're no different than the sound a nail makes when it is pulled from a board, or that a match makes when it is dragged along the lighting strip, or the cawing of a bird high overhead.

They're just irritating sounds.

Someone picked Bellows up – Gam – and someone was worried – Prissy – and the talking dog Anaximander said whatever it was that he said while Dashini and Nathan's mother glowered at each other. None of it went inside Bellows any further than his senses. It was as if the man he had been had burrowed into the mind of the new, withered boy, travelling deep inwards into him, and had made a den in there. The old Bellows huddled in secret darkness, in a place that had no relevance to the world he'd left.

Gam lay him on a cot, pulled a sheet over him and then a soft warm blanket, and put a pillow beneath his head.

Bellows rocked there, rolling at the whim of the sea, until Prissy came and arranged the bedclothes more neatly, tucked him in so that he wouldn't fall out when the waves grew. As an afterthought, she took a glass and filled it with water from a barrel and put this on the ground in front of him. When the ship tilted and the glass slid and almost toppled where it met the gaps between the boards, she picked it back up. Not finding anywhere else to put it, she took a sip herself. 'Where do you reckon Nathan is then?' she said.

Bellows didn't react.

There was the sound of teeth being sucked, lips being smacked, the rustle of shoulders rising and falling in a shrug. 'Master's got him again, I suppose,' Gam said. 'Not much we can do about it.'

There was a silence in which Prissy might have shrugged back, pursed her lips, rolled her eyes theatrically. 'That's just like you nowadays. Very laissez-faire, aren't you?'

'You don't know what laissez-faire means,' Gam said.

'I don't need to know what it means to know that you're it. Takes a very laissez-faire sort of boy to write off one mate without being bothered and an even more laissez-faire sort of boy to let his other mates fall to their bleeding deaths without trying to save them.'

There was a silence in which Bellows, deep in the cave of his misery though he was, could easily picture the hurt on Gam's face, though he didn't understand the reason for it.

This was the last thing the two said to each other before Bellows was left alone.

He didn't sleep, down in there, and when two new people arrived in wherever it was that he had been put, after however long it had been, he heard every word they whispered. First, though, he felt one tug at his blanket, felt himself poked by their delicate fingers, one, two, three times, each touch as thin and firm as dowel rods prodding his flesh. They were checking to see if he was asleep.

'I can sail my own ship, Iolanthe, if that's what it takes.'

'Really, Giles? That would be unusually heroic of you, if only I believed a word of it.'

'Keep your jibes to yourself, you terrible harridan!'

'Why should I? You've been altogether useless this whole time. Here we are, floating who knows where, the best part of a fortune left in flames, and what have you done to prevent any of that? Made endless false promises, that's all!'

'I have done nothing of the sort! Would you rather we'd stayed and been... I hesitate to say what would have happened to us! Burned, probably. Beaten, certainly. Buggered, equally likely!'

'Giles! Don't be so vulgar!'

Then there was a silence between these two, awkward in the face of whatever authority they jointly granted the right to punish their bad speech.

Bellows, though his mood was still low, while the world was still a heartless place to him, felt a reaction to the people in the room. Revulsion is something the body does to the mind. Isn't that right? No one convinces themselves they are revolted, and then feels the emotion. The body says what appals it, and then the mind acts accordingly – withdraws, attacks, whatever needs to be done. Bellows was revolted by these two. The tones of their voices, their cadences, the accents, the words – they were all appalling. In his body he felt a negative kind of energy that was still an energy where none had been until now.

They'd been apart – Giles was much closer to Bellows's bunk than Iolanthe was – but now they came together and for an extended period there was a lot of rustling of dry silks and linens, sighs, and soft sobbing.

'What will become of us?' Iolanthe said, after the above concluded, and he replied without words.

Bellows twitched on the bunk where Gam had lain him, and had to quiet his muscles so as not to draw their attention. His body wanted these two gone, or, at least, to leave himself. Now Bellows was making it known to his depressed mind that the resources required to satisfy it had been made available.

The pair separated again when a third party entered the room, boots clattering on the wooden boards. 'Plans have been made, sir,' said a man with a much lower and gruffer voice. 'Just waiting on your go-ahead.'

'And you're certain they won't be any trouble?'

'Oh, Giles, must you always be so timid!' Iolanthe said. 'They are a renegade, a dog and some urks. What exactly do our crew have to fear from them?'

Urk. Bellows had never liked that word. All the children brought before him were equal in their lowliness, compared to the Master – this is what he had thought – and these pampered aristocrats were just as low. Nothings. At least the slum children knew they were nothing.

The pretensions of these two were sickening, even if his Master had proved false. In his imagination he slapped sense into first one of them, and then the other, and the nerves of his hand let him know that he had the strength to do it.

There was the sound of a man straightening himself – fingertips buttoning a waistcoat, the clicking of heels together preceding the adjustment of posture. 'Whenever you are ready, Simmons.'

The third man – Simmons – went off at a trot.

'We will make for the east,' Giles said. 'My family have land in the old country, in the bogs that the Assembly have ignored.'

'Do you mean the Mecklenburg?'

There was a pause, during which time, again, Giles did not speak.

'Oh, Giles, not the Mecklenburg! It's so tedious!'

'Beggars, Iolanthe, such as we now are, cannot be choosers.'

When they left, Bellows had within him some motivation. However deep his misery, however profound his disillusionment, it was less than his hatred of these two. His body agreed, and though he moved like an animated corpse, he raised himself up and staggered to where the others were, on the deck.

Up from the stairs came first a man apparently on a mission – with a stiffness of expression and walking with brusque authority – and shortly after a pair of furtive-looking aristocrats, holding each other tightly as if their secrets were clasped between them and looking no one in the eyes.

Gam knew a plot in the offing when he saw one, and his instincts told him that the sooner he and Prissy left this ship on their own terms the less likely they'd have to swim for shore. He nudged her, but her attentions were elsewhere.

When Prissy had first met Dashini it hadn't been under the most favourable circumstances. She had been distracted by events; events that had carried on uninterrupted until very recently. Now, though there was still much to draw the attention, there were also the moments of quietude common to all ship journeys that meant that she could pay proper attention to the other girl, which she was doing now, failing even to see Bellows as he climbed, with much use of the rail, up from where they'd recently left him, supposedly comatose.

The look of Dashini was one thing – she had, above her pretty face, the most uniquely wonderful head of hair, which was not hair at all but was like the feathers of a bird. It made Prissy think of that peacock she'd seen in the Zoological Gardens, except these feathers were black.

As Gam spoke to Prissy, muttering something or other, her eyes drifted over Dashini's plumage – there was no other word for it – and though the feathers were black, in the blackness there were patterns of iridescence, bottle-green and violet, or shining black versions of these colours anyway.

Bellows knocked her as he went past on his way to speak to Gam. She tutted, gave him a dirty look. 'Look where you're going! Watch him, Gam, he's still the Master's lackey, even if his nose has gone back to normal.'

'Right you are,' Gam said, but he took Bellows by the elbow, providing the skinny little thing with a bit of scaffolding so his legs didn't give out, and went over to the other side to talk.

Dashini's poise was another noticeable thing – she held herself in a way that Prissy had only seen before... in fact, she couldn't think of any time she'd seen anyone stand exactly like Dashini stood. Her chin was up, her chest was out, her feet were planted firmly apart, and all faced in the direction in which the ship was travelling, with no distractions allowed. Every breath she took was a deep one, beginning in her diaphragm and swelling her bosom, every dip and surge of the boat was insufficient to shake her perfect straightness.

Prissy had seen straightness like this in the aristocrats, but they were also deferential, to each other at least, and Dashini looked like she'd never considered anyone her equal, so there was no one to defer to. The Temple customers had arrogance like that, but it was always of a nasty, unjustified kind, where Dashini's was innocent and factual. She was clever, strong, capable, confident. Why should she defer to her inferiors?

She was one of a kind, Prissy thought.

If Dashini could feel Prissy's eyes on her, she made no sign of it. Occasionally she brushed a feather that came loose in the wind back into its place, but otherwise she was completely fixated on her own thoughts.

Gam came back up the deck, Bellows in tow behind, both inexpertly managing the movement of the ship. Bellows was the worst, one moment struggling like a man pulling himself up a hill by rope, the next braking a run that would have seen him shoot straight past Prissy and over the side.

Gam eventually reached her, grabbing on to a nearby barrel as he threatened to career past, and pulled Bellows with him. They both stood as close as they could to her. Gam wanted Prissy's attention, but when he whispered behind his hand the various stages of a possible plan, Prissy's eyes went back to Dashini, to Dashini's hands, which now made patterns in the air and were never still, as if she was knitting with invisible needles.

Gam's lips formed quiet words, but so did Dashini's, and as she stood, hips against the wood of a low barrier, leaning out into the spray the hull threw up, her red lips glistened odd syllables in the brine, her skin freckled like a stone in the rain.

After a while, when Gam said, 'So, then?' Prissy had no idea what he was talking about. 'So, then?' he repeated, crossly, when she didn't reply with the expected promptness.

'Definitely,' Prissy said, forcing herself to look into Gam's eyes. 'Definitely.'

Gam squinted at her. 'Definitely, eh? Definitely yes, Gam, we'll take the lifeboat before the toffs chuck us over the side and make for shore, or definitely no, Gam, we'll sit tight and see what happens?'

Prissy smiled and reached for his arm – the kind of thing she was used to doing with Nathan or any other gullible sort – but she should have known it wouldn't work on him because he wasn't amenable to that manner of persuasion, nor did he give womenfolk any leeway by virtue of how pretty they were or how friendly, he not having that predilection naturally, and because he'd had pretty house-sisters and a pretty house mother who were free and easy with their fists, introducing that freedom and ease with a distracting niceness up front.

Gam pulled his hand away and turned his own attentions to Dashini, though from the look on his face he wasn't so impressed as Prissy was. 'What's the deal, then?' he said. 'You want to add a new face to the gang? Because it's my preference that we don't do anything of the sort. *In extremis*, I'd say, it's better to keep things in-house. Less chance of funny business.'

Prissy moved so that her back was to Dashini, and she put herself between the girl and Gam. Bellows gaped gormlessly, but she ignored him anyway. 'You know me better than that, Gam. Whatever I do, it's for you and me.' She spared Bellows a glance. 'And Joes... No one else.'

At the mention of Joes, Gam looked at the triangle of boards made in the gaps beneath their feet. 'Alright,' he said, but with such sadness in his voice that he made himself sound like a liar. 'Just, the way you're looking at her, thought you were in the market for a new friend, that's all.'

Prissy pulled a face. 'Just wondering what she's up to, that's all.'

Gam nodded, turned, and fought his way back up the ship.

The moment his back was turned, Prissy looked over again to where Dashini had been standing, but now she was gone, so she galloped after the boy, silhouetted against the bright, gull-filled sky.

Bellows, forgotten, did not follow. Instead, he went slowly and silently to where Clarissa was standing with her dog, up on a higher deck.

Dashini had been gazing out over the water to where she knew her mother's pyramid was waiting.

There is something contradictory about the surface of water. It seems, in a long view, to be a solid mass, like land, so that you feel, when looking out to the horizon, that there's grey-blue ground in every direction. Interruptions to the surface – white breaking waves or broaching fish – are like flowers in a meadow, growing randomly where their seed falls. But, when Dashini had looked down at the bow wave of the ship, this solidity became like a turmoil, like a typhoon, like a hurricane, blowing everything up into chaos, tumbling, turning, frothing as if the texture of the land was being shaken into incoherence.

When she got to the shore, eventually, the Golden Pyramid would be there, over the cliffs, a real place. She had been so young when she left that her memory could hardly picture it. There was perhaps one image that she remembered, and that was of her mother at the line where the dirt met rock, kneeling to put offerings in a niche, gold behind her. If she asked herself why her mother was doing it, there was no answer, so she didn't ask. The image was there regardless. With it there was knowledge that the scene, if she pulled back her focus, would encompass the triangular face of her home. It pointed up, this unseen shape, directly at the sun, sometimes setting, sometimes rising, always directly above.

She turned, and there was Prissy, talking to her friend. He was a crooked and gross child, only recently straightening, and his name she had forgotten almost as soon as she had been told.

Prissy, though, she remembered.

The slum child stood there, a product of Mordew, too short in the arm and thigh, too short in the neck, her hair dirty and unkempt, the expressions that passed across her face too unaffected by any internal nicety of thought. Yet these things, like the sea, had a contradictory effect, because, combined, they made her uniquely perfect. Her neck was strong and solid, her arms and legs were sturdy, the thoughts in her mind were entirely unlike the effete and feckless intellectualism of the books Dashini had softened her quarantine with. Prissy was like a horse bred for cart-pulling: unlike one bred for dressage, coarser, but also simultaneously better, stronger, more solid.

Before Prissy could turn back and catch her looking, Dashini turned away.

She had already spoken the words of the spells that would prepare, in advance, the opening of the way into the first level of her mother's Pyramid.

She turned her mind away from Prissy – her petticoats with the soiled hems, her close-chewed fingernails, her endlessly bitten lips – towards her long-awaited return home.

Dashini wiped the sea spray from her cheeks, wiped her hands on the thighs of her dress, and with her fingers she traced the sigils that would soften the weft, bring into this prime realm the magics that opened her mother's fortress. These things she had never forgotten in her exile.

Magic burns itself into you.

(So far, we have seen Malarkoi, through various descriptions, Mordew, through the eyes of Captain Penthenny and her crew. We have seen Sirius, the magical dog, with Nathan in the past. Gam, Dashini and Prissy we've found in the present.

But what of the Master of Mordew? Where is he? What has he been doing?)

IV

Her Enemy, Part One

NOW BELLOWS WAS DEAD, the Master needed to remake the old vats in one of the secondary ante-chamber realms. This could be done with a very simple spell, and it was included, he thought, in the *Notebooks of Heligon*, but when he went to the library to check, he couldn't find it in there. The Master of Mordew, known to himself as Sebastian, was more than aware of the time that could be wasted searching for poorly remembered passages in hard-to-read books, so he cut his losses, returned to the blank expanse of the other realm, and relied on his memory.

This was, it turned out, a mistake – the replica vat rooms he made, while overwriting the absence he'd needed to address in the secondary antechamber realm, came out inverted, rendering all the sigils useless – and now he was faced with the prospect of scouring the library for the *Heligon* and doing what he hadn't been disciplined enough to do properly the first time, or undertaking the painstaking process of filing down, removing and resoldering twenty-one lines of magical copper lettering.

As he pondered this problem and tried to remember an old-world proverb that had warned about exactly what had just happened, he toyed with the locket around his neck. This he did absent-mindedly, luxuriating in the separation the realm he was in currently had from the passing of time in the horrible material realm. He let the chain slip around his neck, the links cold on the skin his open shirt revealed.

He did this for a while until his thoughts passed into an unblinking blankness that he eventually became aware of. He shook his head – tiredness – and bit his lip. He couldn't remember the proverb, and it wouldn't be much use after the fact anyway. Let labour be the punishment for laziness, he intoned to himself, and was surprised by the near universal aptness of his newly invented phrase. 'Lesson' instead of 'punishment'? Alliterative, but a bit vague.

Anyway.

He got out the biggest file and strode over to the first vat.

Mastery has various consequences on a man, some of which can be countered by limiting the range of possible interactions an intermediate realm possesses. In the material realm, Sebastian had been rendered part of the entirety of his city. When a weft-manipulator uses the weft to create magic, he also binds himself to the objects of his manipulations, and so comprehensively had he used his spells to build and maintain Mordew that there was hardly any of the city left that didn't adhere to or inhere within him. He felt it like a nervous system feels skin – comprehensively and with enormous accuracy. Here, though, in a realm almost entirely separate from the one his city resided in, and with a restricted field of possibilities, he was almost entirely free of the sensation of Mordew, which was a great relief. But it was only almost: as he walked to the vat the solid state feeling of a place in metamorphosis stopped him in his tracks in the way a pinched nerve in the back does when it suddenly catches.

He had initiated a defensive reconstruction of the ruined city prior to his translation into the antechamber, and now, under the influence of the machines he had put in place to carry this reconstruction out, the city was stretching itself into the sky. Simultaneously the gill-men were securing the God chamber, a new Glass Road was solidifying, and the Living Mud was corralling itself into forms that would make the Crusade's passage up to the Manse difficult and slow – all revisions that would allow him to luxuriate in the power of the Tinderbox, strafe the idiot Assembly back into the weft once and for all. He felt his city in its frozen, time-slowed mutability. It wasn't a pleasant sensation – nothing likes to change – but it was possible to ignore it, so that's what he did, shunting the sense of it all into the back of his mind.

Here it sloshed about with all the other things he wanted to forget.

Distracted from the file work, he checked the accuracy of the room. Georgian coving, putty-coloured plaster, picture rails, a black iron fireplace with marble surround and mantel: an exact replica of one of the many rooms the ur-demon Rekka had ruined in his assault on the Manse. It had all been fixable, despite the terrible mess, not precisely with a click of the fingers, but certainly without too much effort, and Sebastian was planning to slot this secondary replica, eventually, into the space in the primary second-floor antechamber realm where the original room still was in the material realm. Obviously he hadn't used that one for years – he had barely set foot in the real Manse since it started giving him migraines – but it suited his prejudices to make these subsidiary realms identical to their parents.

Could you call a copy of something a copy if it was completely different?

Of course not.

The vats – all twenty-one of them – took up most of the space. They were huge inverted bells, identical except in the sigils that decorated their waists, and they were shaped in such a way that though the circumferences of the rims touched, at the base there was enough room to squeeze in a settee, or cram in a drinks cabinet, and in this way he found he could muster enough furniture into place to make himself comfortable in the downtime while he waited for each new boy to cure before moving him to the next vat.

Twenty-one layers were excessive, even he felt that, but this was to be a Bellows, and twenty-three and nineteen were inauspicious numbers, so twenty-one it was.

Nathan Treeves. What a pain in the arse. He twisted the locket on its chain until it started to tighten around his neck and the links threatened to tangle... then he let it go.

The Tinderbox spun there, Nathan spun there – his weft-stuff at least – first all the way unwinding, then rewinding itself. As it did this, the Master kitted the room out with ladders and planks leading between the floorboards and the vat tops, muttering under his breath spells from Ibn al-Sud's *Material Morphotactics*, drawing power from the machines of the Underneath.

When that was done, he grabbed the locket in his fist and held it there. It didn't seem unusually hot, which was a good sign.

The first vat was a softener – the sigils there should have been 'melting ice', 'sunrise', 'how late it is, brother', and a threefold fusion of 'beansprout', 'rooting powder', and 'the Formal Cycle', attached in a belt exactly midway up where the copper bowled out to make the rim. Inverse, it was gibberish, the closest it came to any accepted weft-linked pattern being a fact of the circularity of 'sunrise', though even that was partial, the uneven horizon being uneven in the opposite way. If he'd ignored the fact, saved himself the trouble of, as he was doing now, grinding metal from metal, the vat would either not soften at all, or would harden, making, perhaps, a pangolin-skinned monstrosity of the first candidate. Some use could be found for it – as a guard, perhaps – but that wasn't what he was after. He needed to make the candidate's surface malleable without undermining his viability, so he could move on to the second vat, then the third, through the sequence to the twenty-first, each stage incrementally pushing a fresh boy into a new Bellows.

Working with tools, raising a sweat, good, honest toil, as he believed it was known, made the Master feel real. An occupational hazard, in the weft-manipulator, to worry that everything was an illusion, so he liked this sensation, liked the pain, almost, of banging his knuckles against the metal when the file slipped. Or was this a rasp? He realised he didn't know the difference. Anyway, the effort of it – not some mumbling of mystic syllables or tortured invocation of weft-states, both of which had an intrinsic silliness, he sometimes suspected, compared with manual labour – felt solid in the aching of his muscles.

It would be wrong to say that he was enjoying it – he cursed Nathan, unfairly even he would admit, wherever he was in the immaterial realm, whatever non-life he was living, for the efforts he was having to make – but there was a definite satisfaction in the work.

The backwards 'sunrise' – a semicircle, embellished with three wavy sunrays – once the last smooth, concave meniscus of solder had fallen away, pinged off the vat side with a satisfying wholeness. It fell to the floor, bouncing first off a low chaise longue he'd summoned into being earlier, and when it did, Sebastian realised that he could reuse it, stuck back on the other way, without having to make a new one. It was things like this – small victories – that happiness was made from. Yes, he assured himself, a man's relationship with the objects of the world, and the proofs of his dominance over them, were the bedrock of a satisfactory life.

Where had he put the solder?

On the sides of his tongue, he could feel the shape of the sound he would need to bring a tube of solder into being, in his mind he felt the anticipation of the weft-tone, his blood ached in advance of the Spark sacrifice. No. Take your own advice, he said to himself, find it the old-fashioned way.

He looked around, but he'd overdone it with the decor – hardly any of the floor was visible, hidden behind soft furnishings and low tables. He tutted and let the locket swing into his open palm, something he did with the frequency that a man checks the time on a new watch, which is far more often than he needs to and at the slightest excuse.

He could, it goes without saying, syphon off some of the vast reserve of Nathan's Spark inheritance that a slight, snicking opening of the Tinderbox would release, but he decided instead to kneel and take a quick look across the floorboards. There was the solder, twenty feet distant, under a lamp stand. Such was his pleasure at having once again proved that the simplest method was the best, that he, without thinking, cast the *Venezàmoi*, and had to ignore the fact that he'd done it when the tube sprang into his hand.

The solder was self-melting, and he applied it liberally to the surface. The patina on the vat burned through a metallic rainbow into an eventual sooty grey. Old Bellows could have done this – it was just the kind of work his assiduous nature suited him to – but, though it was better done neatly, the Master splodged more here and there and pushed the reversed 'sunrise' roughly into it. This was a kind of defiance, an angry gesture with Nathan as its object, even though Nathan would never know anything about it.

Small victories.

The solder cooled quickly, once there was nothing moving it around, and when he took his hand away the sigil stuck in place. It seemed to be exactly where it should be, and for a moment that felt like enough. The optimism that goes hand in hand with a job completed smoothly can cause a drunkenness in a certain type of workman – the type that has other people on whom he can offload the consequences of any failure – and the Master knew it well. Hoorah, that optimism says, proof that you are a uniquely skilled artisan and everything you touch will go as well as this seems to have gone! This was precisely what it was saying to Sebastian now, and he recognised its voice. The voice was flattering him, speaking to his scarcely controlled arrogance, but he was wise to its games. This flattery came from that part of him that shirked exactly the kind of work it claimed he was good at – the lazy part. Its aim was to convince him, with some false story about his greatness, that he needn't do what he knew he needed to do, which was to get a three-hundred-and-sixty-degree angle-measure and check to make sure, with a plumb line, that the sigil was on true. Generally, this was a voice he was happy to be convinced by – it made him feel good about himself and saved him work – but 'generally' Bellows was there to tidy up any loose threads when the Master retired for the evening.

That was no longer the case, as was particularly obvious, given the job at hand.

He ignored the voice, therefore, sobered himself up with memories of his previous failures to take the necessary pains, and turned to locate the measure.

In the realms in which any of the completely formed Manses were present, this would have been in the tool room, in the plan chest, but he wasn't in any of those realms. He was in a totality that barely extended past the outer surfaces of the room's walls, such being the useful extent of existence for the purposes of creating this new, replacement vat room. This meant, he wearily realised, returning to the more material realms, facing the progression of their more synchronised passage of time, using magic when he'd decided not to, and in a general and unspecified way doing a lot of things he'd much rather not do.

To what end? To allow himself the delusion that he could manage his affairs by hand? That didn't make any sense.

In a depressed huff, he isolated a Spark-infused part of himself – some semi-vesical volume – and rendered it energetic.

With the energy this released, he first isolated the twenty-one vats, then primed them for translation, and lastly forced them into, and then back out of, an inverted intermediate copy realm. He used, in order:

One: *Sequestrous Lasso*;

Two: a technique of his own devising that there was no pressing need to name now the other interested parties were either dead or sworn enemies; and

Three: a summoning spell of Portia's – though he didn't frame her ownership of it except subconsciously – that she had called *Dragged Through a Bush Backwards*, a name he had never liked since it lacked gravitas and the objects summoned always appeared looking in perfectly fine order, despite the name's implication.

Then there was the room, ready for work, with nothing lost but a small portion of his generative tissue, easily replaced later when he was in his chamber. There was something that smelled like failure in this, and that felt like a bad omen, but then he remembered the 'sunrise' that he'd already corrected the inversion in. There it was, inverted again, and though this was annoying, it was also a chance for him to reclaim some of that sense of just effort that had been quite cheering before. Though it would require the measure...

The Master marched up to the sigil, struck it a ringing blow with the file – or rasp, or whatever it was – picked it up from where it then skittered away under something inconveniently low, marched back to the vat, soldered it back on, and trusted to the accuracy of his eye to ensure its straightness.

All this while, in a glass tank in one corner of the room, the first candidate had been sleeping in a bath of clarified Mud. Sleeping – that is something someone who spends time awake does, so perhaps that was the wrong way of thinking about it. He was a child of about eleven, this candidate, but the last time he'd opened his eyes was... well, the Master couldn't remember when that was. A long time ago, certainly: when he was a toddler, Fetched up from the city and delivered to the hallway antechamber. He'd been in a torpid fugue ever since, near as made no difference, silently growing, steeped in a medium that provided everything he needed – air, sustenance, absolute isolation – and let nothing which could pervert him from the Master's intentions intrude.

Is that sleep?

Probably not, but when Sebastian lifted him from the tank and took him in his apron-sleeved arms over to the first vat, he did very much resemble a sleeping child.

There were worlds, the Master knew, where a man very much like he was carried his own son from, say, a bed in which that son had suffered a nightmare and was fitfully tossing, to, say, the bed the man and his wife occupied. There they soothed the boy's nocturnal anxieties with familial proximity. That was how this child looked, and Sebastian felt, as he squeaked across the floorboards in his newly magicked protective rubber boots, like the attentive father, awake in the night, making things right. That illusion waned a little as he carried him up the ladder beside the vat and it disappeared altogether as he dropped him onto concentrated Mud, its deep, tarry blackness slickly enveloping every inch of the boy's hairless skin as he sank down into it.

When the head was under, the Master swallowed and came down again.

And what did he swallow? The imagination is a powerful thing, and one that is not entirely tamed by the lies the self tells a person. It can see through solid metal, through treacle-Mud, can occupy the mind of a boy it finds there, can see out through that boy's closed eyes, can feel the ingress of thickness if that boy autonomically opens his mouth, can taste it, can swallow. This Sebastian did with his real throat, in a kind of manufactured sympathy, and he represented it to himself as bravery. Look, he said silently, at how my good nature makes me suffer. But below this, as a mirror of the conscious fantasy he tried to force down his throat, an image was provoked – of Nathan, crushed into the darkness of the locket.

(Now the introductions and reintroductions have been made, and we can give ourselves up to events. Things from Part One will reappear in Part Two, threads will come together and pull apart. The Cities of the Weft are like long tapestries: the disparate parts of them cannot be viewed all at once, but that does not mean they are not made of the same cloth, or that they do not tell the same story. Weft or warp, long or short, eventually everything reaches an ending. We know this, and need only wait.)

V

Parting Ways, Part Two

GAM LURCHED ALONG to the cabin, where he'd laid his knives, clubs, picks and tools on a bunk. The unpredictable swaying of the deck and his inability to concentrate on the horizon behind the walls made a ball of tightness in his guts and a burning acid taste at the back of his throat, but it was his new eye that really troubled him. Ever since Nathan had filled his empty socket with this perfect organ it had made a strange and nauseating pressure in Gam's head that was worse than any seasickness.

Still, physical discomforts were a relief to him – they replaced the larger, less dense, but more pervasive weight of the guilt that swelled in his chest. He had seen a great many terrible things in his life, some of which he'd made happen, but he'd seen them only once, and then, one way or another, he'd allowed himself not to see them any more. Now, the memory of his friend Joes dropping into the darkness, eyes wide and mortified, kept taking the place of the normal world. It would come when he least expected it, layered opaquely over everything, almost, but not quite, blotting out everything else. He would blink it away, but when he tried not to see Joes falling, he saw them broken instead, cracked in two, still on a rooftop, spattered with rain.

Then he'd have to look down, concentrate on the toes of his boots.

He picked up his kit and put it all into its rightful places – knives in his socks, clubs in the elastic under his sleeves, picks and tools in the slots in his belt. It takes more than guilt to stop a slum boy like Gam. He knew that, so he felt the pain, all of it, ridiculing himself for being so weak.

Prissy came in – Gam had been keeping an eye on the doorway by its reflection in the glass of the porthole. He turned, gave a brief nod of recognition, and went to go past her.

She stopped him by the shoulder before he reached the stairs down to the other cabins, turned him round. 'We haven't decided what we're going to do,' she said.

She'd been acting odd since Nathan came back from the Manse. Or was it earlier? Was it because of what he'd done to Joes? He couldn't blame her if it was. Every time he told her why he'd done it, it sounded hollower in his mouth. She stopped asking, eventually, but he couldn't stop telling her anyway.

In the end, it didn't matter what he said. It wasn't his right to swap them for her.

She looked like her old self – cross, fed up with him for not answering her straight away, for staring at her, gob hanging open – but he knew better. 'Got time for your old comrade Gam now, have you? Now you've finished eyeing up her ladyship.'

'Shut up!' Prissy said, almost like she used to, taking none of his nonsense. But there was something under it. 'What have you got to say, anyway?'

'Already said it, Prissy – we should go off on our own. Find somewhere else. Perhaps get a ship of our own.'

Prissy snorted. 'You want to be a pirate?'

'Why not?' Gam said, though even he felt a bit silly now the suggestion was made. They couldn't sail, didn't have a crew, didn't know how to navigate, couldn't maintain a ship, didn't know how to sword-fight; in fact, neither of them had the first idea how to do anything except grift in the streets of Mordew. Ignoring that realisation, Gam went back on the offensive. 'No doubt you'd prefer to take off with Featherhead.'

Prissy grabbed him by his collars. 'Now look here, matey, I haven't got nothing but your best interests, or whatever, at art – is that right? At art? – Anyway, it's you I'm thinking about. And me. We can't go back to Mordew, it's on fire, and there's nothing left for us there. Anyone who's got anything to rob has buggered off out of it. I'm not being some lady's maid or whatever, and you're not the kind of boy people are going to want polishing their silver, are you?'

She had a point. 'So, what's your plan, Prissy?'

She let go of him, brushed his shirt back down. 'Well… I don't know. But Featherhead, as you call her, can't we at least see what she's got to say about it all?'

Up the stairs from the cabins below came the pair of emaciated royals, their hair flat and lustreless across their scalps, their well-bred ears poking out from between dull ringlets, looking at each other to spare themselves the unpleasantness of slum urks spoiling the view.

Prissy and Gam waited until they had passed. The royals had so aggressively applied their perfumes that it made the two children blink.

'Right,' Gam said, when they'd gone up on deck. 'Let's go and find Featherhead then.'

Dashini saw the pair return. Gam and Prissy had been together, it seemed, forever, and even though they treated each other with a sometimes weary, sometimes irritated intensity, it was also perfectly intimate, perfectly unselfconscious. He, at something Prissy said, frowned, and she, hearing his reply, pulled a face. The way they did it was innocent of any jockeying for superiority, any attempt by one to gain an advantage over the other.

They saw her looking and moved towards each other. In that moment, barely a fraction of a second, Dashini was reminded of the intense loneliness she had scarcely allowed herself to acknowledge in her long quarantine. She had spent so many years without anything approaching friendship, and to see it in this imperfectly perfect and unaffected state was almost too much for her. Loneliness is like a vacuum – it is an absence that draws anything and everything into it – and in this way Dashini felt herself sucking at these two, at Prissy in particular, like an airless bottle sucks at the things in its neck.

Loneliness, though, like the other feelings, must be repressed for girls like Dashini. Girls with destinies. She beckoned to them, and they came over.

'Hello, Dashini!' Prissy said, in a voice that was several notes higher in pitch than the one she naturally used. 'Are you alright?'

'What can we do for you, Your Ladyship?' Gam said.

'Well,' Dashini said. She could tell something was odd in their behaviour, but she didn't know what it was. That's the other thing loneliness does – it makes it hard to understand other people. When she hadn't said anything for a while, and the three of them were standing there on the deck of a ship, staring at each other, she began to feel awkward. She said the first thing that came into her head. 'I was hoping you two might like to come with me to Malarkoi. What do you think?'

Sometimes a person only really knows what they want when they say it, and this is how Dashini felt now. The two children looked at her, their expressions fixed and unreadable, and though she hadn't known it before, she wanted them to say yes.

'As I have often made clear,' Anaximander was saying as the boy Bellows approached, 'my senses exceed those of a human person in both quality and quantity. So it was, and without their knowing, that I heard the owners of this ship, and their crew...' He paused. 'Should this child be brought into our confidences? He appears innocuous now, impotent even, but until recently he was an eager scion of the Master, who is no friend to your interests.'

Clarissa stepped to where Bellows was standing. He was looking down, like a child awaiting a scolding, and she took him by the chin and raised his face to hers. Anaximander, by virtue of his magical origins, could commune mystically with many animals, and it looked to him as if this was what Clarissa was doing to Bellows, but he didn't hear the words inside spoken in his mind and Bellows seemed entirely bewildered by the process.

'His master has abandoned him,' Clarissa said, eventually, not breaking her gaze into Bellows's eyes. 'I think he's safe.' She let his face go, and while it fell, it only fell halfway to where it had been before.

'Very well,' said the dog. 'Might I make an addendum of my own? Trust, such as is offered to you now, Bellows, is a gift. It is a gift Clarissa has already given to me, and I intend to repay her with loyalty. If you will not also do that, then take yourself away now, since to take a thing with no intention of paying for it is a kind of theft, which in turn is a kind of violence against goodwill. Violence will always be met with violence.' Anaximander raised his lips so that his teeth were visible, making clear the unstated threats and promises that he hoped would guide Bellows in his decision.

Bellows did not leave, and he didn't flinch at the fearsome sight of the fighting dog's teeth. He didn't do much of anything, in truth, but Anaximander took this as an oblique way of him agreeing to be good. 'I heard the owners plotting that they should throw us into the brig and take the ship to a place called the Mecklenburg. This is not a place I am familiar with – the wife thinks it is tedious – but...'

Clarissa put her hand on his muzzle, something she had done many times, to shush him, which Anaximander wouldn't have suffered from anyone else. 'I'm a bit ahead of you... and them. I've got a plan, and I need you to help me.' She took her hand away and pointed up the deck to where a lifeboat hung by ropes, its bolts already loosened and the canopy which kept it dry drawn back at one corner.

Anaximander knew, now his attention was drawn to it, that Clarissa's scent lines went directly to that place. He took a deep breath through his nostrils, then another, and then he frowned, which for dogs is a thing mostly exhibited as a wrinkling across the snout and between the eyes. 'I sense the possessions, such as they are, of we three, including the boy Bellows's book, and items you have gathered as provisions from the stores. What of the others? Dashini and the slum children?'

Clarissa turned and made for the boat, taking Bellows by the hand, making sure he had the book with him. 'They'll have to fend for themselves. We've got work to do.'

•

It was while Gam, Prissy and Dashini were watching Clarissa, Bellows and Anaximander row away that the crew of the ship came up behind the three children.

They weren't big men, or particularly well-trained, but there was one for each of the children, they knew the ship well, and they were perfectly attuned to its movements. Dashini pointed off to the lifeboat, Prissy leaned over the guardrail and Gam shouted, 'Oi!', and the three crewmen, at a silent signal from the most senior, coshed the children out cold.

They lost consciousness immediately, not even knowing they'd been struck.

They were taken down to the brig, the men first stripping them of their weapons and tools and then dragging them down the stairs before bundling them into a secure room.

They locked the door behind them.

Giles and Iolanthe, on hearing their orders had been carried out successfully, weren't too worried about the loss of the lifeboat, and went to the helm. There, luxuriating in the absence of unwanted guests, they stood and turned the wheel together, each with one arm looped around the other's waist, playing at being captains.

'To the Mecklenburg!' Giles cried, and while Iolanthe couldn't quite match his enthusiasm, she had a good go at it. That is what a marriage needs: spouses to try their best under difficult circumstances.

Below decks, in a small, square cabin with no berths and a single barred porthole, the children came round, blinking. Dashini was first, then Prissy, then, as if he was unwilling to emerge from his sleep, Gam. He checked for his things before he opened his eyes, and moaned when he found them all gone.

They all had egg-sized lumps where they'd been hit, grazes and scratches on any bare skin where they'd been dragged, and throbbing headaches. The ship creaked and swayed, and the waves knocked and splashed against the hull.

'This,' Gam said, his fingers gingerly probing the edges of his lump as he sat up, 'is what you get for not paying attention.'

Prissy got up and went to the door. It was heavy and hinged on the outside, with bands of iron to stop it being easily broken down. In the top was a barred window which was too high for her to see through. She jumped up and shouted through it, 'Hey! Let us out!'

No one came. She tried the catch – locked. Without any picks, there was no way she could crack it. She went back to where the others were sitting.

'So, what do you think?' Dashini said, not seeming to pay much attention to their predicament. 'Are you going to come with me?'

If it was meant to be a joke, the other two didn't see the funny side.

'We aren't going anywhere, are we?' Prissy said.

'Not yet,' Dashini said, 'but when we get out.'

Gam went over himself to the door and rattled it. He jumped up, held on to the bars on the window, and pulled himself up to get a good look out. 'Can't see the keys, so we aren't going anywhere.'

'I've spent most of my life in a locked room,' Dashini replied, when Gam dropped back down. 'The best way to survive it is to remind yourself that one day you're going to get out. Sooner, later, it's all the same.'

Prissy, who hadn't really thought about what Dashini had been through in the Master's Manse, found this an interesting point, even if Gam, whose focus was always on the practical necessities of the here and now, didn't seem to. 'Go on then,' Prissy said, 'let's have it.'

'Have what?' Dashini said.

'You seem keen on us coming with you to Malarkoi. What's your pitch? How are you going to convince us to fall for whatever fiendish scheme you have up your sleeve?'

Dashini turned away, blushing, and said nothing.

Up on the deck there was some kind of commotion, the sound of ropes slapping against the hull, the splintering of wood. Gam went to the porthole, and then the door, but he couldn't see anything.

'Sorry,' Prissy said. She put her hand on Dashini's shoulder. 'Didn't mean to get nasty. Why should we come with you?'

The girl's hand was heavy on Dashini's shoulder, warm through the fabric of her jacket. 'It's just I don't think you really know what life can be like,' she said.

Gam laughed mirthlessly, but Prissy sat down on the boards beside her. 'Why don't you tell us then?'

Dashini looked away from Prissy's fingers, up to her face. Was she still trying to be nasty? It didn't look like it from her expression. 'Malarkoi. It's not like Mordew. I don't know what you've been told, but I can guess.'

Gam came away from the porthole and sat by the other two. 'We've been told, Dashini, that Malarkoi is a shithole, and that your mum was, not to put it too finely, a witch. But, luckily for you, we don't believe much of what we're told, do we, Prissy?'

Prissy shook her head. 'No, we don't. Everyone's got some kind of angle, haven't they?'

Mordew was one man's place, Dashini said, the Master's, and while she wasn't telling them anything they didn't already know, they listened carefully. Occasionally Gam turned back to the porthole, distracted, but he was always listening. Mordew – dirty, hard, dark, rainy, a place of streets and work, and private houses, and riches and poverty, abuse and drunkenness, all overseen by an uncaring Master, feeding on the corpse of God. Malarkoi was heaven compared to this. It was, in fact, many heavens, real heavens, all linked together by the Golden Pyramid and overseen by her mother, the Mistress, the goddess of these places all made specially for her people, thousands of them all perfect and forever. With her magic, Dashini's mother made entire realms, perfect in every way, and in them everyone lived endlessly in happiness. It was a paradise, her city, containing world upon world, everyone getting whatever they wanted, forever.

Dashini, as she spoke, seemed to blossom, the feathers of her hair fanning out like the petals of a flower, her face shining at the centre, every word carrying the weight of her joyous emotion.

She told of great trees and flocks of dragons, of Japalura, their god, of ancient forests protected by Druids, endless paradises, magic doors and personal heavens. It was a surprise to her, when she eventually stopped speaking, that both Gam and Prissy looked less than impressed.

'Really?' Prissy said. 'Sounds too good to be true, I'd say. What do you reckon, Gam?'

Gam picked at his teeth. 'You want to tone that down, Dashini. You need to make it a bit more believable if you expect anyone to fall for it.'

'It's the truth!' She looked from one to the other, but they just smiled ruefully.

'Couple of things,' Gam said. 'First, your mum's dead, isn't she? Nathan killed her, right?'

'Yeah,' Prissy said. 'And second, if it's all so bloody marvellous, what are you doing out here? Shouldn't you be in heaven with all the rest of them?'

'Just what I was going to add, Prissy. And third, it doesn't have the ring of truth, does it? It sounds, in fact, like a lot of old bollocks a person might say if they wanted to convince a pair of other persons that they should go along with them rather than going off on their own to become pirates or whatever.'

Prissy was going to point out that becoming a pirate sounded like bollocks too, but from behind, outside on the ship, came a thunderclap. Gam and Prissy leapt to their feet and, quickly and silently, went to stand on either side of the doorway. When Dashini didn't move quickly and silently enough, Gam pulled her over to stand beside him, the index finger of his free hand pressed against his lips.

Dashini ignored him. 'Do you smell that?' she asked.

Gam put his hand over her mouth, irritated and urgent, as if she was some new recruit to his gang who was too stupid to know when to keep her mouth shut. Dashini bit him and he had to take his hand away.

'Sandalwood,' she hissed. 'It's a sign of my mother's magic.'

Prissy and Gam sniffed, and there was a thick, warm, slightly astringent odour that neither of them recognised.

'So what,' Gam said.

Dashini smiled. 'Have faith,' she whispered.

Both the other children frowned – the word meant nothing to them – but then in the corridor there was a muffled thump, the beginning of a scream, cut off, and then the three could hear someone walking quietly towards the door, sliding their feet across the boards.

The planks that made up the door were bound in iron to make them more secure, but wood and metal warp in different ways, and this had made a gap between two of the planks. Prissy pointed this out to Gam, and he immediately put his new eye to it.

When he stood back up his face was drained of blood.

Prissy reached over and grabbed his arm, mouthed 'What's the matter?' at him.

'Anatole,' he mouthed back.

Prissy, unable to help herself, gasped.

It would have been helpful, for Gam, if he could have thought straight at this point, but sometimes the body makes that hard to do. When he thought of Joes, falling, he had his ways of not thinking about it, of stopping his hands from shaking, stopping the memory coming into his eyes, calming himself down. But this way of coping, Gam knew, was a temporary thing. You can put the lid on a pan of boiling water, but eventually it boils over, and now all the shaking, all the memories, all the fear came bubbling up into him when he saw Anatole's face.

It had been Anatole, one of Padge's assassins, who had stood nodding when Padge made his threat to mince Prissy. It was Anatole that smiled when Padge said the only way to avoid that threat was to let Joes fall. When Gam said no, when he begged, it was Anatole that had picked up a cleaver and turned to leave, as if he was going to get Prissy there and then and show Gam how it was done.

Now Anatole was behind the door, no doubt trying to see in, and Prissy was right there, inches away from him.

It would have been helpful, for Gam, not to have developed the shakes, not to have Joes in his eyes, for him to have been able to think.

Unfortunately, that's not the way these things work.

Anatole began tapping a rhythm on the door. It wasn't a knock: it went on too long for that and was too quiet. Then he sang a simple song, to which the tapping was the beat:

> I'm a killer of killing men,
> Out of the Mother's magic earth.
> My quarry's place I do ken;
> Killing's how I prove my worth.
> Map and List, pistol, knife;
> I have come to end your life.
> Do my work, own your sorrow,
> Your friends will live to see tomorrow.

He had a very pretty voice, but it was hard to concentrate on that fact. The three children looked between each other, their eyes wide and staring.

'Hello in there!' Anatole said.

Both Prissy and Gam made shushing signs, but even Dashini knew not to reply, faith in her mother's magic or no.

'Because we're former colleagues, Master Halliday,' he said, putting the key in the lock, 'I'll tell you the meaning of my song, something I don't usually trouble to do. Mr Padge, our mutual acquaintance, now deceased, took out a standing policy employing myself and his other assassins to kill his killer, or killers.'

The children edged back from the door, putting what limited space they had between them and this man.

'We've been provided with a magical list of the people responsible for Padge's murder, a magical map to locate them with, and a magical leg up from the Mother of Mordew, goddess of assassins, to spirit us here promptly. Your name, Gam, is on the list, the map shows you are here, and the Mother has brought me to you. If you kill yourself and spare me the trouble of a fight, I will, in turn, spare the girls you have in there with you. I think you'll agree that's a very fair offer.'

Inside the door, the three looked between each other, not knowing what to do.

Anatole started his tapping again, sang his song, the words of which made more sense than they had done the first time but which still didn't make for an enjoyable performance.

Gam looked like he was going to do as he was told – he'd always been a pushover when it came to Padge and his goons – but Prissy wasn't having any of it. She drew a finger across her throat, stuck her tongue out and pointed at Gam, then Dashini. Then she started quietly sobbing.

Dashini didn't know what she was supposed to do, but Gam did. He lay down silently on his front where he couldn't be seen, arranged his limbs at unnatural angles, and let his jaw hang loose.

Prissy pointed at him urgently, then at Dashini, crying more loudly now.

Dashini got the idea, at last, and lay on top of Gam. Prissy began a con called the Smollett after a writer of stories Gam had read in the clubhouse. Through some very convincing spluttered tears, she muttered, 'Too late. You're too late.'

Anatole stopped, and then turned the key in the lock. 'Is that you, Prissy?' he said. He opened the door, which, by luck, happened to reveal Prissy where she was crouched, weeping, and concealed Dashini and Gam where they were playing dead.

Prissy leapt up, making Anatole step back, but instead of doing anything violent she flung her arms around his neck, sobbing. 'They've caved their heads in!' she cried. 'They've caved them right in,' she said, again and again, more and more quietly, going limp and letting one arm drop so that Anatole had to pull her up to stop himself being dragged down to the dusty boards.

The assassin looked around and there was Gam's hand, a finger caught under the opened door.

Prissy sobbed and sobbed, her messy tears wetting Anatole's jacket, so he took her arm from around his neck and lowered her to the ground, where she kneeled in a ball, wracked with her miseries.

Assassins aren't easily fooled, but they are only human, and it's easy to dismiss a crying child as no real threat. Anatole stepped forward so he could close the door and reveal what he assumed would be Gam's corpse. This gave Prissy the half-second she needed. She'd teased Anatole's knife from his belt with her free hand as she'd sobbed, and now she sprang to her feet and put it against his ribs. 'Nice and easy now,' Prissy said. 'Down on your knees.'

Gam struggled, pushing Dashini off him. 'Don't kill him!' he shouted. 'He'll be booby-trapped.'

Anatole dropped to his knees, as he'd been told, but the look on his face was calm and unperturbed. 'Very wise, Master Halliday,' he said, and began whistling the tune he'd been singing before.

Gam took Anatole's thin belt and Prissy used it to tie the assassin's wrists behind his back with a hobble knot her sister had shown her. Then, gingerly, Gam located Anatole's weapons, concealed and otherwise, and pulled them from their holsters. There was a snub-nosed pistol, which Gam kept, but he threw the rest out of the porthole.

'What's the trap?' Dashini asked. 'Poison gas pouch somewhere?'

Anatole pulled a face. 'Explosive threads in the jacket. Poison pouches are too unreliable, especially when it's windy.'

Gam reached even more gingerly into Anatole's jacket pocket. Inside, there were two pieces of paper. Both were blank.

'Not for everyone's eyes, magic writing,' Anatole said. 'My deal still stands, Gam. Kill yourself, and I'll spare the girls.'

Dashini, not at all keen to be considered collateral in an assassin's bargain, delivered Anatole a kick in the side, explosive vest or no, and walked past him out of the door. 'Who sent you? My mother? Understand this – you're only here for my benefit. She put you on this ship to get me out of this prison, and that's exactly what you did. Lock him in, and let's get out of here.'

Gam nodded, but he didn't leave. 'Are you all after me?' he asked.

Anatole smiled, which was as good as saying yes.

Gam stood there in silence until Prissy took him by the hand and they left, locking the door behind them.

The ship was decorated with bodies. Where some assassins are very workmanlike, delivering death in unflashy and efficient ways – projectiles from a distance, pillows over the face while sleeping, manufactured accidents – Anatole had a reputation for flair: as well as his singing voice, he was known for his close-quarters work. The crew he'd strangled, to keep them quiet, but Giles and Iolanthe were beheaded with a sword where they stood at the ship's wheel. Their fingers were still clasped around the handles, their heads nearby with expressions on their faces that suggested they'd scarcely realised they'd been killed.

Anatole's sword was between them, its point sticking in the deck, and it was ticking like a metronome, the hilt rocking with the waves.

Gam withdrew the sword and threw it over the side, where it splashed and disappeared under the waves. 'If they're all after me, I'm done for,' he said.

Dashini shook her head. 'Didn't I tell you to have faith? My mother sent him here to help me.'

Gam indicated the corpses that surrounded them. 'He didn't help this lot much, did he? We aren't you, even if you're right.'

Prissy couldn't look at the headless aristocrats, but she didn't feel comfortable turning her back on them either. She put her hands on Gam's shoulders and stared directly into his eyes, which was a way of being attentive but which also kept the horrible stuff out of her sight. 'We'll be alright,' she said, but she didn't sound convinced.

'She's not safe to be around.' Gam backed away from Dashini, tried to take Prissy with him.

She didn't come. 'If Padge's assassins are after you,' she said, 'you're not safe to be around either.'

'The Pyramid's safe,' Dashini said. She pulled the fingers of the dead from the wheel. They fell down in a tumble together, and when they were out of the way Dashini steered the ship towards the distant shore, now visible on the horizon. 'No one will be able to get us in the Pyramid.'

Gam didn't believe her, but what choice was there?

VI

Her Champion, Part Two

THE RAIN HAD PASSED, and the clouds had parted, and the surface of the sea was no longer vibrated by an excess of magic. Sirius floated exhausted, and in the absence of the immediate urgency of action that had typified the previous activity – during which time the dog had been living very quickly – he slowed his experience of the world sufficiently to commune mystically with the creatures around him.

There is some variance in the way time passes for animals. It is not quite a rule, but almost, that the smaller a thing is, the quicker it is, and the larger the slower, which is another way of saying that for very small things the world passes by very slowly by comparison with their experiences, while for very large things it is much quicker. This may go to explain why a mayfly lives only a day while a whale can live for many decades.

That said, there is something close to a common rate for communication, and this was the pace at which Sirius now came to operate. This allowed him to make himself known in the minds of those around him being expressed neither too compactly and briefly for his persona to be recognised, nor too drawn-out either.

Sirius took a deep breath, not quite a sigh, and he spoke to the fishes and birds around him with his mind. As has already been established, Sirius did not think in words as much as he did in impressions, and nor do animals understand words and rational thoughts, but that is not to say that there was no exchange of meaning, since there was. It was meaning of a sufficient complexity that a dog with speech such as Anaximander could have translated it into human language with some flexibility and liberties taken.

The fishes and birds indicated to him where enough of the wreckage of the Master's ship might be found floating for him to rest on, and, in response to a polite request, creatures on the seabed where he had recently been reconnoitred the area and gave him to understand that there was a severed human finger there. He asked that it might be brought up to him, but most marine creatures use no ethical framework, and, finding the digit liable to contain nutrients, an oyster clamped it with its shell, intending to consume it over time, ignoring Sirius's prior claim, and this oyster was soon in a mortal struggle with an interloping octopus over its catch, a struggle which neither party was likely to give up easily.

This all became somewhat moot shortly after, when, to Sirius's surprise, the finger communed with him itself, now suddenly containing the essences of both the oyster and the octopus. It had nothing to say other than that it needed darkness, and then it was gone into the silence that generally typifies the sunless sea floor, escaping via a crack in a rock.

From the brief connection with the finger, and from the impressions in the mystical organ which that provoked, Sirius understood it to be Nathan's father's digit, severed, which now, by virtue of its former godliness – since its owner had killed the original God to claim that title – had come alive in the form of an oyster-octopus hybrid, infused with the power of the weft and with a future which would be filled with incident and adventure.

None of these futures felt germane to the business at hand, so Sirius turned his attention towards the fact that the raft of wreckage that he rested on was, quite definitely, being carried out to sea, away from Mordew. He now had time to observe the city, smouldering and clattering on the horizon, steaming like an engine that has split, the water meeting the hot coals and sending dangerous gushes of superheated liquids and gas into the world.

Ships of all types and sizes cut through the waters, and in the hulls, Sirius could smell their cargos – bacon and coal, tin and weed – and their crews, fearful, exhilarated, drunk.

Everything was singed, sails, boards and barrels, and redolent of smoke.

They were fleeing from the city.

As he floated, he heard, he thought, the very distant howling of a female dog coming from the collapsed city. She cried, it seemed, in an exulted type of triumph, delighting in the destruction, as if she was an enemy of the place and had brought its destruction about herself. Sirius turned his head first one way and then the other, listening, but as the wind blew across the waves, the bitch's voice was lost, and in any case his attention was attracted by something closer.

Hovering above the surface of the water right before him a very elderly ghost manifested himself, visible by the eye and to the mystical organ. With the one it appeared as a crooked and elaborately garbed old man, his gums mashing earnestly against each other, saying something that he amplified with an urgent and repeated indication of Mordew with a rheumatic forefinger, and by the mystical organ he was a roughly man-sized patch of magic tending both inwards and outwards, forwards and backwards in time in the manner which Sirius had come to know of intrusions from the weft, and which caused him to growl in pain and annoyance, that reaction having been chosen by the Master in order that Sirius should always seek relief and go to the person who could provide it. That person, the Master, was gone now, and the period when he had valued Sirius was long past, so Sirius was left to his own discomfort.

At first, Sirius attempted to achieve peace by barking at the ghost and glaring – something that very successfully caused living things to flee from him – but the ghost was not at all concerned. Rather than run away, it came closer, urged him more forcefully, and jabbed always to the Sea Wall in the distance. Sirius, unable suddenly to contain his natural annoyance, jumped off the raft and dived at the phantom. It was delighted at this, rather than frightened, but it moved off in any case, towards where it wanted Sirius to go, and then it began its urgent indicating again.

It was in this direction that the dog swam, a little later, but not on the ghost's say-so – if anything, Sirius wanted to defy it – but because that was where he was going in any case.

The choice was between Mordew and eventual drowning.

When the sea works against you with its currents and tides, it is very difficult to make headway at swimming, and it doesn't help when seabirds harry you from above, taking your ears and back as objects to peck at, all the while cawing and screeching and shitting down on you. And then there is tiredness and cold and the constant threat of water inhalation. Sirius suffered all of these hardships, and the hours he spent swimming brought him hardly any closer to land.

He was a magical dog, certainly, but even they have limits, and he was reaching the end of his.

In the distance the howling of the female dog came again. She seemed to call to him, both siren-like and encouraging, urging him to efforts he didn't feel able to make but somehow giving him the strength to make them.

He paddled with the last of his energy, keeping at least his muzzle above the water, and just as the bitch's call faded away Sirius sensed a sudden surge of weft energy that forced the ground up under his feet, pushed him rushing, gratefully, up into the air. It suddenly stopped, leaving what once had been flat and below the waves now steep, beneath his paws and thrust up into the sky.

From nowhere had come a mountain made from the seabed, stretching up through the clouds. For moments Sirius luxuriated in the passing of the necessity to swim and delighted in the ground that supported him – admittedly it was wet and muddy, but there was sufficient solidity to it to make it feel much better, in that moment, than the fluidity of water had felt.

Up into the air the new earth was pulled, as if someone up in the clouds had pinched a place at the middle of Mordew and was drawing it up, like a cook pulls off the gelatinous skin from a cooled gravy before throwing it down to a hungry and attentive dog, waiting by the stove, mouth open, panting. Mordew was not thrown down though, in that way, but remained solid, brown, steep in the centre, before making a slow curve where it met the surface of the sea.

Here was the ghost again, which, not properly understanding what had happened, now stood perpendicular to the surface of this new curve, making an impossible angle. Its urging and indicating took on a comic air, since it didn't seem to recognise the difference that had overcome the landscape. A ghost is not a thing proper to the material realm, and one should not expect it to instinctively obey its laws as a physical person might. Rather, the ghost gradually comes to remember what it did before its death and does those things. For the time it took to remember, and then the time it took to collate those remembered things, and then the time it took to come to a more or less accurate prediction of how it would have behaved in its life – this was several seconds – the ghost remained at an angle. Then he oriented himself to the proper plane – that being 'down' – and now, when he indicated, he did not indicate an expanse of water which must be crossed, but a place up the new mountain, behind the Sea Wall – which was now no longer where it had been but which was slowly tumbling down the hill in pieces.

Then, like the lash of a black glass whip, wrapping around the mountain and solidifying in place, a new Glass Road appeared, tighter to the surface, slicker and more magical, though neither Sirius nor the ghost paid it much attention.

Sirius had a good sense of distances, as most animals do, and he was not interested in the bricks of the Wall since they were still a way away, but he was interested in the direction the ghost was pointing.

Dogs, even those without a mystical organ, make for themselves in their mind's eye a perceptual map which combines elements of memory with the visual, the auditory and the olfactory, each type of sense material informing the other. There might be a tree on which a dog evacuates urine on its patrols through a territory. This tree will have a certain look, will make a certain creaking, and will smell of the evacuations of whomever has evacuated onto it, along with its own natural odours. This tree the dog will remember, since it is an object of interest which it seeks out on its daily walk. If the dog should either see, or smell, or hear, or remember that tree it will, on the map in the dog's mind, join all the other places and objects of its interest in a network of connected experiences of this type, all of which, synaesthetically, make the world in miniature inside the dog's mind and form a thing that can be manipulated and queried internally.

A dog might ask of this map: 'Where is the dog that emitted this unusually pungent secretion on this tree yesterday?' – not using words, but feelings – and if that dog is present to be sensed it will be obvious to the questioner where in this miniature representation that dog might be. It will allow him to go there in the material world and do whatever it is he pleases there.

Of course, this is merely a metaphor for the experience of a sense that man does not possess, but nonetheless there it is.

While he had been at sea – which is so mutable and unfixed that it makes even instinctual cartography, at least of the surface, pointless – he hadn't needed it, but this map now encompassed where things were and what they looked, sounded and smelled like. It combined this with memories of times he had been to this place, and Sirius knew that the place that the ghost was indicating was the secret den that Nathan and his playmates had occupied from time to time, and in which Sirius had encountered these ghosts before.

Back then he had tried to bite them in his anger and frustration, and there was nothing in this present ghost's demeanour that convinced Sirius that the same course of action was not now justified. Yet the memory of that previous visit, and the still, it seemed to Sirius, extant service-pledge established with Nathan, meant that this place – where Nathan had been and therefore could be again – seemed to the dog to be a good place to go, and the ghost seemed to be leading him to it. He put away his desire to disrupt the thing's material presence by harassing its image, and instead followed him at a run, the ghost always maintaining an exact distance away from him and never drawing any closer or further away, no matter at what speed Sirius approached it.

When Sirius had reached the Sea Wall he was already splattered with simple, innocent silt, but once he passed the first pile of partially disassembled brickwork his paws hit clumps of the Living Mud, slowly slicking down the new slope towards the sea. His mystical organ detected within the Mud writhing potentialities of ill-portent. Sirius had experienced the Mud before, but then it was generally passive, and what active things there were in it were small, mostly, and unthreatening. Now it seemed to have a will of its own, an intent towards violence, and the things that thrashed in it were larger, and all claws and teeth, red-eyed and wailing.

Up ahead, between tumbled brickwork and toppled shacks, there was a thing as high as Sirius's shoulder built of all the aggressive parts of a beast or insect – horns and fangs, stings and pincers – these bound to each other by strips of ligament and articulated by muscles intent only on operating whatever organic weapon they were attached to. This thing could not move around, but eyes from within it watched Sirius as he passed, angrily staring, and it made a sound like the hissing of a fearful cat. Then a poisoned sting at the end of a multiply jointed limb lashed out at him, though to no real effect.

This monster was not unique – there were many of them all around, some perched on piles of rubble and collapsed shacks, some half-emerged from the mountainside. None of them would commune with him, and his organ only sensed in them a spiteful and piteous bitterness.

When the mountain that Mordew now was had grown up out of the sea it had not done so by virtue of some natural movement in the plates below it, or by some gradual buckling of the crust; it had been forced up by magic and this had stretched the matter it had raised so that what had once been the slums – the ground, the dwellings, what passed for roads – was deformed upwards and made higher. Some parts were almost as they had been, the effect being unevenly distributed.

Sirius came to Nathan's parents' shack, which had been close to the Sea Wall, but the planks that had made it were now represented in the world as great long strips of wood, tens of feet in length, and these rested precariously together, more of a tepee than a shack. He slipped inside, between the gaps the stretching had made. Some of their small things were longer too – pillows, bedsteads, fire grate all pulled into shapes as if made from thick treacle gone solid, or from the sap of tree left to drip, or even like stalactites that stretch down with impossible solidity from the ceiling of a cave – while other objects were almost the same.

Sirius sniffed at a keepsake of Nathan's mother – one of her son's milk teeth, kept in a wooden box, that had fallen from wherever she had secreted it to rest on a table that had once been sturdy but which now had two elongated legs and two untouched ones. The table toppled when his snout touched the box, and tooth and box rolled into the Living Mud and sank into it.

There was something about this that made Sirius unhappy, so he lurched out of the remains of that place and ran here and there, not knowing how to escape.

Anything that was warped was warped in the same direction – up, towards the far distant Manse – and the disparities in the transformation undermined the foundations of anything that still stood, making structures rattle and list, all weak and prone to collapse, as Sirius passed.

Within this strange new organisation of the world, the clawed stinging flukes were dotted, and others like them: smaller, scurrying terrors; abominations that flopped and rolled in the filth; half-formed hybrids that jumped, hoping to hop, seemingly, into flight, only to splash down, growling. They were all lit in the same evil light, and all equally furious with the state they found the world in.

Prey they appeared to have found, despite their ineffectiveness, in the form of worms the size of a dog's forelimb, lungworms like those Sirius had seen in a bowl once, and which parasitised on anything, boring into flesh and eating it from within.

Then Sirius saw something that made him bark in excitement, though he was soon disappointed. A Nathan fluke came down the slope, its silhouette so like his service-pledge, slipping easily between any obstacle, gliding quickly without seeming to lift its legs. It was the size of Nathan and his shape, down to the smallest detail, but rather than a boy, who possesses disparate qualities, who wears clothes and is, materially speaking, differently textured in places, this fluke was made of all the one matter – a kind of shadowy, firm, blubbery putty, all smooth and dark like a dead porpoise, except for its fiery blue eyes.

It gave an aura of hostility, so Sirius did not try to commune with it when it stopped a hundred yards away. It picked up an object – something that had once been a kettle and which was now an attenuated lozenge of iron, six feet or more in length – raised it high, then brought it down in the midst of one of the sting creatures. The blow provoked a long, gurgling ululation that became a sickeningly choked-off silence when the Nathan fluke brought the iron down again.

Then it made its way towards Sirius.

The rules of the service-pledge are binding, but not definite, and for a moment Sirius was unsure, in his actions, how to manage the Nathan fluke as it approached. It had the form of Nathan, and had, as far as the dog could determine, been born out of his Spark energy. While a person of the material realm may not understand this, the kind of creation that Nathan used to make these flukes requires a certain passing of rights and obligations to bring about. These rights are analogous to the bond established during procreation between the parent organism and its child, though even more closely, the child being a thing of its own whereas the fluke has no such claim to individuality. It is very much more its creator than it is anything else. But just as a tumour is not equal to the person from whom it has been removed, nor is matter expelled, mucus for example, the same as the person who has expelled it, Sirius felt that he did not owe this fluke any particular service since it was something Nathan had made and then abandoned, and was not like a lost child, or a thing his service-pledge needed for his health or happiness.

This feeling was not one the dog came to instantaneously, though, and in the time he used to come to it, the Nathan fluke came before him, iron in hand, taking him presumably for one of the excrescences from the Living Mud that the previous creature it had dispatched had represented.

Regardless of the absence of any obligation, Sirius still found it difficult to countenance biting out the throat out of something that bore such a close resemblance to Nathan, though imperfectly, and certainly more difficult than running away. So he ran.

The Nathan fluke followed him for a little way, but soon found another target for its violence – a mix of man and pig lolling and retching in the mire – and while it was staving it in, thereby killing it, the ghost had left the vicinity, satisfied, possibly, that Sirius had understood his message.

Sirius made his way upward in the direction the ghost had been pointing.

VII

Boy, Book and Dog, Part One

BELLOWS AND ANAXIMANDER – using his mouth, the muscles of his neck and back corded and rippling – sculled the boat across the water in the direction Clarissa steered with the rudder. The waves, such as they were, were low, and the sun was high. In the distance the world was as if paper folded in two, both halves blue, sea and sky divided by an inked horizon.

Quite where they were going, except away from Giles and Iolanthe, neither Bellows nor Anaximander knew. Clarissa seemed to have some definite direction in mind, and kept their course straight, but she was very quiet about where they were going.

Because he didn't use his lips to speak, and didn't need to work his jaw, Anaximander could still talk, which now he did. 'As a dog who has lived exclusively in a city, I am not used to this ubiquity of water. More often I have seen quantities of it confined to containers, or had it falling in drops from the sky. Thence it gathered in puddles, or flowed through fountains, but never have I seen it agglomerated so universally.' As he said this, he pulled and pushed, and his molars dented the wood of the oar.

Of the two rowers the dog was the most powerful, young Bellows having arms like pipe cleaners and a back that bowed under the weight of his efforts. Clarissa needed to adjust her steering to account for the discrepancy in their strengths, and the frame and the planks creaked with the revision.

They moved slowly, but the ship they had left behind travelled in exactly the opposite direction, and soon there was nothing but a splinter of it, safely far off.

'While my knowledge of natural philosophy is extensive,' Anaximander went on, his oar blade cutting in, then catching perfectly, with a minimum of splash, 'it is all from book learning, even if of a magical kind. If we had the leisure, I could think of several practical experiments I would like to undertake, and thereby broaden my technical understanding with experience.' Pausing, he put the oar under his paw and looked back over his shoulder at Clarissa. She didn't, as he might have hoped, assure him that there was plenty of time for him to satisfy his curiosity, but rather she ignored him completely, so he clamped the wood between his teeth again and pulled, saying nothing for a while but thinking a great deal.

What is the extent of this sea? What lands does it border? What lies under the water?

A thinking dog wonders these things.

The placid, mirrored surface hid everything, and his other senses could not penetrate the omnipresent and consistent odour of brine. Abstractly, the texts that had been burned in the vats of Anaximander's education contained answers, and these answers came into his head when he posed the questions. They were informative, but just as a diagram is not the thing itself, and nor is a definition, he knew that the maps of an atlas and the etched and coloured plates of urchins and cetaceans and sharks and Cephalopoda that came to his mind's eye were qualitatively inferior to real examples of these things, some of which were under the planks of this boat, waiting to be observed.

To know things only magically, and from books, he thought, is to scarcely know them at all, except for the purposes of recognition. Recognition is only the beginning of knowledge and is no substitute for comprehension. If he paused now and put his face under the water, past the snout and down over his eyes, he might see wonderful things. Without stopping in his work, he tried to look back at Clarissa again, but it wasn't possible.

He knew, he felt, what her answer would be anyway.

Still, he was not a dog to be put off. For many long days and weeks and months and years he had been deprived of any ability to do the things he would have preferred to do, by virtue of his service to the merchant's wife, but that did not mean that his wishes went away. Anaximander, it must be remembered, was a dog with reason, and with memory, and with language, and all of these to a very high degree of sophistication, so when he was unable to act to make his wishes come true, he did what all reasoning beings do – he made a list of the things he wanted, memorised it, and determined to do what he could to bring them pass at his earliest convenience.

As he rowed – Bellows puffing and straining beside him, the book between his feet – Anaximander determined that he would one day:

- Place himself in a diving bell and drop it into the sea so that he might see submarine creatures in person, having set up an automatic system to provide him with air to breathe;
- Use a very bright light to illuminate the surface of the seabed and thereby make a map in his memory of the hidden features of that place, with the aim of transcribing it to paper later;
- Attempt conversation with the larger mammals and learn their lore;
- Divide the sea into a cubic grid, and give each unit of it a name so that he might monitor it and see how each part changed over time; and
- Build for himself an underwater home, fill it with air, and live there for a period, preliminary to reporting the findings of an extensive survey undertaken from therein.

In his mind he imagined the swaying of the seaweeds that made underwater forests, followed the twist of a narwhal's tusk, and learned watery secrets that he could not adequately formulate to himself, not knowing anything about them except that they were hitherto unknown. In this way he entertained himself where Bellows did not – that boy looked forlornly at his brother, caged in paper, and buried first one, then two, then a hundred memories of his betrayal at the hands of his former Master – and the salt spray from the prow of the boat was cool on Anaximander's snout, and his service-pledge was very much in control.

Consequently, it was all quite pleasant for a long while, particularly in comparison to some of the recent events of his experience.

The water hadn't been choppy, but eventually, after some hours of rowing, it became entirely still. There was no wind to ripple its surface, and one pull of the oars was enough to send the boat gliding. When Anaximander looked over the side, hoping to see schools of fish, or perhaps the tumbled ruins of an Atlantean temple, but expecting the depth of the water to reflect his features back at him, he saw instead what looked like the ground one sees above water, in a park, say, or a garden, except submerged. Occasionally, as they slid through the water, the bottom of the hull knocked on something – a rock perhaps – and sounded hollow in his ears.

There was land beneath, only a few feet below, perhaps territories that had only recently succumbed to a rising tide, and in the distance was a landscape of marshy, undulating hills, with drumlins and hummocks and a few lonely tors.

The boy Bellows was as lost to his thoughts as he had been all afternoon, and Clarissa's expression was fixed between boredom and indifference, so there was no one with whom the dog could discuss this observation. Regardless, he put his oar down, and used his newly freed mouth to lick the surface of the water. It was, possibly, less briny than it had been earlier, and was filled with the flavours of plants. There was dandelion and burdock, aniseed and nettle, daisy and bluebell. He put his paw out and let it drag in the water, and beneath it – just beneath – there was a trodden path cut into grass, surrounded in its turn by gorse bushes and heather, drowned but still in flower.

A while later, when the water had given way mostly to grass, Clarissa stood in the boat, letting the rudder list over, and announced, 'This'll do.' She stepped off onto the drowned land they had been drifting over, leaving the others where they sat.

The day was warm and rainless.

Bellows looked gloomily off after Clarissa, but Anaximander leapt up excitedly and followed, circling her first one way and then the other, rising onto his hind legs and then splashing down near her feet, all the while looking at her and panting. This was his way of performing enthusiasm, and though his experience of her had been relatively brief, he knew this was more liable to make an impact on her behaviour than speaking tended to. Against words she always had a defence, but his postures and phatic utterances were less easy to dismiss.

He got what he wanted when she turned, kneeled in the inches-deep sea and grabbed his scruff affectionately. She was, he knew, a troubled soul, but her troubles were in the domain of thought, mostly, and she seemed to feel them less keenly if she could be kept away from thinking. He lay so that his belly was flat on the soft, wet ground, flanked by bays of daffodils, and made the sort of smile that dogs have, displaying a considerable acreage of red and glistening tongue.

When he wagged his tail, it made ripples.

She took his muzzle in her hands. 'We can leave the boat here – we won't be needing it now.'

As if this was an order, Anaximander sprang away and went to where Bellows was. 'Stand,' he said, 'you sullen child! And bring your brother-book with you. This vessel we here abandon, at the suggestion of my service-pledge, and there is nothing to be gained from sitting there any longer, oar loosely in hand.'

The boy looked at him, his eyes as big as owls' eyes and equally staring, but despite their size no comprehension was in them. Nor was there that telltale glistening of an animating purpose. Instead, everything was clouded and distrait.

The book, though it was magic, gave off a turbulent and disorganised rattle, as if the pages inside were clattering against each other and twisting.

Anaximander turned back and there was Clarissa, moved to a piece of higher ground which was all above the sea. Between her toes were daisies, and the rain from the hem of her dress fell around them, as if she was some huge and primal god at large in the early days of her own creation, bringing rain to quench its thirst.

The dog grabbed Bellows by his trousers and pulled him out of the boat. He did this gently, not wishing him any harm, but the action was entirely unavoidable by such an enfeebled specimen as Bellows was, so it was aggression of kind – that which acts against the will.

Bellows was made to stand where the boat had stopped, but he picked up his book of his own volition, and this made Anaximander feel, briefly, as if the child had been roused, but when the dog went over to Clarissa, Bellows didn't follow. Instead, he stood as if he was in a fugue, his lips parted and his hands at his sides.

Clarissa looked back at Bellows, but her vision fell on him for hardly a moment, as if he was nothing more than a shape a bush might make in the wind, or a shadow. She turned back and Anaximander knew that she would leave the boy there if he didn't follow by himself.

Dogs who have known hard labour, first in the vats of a Master, then in the training pits of a dogfighting trainer – Anaximander's was Heartless Harold Smyke, whose name was just about right for him – have a low tolerance for certain types of behaviour they feel are self-indulgently negative.

Certainly, it's acceptable, they think, for a person to experience unhappy emotions. Not to do so is indicative of illness, or of developmental arrest, but they also know that these emotions can only be banished by a person's internal resources. Yes, they admit, sad thoughts rob a mind of its usual resourcefulness, but that's not to say that a certain bucking-up-of-one's-ideas is not desirable in any case. They think this not out of some moral judgement about the rights and wrongs of certain frames of mind, that it's necessarily better to be positive of thought and active than to give in to the lassitude of misery – no. They think it out of raw experience, knowing, as Anaximander did, that there's no benefit to be had from dwelling on pain, and that no matter how inevitable misery seems, and how all-encompassing, this is an illusion the unhappy emotions baffle the mind with, to their own self-proliferating ends.

For example, when faced with immediate physical danger – let's say Heartless Harold Smyke had decided, for the amusement of a wealthy patron, to introduce an enraged and rabid badger into the training ring one winter's morning, its hot breath panted out and billowing up, its eyes blank with fever – even the most self-pitying denizen of that trainer's maudlin house of pain, even the most long-servingly depressive inmate, even the closest dog to death, shivering by a grate of coals long gone out, was capable of one last, frantic effort to save their life. They would rip at ears, clash teeth and claw the liver from the side of any billowing badger with an energy that's unmatched, rather than accept their own murder. Which is not to say that an animal cannot be injured past its ability to fight – Anaximander had seen a great number of his kin in exactly that position – but only *physically*. The body is limited, but the mind is not, and any mood can be shaken off when death is near.

Anaximander, for whom death had always been near to that point at which he felt it would always be near, could remind himself of the terrible things that might befall him at any time and thereby shake off from himself from any mood, no matter how profound, by understanding that a dog like him had no need for it. To see Bellows – who had never, to the dog's knowledge, so much as disembowelled a ferret in anger or had a starving one set upon him – moping and biting his lip stirred an irritation in him. It was this irritation that informed what he did next, though it was with the best intentions: he bit Bellows hard on the buttock, piercing his skin.

To Anaximander, as an observer, Bellows's face of wide-mouthed, wide-eyed surprise, his immediate propulsion two feet into the air, and his eventual bent-kneed loping in circles, rubbing and rubbing, was a most amusing picture, though it was clear that Bellows was anything but amused. Sometimes a person so startled in this way will catch sight of themselves in all their ridiculousness – say in a nearby window – and the sight will serve, perhaps after a playful chase-about, to cheer them up, making their previous unhappiness a memory – that was certainly Anaximander's intention. While the cheerfulness will be temporary, it forms in the mind a template for future changes of mood, the memory of the pantomimery available as a spur that obviates the need for the bite.

Anaximander hoped such a template was now formed, but he rather doubted it – Bellows went onto his knees and elbows and was weeping down onto the book which rested on the ground beneath his face.

Anaximander turned to Clarissa to see that she had moved some distance off, up the side of a hill that swelled gently above the surface of the water. Into the grass where her feet had rested were pressed soft indentations that led through a bank of speedwell and irises, and her fingertips brushed lone blades of wild wheat. In the sky a haze of midges made a cloud above her, and a heavy dumbledore rose and dipped and rose again, buzzing at her shoulder.

Anaximander gave a sharp yap – the sort a dog would use in the place of the word 'hey!' – but she didn't acknowledge him. Instead, she cut a gentle swathe through the foliage of this place, tending ever towards a pink and mellow sunset.

When the dog turned back, Bellows was entirely prone, and it was Anaximander's turn to feel unhappy. He now realised, as a dog of his intelligence inevitably must, that just because he did not feel the validity of this child's pain by sympathy and intuition, his reason, faced with the facts, must surely recognise its reality. Bellows was sobbing deep down from his insides, convulsing at the gut, wracked across the muscles of the back and shoulders in ways that cannot simply be described as 'spoiled' or 'self-indulgent'.

He went over to him. 'Young Bellows,' he said, 'your insistent low mood, and now this immunity to tried and tested remedies, lead me to believe that you have entered a depressive state of mind from which you cannot easily be coaxed. Is this a fair summation?'

The boy didn't answer, but there was a quality to his sobbing that indicated that, possibly, he agreed that Anaximander had it right.

'While a fighting dog, such as I was raised,' he went on, 'who behaves as you do will find himself pitted against far superior opponents than he can be expected to defeat, in what is known as an exhibition match, and so test his lethargy against the very real and immediate presence of torture, I know that you are not such a creature. The lack of kindness shown to said fighting dog during his upbringing is not a recipe conducive to every man's mental health. So,' he said, nuzzling beneath the boy and coming up under him, 'let me carry you where my mistress goes. She would lead us where her wisdom takes her, and I cannot leave you here to be washed away with the next tide.'

Bellows allowed himself to be lifted so that he lay on the dog's broad and muscled back, his arms and legs as limp either side as a near dead cavalryman's are when he returns wounded from a charge, the horse taking on the responsibility for his balancing. The boy did not even pick up his book, so Anaximander took it between his teeth.

Immediately, and without warning, Anaximander's sensorium was lit with images so bright and magical that they effaced the images of the mundane world, and in his ears were a thousand voices, saying a thousand things, and for a moment he was confused and dizzied, and he stumbled forward and let Bellows slip.

Fortunately, a dog of Anaximander's sort is not entirely overwhelmed by sensations of this kind – quite the contrary, since he's made for magical work, and it often comes in strange ways – and soon he picked out that each image was the same, a thousand times overlaid, and each voice was the same, a thousand times overlaid, and while he trotted after Clarissa, having resettled Bellows on his back, he performed a magical translation like that he'd often performed when understanding Sirius's mystical visions – which is to cohere disparate utterances into one unit, so that they can be dealt with rationally.

Clarissa was ascending ever higher up a hill she had found, following a path that sheep or goats had cut into the landscape with their grazing and the trampling of their hooves to get to new and fresh vegetation. Her hands sometimes pushed against her knees to give her purchase, and the sky went to streaks of red as the sun approached the horizon.

Anaximander followed her with Bellows. What were the images and sounds that the dog received from the book? They were depictions of veins and ligaments, strung on a loom, of teeth, ground in a pestle with a mortar. The voice was a recitation of the alphabet and the numbers in base ten. Across them all was a hex, simple but powerful, that made puzzlement fill the pages of this book. A hex was something Anaximander had known before, in the merchant's house, and while he couldn't remove it, he felt that Clarissa might be able to do so.

He galloped up the hill to her, expecting to ask for her assistance.

Before he even arrived by her side she turned and knelt before him, gathering her skirts, and put her hands to either side of his face. This he took as an act of affection – like the one she had exhibited earlier, and which had made his heart warm with pack-happiness – but the book was in his mouth and this she touched instead.

She looked Bellows in the face, and there came into her expression a softness familiar to Anaximander, a sad pensiveness he had seen by the fireside on long silent nights in the Merchant City. Perhaps Bellows, the frail and anaemic boy he was now, reminded her of her own son, Nathan, evoking sympathy in her, or perhaps it was something else, but she took the book from the dog's mouth and held it in her hands as if it was a wounded bird, found by the roadside.

Those who are not familiar with mystical communication, or the realms within which magic operates, may not know it, but when a person who resonates with weft-Spark makes mystical contact with a magical object, other magical creatures in contact with it can also feel it – and know it with their other senses – so clearly that it's as if a place opens specifically for that experience. It would be as if, to a non-magical person, a chance meeting between three or four friends were suddenly to occupy the most suitable room for it – a drawing room, say, over cigars – rather than the physical place one happens to be – in a side road behind a brothel.

When Clarissa communed with the book, she, a weft-manipulator – though a secret one – Anaximander, a magical dog, Bellows, a boy whose previous existence was facilitated through magic, and Adam Birch, a boy turned into a book by magic, all went to a magical realm. To use the technical language, we might say it was a limited, ad hoc, intermediate realm. There they appeared to each other in the way magical beings tend to appear to each other, which is in the form of a perfected exemplar of their self.

Clarissa was unchanged, being, presumably, perfect in her own eyes even in her most material form, Bellows was as he had been before the red concentrate had reflected onto him, which is to say the large-nosed, briar-limbed, middle-aged factotum of the Master of Mordew, Anaximander was a dog very like himself but perhaps larger, leaner and taller, and Adam Birch, the book, was a handsome young man in his early adulthood, clear-eyed, straight-limbed and athletic, wearing a very smart navy blue uniform.

To describe what happened next is only possible through use of simile and metaphor, since there are no appropriate non-magical modes of language that can capture mystical communication of the sort that magical beings are capable of. They have modes of expression and comprehension that material beings cannot possess, these being almost entirely combinations of the immaterial realm and the weft, with only a token material component, but since the weft contains everything, and timelessly, and the immaterial realm knows all concepts, this exchange between the four was done primarily through a perfect comprehension instantaneously of everything there was to know and gather about the situation taking place in a moment. True, attempts to operate on this information, particularly by the rational sense, which is tied in material people to their brains, which are a species of object, was limited by virtue of the loss inherent in translating from primarily immaterial methods of comprehension into material ones. Still, significance was exchanged in a vast and complex network, information from which could be used for thought.

The following is a poor and vulgar translation, but it was as if Clarissa was become a great and encompassing mother, warm arms around all, the scent of the skin of her breasts making the spirits of the others both drowsy and fulfilled, and each of them with a teat of their own, on which they paddled with their hands and paws. She gave forth sweet trickles of milk, all analgesic for any pain they might have. The milk of her breasts was also, simultaneously, the roots of her tree, and unlike a material tree which draws water from the world, she was giving of herself to them, so that they all knew her to be a kind of god for them, capable of anything, and they need only pledge their allegiance to her for all desirable things to come to pass.

Anaximander, like a black polyp on Clarissa's root-teats, was already part of her, and all that was required for Bellows and Adam to receive her full munificence was to express the willingness to do so, which they happily did, her acceptance gushing into their mouths like the first milk a baby gets, which can make it posset, the flow coming too greatly.

In their drinking they understood that Clarissa could correct all things, and she divined from them what these things were, and the first was that Adam should retrieve his mind, which he then did.

In the material realm, the book regained its syntax – the machinery of it was repaired, and his endless hex-induced focusing on the trauma of his making was relieved just as the hex was cleared away.

In Bellows, the loop of sad thoughts, each leading in a negative chain to the next was broken, like a daisy chain is easily broken by snapping a single stem. He looked then at his brother's face, drawn on the first page of the newly sensible book and the plan was made whereby, with Clarissa and

Anaximander's help, Adam should be returned to his boyhood, and the two brothers should live on together, where they might enjoy each other again.

'I never learned the spells that reincorporate an incorporate person,' Clarissa said, returning them to the material world by disengaging from the book. 'That's Portia's speciality. Mine is transformation of the weft.' She stood before them again, and they were back in the half-drowned landscape, Anaximander much as he was but Bellows much more lively and attentive and the book vibrating with magical colour, fluttering its pages. 'I can,' she continued, 'do the same work. But I need a relic. Will you help me to find it?'

Since he couldn't see what earthly use the other two might be, Anaximander thought that this request was for him. But if he could have seen into the thoughts of Bellows and Adam, he would have realised that they both thought the same about themselves.

'When we have it,' she said, 'I'll be able to make everything right, for everyone. Friends, enemies, they'll all get what they deserve.'

VIII

Her Enemy, Part Two

TIME PASSES STRANGELY across the realms, and there were now, on one wall, clocks, each running at different speeds. Twenty of them, four rows of five, suddenly there where they had not been before. A weft-manipulator can create realms and make them so that they have certain properties – this is obvious – and the Master had made this one so that it would, when a candidate was introduced to the first vat, begin a timer. This was because softening took time, and the clocks, measuring it, could be used to judge how much of it was remaining.

The clock that represented this realm – the first on the left of the top row, naturally – was running at a normal pace, the second hand ticking round in that reasonable and familiar manner of clocks. It was set at two o'clock and no minutes, indicating that ten hours would elapse before the first vat work was done. The clock next to this, on its right, was almost static, none of the hands seeming to move at all. This was the passage of time in the material realm, and it was set to a time that was matched by the rest of that row of clocks, each of which were the primary intermediate linked antechamber realms relating to the Manse. This synchronicity was a function of their necessary interrelation – an interrelation that this secondary intermediate antechamber realm didn't share, or need to share, since it would be dissolved once the vat work was done, and the room removed into the Manse proper.

Time as it passed in this realm did not contribute – much – to the passage of time in the primary realms. The Master had recently designed a reactive chronologue, weft-keyed to the future arrival of the Eighth Atheistic Crusade at the borders of Mordew, and he instanced one here for convenience's sake. Like the other clocks it had a face, but this one had more divisions, and the hands moved in reverse. He was pleased to see it stalled one minute into its nominal twenty-four-hour countdown to the Assembly's arrival. He could live ten lifetimes here – providing he cast the necessary rejuvenating spells – and the minute hand would not make a single circuit.

This was all to the good, but a man does get bored, waiting around for ten hours for a boy child's immanence to reduce in consistency to allow his essential form to be manipulated in the way the Master needed it to do, so on the second row the first clock was, again, this realm, but the next four clocks were realms subsidiary to this realm where the passage of time was faster, and each by a multiple of the last: the original clock being one times' speed, the next two, the next four, and so on. The third row continued these multiples, and the fourth began the same sequence, but slower rather than faster. Beneath each clock was a little button, the pressing of which would activate the presser's translation into the relevant realm. It was systems such as this that the Master had invented over centuries, and which he now couldn't remember having lived without.

He pressed the button beneath one of the clocks and was taken out of the vat room realm and into a realm with the same dimensions, but with a chair, a side table, a decanter with wine, and a glass.

An auditor of the Master's practices, though there were no longer such things, would have pulled him up on the profligacy of having made so many furnishings for the secondary vat room if he was going to run out of time in this realm, but that auditor would have been mistaken, since not all the vats could be left while they did their work, and certain ones could be more or less left alone, but an expert hand would be needed on occasion to attend to something. Anyone who has troubled to learn to cook will know that a hard-boiled egg can be made without any attention other than ensuring the water doesn't boil dry, a casserole can be left on a low heat for hours, but most cream sauces need constant agitation, or they will stick, or split, and it was the same with the vats. The furniture in the vat room was for those times.

He took a seat, poured himself a glass of fortified wine, which turned out to be a rich and chalky port, and, with one eye on the sole clock – which told the time in the vat room and was whirling at speed – turned his attention to the condition of his nails and cuticles, some nagging anxiety about which he had felt all day.

There was a whitlow on the ring finger of his right hand, specks of white in all the nails, and Mud engrained under some. The side table had a drawer, and in this draw was a manicure set – amongst other things – so he took it out, opened it, got the scissors and tried his best to remove the whitlow without tearing the skin back and opening the nerves to the air. This could be very painful, he knew, even if that pain was a minor sort of pain, so he made sure he wasn't joggled in any way by leaning his elbow on his knee to prevent any unexpected movements.

It was in this state of exaggerated stillness that he first noticed what went on to be an irritating fact for the rest of the day: the locket, dangling from his neck and under no possible influence, was jerking. Perhaps kicking is a better way of saying it.

When a mother is reaching term, though it is disturbing to see it, her baby will turn in the womb, or stretch its legs, and this can be observed through her skin, if she is naked. If the belly is instead covered with, say, a loose smock, then this clothing can be made to move, the energy from the child's movement enacting change on the things of a realm outside its experience and direct understanding. This is how the locket moved – as if there were a baby within it, transcending its realm.

Sebastian put down the nail scissors, but then remained absolutely still, the whitlow temporarily forgotten. He watched the locket as a visitor to a pregnant woman is often asked to watch her covered bump – waiting, seemingly in vain, for a movement recently felt to be repeated – and the event eventually came to pass – the locket moved again, without him having influenced it in any way.

Anyone trained in the creation of a Tinderbox will know that this is not possible. Anything contained in an interdictory realm cannot influence the realm from which it has been separated – that is axiomatic – so whereas the lack of heat that the Master had previously noticed had been a good sign, this movement was not a good sign at all, though he had to admit to himself that such a movement was completely without explanation, positive or negative.

He took the locket off and lay it on the table – this he did with one hand, while the other he used to pick up the glass and drain the port in it down to the silt. He put the glass down with a click, then slid it to the far edge of the table. With an unimpaired view, he maintained a wary surveillance of the locket and its chain.

Nothing happened for the several brisk revolutions of the clock's minute hand, time as represented in the vat room, representing almost none in the secondary material realm or in the material realm proper. But what about the interdictory realm? The synchronicity and speed of that place was something that he hadn't considered, he had to admit that much to himself. The issue should not have been relevant, given that anything contained there was forbidden, by the nature of the process indicated by its name, from interfering with the material realm – or indeed any other intermediate realm – until its creator opened it. Then, of course, it would almost entirely 'interfere' with it, to the great detriment of anything not prepared to be interfered with in that way, but up until that extremity, it could be considered irrelevant.

So, what was the issue?

The locket moved again. It set up a spinning that was only slowed and stopped in a revolution by the chain and the friction of the highly polished table. The interval between that movement and the last was approximately half a vat hour – the Master had thought to note the first instance almost instinctually. Perhaps noticing small details like that was paranoia, perhaps it was an abundance of observance, but he noticed it either way.

In the time the clock took to mark another half hour, he thought through some possibilities. If time ran more slowly in there than here, and more slowly in here than the vat room, and the material realms, then there was no issue – nothing could, in any way, be taking place there, time being necessary for events to happen in. That was one, it seemed to him, of the available options.

If it was running at the same time as this room, then there would be insufficient time for anything much to occur in the material realm. Sebastian had made weft-stuff of Nathan, vibrating at his Spark-infused frequency, and when confined to an interdictory realm, that would be almost inert and consequently not malleable in the short, medium, or even long term. But what about the very long term? What about on an epochal scale? Tinderbox weft-stuff, Nathan-infused or otherwise, was only almost inert. There would be that slow and fundamental vibration, its weft-resonance, that was a part of its power. That, over the course, of an entire realm's life cycle, could be said to be 'change'.

Into the Master's head came a memory of his life as a boy. This was impossibly long ago, but it was there clearly in his thoughts. He had, in the corner of a page of his schoolbook – French dictation – drawn a crude picture of a clothed woman, facing away from the viewer so only her back could be seen. She had a skirt, high-heeled shoes and a short-sleeved blouse. He turned over the page and in the exact same place he drew the exact same picture, except that this time the arms protruding from the short sleeves were reaching back, the hands coming up from beside her thighs. On the next picture she was reaching for her hips, and in the one after that her hands were on her waistband. Over the course of twenty-five or thirty pages, the woman pulled down her skirt to reveal her underwear.

The teacher came, as he was drawing the lace frills on her knickers, and rapped hard across the backs of his knuckles with his cane, making young Sebastian drop his pencil, but nonetheless the Master realised the significance of the image: even something almost immobile can, with time, expose something, to his detriment.

If time moved at all in there, it might have unpredictable results.

When the half hour of vat room time was passed, the locket moved again.

He got up from his chair, scooping up the locket and chain as he did so, and marched over to the door that led back to the vat room. The moment he was in the vat room, he translated himself to the secondary material realm in which he had placed the material realm-dependent Manse. There, where time was running at a set speed, neither slower nor faster than it ought to, he reckoned he had already slowed down the passage of time in the locket, the case of which reacted not to some universal time pace but to the multiplier built into the realm from which that realm was dependent.

He waited for half an hour by a clock in his library, and, as he expected, the locket did not move. He went to his study, moving with a brisk familiarity that brooks no obstacle, and, knowing he would not find Bellows waiting to enquire of his needs, found nothing to stop him putting the locket in the top drawer of his writing desk. There was a secret compartment – the desk-maker had made one because such a thing was standard in those days – so the Master put the locket in that, ordered a phalanx of fresh gill-men to stand guard, and returned to his work in the vat room duplicate.

He took the softened candidate out of the first vat, wiped him down, and, with a wooden clothes peg, pinched and pulled his nose until it stretched like saltwater taffy made into sweets. Then he put him in the second vat to set, which was filled with a mixture of quicklime and water, and then into the third to grow.

When you want to make a cutting sprout, you put rooting powder on it – any gardener can tell you that – and this third vat was filled with the rust of a metallic plant that did the same thing, but for people and animals, and into this he planted the candidate so his feet stuck out over the rim of the vat.

During this time, Sebastian kept thinking of the locket in the drawer in his study. Was that a sensible idea, to put it in the heart of his domain, in the room where he kept his most puissant things? Time is one thing – it can make things change... it is, in fact, change distilled – but other things can have effects too. Magic can cause all sorts of mayhem. A weft-manipulator is familiar with his manipulations, knows how things interreact, but add an unknown factor? That was a recipe for disaster.

What was an impossibly moving Tinderbox locket if not an unknown factor?

The candidate was due for removal into vat four in fifteen minutes. If the Master didn't follow his known recipe, there might be a problem.

Or there might not.

He went back to his study – it would only take a moment, so he comforted himself – and it was exactly as he'd expected it to be. Again, moving around without conscious deliberation, he found the locket. It was cold, still and entirely neutral-seeming. There were no undue vibrations, no unearthly tones to indicate dangerous seepages into the real. Still, what was the downside of putting the locket in the safe? His agents had instructions to inform him when the Assembly forces passed certain way-points, he could not be caught off guard to the extent that the short time he'd need to retrieve the locket would be crucial.

He went to the safe. It was behind a potted palm in one corner of the room, covered with a knitted doily on which another plant had been put. He realised he didn't recognise the species of this other plant. Orchid? One of Bellows's favourites, perhaps?

With a few gestures the arcane lock was opened, and he took an invalidation cube – like a musical box but treated to negate any unauthorised magic – put the locket in it, then put the cube back in the safe.

Which was a relief.

IX

Her Heir, Part One

THEY GROUNDED THE SHIP on the coast of the Island of White Hills, holing the keel beneath the waterline on the rocky shore, making the hull list in the shadow of chalk cliffs, white for a hundred feet before they met grass. Overhead, gulls squawked and glided, circling above land that looked as if it had been spooned away or carved carelessly, its edge left to crumble into the water. The sun was barely risen, the air was blustery and cold, and dark brine was rising below decks.

'Shouldn't we fix that leak?' Gam said, not really knowing anything about it. 'Looks like it'll sink.'

'How do you fix a boat?' Prissy said, pointing at a wide and jagged rent through which water was bubbling.

Gam had to admit that he had no idea.

The assassin was still in the brig, singing, because none of them had the courage to go in and shut him up.

Prissy risked a look. 'Do you think he'll drown?' she whispered.

'I don't reckon we're that lucky, do you?'

Gam had retrieved his stuff – it was in Giles and Iolanthe's cabin, in their linen chest – and Dashini had found the Nathan Knife in one of the crew's thigh straps, but that didn't mean either of them was confident they'd get the best of Anatole.

'Set fire to the ship?' Dashini offered, but it's not easy to burn something that's half soaked in sea water.

Eventually they checked the door was locked, left him where he was, and made their way to the beach.

There was, in the sand, a strange and partially covered series of black stepping stones making a vague sort of path that led to the land. Gam poked one of them with the toe of his boot and pushed it back and forward. It moved a little bit, as if it was buried deep enough to keep it in place but not so deep that it couldn't be dug up.

Dashini came up behind him and looked over his shoulder. 'What have you got there?'

'Don't know,' Gam replied. 'Is that kind of thing normal?'

Dashini poked at it with her own toe. 'Well, beaches are funny places. It might be sea coal?'

Gam looked at her. 'Don't ask me,' he said. 'Not really my forte, never having been on a beach before.'

'No, he hasn't,' Prissy said, 'And neither have I.' She knelt in the sand, dug round the stepping stone and pulled out a chunk of what looked like jet – an irregular block of dark glass the size of a discarded shoe, with a sharp end poking underneath. Not being much impressed by it, she threw it aside. It thumped down, point up. 'It doesn't look like it's going to do much harm. Assassins, on the other hand...'

Prissy set off across the beach, hopping between the stepping stones, towards the cliffs.

There were no obvious pathways, only dips worn down where the cliffs were lower. On one of these, sheep were grazing. The muzzle of one of the sheep pulled grass up by the roots between two chunks of the jet, sea coal, stepping stone stuff. The creature chewed silently and dipped its head, as if children like Dashini, Gam and Prissy were the kind of thing it saw every day.

Prissy walked over to it, but when she got close enough to reach down and pet its head it trotted away to where its comrades watched sidelong.

'Suit yourself,' Prissy said, but the sheep had already turned back to the grass and wasn't listening. She took what looked like a path and the others followed closely behind.

'The Pyramid is beautiful from the outside,' Dashini said, as if to keep all their minds off the possibility that Anatole was already free and chasing them. 'That's nothing compared to the inside, though. Every level is its own world, with its own sky, sun, clouds – everything. The first one is given over to the cattle-headed people, the second to the person-headed snakes. Frankly, I can take those realms or leave them. But the third level belongs to Japalura and her dragons. Do you know what a dragon looks like?'

Slum children of Mordew find it difficult to imagine a warm and dry bed at night, so Prissy felt very confident in her reply that, no, she had no idea what a dragon looked like.

'They're incredible,' Dashini said. 'Beautiful. You're going to love them.'

Prissy smiled, largely because Dashini seemed to care whether she might love something or not, but Gam wasn't so easily enticed. 'Never mind all that, why isn't your mum dead? I thought Nathan killed her.'

It was Dashini's turn to smile. 'Avatars, Gam.' The word went nothing to him, so she had to go on. 'My mother's a goddess. The woman Nathan killed was just a material realm aspect of the true Mistress. She lives in her own world at the top of the Pyramid.' Dashini's eyes seemed to focus on things the other two children couldn't see. 'She's goddess to the faithful people of Malarkoi, protector of their sacrificed children, maker of their heavens. Her avatars are everywhere. Anatole, when he was talking about the assassin goddess, he meant the Mother of Mordew – my mother again. She directs the affairs of men.' This thought seemed to bring her back to her senses, and she looked between Gam and Prissy. 'When we get to the Pyramid, I'll take you up to her realm and she'll explain everything.'

Gam was never the easiest boy to impress with good news, and now was no exception. 'And the best help she can send is a trained killer? Are you sure she's not trying to get rid of you?'

Dashini took a step towards Gam, hand at her belt as if she was going to take her knife to him, but Prissy stepped between then. 'How come you had to leave home?' she asked. 'You were only little, weren't you?'

Dashini relaxed. 'It's all part of the plan,' she said. She marched ahead and the other two had to jog along behind her to keep up. 'I've already prepared the doorway,' she called back to them. 'Not long now.'

Gam looked back behind them.

Thankfully there was no sign of Anatole.

They walked past empty, fenceless fields, only discernible by the colour of their vegetation, most of which was burned down to stubble but which here and there sprouted dry and thin. Occasionally, what looked like bundles of tent poles and scraps of fabric interrupted the emptiness, but otherwise there was no sign of people or the kinds of places people lived in.

Gradually, the fields became smaller, and the remains of tents more frequent, and then, beneath their feet, over at a distance, right here, over there – everywhere – were bones. Skulls, femurs, ribcages – they crumbled to dust when the children kneeled to touch them.

Gam and Prissy turned to Dashini – in the slums, death was common, but this was everywhere.

Dashini shook her head – if they were after answers, she didn't have them. 'Something bad happened here,' she said.

'We can see that,' Gam said. 'Surprised your mum didn't sort this lot out.' He cleared a pile of bones out of the way with a sweep of his boot and they became a smear of ash on the dry grass.

Dashini didn't rise to the bait. 'The Pyramid is just over the next line of hills, a couple of miles at most,' she said. 'She'll explain everything.'

As they grew closer, amongst the animal remains there were human figures on the ground. They were corrupted, lying as if they'd been made sand dunes of – one side of them disappeared, the other piled up, wind blown into odd half-things, no whole person anywhere.

On the path in front of them was a bell, bisected by the ground, pooled by melting so that it seemed to be buried, like the stepping stones on the beach had been.

They came around a hill, barren of all vegetation and studded even more frequently with piles of bones, and emerged into the bowl of a great valley, smooth and round.

The Golden Pyramid of Malarkoi was exactly as Dashini had described it, as brightly sparkling in the sunlight, a wedge of perfect triangular geometry and weft-magic cut into the natural world. Each side was entirely smooth, clad in a single sheet of glistening metal that wrapped the structure without seams, mirroring in gold the hills, the clouds, the alabaster pathway that led up to it. Only the entranceway interrupted the regularity of that surface: a depthless square of black.

But everywhere around was scorched ground: no tents, no bunting strung between high poles, no staked goats, no flotillas of kites, no dragons of paper, no scaffolded sculptures. No people at all, except near the entranceway, and here there were only remains – a chalk bonfire of fragile and ruined skeletons, ever clambering, eroding and still.

Dashini spat into the dust. She didn't need her mother to explain. This was Nathan's doing.

He would have scoured the place clean when the Master sent him into battle. How else could he have defeated her mother?

Dashini swallowed, focussed on the Pyramid. That was the same as her memories, so often pictured, now real. But different.

'There's something wrong,' she said, almost too quietly for the other two to hear her but not quite.

'That,' Prissy said, 'is an understatement.'

'She means that weird colour round it.' Gam could see a viscous rainbow of light clearly with his new eye. 'What is it?' he said.

The three started down together, Dashini slower, wary.

'Is it in the middle of a glass ball?' Prissy said. That's what it looked like to her when she caught sight of it at an angle – a hemisphere of glass, or a bubble resting on the ground, big enough to fit the whole pyramid in, only just visible when the light hit it right.

'The Master's been here, too,' Dashini muttered. In her stomach she felt magic fear, and no amount of calm breathing removed it. Back in the time of her imprisonment, the Master had left his Manse, gone to Malarkoi with Bellows, leaving her and Nathan to wreck Mordew. He'd sailed away in his black ship, and now Dashini knew what he'd done.

He'd surrounded her home with Spark glass, quarantined the Golden Pyramid as he had quarantined her within the Manse.

'How's your faith now, Dashini?' Gam said.

She walked up to where the glass met the earth, ignored the bones, dug at the border with the toe of her boot; the quarantine went down below the loose soil.

'Is it supposed to be like that?' Prissy said. 'How do you get in?'

Dashini didn't reply. The entranceway was at the end of the approach, but the path of alabaster slabs leading to it was interrupted by the curved surface of the glass sphere. Even the bones were displaced by it.

Everything felt corrupted, wrong.

Gam rapped on the quarantine with his knuckles, as if knocking on a door, and rainbow ripples spread out through the solid energy, making a sickly, oily display but not achieving anything much, practically speaking. 'How are we supposed to get inside?'

Again, Dashini didn't reply. None of this was the way things were supposed to be. This wasn't the plan.

Her homecoming was ruined – she felt childish feeling it – but after so long? She couldn't help it.

What if she circled the Pyramid, checking for flaws?

What if she made a spell to open a gap?

She knew well enough from the time she'd spent trapped in the Manse that it wouldn't be any good. The Master's quarantines were essentially unbreakable without demonic or angelic assistance, and those things came with problems of their own.

Now Prissy and Gam were speaking. 'What are we going to do then?' they said, in various different ways, with more or less anxiety, as she tried to think.

When Dashini was on her own in the long years of her isolation in the Manse, she had dreamed of having people around her. How wonderful it would be, she'd thought then, to be surrounded by others. All their faces, the voices, the needs, the opinions.

She blew the air out of her lungs and held her breath. The other two kept talking, and now Dashini realised that she needed to block them out, these others, so she could think. Loneliness is bad for a person, she knew this, but when you've grown up alone it's hard to think with everyone wittering on.

Now Prissy was in front of her, saying something idiotic.

Dashini shut her eyes. She could, as she'd done before, summon a demon to destroy the Spark glass. But that would mean locating the necessary magic books, most of which were either in the Master's Manse, or in the Pyramid, or chained in an Assembly reliquary, none of which she had ready access to. Even if she'd had the spells in front of her, the kind of demon required to do work of this kind would be impossible to control; there'd be no guaranteeing it wouldn't destroy everything else but the quarantine, and that was only after it had killed her, which is what it would try to do first. You couldn't really tell them what to do.

Gam put his hand on her wrist, so she turned her back on the both of them.

She could develop an object capable of drilling a passage through the barrier – she'd had a little success with this in the Manse, making a hole about an inch deep over the course of a month. But at this thickness? It would take decades, and what would they all do in the meantime?

The other two were in front of her again, shouting, so she went down into a ball on the ground.

They could ditch Malarkoi and go somewhere else, but where? There was only one real solution – the back door –

but the consequences of that were serious. Fatal, even. For them.

Everything was going wrong. Why was her mother letting this happen?

Prissy slapped her hard across the face. Dashini reflexively stood up, opened her eyes.

'Look!' they both shouted.

The Pyramid was nested between two slopes which made a valley that had once had a river running down through it. On one slope, two or three hundred yards away, silhouetted against the sky, there was a man.

Gam had seen him first with his new eye. There had been a clap of thunder, just like the one they heard on the boat before Anatole arrived, and it took a moment before Prissy could see him too. Then he came up out of the ground leaving a mound of earth behind him, like a molehill, and now he was moving like a rat, scurrying and twitching, looking from side to side. 'He's watching us,' Gam said.

Dashini bit down her thoughts. He didn't look like a Malarkoian – he was too crooked, too dark, too solitary. Who was he?

She was thinking this was another problem, another failure of things to go the way they should go, but then, on the breeze, the odour of sandalwood. 'Do you smell it?' she cried.

Gam did, but he pulled out Anatole's snub-nosed pistol anyway. 'I can see his face with my new eye,' he said. 'But I don't recognise him. He doesn't look like one of Padge's.'

'They like disguises though, don't they, assassins?' Prissy stepped behind Dashini, who drew the Nathan Knife. 'And didn't Anatole say something about coming out of the earth?'

'His mother's magic earth,' Gam clarified.

'Right.'

'If my mother sent him, why is he staying up there?' Dashini said.

'What's the hurry?' Gam replied. 'He's probably waiting until it gets dark.'

'He won't be able to kill us, even if he tries. Not if he's my mother's pawn.'

Gam shook his head. 'He won't be able to kill you, perhaps. I'm not sure we have the same privilege.'

Prissy turned Dashini round to face her. 'He's giving me the creeps, and that's saying something after all this. Can you get us into the Pyramid or not?'

Dashini looked from Prissy to Gam and back. 'Not by the front door,' she said. 'The Master's put pay to that. But if he thinks he's kept us out, he's wrong. He's not as clever as he thinks he is, and my mother isn't as stupid. She made a secret back way. Same levels, only more difficult to access – we'll have to take them all, one at a time, in order, before we get to the top. But we can still get there.'

Prissy was used to there being a back way – there was one in and out of most places – so that sounded like something they definitely ought to do, but Gam noticed the choke in Dashini's voice as she spoke. 'What's the catch?' he said.

Dashini looked up to the distant silhouette of the rattish man. He was sitting on his haunches, peering over at them. 'Couple of things,' she said. 'The first Door's half a day's march from here.'

'Doesn't sound too bad,' Prissy said. 'If we can keep ahead of him up there. What's the second thing?'

A dark look came over Dashini's face, and in her hand the Nathan Knife flickered with the black flame in anticipation of what was to come. 'The Doors demand blood sacrifices,' she said, 'which might explain why she's sent some for me.'

Up on the hill the ratlike man stood silently watching.

They set off away from the bones, away from the quarantine, away from assassins, and away from the Golden Pyramid of Malarkoi.

Over a hill, sheltered seemingly from Nathan's scorching of the world, began a patchy but high forest. Dashini took them through there.

Gam objected at first – it's a double-edged sword, cover of that type, just as likely to hide a hunter as it is its prey – but Dashini pointed out it was the straightest route to the back door, and, if they needed sacrifices, they'd need them to follow anyway.

Gam paused, looked back and put his hand over his old eye, let the magic one see what it could see. It wasn't like a telescope, bringing everything closer, but when he concentrated on something it made it more detailed somehow. He turned it on the rat man's face. There was something familiar about him, but he couldn't think what it was.

'Come on, Gam! What are you waiting for?' Prissy called from down the path that led into the woods.

Gam put his hand down. Recognise him or not, there was no doubting he was trouble, regardless of what Dashini said. Whatever faith Featherhead put in her wonderful mother, Gam didn't share it.

The day progressed, the sun passing through the canopy overhead, and they went deeper into the forest. The slum children hadn't had much experience of places like this; plants and trees tended to be behind fences in Mordew, safely protected from people like them, reserved for the use and pleasure of their betters.

'What are all these things?' Prissy said. She meant the bushes and saplings, fallen branches and lightning-struck trunks, the bracket fungi and scampering woodland creatures. Every new thing she saw she recoiled from, put her hands to her mouth like she would have done from Living Mud flukes.

Gam wasn't so bothered about all that; what he cared about was line of sight, and he walked briskly between the least dense parts of the forest, never relaxing his vigilance.

Dashini understood their reticences, but to her, despite everything, there was a poignant nostalgia about this landscape: everything was full of things she'd forgotten. The shapes, the smells, the quality of the light, the texture of the earth – sometimes soft and loamy, sometimes sun-baked and hard – the random and unpredictable undulations of the path, copses, dells, nests in the treetops: everything was familiar, infused with memories she'd not allowed herself to think about in captivity because they'd made her unhappy there. Here, though, she could hardly keep her mind on the work at hand.

'How much further?' Gam barked, nervously peering around from a patch of higher ground.

Dashini looked at the sun as it sank in the west. 'Five hours? Six?'

'Too long.' He ran to where she was. 'He's going to pick us off in the dark. I think either you or your mum has made a mistake. You say she's sent Padge's assassins as sacrifices, but what if she's sent them as assassins? What if she's under-estimated them?'

Dashini turned her back on Gam. 'You forget who I am.'

Explaining the limits of her abilities to Gam and Prissy wasn't easy, and Gam kept them trotting forward, forcing the pace, never giving her the chance to take the time they needed to understand her.

They kept asking why they couldn't just fly to the door and be done with it, or turn themselves invisible, or make another Door, or do any number of things that Dashini just couldn't do, and when she tried to tell them why, she got bogged down in Spark mechanics and weft-lore, none of which Gam and Prissy understood in the least.

As they half ran, half walked through the growing twilight, she explained that during her time in the Master's Manse she'd developed some techniques. As the Mistress's daughter she had some natural affinity to the weft and—

'What's the weft?' Gam interrupted, sparing his attention from the road behind.

Dashini couldn't think of an easy way of putting it. 'It's everything that is and was and will be, everything that might be, might have been and might come to be, all possible matter and energy, all existing at once and forever, facilitating the world that we live in.'

They both looked at her blankly, so she pulled a twig from a nearby branch. 'This twig is here, right?'

They nodded.

'It could have been here...' She moved it over to the side about twelve inches. '...Right?'

She moved it around a few more times until she was sure they'd got the gist. 'It's the weft that makes that possible. The weft contains all the versions of this stick, and all the places it could be at all the possible times.'

Gam and Prissy looked at each other and Prissy put her hand up.

'Yes?' Dashini said.

'What's that got to do with magic?'

'I'll get to that.' Dashini picked up a stone and held it next to the stick. 'Now,' she said, 'the weft contains all the possible instances of this matter being a stick, but it also contains all the instances of the matter being a stone instead, since it's possible for it to be either a stone or stick. Right?'

Gam put his hand up now. 'What's "instances"? And what's "matter"?'

Prissy nudged Gam supportively with her shoulder, as if she didn't know what those things meant either, which she didn't.

Dashini thought for a bit. 'Never mind,' she said. 'This stick could have been a stone, that's all you need to know, and because of the weft, I can, with enough magic, make it into a stone.' She could have pointed out that to do this she'd need to instantiate a weft-state in which the stick was instead a stone, mediating that through the immaterial realm, and then anchor that state in the material realm with an expenditure of Spark energy, but she thought that was a lesson probably best left for another time.

They both put their hands up now. Dashini pointed to Gam. 'What's the point of that?'

'There wouldn't be one.'

Gam looked around. 'I hate to be the one who reminds you, Dashini, but we're being followed by at least one, probably two of Padge's assassins. I don't think sticks and stones are going to help us much. And it's getting dark. Can we please hurry up.'

Gam ran off to higher ground, sparing a few dismissive, muttering glances over his shoulder, and put his new eye back to work.

'The gaps that are left,' Dashini said a little later to Prissy as they walked together, breathing hard from another of Gam's forced sprints, 'the impossible things that never happened, and which never could happen, make a person called the weftling. He takes up that space – it forms his body, it forms his nerves. God, some people call him.'

'And you've got finity to him?' Prissy said, one hand on her hip where she'd got a stitch. She seemed to learn better when Gam wasn't around to confirm her ignorance. He was up ahead and, in the growing twilight, increasingly difficult to follow.

'It's affinity,' Dashini said, increasing their pace a little to keep up with Gam, 'and no, I've got no affinity with him. He's dead. Nathan's father killed him. When the weftling was alive, he had control over the possible, and he made the world we live in. The energy of the weft, the Spark, was the same as his Will. When Nathan's dad killed him, his control of the weft went with him. My mother has taken control of some of it, given herself affinity with the weft, which is how she makes her heavens. I'm her daughter, so some of her affinity is also in me because we're tied together by our concepts in the immaterial realm. So I can change the world, a little.'

'I didn't understand a word of that,' Prissy said, 'but that was what Nathan was doing, right? Changing things with his affinity?'

That wasn't right either – Nathan had inherited the majority of God's Will on his father's death and could force the world to evolve in concert with it – but Dashini let it slide. 'Yes, I suppose,' she politely lied. 'The problem for me, though, is that I don't have any Spark except my own life. And you need Spark to do magic.' She took out the Nathan Knife and concentrated on it. 'This is made from Nathan, my mother created it, and the black flame is a kind of Spark.' As she concentrated, the Knife flared. 'I can't use it for magic, because its Spark is being used to keep it in existence in the material realm, but it can free Spark for my use.'

'How?' Prissy asked, but Dashini suspected she already knew.

'Killing people,' she said, and she tried not to make that sound too awful. 'Everything with a will has Spark – we're all born with it; it's the energy that keeps us alive – gradually it leaks back into the weft and when it's all gone, we die. But we all have it. The younger we are, the more we've got. Some animals have it too. The more intelligent a thing is, the more like God, if you want, the more Spark it has. If you release the Spark, you can use it to change the world if you know the spells.'

Prissy stopped in her tracks. 'So you can do magic if you kill people, the younger and cleverer the people the better?'

Dashini nodded.

Prissy looked over to where Gam was standing, stiff as a hunting dog, alert suddenly. 'Well, we'd better watch ourselves then, hadn't we?'

It was getting dark when Gam beckoned them forward, urgently.

The rat man was a hundred yards away, perhaps less, standing between two fallen trees. Gam had reached the end of the forest path and found him there, waiting, the blooded sky of the sunset behind him. He should have expected him – no child can run as quickly or steadily as an assassin, and Prissy and Dashini had been dawdling.

The rat took a whip from his coat and slapped it against his thigh.

Now, from behind them, came a familiar voice, singing.

There were three birds that flew a snare.
Over hill went they for a night and day.

208

Bad men found them unaware.
And one by one they made them pay.
Though birds may tweet, and birds may fly,
The day must come when birds will die.

'No deals now,' Anatole said, when he'd finished. 'You've missed your chance.'

Gam had already come to this conclusion himself, but then there was another thunderclap, a flash of light in the sky. Everywhere smelled of sandalwood, something Gam now recognised immediately. He looked up, and there, sitting on a high branch, was a white-haired man, jacket off, his sleeves rolled up. On his arms were tattoos – the left one a spear, the right a falcon. 'Montalban,' he said, reflexively: another of Padge's assassins. 'If you're planning on turning any sticks into stones, Featherhead, now's the time to do it.'

When Dashini didn't fix everything with a click of her fingers, Gam fired Anatole's snub-nosed pistol directly up at Montalban. The was a cloud of black smoke, and he took Prissy's arm and ran with her directly at the rat man, trusting Dashini would follow, which she did.

There was a splintering crack from behind them and, when the smoke cleared, there was Montalban in a mess on the ground, one side of his shirt tattered and bloody at the shoulder, but definitely not dead. Perhaps the range was too far, or the ammunition was cheap, but, whatever it was, Montalban had lived through Gam's shot and the fall.

The rat man approached from the front, so Gam delivered another shot at him. This did more harm, taking the man's ear off, but it also exploded the weapon, which fell to scalding pieces in Gam's hand, so that he had to drop it.

'Simon!' Anatole shouted.

That was where Gam knew him from – he was another of Padge's assassins. It was certainly an impressive disguise, but he didn't have time to appreciate it – the rat man lashed out with his whip, and it split Prissy's skirt, delivering a slit the length of a hand to her thigh, making her stumble. Simon was the kind of man that liked to hurt girls, but he also knew that the best way to slow down a person is to attack their weakest friend.

How could Dashini imagine these assassins were help?

Gam stopped in his tracks, drew a pair of knives, and ran straight at the rat. This was almost certainly a mistake, but Gam wasn't thinking. He'd frozen when Anatole had come to them on the ship, and that had been a reaction his mind and body had made between them; this was the same kind of thing – automatic, thoughtless, spurred by previous experience and emotions.

There was something like fifteen feet to make up, and Gam was quick. Simon had only just enough time to drop his whip – useless at short range – so that he could extend his claws and slash for Gam's throat, meeting the boy's knives, making both attacks ineffective.

Montalban, twigs in his hair, charged Dashini, while Anatole went for Prissy where she'd stumbled and rolled onto her back. Neither assassin got what they were hoping for – a hostage. Dashini used Montalban's moving bulk and an armlock to send him crashing back into a tree trunk, provoking a storm of falling leaves, and Prissy, who had learned more than a few dirty tricks in the slums, kicked Anatole in the bollocks through his skintight suit. 'Ignore the sausage,' her sister always told her, 'crack the eggs,' and this is what Prissy did, very successfully.

This first round of the fight went well for the children, but no one can expect to stand against assassins for long, even if those assassins have underestimated them. A drunk in a bar fight will, once fighting, continue until they either win or lose, letting anger goad them into action, but assassins aren't like that. If they meet resistance, they retreat and regroup.

Gam, furious and wanting to punish Simon's whipping of Prissy, ran at him, but the rat man scampered off, nimbly dodging branches and roots, smiling an ugly smile. Montalban walked slowly away from where Dashini was, circled, pulled a slingshot from his pocket. Anatole had no breath for singing, but minced to the side and searched his pack for a suitable rejoinder.

The three children came together and backed away.

'Magic?' Gam said, but to Prissy this time.

'She can't do it without killing someone.'

'It only needs to be one of them,' Dashini said, 'but I have to land the killing blow with the Nathan Knife.'

Gam sniffed. 'It's not very practical, is it?'

Dashini had to admit that it wasn't.

'How far to the back door?' Prissy asked. 'Can we run for it?'

'Half a mile?'

'No chance,' Gam said. 'The moment we turn, we're dead.'

It was with this fact still in their minds that, behind them, they heard a fourth thunderclap, smelled sandalwood again. Gam and Prissy knew not to be distracted and kept their focus on the immediate threat, but Dashini knew better.

'I told you!' she shouted.

Behind them was a man, half-emerged from the ground, soil in his mouth and eyes, one arm out, clawing at the grass for purchase. Without a pause, even for a moment, Dashini ran at him, the Nathan Knife in her fist, and plunged its blade into the top of his head. A normal knife would have slid off the man's skull, sliced through the scalp and made a nasty but survivable wound, but the black fire was better: it flared and burned through the bone, killing him in a moment.

No time that Gam and Prissy perceived passed, but in that uncountable moment the Spark that remained in the man – he was another of Mr Padge's assassins, Mick the Greek – was released.

Simultaneously, Dashini, with a spell she had prepared during her long exile – she planned to call it the *Convenient Substitute* when she had the chance to write it up – summoned a weft-state in which the air behind them was not air but was instead a growth of thick, dead brambles, a hundred feet high, fifty feet deep and a mile across. She chose this state because dead things need less Spark, as do porous things, as do natural things. It was also one of the first substitutions that came to mind. She instantiated it in the material realm, where it would exist until it was destroyed, blocking the path behind them.

Gam and Prissy, because they hadn't been distracted, saw the brambles suddenly come into being between them and the assassins with a rush of displaced air that blew them off their feet. When they'd regained their senses, they got up and followed Dashini, who was already running.

From then they never looked back.

They left the forest and the brambles and the assassins behind them – three of those who were still alive – and they fled the half mile to a high hill that had been hidden by the trees. At the base of it, where the slope rose up, there was an entranceway. It was almost like the one at the base of the Golden Pyramid, except this was more rugged, a stone frame built into the hillside.

Dashini sprinted and the other children couldn't keep up with her. When she got to the Door, she waited for them, turned.

Prissy was out of puff – there wasn't much call for running about in Mordew, or the wide open space to do it – but she forced herself on. Gam fell behind and she put out her hand for him, but when he took it, he dragged her back.

'What the hell are you playing at?' she said.

Gam shook his head, didn't say anything. He was looking at Dashini where she stood framed by what must be her mother's secret back door to Malarkoi. She had the Nathan Knife in her hand, its fire burning black.

She was waiting for them.

Gam was about to tell Prissy why he'd stopped her, but then out ran Anatole from the straggling treeline. He must have taken a shortcut, gone left around the brambles and made for here, sent the other two right to intercept them. Or he'd cut his way through. Or climbed over. Whatever it was, he was there, and he collided with Dashini, knocking her off her feet, in one swift motion looping a garotte around her neck, tightening.

Prissy screamed, the sound drawing Anatole's attention. It is a reflex to turn towards a scream, and this was a fact that killed Anatole, because Dashini used his distraction to put the Nathan Knife through his chest, sliding it silently into his heart.

In another blaze of black fire, Anatole's Spark was released.

Dashini struggled out from under him, cast the opening spell with the freed Spark and the first Door lit. 'Get in!' she cried.

Prissy, oblivious to anything but the death of their tormentor, wanted to stop, to sing a song like Anatole had, but she couldn't think of a rhyme for 'bastard' and, anyway, the Door might close again, so she left it.

When Gam came, he tried to catch Dashini's eye, to let her know he had her number, but she wouldn't let him. He went in anyway.

After they had gone, things were quiet. A bird flew down, rested for a little while, then flew away again. The wind rustled in a bush. Clouds passed overhead.

Above the Door, in carved letters obscured by lichen and weathering, were the words 'Secundus est Pretium Caeli'. None of the children had seen it before they left, and only Dashini would have known what it meant, but the words were there whether or not they were seen or understood. They meant that the second, or the lucky, or a person or thing called Secundus, was the price, or the cost, or the ransom, of heaven, and were a reference to the Mistress of Malarkoi's practice of taking the second-born children of her devotees to use in her spells.

Montalban and Simon, when they caught up with Anatole, were also unable to read the words, but then they had other concerns, and hardly paid them any attention.

The first level had always been a quiet realm, dark and sleepy, thick with the smell of milk. When Dashini had decided to take this route that's what she'd expected: a simple, uneventful trip through a realm she remembered from her earliest childhood. An easy trip to the next Door, warm and happy.

But now? Whatever renewal of her faith in her mother's magic the appearance of Mick the Greek had made disappeared.

Where there had once been a hollowed-out space inside a hill, gently filled with the herd of the cattle-headed people, sheltering in the dark from their enemies, safe under the eye of their patron god, now the whole volume was crammed tight, and each of the naked cattle-headed men and women had grown enormous, as if fed for exhibition.

Up, down, left and right, there was nothing but flesh, and in the remaining air the musk of inner thighs was sickening – the tang of armpits, the taint everywhere of milk and flatulence, grass and dung.

It was hot from so many bodies, and the air was motionless.

Had her mother been here recently? Dashini couldn't believe she had. It was as if, during all the years Dashini had been quarantined, the realm had been left to run unchecked.

Dashini reached until she found Prissy's small hand and pulled her over between the belly of a cattle-headed woman and the back of a cattle-headed man, both slick with sweat and steaming. Everywhere was the body-heated lowing of these people, meaningless and omnipresent. Gam, grabbing Prissy's hand, pulled himself too, then pulling her elbow, then her shoulder, until his head was between hers and Dashini's, his hair wet with cattle-headed people's sweat.

Prissy pushed him back again, not liking where his face had ended up, pressed against hers. 'Watch it!' she barked, and the cattle-headed woman beside her lowed at the sound.

'What do you expect me to do!' Gam shouted. 'It's not my fault. Where would you rather I put my face? In something's arse?' He turned the best he could to Dashini. 'You call this heaven?'

Dashini pinched her nose and said, 'Something's gone wrong. We need to get out, right now. The Door out is up. Just keep going up until you meet rock, and then follow that upwards as far as you can go.'

'How far is it?' Prissy snapped. 'Because if it's further than going out the way we came in, I vote we go back. I can't breathe in here.'

'I agree with her,' Gam said. 'This isn't going to work.'

Dashini shook her head, as much as she could. 'The Doors are one-way.'

A particularly well-fed cattle-headed man squirmed between them, his tongue rolling out of the side of his mouth so it licked Gam across the face as he went, making him close his eyes and mouth until it had worked the whole length of its front across him and its back across Prissy.

'Can't you get us out by magic?'

Dashini would have tried to explain, but now there was a knee under her chin and a huge, mottled buttock against her cheek. 'Realm already magic, mine doesn't work.' Then she was gone into a mound of flesh, subsumed under rolls of fat, and there was nothing the other two could do except make for the top and try not to think about what they were grabbing to pull themselves up.

Soon Gam lost sight of Prissy, and the endless lowing sound of these cattle-headed people blocked out all other sound; if she was calling for him, he couldn't hear it.

'I'll find you at the Door!' he shouted out, but his words were lost in the mass.

He turned away, back to where the entrance had been. He couldn't see the way they had come in, but up, through the freckled, moist, nippled wall of flesh, he caught sight of a patch of stone. He forced his way towards it, pushing his boots into cattle faces and bloated human midriffs, getting purchase on whatever he hoped was an arm, or a foot, and pulling himself across to the rock face that he hoped Dashini had meant.

It was rock, and mud, tree roots, earthworms and ants, but never had he been more grateful for any of them, regardless of what they were, because at least they weren't flesh. He waited there for a moment, breathing the scent of soil as if it was of roses, and then, pressing his back against the naked, cattle-headed crowd, he climbed the wall, putting them all out of his mind.

His clothes were so wet he wished he could take them off, but the thought of their bodies on his was too disgusting.

The wall had levelled off, and while it was difficult to tell up from down in there, he felt that he must be getting near to the top, if that wasn't a lie he was telling himself. He was on his back most of the time, and had convinced his senses, mostly, that the bodies under him were just some enormous and sticky cushion covered in hot leather.

He grabbed a rock at the end of his reach and pulled himself along the wall. The cushion tended to breathe in concert with itself, and to breathe out after, and when it breathed out it made space so that he could put himself into it, that space disappearing when the cushion took its breath, so he made a gradual sort of progress, when he wasn't being pressed into the wall.

Eventually he found Dashini. She was at the centre of a square of rocks, just like the ones they had come in by, and when she saw him, the only human face in a seethe of cattle heads, she reached out for him.

Gam had never seen her look like this. She was panicked, out of control, frightened.

'Under me!' she shrieked. 'I had her hand, but she let go.'

Gam didn't need her to clarify, knew precisely what had her rattled. He dived down into the bodies, swimming violently through them, forcing his eyes open no matter how much the sweat of these people stung them, grabbed, pulled, strained, kicking down to where Dashini had seen Prissy fall.

Not another, his mind told him.

Not another.

Down, into them, fingers in their mindless eyes, their mindless nostrils, tugging their mindless ears.

There she was: wedged between the parts of creatures he couldn't even separate. Her arms were above her head as if she was a toddler, waiting for her sister to undress her for bed.

Her eyes were open and so was her mouth, but she said nothing and was blind to him.

She wasn't breathing.

Gam took her by both wrists and pulled. She came up easily, limply slipping between lubricated bodies into his arms. 'I've got her!' he cried, kicking his way up to where Dashini would be, where the Door would be, where escape would be.

Now he tasted blood. Where before he had tasted sweat, now it was blood.

He scrabbled up, pulling Prissy's dead weight with him, and there was Dashini, cattle hair in her hand, a head pulled back, the knife wet.

'It's not working!' Dashini turned to another one, another sacrifice, her clothes dark with the first one's blood, her hands and knife tacky with it. She stabbed into its bovine eye, cut into its neck, making it bellow like a bull, briefly, before it silently pumped the contents of its arteries into the scarce few gaps remaining. 'I've made the sacrifice, but the Door won't open!'

'Put her through!' Gam barked, desperately, but even he could see it was no good. Prissy's lips were blue, and her eyes stared lifelessly.

Gam spared one last glance at Dashini, but she had no hope for him. She was clawing at her own mouth, drowning in the sacrificial blood, crushed by the panicked writhing of the cattle-headed people, the blade of the Nathan Knife scoring its way needlessly through whatever flesh was nearby.

All Gam could do was hold Prissy's body tight to him and wait for a better heaven than this one had turned out to be.

X

Her Champion, Part Three

THE SLUMS, the sewer grates, the sites of pitched battles, bonfires, broken buckets, clothing on washing lines – singed and charred – carts, bridles, tanning tools, forges, chimneys, discarded carrots left uneaten, packets of bacon – empty – piles of wet wood: things that had been solid and inanimate and of a definite shape and size were now stretched unevenly into new shapes. Some were made thin and long and narrow and pointing upwards, still strong, still heavy but stretched, some beneath them were incongruous in their lack of change, the whole city balancing precariously. Between the chaos and flukes, those people who had not already fled stumbled in their confusion, blinked and raised their arms against the sight of things that must surely fall and crush them.

Sometimes, if Sirius went straight up then met with an obstacle that prevented him from following the shortest path to the den, the rules of perspective and foreshortening made this object seem to the eye as it had been before. By concentrating on the sensations of his mystical organ, or by going up closer, or moving to one side, he knew that was not the case. Then there was always the elongation, the stretching.

Sirius's companion Anaximander might have, by virtue of the abilities in rationalising that went with his possession of a man's voice, made conclusions as to why these objects were stretched the way they were. He might have posited the idea that the Master, returning to his Manse, had made magic that softened the world and then plucked himself upward, dragging everything with him into the sky until the Manse was at the height he required, and then done magic to harden the world again, so that his home could rest on solid ground and not collapse down into what lay beneath it. Having made this thought Anaximander could have communicated it to his companion in a comprehensible way. But Sirius had no such rational facility of his own, so no such conclusions were reached – it was enough for him to know that the transformation had occurred and that this was, for the predictable future, the way the world around him was, and that he should deal with it on these terms. That was what was useful about being an animal of Sirius's type: there was almost nothing trivial to distract him from his purpose, which in this case was to find a way of serving Nathan, even though that child was seemingly gone.

In his heart, even as he ran through this strange landscape, Sirius felt sadness. A dog that is separated from his service-pledge pines and will eventually die, unless he forgets his bond first. If he finds a new master, or suffers an injury to the head that disrupts his memories, then he may recover from the wound to his emotions, but it is rare, so strong is the connection he makes. Every moment he is apart is like an aching to him, and this aching grows stronger, becoming more and more like physical pain. Someone who suffers endless pain becomes exhausted by it – he must move in ways that are unnatural to him, behave in ways that do not take his health into account, and in every other way follow the dictates of his anguish and not do what is best for him.

It was too soon for Sirius to have properly suffered the effects that this situation provokes over the long term, except in his mood. At first, he had been carried away by the urgency of Nathan's disappearance – the body makes itself excited, and this excitation obscures the emotions – but now as the body sought the necessary respite for its nerves and let the excitation wane, so Sirius's feeling of loss grew.

He stopped and sat in the Living Mud, surrounded by corrupted flukes and distorted objects, the spiral of glass above him, and howled up into the sky: a long, high, wavering, tremulous howl of grief.

When that was done, he ran off. A dog does not dwell overlong on his misery and howling will overcome it, but this is not why he moved from one state to another with such facility. Here was the ghost again, and it stood, hands on its knees. This is the sign a man gives to a dog that he wishes him to come near.

Sirius was not attracted by this pose, though he came as if he was. Rather, he was moved by the strong sense from his mystical organ that there was something approaching from the future, coming backwards in time, and that he must meet it where this ghost directed him. Presently this was at the entrance to a long black scar in the earth, a black and depthless oval cut into the Mud. Around it, in the material realm, were blistered and reaching creatures, sticklike and crab-jointed tangles of blackness with eyes blacker still in their centres. They longed to commune with him, these things, but in the way that an illness longs for you – so that it might bring you low for its own purposes. They were like the sores that surround the lips of a man with the pox and the entranceway was his open mouth. Sirius was not put off by this similarity: he recognised the likeness, surely, but it gave him no pause, because the future echo was coming stronger now, and no simile or metaphor can overwrite the sense of destiny that such a sensation gives.

It comes looming, fate, out of the possible, and even if you do not quite know *what* will happen, if you are sensitive to its signs, you can know *that* it will happen. Sirius was very sensitive; indeed, he had been made to be sensitive to this sort of sensation.

The ghost went between the pox lips, untroubled by the long reaching claws of the sores, and in where he went there came a vision to the dog's inner eye of himself, grown to enormity, rearing up. So definite was this vision, and so powerful was the mood it gave off that Sirius would have gone to it under any circumstance, but he also wanted to do it, feeling that the solution to the problem of where Nathan now existed was tied in closely to this premonition. So, he followed.

The scar gave into a sewer, and if it had not been for the extreme transformation that it had undergone, Sirius would have known it for the same one he and Nathan had once entered together. Only, before he could go in, he had to contend with one of the tangled things, which had tumbled into the entrance, blocking it.

While the dog was thus occupied, there came in the distance an army of gill-men, a thousand strong, sliding and slipping and creeping between the standing buildings, down the hillside from the Manse. They were still some way off, but he could feel them coming as he rooted down to the centre of the spiked fluke and found in there what passed as its mind and chewed it to pieces. It scraped at him and gored him with spines and screamed for its brothers and sisters while he did it, but as a foe it was scarcely any trouble.

The gill-men came down, the babble of their thought-language in Sirius's mystical organ like an argument heard before dawn, down in the street. On their backs they carried packs of tools and material – shovels, barrels, stones and staves. The tangled creature was a weak thing, brand new and lacking fighting tone, and the little attention Sirius required to dispatch it was too little to distract him from the gill-men, some of whom carried between them, in gangs, lit braziers, barrows of concrete, struts and rails.

They all stank of the Master, and of Living Mud, refined and purified.

The ghost was in the darkness – and the vision, and the sense of oncoming fate – but Sirius spared time for the gill-men and performed an anticlockwise lap of the entrance, putting to death the other pox creatures while watching the army take a course that missed where he was by half a mile. They gathered a way off in a deep patch of the Living Mud which seethed with the same putrescent glow he had seen in the undersea vent earlier.

If he had decided to continue his observation of them, he would have soon, he felt, been sure that they were constructing an earthwork or building, or that they were filling in the hole that led to the God chamber, where Nathan had been before he returned from the Master's Manse.

This certainty was sufficient for Sirius, once he had seen into the intermediate realms with his mystical organ, to allow him to take this fact as read, and to continue into the mouth after the ghost to meet his oncoming destiny. If his companion Anaximander had been present, he would have urged all this information into him so that dog's rational mind could codify and stratify and collate it, ready for remembering and speaking. This is a very freeing thing to do, to sense but never have to make sense, but his inability to do it here was not an indication that the experience would be lost since he had in his heart, or in some other internal place, a kind of pocket or pouch into which he could squirrel away unresolved things of this kind. Though it swelled inside and made a kind of biliousness that ate at the contentment a dog might otherwise feel, he put it all in and dived into the blackness.

Here the transformation that had come over the world was written clearly in the brickwork of the sewer pipes. These pipes are usually made of a great number of uniformly rectangular blocks of baked clay, glazed and mortared together. In their natural state they form vertical and horizontal lines of near perfect uniformity, but now these lines were warped and elongated, made spheroid in places, or performed long parabolas, bulging into and out of the volume of the cylinders the sewers had been. The effluvia that were carried through the pipes ran in unruly eddies and currents, gathering and interfering in ways that suggested the white water at a cataract, or after a weir.

Similar perversions of the familiar had been made to the rats that called this place their home, making of them uneven, hairy, red-eyed snakes, drooling, with vestigial stubs of limbs, scarcely useful for anything. These mostly thrashed in agonies, solitarily and consumed by their own misfortunes, and when they lurched at Sirius, hoping to clamp their jaws on him and make themselves whole with an infusion of his untainted blood, it was the work of a moment to crunch their skulls and toss them away. He made a general communication to all nearby things, but received only the ache of their pain, returned to him through his empathy.

Fate was becoming less of a suggestion and more of a promise with every loping stride Sirius made towards where the ghost now stood by the entranceway to the gang children's den. This was the only place untouched by the change in the sewer's geometry. The bricks around the door were even more distorted than all the others, spread so thin in the world that they seemed as if they might tear and reveal beneath them the fabric of the weft, but the door itself was perfect and right, though that rightness itself was strange, so consistent was the wrongness the rest of the world exhibited.

The door had a lock that Gam had previously opened by some dexterity that Sirius's paws were incapable of, magic or no, and ghosts cannot, generally, interact with the things of the material realm, but as the dog approached the door it clicked and opened inward of its own accord.

There, unaltered from the way it had been, was the spiral staircase that led down into the depths.

The ghost went down the stairs, though unconvincingly; sometimes it was an inch or two above the surface, and sometimes its feet seemed to go into the steps.

If it had been a solid person, when Sirius went down beside him, overtaking him in the sudden conviction provided to him by the mystical organ of where it was that he had to go, the ghost would have been knocked off its feet. Instead, it shimmered a little, dimmed, but was otherwise unaltered.

Sirius didn't concern himself – instead he was off through the rooms, pawing at the door handles and putting his weight on them, rushing through furniture, toppling side tables and dragging rugs out of place.

There had been a door with a stuffed ram's head above it when he had come here with Nathan, and it would not open, though Sirius had sensed a terribleness behind it, and this was where he knew must take himself. Through the world rippled the effects of whatever was behind that door. Through events it shone, back from the future where he would find it. In Sirius's chest it vibrated, as if the clapper of a bell was there, striking against the nearness of this thing in time and space.

After turns and stairs, here was the door in question.

Sirius pounced at it, hoping to splinter the panels or take it from its hinges, but it was made of iron with none of the warm give of wood, only the implacable and oxidised immovability of a weight of old metal, painted and bolted into place. Sirius sniffed at it and panted, whined in a way that would have brought Anaximander to his side, but his companion was elsewhere. Instead, the ghost came to him. It made gestures and spoke words, but if they were information-bearing Sirius could not gather anything from them.

Perhaps there was some magical thing that he could have done – searched inwards and found some immaterial method to open the lock from the other side – but a dog in his enthusiasms and needs is not like a man: he is not put off and nor does he know that a door is the only way into a room. These facts, and the natural tendency a dog has to burrow, explain why it was that he scratched at the wall in which the locked door was put, sending first a cloud of plaster dust, then a collapse of the dado rail, then splinters of the wooden frame on which the plaster had been set, and then red brick dust.

This was the first thing that caused Sirius pain, but pain to a dog trained for fighting is no great deterrent, and though it eroded his claws, and cut at his pads, he dug into the bricks regardless. When the pain was too much, he rested by barging at the wall with his shoulder, shuddering the mortar from between the bricks, and then he clawed at the gaps again, bloodying but loosening them until they gave way and the wall fell partly to rubble.

The way to the room within was thus opened.

When a curtain flaps in a gale, after the closing of a window has been overlooked, it makes a slapping, rustling, whooshing sort of sound, with sometimes a tearing – this sound came from within, and a painfully high and insistent tone with it. It was foreboding and wrong, lit with a nacreous aura, ever-changing, and the mystical potency of it threatened to overwhelm Sirius again. Despite that, he did not falter – he scrambled through the gap in the wall the collapse had created and squeezed himself into the locked place.

XI

Boy, Book and Dog, Part Two

CLARISSA'S WORDS had blown through Bellows like a fresh dawn breeze after a long, hot night. This night, to him, had been one of many testing dreams, with visitations of phantoms, the chanting of choirs of chiding voices, each alerting him to his inadequacies, both in prose and in verse. It had seemed to go on forever, all anxious and fevered. But now, since she had come to him, the sun had risen, and lo! – he thought to himself, joyously – he was newly awoken, coming back to himself at last.

When he looked at his hands, pale like radishes – red on the bulbs of his palms, white on the tapering roots of his fingers – he sensed the sadness again, but this was something he remedied by putting his hands in the pockets of his smock. If he caught sight of himself in the mirror of a still puddle and saw his ludicrously flat face something similar happened, so he only looked forwards and a little up. This had the effect of raising his chin, which a certain type of boy finds ennobling of himself.

Clarissa – he tried not to think of her as a female version of his former Master – was ahead of him on a grassy knoll carpeted with bluebells, attended to by the talking dog. After the day's walk, which had taken them through mile after mile of low hills, flowers and flooded plains, they were discussing something.

Bellows ran after them, interrupted them. What was so necessary in the speech of a lower animal? 'Madam,' he said. Then 'Madam!' louder, when the first attempt to get her attention failed, putting himself between woman and dog.

She turned to him, and the dog fell away, so Bellows went on. 'What relic is it that you require? In my former position

I had access to a library in which maps and surveys of His enemy's territories were made. If you name the object of your interest, I may have heard of it? Or know where it is? Or know a quicker route? I am very eager to please.'

He expected a reply from her at this, but the speaking dog spoke instead, not to him, in a loud faux whisper that did not trouble his slavering lips and which had a conspiratorial and familiar tone that Bellows found irritating. 'Should you trust him? He is a thing of the Master and I recognise the scent. I associate it with menace.'

Bellows baulked at this. 'I am a thing of the Master? What, then, are you, who was birthed from his vats?'

Anaximander looked at Bellows, swallowed, then turned back to Clarissa. 'His point, while not directly answering the question, is well made. Except that I, your service-pledge, have proved my faithfulness by action, where he has not.'

'I have not had the opportunity!' Bellows said, interposing himself between woman and dog again, since Anaximander had come closer. He was just about to continue speaking – to offer some promise that would demonstrate his earnest desire to serve – when Clarissa shushed them.

'You're both things of the Master,' she said, any sympathy she had in her expression gone, 'and you always will be.' She turned her back, leaving them to look at each other.

And what was Adam? He'd been born in Mordew, like Bellows, but he was much more a thing of the Mistress. This he knew in the way that someone who has once read a book knows what's inside it – in summary, not in detail. In the same way that the owner of a book can open it, turn to a particular page and remind themself of the precise wording of the story contained within, Adam could have, if he'd chosen to, re-experienced exactly what had made him. But the book of his life was a terrible one, horrific, some chapters still raw as open wounds, and deep, so deep, that he had only recently been able to experience the world outside them. Pain is like that – it draws the mind to it, since its purpose is to alert the self – and once it can be ignored, that's an effort that must be made, continuously, if one is to live outside of it.

That evening, all gathered around the fire, open on Bellows's lap, Adam did not turn to the pages in his memory where his making was preserved, nor did he turn to the pages before or after it. Instead, he turned to a blank fresh page, and here he wrote new words, new lines, drew new illustrations, and he spoke while he did it, narrating the life of the present, which, regardless of what it was, wasn't the past, to people who, even if they weren't interested, were not his wounded self.

'Here we are,' he said, 'on the Island of the White Hills. It got this name long ago, before the flooding made it what we walk on now – thousands of islands. The name was always wrong, even then, since the white hills were only at its southern edge, and those dissolved away under the action of the sea as it surged up in defiance against mankind, and where it still remains, drowning the world of the ancients.'

Anaximander, for all his rationality, was lacking in data of this type, in lore and facts, and though he had questions he kept them to himself, so he didn't interrupt the book's information. Neither did Bellows, who was astounded to hear Adam speak at length and recognised his brother's voice in the words, which was both thrilling and melancholy. Clarissa, had Adam known it, predated even the period Adam described, and knew more than was contained in his pages, but she chose not to share this fact. She listened in silence for a while, and then wandered off into the darkness.

'These flowers,' he continued, drawing a plan map of their gathering and highlighting those that surrounded their circle of fire stones, 'so beautiful in their variety, aren't entirely natural to this environment. That blue one, by Anaximander's paw, would be dead if it was unaltered. The sea is full of salt, and salt will kill most plants. How does this plant live? The people of the past spliced into it the resistance sea weeds have to brine, using a technique that drowned with them.'

'Why,' Anaximander said, interrupting, 'if they knew how to preserve life against brine, did they not apply the technique to themselves, and so prevent their own drowning?'

Bellows nodded that this was a good question, but the answer did not seem to be in Adam's pages, no matter how many he flicked through, so Anaximander added it to the growing repository of questions he would determine the answers to, if and when he had the leisure.

'The mystery deepens when we realise that the same alteration is true of that plant, and that one, and that one. The same is true of all of them.'

On his pages he sketched the plants to which he alluded, each with notes and keys, one to a page, pencilling a diagram like a naturalist might make, then water-colouring it, before turning the page over and replacing it with another. The width of the book grew, by increments, and put that distance between Adam's thoughts and memories, making a buffer of experiences he could recall without anguish. 'Below the water are ancient roads of black stone, the foundations of ancient cities, sites of even older ritual places. Clarissa' – she was some distance away now, and Bellows and Anaximander looked up from their imaginings of the submerged artefacts of these lost times – 'she follows a twisting path that would have been very straight, once.'

Adam paused, and in the gap Anaximander's curiosity got the better of him. 'Where,' he whispered, in a slightly conspiratorial tone indicating that he knew that to seek knowledge his service-pledge had not seen fit to trust him with was a small betrayal, 'is she going, do you think, book?'

Bellows, pursing his lips, pulled the book away from the dog. 'How dare you question her actions? She exceeds your knowledge, and this is how it must be. It is your place to do what she wishes you to do, not for you to know what she knows.'

Adam drew a line on a page that traced the path they had taken, and he might have filled in the names of places, or made a supposition of their destination, but Anaximander interrupted again.

'A dog may ask questions, even if he does not expect answers, and an enquiring mind is not the same as a disobedient one. Indeed, he who knows his own strengths – in my case intelligence and wide-ranging senses – and then does not request knowledge that might help him to use them, isn't he, in fact, holding back from the entirety of his possible service? You yourself, Bellows, only today asked Clarissa—'

Bellows shut Adam and held him closed. 'Whatever your arguments, he is not yours to question,' he said, and went to put his brother into his jacket.

'Nor is he yours to hold shut without consulting him.'

Bellows, to his credit, immediately recognised the truth to this, but when he opened Adam back up again, his pages were blank.

When Anaximander stretched and rested his head on the ground there was something there that disturbed him. He got back to his feet, circled one way and then the other, and lay down again, stretched, but when his neck and the underside of his chin met the earth, he felt it again.

He looked over to Clarissa, who was also preparing for the night. She was gathering her objects, those things she habitually gripped while she was sleeping – a twisted rag, a folded piece of paper, a cracked glass bead – and because he didn't want to disturb her, he tried to ignore the feeling.

He could sense, deep below, the possible presence of another magical dog. It was very faint, like half recognising someone and not remembering from where. To his knowledge there was only one other in the world, his companion, Sirius, and perhaps he was wrong anyway, so he put his head on his paws where the sensation was less, and so it went altogether, allowing him to sleep.

XII

Her Enemy, Part Three

THE MASTER HAD been late getting the candidate out of the fourth vat. He knew it, but then again, what was the margin of error in work like this? It was not documented, so it might be anything. It might be that a minimum exists for the process to initiate, but no maximum exposure. Almost certainly that might be true. That would be fine.

The fifth vat had sigils relating to noses, the sense of smell, odours and women, none of which the Master troubled to look at since he knew what they were and what they did. This vat was filled not with liquid, but with gas, and was covered with an airtight lid. He took the peg he used to draw out the candidate's nose and put it over his own to prevent the ingress of the air the vat contained. This air was redolent of a female creature's oestrus, so he made sure he kept his mouth shut as he levered the lid off, and even once it was off, he only lifted it the distance necessary to slip the naked and slick child in through the gap. Then he sealed it up again, carefully, and once he was sure, he removed the peg. The waft was still there, so he sprayed an atomiser of concentrated verbena all around, putting some, lastly, on his sleeve, which he kept up to his face.

Would, he then thought, an invalidation cube weaken the seal on the Tinderbox? Had he done exactly that thing he'd hoped to prevent? By being overcautious, had he undone his own hard work of years?

Almost certainly not. No invalidation cube could work so quickly, and it only prevented unauthorised magics. It would isolate the locket, prevent it from interaction, but it wouldn't undo the magic it was isolating. Would it?

He gritted his teeth and pulled a face, then did the necessary translations until he was back in the study.

Repeated transition between realms is an occupational hazard for a weft-manipulator, and, like a drinker, or a smoker, or a taker of strong drugs, the Master was used to it. But, like a drinker, smoker or drug taker, it still had some effect, even on the hardened, and now, as he looked at the safe, he couldn't quite remember the combination. An arcane lock doesn't work like a rotating combination lock: a string of numbers, left and right, easily remembered, will not undo it. Memory is required, and manual dexterity, and either one or other – possibly both – of these things eluded the Master, dizzy as he was now from too much translation. The mystical chambers swam before his vision, and it was only on the fifth attempt that the door clicked and eased open.

He took the invalidation cube out, opened it, and there was the locket, perfectly unaltered as it should have been.

Except…

Sebastian went over to his desk and pulled the lamp into a convenient position. It was engineered so that, by a combination of springs, joints and hinges, it could illuminate things from any angle, but he manipulated the locket with his fingers instead, twisting it and turning it so that he could see it from all sides. When that wasn't sufficient to confirm or deny his suspicions, he went and took a magnifying glass from a vase into which he had previously placed it in lieu of the more usual bunch of flowers, or arrangement of fragrant sticks. Onto this he cast a simple fluence, so that it was several times more resolving, and then he looked again.

Time passed in his looking.

Men as old as the Master was, and who are prone to his unselfconscious and shameless self-interest, will generally have come across every curse and expletive the local populace has available to throw at him. Those that Sebastian remembered, in every language he could still speak, he rehearsed suddenly, under his breath, accompanying their delivery with the rhythm of his fist pounding against the green leather of his desktop.

The locket, he'd seen, was marbled with innumerable minute cracks.

These cracks were almost entirely invisible, but they were there nonetheless, approaching the infinite in their small-ness. To a person unfamiliar with magic, this would not be a serious matter. What wrong, after all, could come from such small cracks? Would a small mouse or rat emerge from them? Of course not! Would a very small volume of water leak into them, spoiling the contents? No! The surface tension of a liquid prevents it from operating at such a scale. There was nothing worth worrying about, to a mundane man, with imperfections of that size.

But Sebastian knew all about magic. He knew about things so small that they existed only as the concept of themselves, with no physical dimension at all. Moreover, he knew that Nathan was one of those things, occupying, if the term was not too *life-specific*, the immaterial realm of concepts. He was exactly the kind of thing that could make his way into and out of cracks like that.

More worrying still was the fact that such cracks don't make themselves – they must be made. And, if so, by whom?

The fact of the cracks, the fact of the locket's movement, the fact of the Tinderbox's centrality in his defences against the oncoming Crusade – those facts and a host of other facts closely related – meant that this could be no coincidence.

So, what to do?

He pulled at his lip, searched around the heavily laden study shelves, higgledy-piggled with implements, parchments, orna-ments and the magical ephemera of centuries, pausing now and then to rub his eyes and settle his stomach with brandy.

Why break with recent habits? he thought, after nothing on the shelves suggested itself as an alternative. A quarantine would do the trick.

Admittedly, unlike the cube, this would be an inconvenience in a hurry. Also, it was a time-consuming and fiddly business, erecting a barrier so powerful and yet so small. But it would undo whatever this plot to crack the locket was designed to do.

Such a quarantine would require returning to the primary Manse – they worked out from the material realm, into the weft, cascading back through any secondary and intermediate linked realms and up into the immaterial realm – but once the spell was achieved there would be a two-way impermeable block in every realm. Nothing in or out, without a prohibitively large expenditure of effort. He could then protect against any Rekka-like demon attack by keeping the locket on him again while he did his work.

His work!

He checked the gold, atmospheric carriage clock on top of one of the stacks, but too much translation tends to muddle the mind, and he could not calculate the vat room time.

He cursed again, repeating the favourite from his childhood he'd only recently used for the cracks, and made his way back to the vat room.

The candidate was too long steeped in the oestrus, there was no ignoring it. He was brown with it, as if he'd been left in a pot of tea with several scoops of lapsang souchong. If only the smell had been so pleasant...

The Master, pulling his rubber gloves up to his elbows and reattaching the nose peg, lay the candidate out on a nearby table and saw what could be salvaged. With a counteractant wash, he might be able to undo some of the damage.

Improvising, he filled vat six not with the briny solution he favoured at that stage but with a light peroxide, diluted with distilled water and unlikely to cause any serious burns or tainting of the already sensitive olfactory organs.

'Unlikely', though, wasn't good enough, so he made wax of two red votive candles, waited until said wax was cool enough to handle, and then plugged the candidate's nostrils with it.

He smoothed as the plugs cooled, and soon there was on the table a large-nosed boy with red nostrils, too brown a complexion, and an extended period of containment in a bleach vat ahead of him.

And the Tinderbox was still not quarantined.

The Master's chambers in the Manse in the material realm, to any observer in that realm who could correspond with their counterpart in the Master's secondary antechamber realm, was identical in every respect, and no amount of cross-checking and comparing of details would have proved otherwise. The two realms, up to the limits of the edges of the building, were identical. Except that, for the purposes of some spells, it was necessary to be in the material realm proper and not in the secondary antechamber realm, since that secondary realm had physical limits in various directions and consequently did not have the full breadth of the weft at its disposal. This Manse also had its own Master, and now the real Master took the prescribed route as so to arrive at exactly the time to replace the material realm Master as he translated himself out into a tertiary realm Manse to do what this Master was planning to do here, there, where he could do no harm.

Because the secondary realm was for all practical purposes, real, to use the Assembly's terms – though they would deny it – the Master didn't want the replica Master to tamper with anything there, so he'd made the tertiary realm for him to act in so that there weren't any inconvenient disruptions in the synchronicity between the realms. This material realm Master was necessary, even though it would have been less complicated and less taxing on the imagination if he hadn't existed. The existence of an exact duplicate of yourself casts some doubt, ontologically speaking, on your own reality, but for certain reasons relating to the extreme unpredictability of the movement of particles at a small scale, the other Master needed to be there for the machinery of that Manse's reality to keep on ticking.

But his necessity was a practical fact only, and Sebastian had, immediately on instantiating him, rendered him a puppet, conceptually speaking, by isolating him from his immaterial component – by a process known as shuyet binding – and forcing him, unknowingly, to mimic the real Master's every thought, movement and action. Because the material realm Manse was isolated from the material realm in the outward direction, the influence of which the secondary realm undertook in its place, the puppet could have no influence on the events in the material realm proper.

This made things much easier, though even the Master had to write it on a blackboard with chalk in order to understand it all.

Suffice it to say, the material realm could still be influenced – an invasion or an explosion could damage, even destroy it – but any issues could easily be corrected from the secondary realm and return the place to a state of perfection without anything much more than a little elbow grease.

Here he came, the unknowing Master puppet, directly down the translation corridor, walking towards the mirror that would translate him to the tertiary realm that he took for the material real but which the real Master knew was a tertiary falsehood. In this realm the real Master had made the mirror non-reflective, so he could make sure there was nothing awry in the matching, and as he walked towards the translating frame, he was pleased to see the same pleased look he was wearing appear on the face of his counterpart.

When at the frame, neither felt the other, and one went one way and the other the other, mimicking each other as a reflection mimics an ordinary man as he dresses himself in a wardrobe mirror.

In this way the Master went to the material realm Manse study, which was identical to his secondary realm, and began work on the quarantine for the locket, first tying a ribbon around his finger to remind himself to mirror the secondary realm's chambers on the material realm's Manse after he translated, or find everything falling out of sync in short order.

This made him think, sadly, of Bellows. He wasn't there, which made the whole thing much more convenient, but it was a convenience he would have given up in a moment if only to have his friend back. He would have isolated, maintained, mirrored and returned ten times over if only he could. Now there were only the gill-men to worry about – even Cook and Caretaker were gone – and there was no necessity to take their lives into account. He'd just instantiate material realm replicas and attach those to the immaterial concepts later.

With these sad thoughts circulating, Mr and Mrs Sours – the married pair of mechanical mice that did small cleaning jobs about the place – came over to see if he was alright. It was very like them, recently, the Master thought, to make a mistake like this. He'd designed them to seek out problems, and for a very long time they'd understood this to mean things like a pile of dust in a corner, or a dead beetle shell. Now they were alert to a wider range of issues, and it had got to the point that if he sighed too loudly they'd wheel and nudge at his boot.

Evolution was an irritation in things like these. He'd have to wipe their minds and begin again, but there was no time for that. To demonstrate that he was fine, Sebastian returned to his work; he took a chrysoprase-studded iron chest from a high shelf and opened it.

Inside was the tabard relic of the hermit saint Zosimus. Quarantines isolate, hermits are isolated, hermit saints are weft-infused, weft-infused relics can be used as the material for spells, so he pulled one of each of the warp and weft threads from the tabard, then closed and resealed the chest.

Mr and Mrs Sours seemed satisfied with this, returning to their hole in the skirting board, and the Master went and sat at his desk with the threads. Here, he braided them together, something that was a little fiddly and needed a steady hand. Once it was done, he snipped the braid in half and braided the two parts. He slit his thumb, sealed the ends of the new braid with his blood, and burned the lot in the flame of the candle in one of the desk lamps.

Then he inhaled the smoke and held it in his lungs.

Nathan Treeves really did have a lot to answer for. And Dashini. The pair of them together were real menaces, and now Bellows was gone, dead at the hands of Padge, of all people.

Still, wasn't that appropriate – Padge was a Malarkoian spy, after all. He had a mind to bring him back – a replica at least, he was no Nathaniel – and punish him for his crimes. But what would be the point?

When Sebastian was forced to breathe out – a man can only hold his breath for so long – it was not breath that came out but a kind of soft ambergris, or very solid ectoplasm, and this he took to a cloche he had for just such occasions on a small balcony.

Out here it was raining, and he shielded the formless blob of material from the water. Up in the clear parts of the sky it was a deep blue transitioning from day to night – some gloaming time between dusk and twilight, untroubled now by bird-death – which was a perfectly suitable time for planting. All the while holding the blob under his jacket with one hand, he used the other to dig a small excavation in the soft soil under the cloche glass. It was about the size of a teacup, and into it he put the ectoplasmic ambergris – he would have to name it one day, at least to save him the trouble of trying to come up with something each time – covering it again with soil after.

A green spider, a representative of a species Sebastian had bred as gardeners and tenders of plants, inspected the planting site. It found the Master's work mostly satisfactory, but flattened the surface here and there with its delicate forelimbs.

Sebastian closed the cloche lid and went for his copy of *Accelerants and Decelerants, volume III – Sprays and Mists.*

While he looked for it on the shelves of the library – it was somewhere on the second level, near the chimney stack – anxiety crept up. This New Bellows. This first candidate. He felt that it was already ruined. Should he begin again?

The reactive chronologue was in the vat realm, so he did a rough calculation on his fingers of the time it would take, of the time he had lost, of the time he would lose, his thumb marking the numbers in leaps across the digit tips. He gave up before the sums were done; it would take too long to begin again. He was already risking a prolonged post-translation syndrome, and the only way he'd have enough time before the Assembly arrived would be to double this risk. Not worth it.

He'd have to hope for the best.

A+D, vol. III was mis-shelved, placed spine inward, which was why it took him a while to find. Once he had it in hand he went straight to the laboratory, letting the glowing pages fall open where the spine was cracked. It was a spell he'd consulted many times before, but there were just one or two steps too many for him to encapsulate it in his head, at least in a way that would last between uses. Laid out in front of him, as it soon was, beside an Erlenmeyer flask/titration burette combination and the bank of gas nozzles for the burners, the words – all as elaborately coloured as an ancient, illuminated manuscript, and archaic in spelling – were immediately familiar. The Master could, he suspected, have made a slight alteration to his mind's recall, and thereby saved himself the trouble of having a library at all, but that was a dangerous route to go down. Ask Clarissa. Ask Clarice. Ask any of them, really, with the obvious exception of Nathan.

No, he thought, tracing the line of the incantation with the index finger of his left hand, better to suffer a minor inconvenience to avoid a major catastrophe.

In the long and distant past there had been a machine that had read sounds inscribed on a disc with a needle which magnets converted into vibrations and so music was made, and Sebastian's finger acted in this way, resonating his vocal chords under weft-influence and setting off in his immaterial counterpart a chain reaction that had the effect, in the material realm, of making in his finger a superfluity of the concepts around 'speed' and 'vegetation', and once it was green with it he rushed round to the other side of the table, tinkling glass tubes in their racks in his pounding hurry, to where a litre of distilled water was in a glass jug. He doused his finger, and the liquid went like crème de menthe thick and shiny. He put this into an atomiser and took it back out to the garden.

It was full night now, the stars in the moonless sky barely lighting anything, but they didn't have to – the ambergris ectoplasm had already sprouted, and the plant it made was as bright as a firefly's belly. Bioluminescent, some of the older books characterised it. With two puffs of the atomiser, it was not only bioluminescent, but greenly so. It expanded, the sprout, into a cotton-like plant, and the Master picked the bolls and went back to the lab.

Was he this lonely?

The thought came to him out of the blue. It was almost audible, like a word heard on the near edge of a dream that startles a tired man away from beginning a night's rest. It wanted to know, this thought, whether a self-contained, self-controlled, self-aware man ought to go to this amount of trouble to replace a manservant.

Well, Sebastian thought, the thought could mind its own business. He was exactly as lonely as he was, and if that was so lonely that it made him do this kind of thing, then what exactly did the thought want him to do about it?

Cotton thread is made from the innards of a cotton boll and a quarantine is made from the thing he now held in front of him, which was a near invisible tangle of clear fibres. Once he'd have spun this by hand, but he'd made enough quarantines now that it had been worth making a machine that did it for him. It was scarcely worth firing it up for one this small, but he'd cleared the small loom off to a place that wasn't immediately leaping to his mind – Bellows, of course, would have known – so he cranked the mechanism, waited for the flywheels to catch, tapped the gauge until it registered one bar, and dropped the fibres into the compartment.

As the machine laboured over its spinning, he took the locket out of his jacket. He didn't need to look closely – he knew the cracks were there, and anyway, that would be remedied in moments – but there was something odd about it, even when he chose not to turn its attention to it.

A smell was leaking out.

It's hard to avoid a smell. You can block your ears, close your eyes, shut your mouth, put your hands behind your back, but because you must breathe, smells make themselves smelled despite you. They come in with the air you breathe. This smell was of sandalwood. Possibly patchouli. Not lemon balm. No, it was sandalwood.

239

The gauge crept up to one and a half bars, so the Master loosened the Duckbridge valve on the side and held his breath as it edged back into the safe zone.

When he breathed in again, the sandalwood was still there. Was he expected to understand from this that sandalwood-scented gas was leaking from the weft-stuff contained in the locket? Was Nathan, caged in the infinite but unmoving immaterial realm, influencing it to make a sandalwood-ness in the materials of the Tinderbox? To what end? It was true that Sebastian had no liking for that smell, but nor was he particularly bothered by it. Was it the by-product of something else? The same thing that was making the cracks?

Irrelevant, because now, at the rear of the machine, the exit compartment made a ting like a tiny bell being struck, and when he went around there was the flexible glass that quarantines were made of, once a sufficiency of Spark was infused into it. He took the glass out and it was like a frog's egg, enlarged, but without the tadpole in the centre. He Scratched in Spark as he sang his maker tone, Scratched more as he sang the dissolving harmony, and when there was enough Spark to make it glisten, he poked the locket, chain and all, inside the egg.

Once it was inside and safe, he smoothed the gap, shook it a few times to get any air bubbles out, and wiped his finger on his trousers. It was a perfect sphere, so he struck the spinning machine with a tuning fork, which set the quarantine in place permanently.

And that was that.

XIII

Her Heir, Part Two

THE DOOR INTO the second level of the Golden Pyramid, home of the person-headed snakes, was not open to admit Dashini and Gam because it had fallen into disrepair on the first-level side. The words 'Secundus est Pretium Caeli' had almost entirely worn away. Prissy was dead, suffocated by the flesh of the cattle-headed people, and the other two weren't far behind.

So, what now?

What of Dashini's faith in her mother?

These trials would be insurmountable obstacles in the material realm, but Malarkoi was not in the material realm. Here, in the heavens made by its Mistress, there was always more than one way to skin a cat, and goddesses work in mysterious ways.

In the absence of their deity, civil war had broken out amongst the person-headed snakes of the second level. Those who still observed the religion fled into secrecy, the priesthood hiding their mitres, the litanies mouthed silently, and along the verandas, and around the shaded bowers, and beneath the jewelled gazebos, they disavowed Cren to the mobs and wept for their weakness later.

When a handful of them met, their beautiful churches substituted for cellars and abandoned places, their furtive conversation was all of faith and prayer and rebellion.

'What is to be done?' one of them would whisper, sibilantly, and more often than not there was no answer.

In a shadowed and collapsed veranda, or within a forgotten annexe, these person-headed snakes would half-undulate, their necks nervously straight and as close to the ground as they could be held, and whichever one of them had some plan they would offer it to the others.

'Devotion,' one of them said, 'is a necessary quality that the righteous possess. All we person-headed snakes who worship Cren can recognise and agree. It is a necessary truth. If one says to another, "I am devoted," that is a good thing. And what is devotion if it is not devotion up until death?' The person-headed snake looked nervously to see if he was overheard, but only briefly, since it would be contradictory to make such a statement in fear.

The others gathered there held their rattles erect and let off susurrations with them to indicate their agreement.

Another snake – this one woman-headed – said, 'Devotion to Cren even until death is righteous, but isn't it better to live and further Cren's cause? Further, righteousness in and of itself is a personal good, but can it not be said that to benefit Cren, even at the sacrifice of one's own righteousness, is a communal good? So, might it be that righteousness that stands in the way of doing what must be done is not a good? Perhaps this is why Cren has deserted us. We cleave too closely to the Cren-lore and our enemies' benefit.'

The huddle made an approving hissing at this, even those who had yet to understand the ramifications of the argument. These person-headed snakes joined to make an ellipse around the debating pair, each of whom went to the foci and faced each other.

'I did not say that death was desirable,' the person-headed snake said, 'nor that righteousness was easy to judge. There is a transcendental quality to both concepts, and we person-headed snakes are not capable of knowing that which only Cren can know. This makes us prone to error, and so we must obey the Cren-lore to the letter, since it is the word of Cren and one cannot go against it.'

The woman-headed snake recognised this truth, slithered back, nodding, so that her debating partner could continue.

The person-headed snake – let us call him Sorax – expounded to the woman-headed snake – let us call her Arinne – 'Cren says that no person-headed snake may kill another person-headed snake, and so we do not kill. Cren says that no person-headed snake should act out violence on another person-headed snake, so we are peaceful. To be otherwise would be to do evil in the world.'

It was a cloudless day, warming to the blood but not too frantically hot. In the sky behind their gathering place – the remains of a warehouse, destroyed in the purges – smoke rose in the distance. Arinne risked rising up, her posture a kind of rhetoric, convincing in its boldness. 'And yet the secularists burn our churches, chase our priests through the boulevards. The scriptures they deface, and mention of Cren is punished by summary execution. Our devotion is up to the point of death, but only our own. To defend Cren and Cren-lore we must be willing to break its prohibitions. This is the paradox. Violence contravenes Cren-lore, but without violence Cren-lore will be destroyed. What if to sacrifice our righteousness in the name of Cren is devotion of the highest order? What if it is our obligation?' Arinne's words echoed through that ruined place, and the person-headed snakes there were silent in the reverberation of her heresy.

She had gone too far, and now the others left, looking back with slit eyes, spitting on the ground.

Only Sorax remained.

He came up to her. 'You must be wrong in what you say: to contravene Cren-lore is to deny Cren,' he said, 'but I cannot find fault in your reasoning. Where does it end, your argument?'

Arinne turned away from him, performed a rotation of her head that allowed her to see all around, and then rotated back so that she didn't twist herself in a knot. 'Follow me,' she said.

There had been no recent census of the second level, but the city where Arinne and Sorax dwelled was thought to have been occupied by at least a hundred thousand person-headed snakes before the secularist massacres began. Perhaps one in ten of those once living had now been killed, and double that number had been wounded.

They kept back from the boulevards, taking side streets half destroyed by fires, skirting displaced person-headed snakes, slithering between potholes and piles of rubble.

Arinne said nothing until they reached her rooms, which were behind a disreputable-looking theatre, up a spiral stair.

They went in and the first thing Sorax saw were her books – there were hundreds of them, jumbled in piles.

Arinne curled her scales around one pile as if they were a nest of her eggs. 'They are refugees, all these scriptures, all these piles, from the ruins of the Great Library.'

Sorax gasped. 'I heard that the library at Glastonbury had been burned and all its works destroyed.' He went to them and there were tears in his eyes – the books were a gift from Cren. 'Is this where you learned the lore you preach?'

Arinne smiled but said nothing.

She took him to the dark food store of her place and there raised a piece of inconspicuous sacking in a shadowed corner. Revealed beneath it was a hatch which opened onto a crevice. Into this space had been lowered a chest, banded with iron.

It did not have a keyhole, this chest, since a person-headed snake cannot easy hold a key or turn it in a lock, but there were dials which Arinne shielded as she clicked them with her tongue, hiding the numbers until it opened. She slithered back and raised herself up, so she was right beside him. 'Inside there,' she said, pointing with her silent rattle, 'are forgotten works of Cren-lore.' She looked at Sorax, examined his broad cheeks and sunken brown eyes for signs of his trustworthiness. She must have found some, because she went on, 'They are *Fragments Towards a Natural Philosophy of the Weft, Practical Theology,* and *The Incomplete Proceedings of the Meetings of the Society of the Weftling Tontine.*'

If his eyes had held trustworthiness this must now have been replaced with incomprehension – it was clear from his lack of an intelligent response that he did not recognise the titles, and there was nothing about them that allowed him to guess at their contents.

They took the books back into the living areas of Arinne's den and she laid them out on the flat ground there in the grid that formed the semantic backdrop of the person-headed snake's writing system. She insinuated herself into a pile of pillows, leaving Sorax to ponder the meaning of the arrangement in front of him.

It was some while before he looked up, and the tentative glint of knowledge in his eyes often receded in the face of his ignorance and doubt, the two things coming like the peaks and troughs of a wave, a stillness in the waters of which would have indicated full comprehension. 'I...' he said, pausing, and Arinne took his lack of a complete utterance to be a sign of an absence in him of wisdom.

She emerged from the pillows in a high and stiff annoyance, but when she saw he was cowed and sorrowful in his expression, she decided not to give him a lecture on his stupidity but instead to foment what understanding there might already be in him by giving a practical demonstration of the things he might have been expected to understand, such reification of an idea being a useful pedagogical technique, particularly when teaching a person unfamiliar with one's own discipline.

In the *Incomplete Proceedings*, there was a spell called *The Opening of the Eyes*. This spell Arinne cast on Sorax, reciting the tones from a page of her notes, the energy cost being paid by one of a cage of captive mice that had recently been born and which simultaneously provided her evening meals and the motive force of her magic.

For Sorax, the veil of the real ascended to reveal the weft behind it, which to a person-headed snake was a dark and writhing field of potentialities within which facts and truths emerged and receded, shapes and forms became recognisable and faded into nothing, people and events coalesced and dissolved. Across this, like an image made of a thousand other images, the form of Cren could be made out: there was its mitre and there its crook, there were its good red scales and there the evil yellow, there was its base neck and there its elevated chin. All these things were present only briefly, the form of the weft obscuring its features, consuming it in its endless purposive meaninglessness, but before they left one thing was perfectly clear – Cren was dying.

When the real re-established itself after a few minutes it formed by degrees out of the weft in a way which represented itself to Sorax as indicating the true eternal sources of the temporary forms of the real. This effect remained for a while, showing Arinne and her coils as a physical manifestation of vibrations contained by states of the weft. The spell had been formulated to do exactly this work, allowing a weft-manipulator to make changes in the real that influenced the frequencies of weft-stuff, and thereby facilitated the crossing of things and concepts from one possibility to another in a manner that the scriptures told them were miraculous.

When eventually Sorax came down to a level that allowed him to speak, the first thing he did was to abase himself anew before Cren. He prayed so rapidly and ecstatically that the words came out of him as an endless high exhalation, force-fully delivered, until he had no energy remaining to keep him upright and fell thrashing to the floor.

'Do you see now,' Arinne said, 'the importance of our devotion, and the limits it must exceed?'

Sorax was too exulted to reply.

Later, when Sorax had recovered, he said, 'What can we do to save Cren?'

Arinne did not wait a moment. 'We must go to the rue Barbauld.'

This was a place that Sorax had not visited, but it had a reputation for the worst excesses of secularism. He nodded slowly and warily. The rue Barbauld was frequented by Crenless person-headed snakes of a bohemian type – young, intelligent, iconoclastic – and the kinds of behaviour to be expected up and down that street were anathema to his Cren-fearing beliefs. Yet hadn't he seen things that put his old truths into doubt? Didn't he require a reformation of his faith?

They left and joined the moving pavements – the boule-vardiators – outside Arinne's dwelling that accelerated them from one side of the city to the other and which existed here where vehicles might have done in other realms.

A man with legs would topple at the speeds these conveyors transported person-headed snakes – but Arinne and Sorax coiled close to the ground like compressed mattress springs and rested their cheeks against their scales, thereby preventing any chance of slipping or concussion.

They observed each other from this position with sideward eyes as they sped through the arrondissements in an intimate and conspiratorial proximity: the towers of the Fifth Borough went by, their light-play overlooked; they did not hear the terrible cries from the Tribute Ring; and the aqueducts of the Eighth, choked with bodies, were nothing to them; they fixed their gaze on each other's eyes and ignored the new horrors of this war-torn world.

The rue Barbauld was a place of unrestrainedness, where Cren-freedom was elevated to a deviant art form and those there cavorted in blasphemous indulgences that would have driven the priests of previous ages to the construction of engines of punishment. Amongst the tall buildings – simultaneously grand and crumbling, bejewelled and shabby – person-headed snakes writhed in lamplight of a thousand colours, and the thudding of head-drums competed with their cries of exultation and ecstasy.

'Try not to look,' Arinne said. 'We'll be there soon.'

Where 'there' was, Sorax was unsure, but before his half-covered, appalled eyes, person-headed snakes of all thicknesses and lengths, all sects and casts, all breeds and none, circled and pulsed along posts that had been driven into the cobblestones for just this purpose. The boulevardiators had been thus halted and there was a sickly and perverse lack of forward motion, as if everyone there was waiting for the noon warmth, stewing in their lethargy, jaws slack and drooling. Cloacal transfer was taking place everywhere, Sorax was mortified to see, and now passers-by laughed at him openly, seeing him and despising his discomfort.

'How far—?' Sorax began, but Arinne did not let him finish and instead urged him with her loops off down an alleyway, where the hubbub was lesser.

Some distance along this, she went down to an unmarked cellar, steps slick with moss and dripping gutter water, and when she was there she made a coded rattle and waited. Sorax came to her without urging, hearing something clatter in the darkness behind him, and, when the door opened a crack, he was in head first and his ear caught on the door frame.

'Sorry,' Arinne said to a person who, Sorax realised, was risen before him. 'We're here to see the Seneschal.'

The person-headed snake in the doorway slid aside and indicated with a jerk of his head another door to his right, which Arinne went through without delay, Sorax coming at her side.

The corridor Arinne eventually arrived at, after many ascensions and descensions by pole, had several rooms off it, with identical doors. It was like a cheap hotel, and just like one of those there came from within the rooms a variety of sounds, each seemingly belonging to some tawdry melodrama being played out in the imperfect privacy of thin walls. There was shouting and crying, banging and moaning, and the lights flickered irregularly, lending everything a peculiar and dangerous atmosphere.

Sorax was not the kind of person-headed snake who was immune to anxiety. He had led, it now seemed to him, something of a sheltered life, and when two person-headed snakes fell out of an open doorway and twined across the hall, head-butting each other and shrieking oaths, he almost turned back. Arinne had to look at him imploringly, making him know by her expression that she understood his reluctance, but that it would all be worth it, for Cren. Still, how was he to continue, now his path was blocked?

Thankfully, the obstacles removed themselves as they fought, their wrestling taking them back into their room, the door slamming behind them. Sorax slipped around the blood-ied carpet and followed the back of Arinne's retreating form.

She stopped at the end of the corridor and uttered words in a language he did not recognise. The door opened and here, filling the doorway, was a louche type of woman-headed snake, or perhaps a very woman-headed type of man-headed snake. When he or she spoke, the issue was not resolved, the idiolect used being a mixture of the feminine and masculine forms and spoken in a low, whispering, gravelly voice, indicating abuse of shisha over years. They wore – Sorax settled on a neuter pronoun in his mind – woman's face powder, this person-headed snake, but their skull shape was bluntly masculine, and there was an aura of violence about them, accentuated rather than hidden by the over-application of face waxes.

'This,' Arinne said to Sorax, having communicated with the person for a little while in the unknown language they shared, 'is the Seneschal.'

The Seneschal – the word meant nothing to Sorax – looked him up and down, darting their tongue in and out between their lips and blinking rapidly. Their eyes were rimmed red and bleary, their teeth stained. 'Bring him in,' they said.

Arinne did as she was told.

Inside, rather than finding what Sorax had imagined would be a sordid and untidy hotel room, dotted with vermin and black mould, cluttered with empty bottles and narcotic para-phernalia, there was instead a very neat Cren church, of sorts, with hassocks, an altar and a pulpit. The room was several knocked into one, perhaps three deep, and while there was no natural light, an electrical light box had been erected against the far wall with bulbs that shone through stained glass.

Sorax was surprised to see all this, obviously, and the Seneschal's appearance was also unusual, but it was the scene the lit panels contained that occupied his attention the most.

On it there was a unique and terrible being depicted. She was like a woman-headed snake, except that where such a person might be expected to have a snake's body, this one had four limbs, two vertical and two horizontal, held so that she formed a cross. Her head and neck rested in the crook of the upper limbs, her scales were uniform and undifferentiated, bleached, and from her head spikes emerged. Around her were shapes that followed the grid of a sentence but were not words as far as Sorax could recognise them, and below her, much smaller or further away, was a representation of Cren, cowering on the ground.

He did not know why he did it – there is something powerful in fear that motivates a person-headed snake even without them knowing why – but Sorax backed away from the image. Superstition can make one retreat from a blasphemy, as can fear of divine judgement, but this was more of a simple repulsion: the cross-figure was an abomination, lacking even a single curve, appallingly straight in every direction.

He backed into the Seneschal, their hard-softness stopping him and enveloping him all at once. 'She is the Mistress,' they said, 'mother of Cren. We must bring her here, so that she can punish Cren's enemies and re-establish his rule. Is this something you are willing to do?'

Sorax didn't know what to say, so he said nothing at all.

The Seneschal slipped round to the front of him. The light from the stained glass coloured their already coloured face and glinted off their scales. Arinne replaced the Seneschal behind, put herself against Sorax and pushed him forward. 'We need your sacrifice, Sorax, proof of your devotion, even though it defies Cren-lore.'

Whatever communion Sorax had thought had passed between him and Arinne he now knew for something else. This woman-headed snake was a devil – she meant to murder him. The rue Barbauld? He should have known it was a trap.

The Seneschal and Arinne made between them a cage, their coils binding him between them while they exchanged a long glance full of sinister meaning.

'Please,' Sorax said, suddenly seeing that the altar was stained not just with red light but also with blood. 'Please! If there is a shred of Cren-love in you, release me. You have lost your way, turned your back on Cren-lore, mistaken the scriptures.'

Arinne pushed him forward. 'It is you who are mistaken. With your death we will summon the Mistress, return Cren to its rightful place.'

The Seneschal stretched to their full height, and from their head-drum there issued a thudding rhythm that shook the stained glass in the light box and sent shadows dancing across the pews and altar. 'The time has come.' The Seneschal came forward and writhed in front of him.

Arinne took a curved knife, held it clumsily in her coils, while the Seneschal recited lines they had found in the *Incomplete Proceedings*.

Sorax tried to slither away across the ground, but Arinne was too quick for him.

She slashed and stabbed him with the knife, her inability to hold the weapon tightly making cruel and ineffective wounds, but when Sorax eventually succumbed to her attacks suddenly it was as if the room had been subjected to a lightning strike and an earthquake, one following directly on the other.

The two living person-headed snakes twisted to face the sound, ignoring the splinters and shards and fragments of glass that invaded their scales.

There, lying in the rubble where the altar had been, were three people like the woman in the stained glass, each with the four strange limbs. They were slumped over, breathing heavily, bloodstained and panting for breath.

One of them, after a while, was the first to stand and the first to speak.

'What the bleeding hell is all this?' Prissy demanded.

There were two very weird-looking things, each with a bobbly head stuck on top of a stripy-looking worm. They were swaying all over the place – which was like some kind of gin-house with no customers and cushions instead of seats – their mouths and eyes wide open and their tongues poking out.

Prissy turned to Dashini, even less impressed than she had been by the cattle-headed people. 'Is this supposed to be heaven too?' she said.

Dashini, blinking from the summoning, not sure how or why Prissy was alive, nodded her head and said, breathlessly, 'Should be.'

Prissy put her hands on her hips. 'I don't know why your mum bothers. You two,' she said to the person-headed snakes, 'look bloody ridiculous. Honestly. Have you seen yourselves?'

She didn't wait for them to react or reply and instead marched right down the aisle of the church. Prissy was head and shoulders above the person-headed snakes, and the top of her hair touched the chapel ceiling. As she walked, the floorboards creaked and buckled and she was first blue, then red, then green, then yellow in the stained-glass light. When she stepped over the corpse of Sorax she boggled in disbelief. He was like one of those things that come out of a jack-in-the-box – a jack, she supposed – once its spring has stopped.

She opened the door at the far end and, seeing nothing worth noting, slammed it and came back – yellow, green, red, then blue again. 'What a dump! And why are we here anyway?'

'Summoned?' asked Gam, who was staring at Prissy.

'Summoned,' said Dashini, in agreement.

'Summoning brings people back from the dead, does it?'

'Not usually.'

'So, this is a miracle then? From your mum?'

Prissy looked at both of them, but particularly at Gam. 'What's the matter? You both look like you've seen a ghost.' She searched his face waiting for his answer.

Gam looked away. 'I'm fine. Just pleased we got out in the nick of time.' He turned to Dashini, something in his mouth like an apology about to be spoken, but Dashini went up to Arinne. 'You,' she said, 'where is the outward Door?'

Arinne understood their words – this was the secret language she and the Seneschal used for occult matters – but whatever words she might have wanted to speak, this acolyte

252

of the Mistress's cult, they stuck in her throat in the face of her deity.

Thankfully, the Seneschal was a little less intimidated. 'Mistress, the Door is Cren's Seat, in the holy cathedral of its priests.'

Dashini beckoned Gam and Prissy to come over to where she was, which they did. 'Take us to Cren's Seat. Now!'

'We can't,' the Seneschal said. 'The secularists have taken over the place and no one is allowed to enter.'

Dashini frowned. 'Secularists? Aren't you all Crenfolk?'

Now Arinne got her voice, and out rushed an impassioned lecture on the civil war, the massacres, the moribundity of Cren, her transgression of Cren-lore, and, eventually, the recent sacrifice of Sorax. She prostrated herself on the ground. 'Forgive me my trespasses,' she said, 'and deliver Cren back to us!'

Dashini bit her lip. What was going on? Another realm where things were falling apart... what was her mother playing at? Gam was clearly convinced she was a goddess, but Dashini couldn't help but feel differently. 'I'll do my best for you,' she said to Arinne. 'Take me to Cren's seat, and I'll send you straight to the woman who can sort this out.'

The person-headed snakes, after a momentary exchange between them, turned and went to lead their summonings there, but Prissy grabbed them by the rattles and pulled them back in a way that was, for this realm, impossibly rude and insulting. 'Can we have some water first? I'm gasping.'

Dashini nodded, and the Seneschal went to a kitchenette off to the left of the altar and returned with the end of the water pipe, valved shut.

Prissy wrinkled her nose at this. 'Don't you lot have glasses then?'

The Seneschal didn't understand. Instead, they prodded the tongue-button and passed by mouth the activated spigot for Prissy to suck on.

Prissy blanched at it, but Gam came over and grabbed the hose by the neck. 'How is it going to pick a glass up? It hasn't got any arms, has it?' He put his head back, made an airlock with his thumb over the pipe hole, released it, and let the water gush down into his mouth from above. When he'd had enough to wash the taste of the cattle-headed people away he passed it to Prissy.

She didn't take it. 'What do I look like? Someone who'd suck water out of a pipe?' She crossed her arms and turned away.

Gam, not seeing any other option, passed the apparatus back to the Seneschal and bowed his thanks, which they reciprocated with a bow of their own.

'When in Rome,' Dashini said to Prissy, 'it's a good idea to do as the Romans do.' She took the pipe and drank herself, first wiping it with her sleeve.

Prissy, either not knowing what a Roman was, or not caring, yanked the pipe from Dashini's hand, went over to the back of the church where a baptismal font had been erected. She filled it with water and drank from that. 'Do Romans do that?' she asked.

Dashini had to admit that she didn't know. 'Disciples!' she cried to the person-headed snakes. 'Now is the time for you to take us to the place appointed.'

Prissy took her head out of the font, the ends of her hair dripping. 'Let's get out of here. These things are giving me the heebie-jeebies.'

Even on the rue Barbauld, where unusual sights were delighted in, even in the middle of a civil war, something that brings new and frightening experiences, three persons of Prissy, Gam and Dashini's type were a monstrous sight. No unlimbed creature looks on a thing with legs and arms with pleasure, unless it's food, and to see these great galumphing monstrosities at large was a challenge to the religious and secular alike.

Some cowered from them, others shouted curses or pro-pelled at them whatever they could mouth and fling. One tried to trip Gam as he followed Arinne and the Seneschal to the boulevardiators, and another threw a dead rat at him.

Gam did not take kindly, as anyone who knew him well would admit, to violence directed at him, and recent events had done nothing to soften him. The anxiety he had suffered ever since the death of Joes, the flight from the assassins, the death and mysterious rebirth of Prissy, all of these things had built inside him a pitch of emotion he could now no longer control. He charged at the person-headed snake who had hurled the dead rat and kicked it hard in the teeth. Because a person-headed snake isn't naturally balanced to prevent movement prompted by a kick, and because it wasn't used to it since no one in its realm had legs to kick with, it found itself flying through the air. In the satisfaction of that reaction – who wouldn't find a sickly kind of delight in kicking a person-headed snake twenty feet across a street? – Gam felt the burden of his anxieties leave him, and he went where he could, berserk, performing the same manoeuvre on anyone who gave him the evil eye, until there was a rain of person-headed snakes in the middle distance.

Further away, there was a building that stretched up, snake-like, until the tip of it – arrow-headed like a viper – was by the moon, which was now risen to its noon point. It wove its way behind the cityscape, above the smog of war fires, clad in silver scales, edged in gold, and on the point of the arrow was a huge diamond which shone down moonlight across the city and beyond.

'The Tower of Cren,' Arinne said, and led them there by boulevardiator, Gam following violently behind.

The secularists were ten deep at Cren's Seat's Gate.

They wore equipment made of tubes that split so that one of three ends went in their mouths, another went to a repository of envenomed darts, and the last allowed them to direct the passage through the air of the projectiles to shoot death at any Cren-worshipper who dared emerge to worship. So, when Dashini and her company slipped across the boulevardiators, they were met with a volley of darts.

These were mostly blocked by the clothes the people were wearing, but one struck Gam on the neck.

Gam had been stung by many things in his life – spiders, wasps, ants, even flukes with that capability – and had learned

to ignore it, but, because it was poisoned, this sting immediately filled him with a very strong and burning agony that
spread up into his jaw like the pain of an abscess or a rotting
tooth. That kind of discomfort, so close to the mind, where a
person situates themselves, is not so easy to ignore, and with
all his traumas still at the forefront of his consciousness he was
filled with rage. 'Right!' he hissed to himself, and with the pain
of the dart motivating him – now added to by a ripping of his
skin where he pulled it out, there being a barb spitefully built
into the end – he marched over to the secularists.

He grabbed the nearest one by the rattle and cracked
him like a whip, sending a wave down the length of him so
that, when it reached the heavy and bulbous man-head at
the end, it broke his spine at the neck and made his eyes roll
back into their sockets. This horrible sight would usually have
been enough to bring Gam back to his kinder self, but the
venom was spreading up to his ears, inveigling its way into
the sensitive tubes that exist there and making him angrier
still, so he swung the dead body around, and, using it like a
mace, battered the others with it, tomatoing noses and cau-
liflowering ears.

While the secularists were certainly surprised by this turn
of events, not all of Gam's victims were paralysed by it. They
focussed primarily on him, and more of the next volley of darts
found their mark. Now the backs of Gam's hands prickled
and so did his cheeks, and he rampaged from one side of the
decorated arch of Cren's Seat's Gate – where Cren made first
the cosmos and then the flat Earth – to the other – where Cren
laid out its commandments in a grid – the venom pumping
through his veins.

Gam whip-cracked another secularist when the head fell
off the first one, and then did a third so that he had one in
each hand, and, to the delight of Arinne and the Seneschal,
destroyed the guards at Cren's Tower like an avenging angel.

Dashini and Prissy watched, united in a kind of sickened
fascination.

There was a rearguard of secularists inside the cathedral, but Gam made short work of them too, roaring in pain and anger. Cren's Seat – the second Door – was right in the middle of the tower. From the inside, the structure was filled with the holy light of Cren, beamed down from the gigantic diamond above by a series of angled and coloured mirrors.

Dashini half-ushered, half-pulled Arinne and the Seneschal with her through the dappled light to the Door, stopping in the space in front of the archway.

'Well,' she said, 'I promised I'd send you to the Mistress. Now is the time.'

The two person-headed snakes looked at her, then at each other, then back at her. When neither of them said anything, Dashini carried on. 'Just like you made a sacrifice to bring us here, now it's my turn.'

The two of them pulled away – there's a difference between killing and being killed – but Dashini had stood on their rattles when she gathered them together, so they didn't get very far.

Now, in the doorway, there was a gathering of person-headed snakes, a tangle of them.

'Get on with it!' Prissy said, and Gam pulled up his sleeves as if he was about to begin another rampage.

'I'll send you straight to heaven,' Dashini said, without any more waiting. 'You can intercede directly with my mother, I promise, and she'll bring Cren back.' Dashini raised the knife, making the two sacrifices cower, but then she brought it down again, because she'd thought of something. 'While you're there, can you pass on a message? Tell her Dashini and friends are on the third level and need collecting. Can you remember that?'

The two nodded, uncertainly.

'Thanks,' Dashini said, and then she killed them with one swipe, freeing enough Spark energy to open the Door to the next realm.

XIV

Her Champion, Part Four

THE ROOM WAS COLD, as was clear from the plumes of breath that billowed from his nostrils, clear from the chill on his lips, on his gums, clear in the pain like needles in the pads of his paws where they made contact with the flagstones, themselves dusted with ice and tacky against his fur as he walked tentatively forward.

When he had been in the merchant's house, and the merchant had taken his family to visit with another merchant family, then the servants, sensing the oddness in the pair of magical dogs, would lock Sirius and Anaximander in a root cellar. Down in the dark, this room was kept unheated so as not to provoke the tubers to sprout, or make them rot, and the two dogs would huddle in a corner and commune together, mystically and with words, each by the method allowed to them. When Sirius had dived into the sea to find Nathan, it had been as cold and dark as that tuber cellar, and wetter. Once he had come out on a winter's night and danced in the snow, buried his snout in a drift and rolled on his back before being taken in by the collar. None of those times, memories in him whole and vivid, were anything like as cold as this room was, and since these were the coldest times of his life until then, this was the most coldness he had ever known.

It was sharp, too, this chill, spiked and crystalline. In his lungs ice made incursions into his insides, so it felt, chilling him from within. This was the worst of it, since his fur protected, mostly, the outside of him, and protected him from the cold's ingress, whereas his lungs needed to take the frigid air deep in order for it to feed him with breath.

The ghosts did not shiver as he did, neither did the man they all surrounded, who was a corpse standing on a table.

The room was neither very large nor very small, but was the size of a drawing room or a parlour in a merchant's house and it was decorated like it too, with papered walls depicting a girl on a swing in a garden, in blue, repeated over and over, and below that, divided at the dado, a plain and soothing beige colour with high skirting boards, but everywhere was blurred and frosted with cold and there was only the one piece of furniture: the table, which was towards the middle of the room.

The ghosts were too many to count, stood to attention around the walls like soldiers parade drilling. The dead man on the table faced the locked door. He was the size of an average man of Mordew, perhaps a little smaller, but certainly not by much. He was dressed plainly, unlike the ghosts, with no ruffles or frills or ostentations of costume.

Some of the ghosts wore expressions of anxiety and horror, others were eager, others still turned their attention to things that were not in the room: speaking to people who were not there, manipulating absent objects. Sirius's mystical organ, had he directed it to these invisible things, could have, if he concentrated on them, resolved some of their details by sensing into the intermediate and immaterial realms where these phantoms partly resided, but this he did not do.

The corpse in front of him was impossibly deep, and this deepness drew all of Sirius's attention. A thing has a surface, and this the eye scrutinises, since that is what an eye is made for. As an organ of sense, an eye has the function of knowing the superficial appearances of the world, and that is why sighted men are so often superficial creatures. Anaximander had made this argument once, and Sirius had not been able to disagree. But an object also extends inwards. Which is to say that it has an internal volume but also that it possesses a microscopic extension down, through and into itself. Most things extend only a little way: objects mostly resolving at a particular scale, demonstrating uniqueness for a period of examination, before giving way to that undifferentiated common stuff that makes up the material realm. But this corpse seemed to go inward forever endlessly, dividing into smaller and yet still particular things, patterns which formed in Sirius's understanding until his mystical organ represented this to him as possessing the same complexity as everything there was.

There was a fascination for this complexity which the mystical organ desired, but Sirius denied it, and this because the cold vied for his interest and he also knew better than to be overwhelmed again. Sirius could overwhelm himself with the abundance the mystical organ provided for him, and so he turned his attention to the material realm.

The table was of broad and heavy oak, but with chamfered edges and elegantly turned legs that ended in ball-and-claw feet. It was like the one he was often banished under in the merchant's house. Like that other table, this seemed to have been made for a specific purpose and was not at all designed to have a frozen corpse standing upon it. Indeed, the varnish had become milky and opaque in a corona that surrounded the edges of the corpse's feet. Nor was the corpse ideally placed: it stood off-centre and very close to two edges. Moreover, the corpse had no support – the suits of armour that had decorated the staircases of his former mistress's house had depended from a stand, that being a rod of iron tall enough and hard enough to give the individual objects of which a suit of armour is constituted the appearance of bearing the shape of a man standing by himself. This body had nothing of that sort – it was as if in death the cold was doing this work, taking over from the physical processes that keep a living person upright.

Its feet were bare, blue and mottled, the veins even more blue, almost black with the settled blood inside them. The arches were fallen, the ankles swollen as they joined with the legs and disappeared into the trousers. A live man's feet are not like this – veins snake across the surface, pulsing, tendons present themselves tautly and the whole shifts weight from one place to another, deforming the anatomy of the bones in response to the requirement to keep whatever is above in balance. This corpse was entirely still, but not like a marble statue is, which is so clearly made of stone.

If this corpse was not a corpse – though it very obviously was – then it might only have been a representation of a man's body carved in ice and then dressed in a man's clothes, but it was a corpse because Sirius could smell the slow decaying of it even if that was retarded by the cold.

A dog pays no particular attention to the clothed parts of a man since he has no understanding inherent in him regarding what clothes are for, and so he next looked at the corpse's hands, which were ringless and unornamented. The indentations where rings had been were present, though, on all fingers and even the thumb. On the backs of his hands there were tattoos: the ends of designs as they emerged from his sleeves, different on both arms. A dog like Sirius, untrained in the abstract representation of ideas as words and images as signs, would have relied on a speaking dog like Anaximander to decipher the meaning of the marks written on these hands and wrists, but without such a companion they meant nothing to him except that they were over and sometimes alongside scars on the corpse's skin. In fact, they may have been congruent with them, as if the tattoos inked in the scars, the two parts making a whole that the dog could see as such, even if he did not know what they meant.

Its nails were neatly trimmed, and its hair was plainly cut and black.

The face, lastly, was something that Sirius could scarcely direct his attention at – it was too magical to be seen straight on – so he looked a little to the side, tilted his head, stifled the mystical organ, which was attempting to flood him with an excess of sensations, premonitions and immaterial significations.

At the edges, by the ears, was bare white bone, scraped into fleshlessness like the ones he had been given at the merchant's house as reward for good behaviour. There was hair still, behind, grey with frost, and the skin that covered the rest of the corpse was under it. He could determine from the join that the skin of the face was of a different flesh to the rest. The very edges where Sirius peeked were filled with warm blood, this much he could know without provoking his mystical sense: blood was in the capillaries, not flowing, but not congealed, as if it could both flow and remain at rest simultaneously, and this, by a bright and vibrant magic that Sirius knew, if he looked at it, would coruscate with impossible aurorae.

Sirius was not a thinking dog, as has been said, but for a thoughtless creature he had in all possible abundance the sort of intelligence that type of thing can possess, and his world had always been filled with mirrors: his mistress was often having them polished, arranging things in front of them, and, when the mood took her, examining herself. This room had one on a wall. Some sorts of magic are like light – the red and blue concentrates, for example – but some sorts are not, and are not reflected by glass. This fact did not occur to Sirius, but his natural intelligence led him to look in the mirror in much the same way as if it had done, he having developed a tendency to do right by a process of reinforcement through positive reactions the world gave to the thoughtful-seeming things that he did. With his mystical organ stifled, and by not directing his eyes at the face itself and thereby keeping the magical sensations at bay, he was able to see the face in the mirror, though it hurt him a little, more so as he stared.

The face was like Nathan's – that was the first thing he felt – but older. A dog is not easily fooled by similarities of appearance since he has so many corroborating senses running at once, but he did see the resemblance and let out a small whimper of longing.

The second thing was that the face did not fit the bones beneath it. It sagged in places and bulged oddly in others, and the more he bore the pain and examined the visage, the more he could see that the Nathan-ness of the appearance was a function of the bone structure beneath, and perhaps some remaining muscles and cartilage, all deforming the skin into the semblance of Nathan, or an older version of him.

The third thing, and lastly, was that the face was alive, where the rest of the corpse was dead. There were no eyes in the sockets, but the empty-lidded gashes behind which those things would normally shelter blinked and widened, squinted and pinched. There was emotion there, but Sirius could not match it to a person's feelings, not even with the movement of the nostrils, unevenly scaffolded on whatever was beneath, and the drawing back of lips which made the shapes of words no dog except Anaximander could be expected to read.

The ghosts, seeing that Sirius was where they had led him, and that he was alerted to what they had wanted him to be alert to, all as one dropped to their hands and knees, sniffed and circled, bared their fangs, making between them a pack of wolves in human form. To a man they would have seemed ridiculous, all dressed but feral, all play-acting at being things they weren't, but to a dog a pack of his peers is a powerful determinant of his mood, and he did not find them ridiculous at all. If ridicule was something that he was capable of, and very few dogs were, then it would have been reserved for upright men, not these crawling fellows, jostling and growling and snapping their jaws at each other, since a man is a fool when he damages his back by standing with it.

There is communication in the movement of a pack, the motions of which, in their smoothness and abruptness and excitements, tells each member of it the collective intent. These dogs, these men, were ready for a fight – the dance they performed together told of an enemy in their midst, and the way they came up to Sirius, taunting him and deferring in turn, made Sirius want to find who it was they wished to attack and lead them into that fight. They did not smell, these ghost-men-dogs, and they were silent, but he knew what they wanted, and because he was a dog from whom fear had been eliminated by generations of breeding, he did what it was – he leapt at the corpse, toppling it from the table.

When it fell to the ground it shattered on impact, the frozen flesh falling into chunks of ice in place, leaving an imperfect skeleton behind. The skull rolled away from the spine and the living magical flesh of the face was left inside out, half smeared onto the floorboards, half sticking amongst the fibres of the dusty and unswept rug that was underneath the table.

With it looking the other way, Sirius was free to do whatever his instinct told him, whatever the pack had inspired in him, and he galloped over to where the face was, and though it wriggled where it had fallen, he ate it up as if it was a portion of tripe given to him for his dinner.

Though he did not know it then, he consumed in that moment the living face of the weftling, of God, which had been secreted here since before Mordew was made. The corpse was of Nathan's older brother, preserved in this room against decay by magic and the cold. This unfortunate sibling never took on the mantle of God, though that was the intention of the spells these ghosts, when men, had cast, but in consuming this God-Flesh, Sirius made of himself the divine creature some later sacrilegiously called 'Goddog'.

XV

Boy, Book and Dog, Part Three

ANOTHER DAY PASSED in travel, the relic presumably coming closer, Adam remaining silent on the topic of their destination.

Anaximander, to occupy himself in a different way, wondered what the history of the place they were walking through might be. There were hills, and plants, and natural things, but occasionally there were remnants of fallen-down buildings too.

He trotted over to one, mid-afternoon, and though Clarissa didn't stop, Bellows did, so the dog asked him, 'What do you make of this?'

It was a square of brick walls, perhaps twenty feet to a side, fallen over and mossy. In one side what looked like the space for a window half-emerged from the ground, and on another there was pipework in copper. 'I think it might be the remnants of a room, buried in the earth,' Bellows said.

This chimed with what Anaximander thought.

They saw other things of this type as they followed Clarissa at a distance, and once the headless statue of a person with its arm raised, weathered down so that all of its other features were vague and indistinguishable.

If there was a quality everything shared, it was that it was buried, as if the surface of the world it had been extant in was lower than the one that currently existed.

Bellows, while interested, was occupied mostly with thoughts of his own, so Anaximander, looking first towards his service-pledge to ensure that she needed nothing from him, made another list.

He determined that he would one day:

- Select an area of flat land and mark out a boundary with rope and staves;
- Dig out of that area a volume of soil and vegetation to a depth of, say, twelve inches;
- Carefully excavate the ground beneath the topsoil, being sure to set aside any objects and artefacts thus discovered;
- Make a record of what was discovered where; and
- Use the results of the above to determine what had occurred in this place in the past, and so come to know why it is that things are the way they are in the present.

Having made this list, he paused and looked over the entire vista of the landscape – it was a panorama of unique places and things as far as his vision could resolve. A feeling of the enormity of the run of time combined with an appreciation of the sheer breadth of space that the world occupied made itself known in Anaximander's chest. It took the wind out of him for a moment, and in that moment he felt himself to be a very small thing indeed.

When he looked back to where Clarissa and Bellows had been, they were no longer there, so he stopped his thinking and galloped off to where they might have gone.

That night, the sensation of the presence of another magical dog was there again, unmistakeable in Anaximander's mind.

Clarissa was on her side, but Anaximander could tell from her breathing that she was awake, and now there was no denying the information his senses were providing him, he trotted over to her. 'I am sorry to disturb you,' he said to her back, 'but I must inform you of something.'

Clarissa rolled to face him, her hands clutching her sleeping objects. 'What is it?'

Now Anaximander felt anxious, wondering why it was he had not told her on the previous night. 'There is another magical dog in this place,' he said. 'I felt him yesterday, but was not sure. Today, I am sure. He is beneath the earth.'

Clarissa nodded but said nothing in reply.

In the absence of her words, the dog pressed on with his own. 'It is possible that it is Sirius, my companion. Do you know why he might be here?'

She looked, Anaximander imagined, momentarily relieved, as if she had been spared a difficult conversation. 'Your companion is pledged to my son, Nathan. He might be looking for him in the other realms. Perhaps you sense that? The weft is a confusing place, linked to the material realm erratically. If Sirius is intervening in the weft, then you might sense his presence anywhere.'

Anaximander saw the truth in her words. 'And the weft is where you go, during your dreaming?'

Clarissa smiled. Her grip on her objects loosened, and the always present tension that knotted the muscles of her shoulders relaxed. 'You are a very clever dog,' she said.

Anaximander filled with a warmth so physical it made him pant. 'Thank you,' he said.

Clarissa opened one palm and showed Anaximander the folded piece of paper she took to bed with her each night. 'Written on here is a spell. I use it to go into the weft. I can't tell you what I do there, it's a secret, but it takes all my energy, all my concentration. If it works, I will be able to make everything right again. For all of us.'

Anaximander didn't know what she meant by 'make everything right'. In that moment, still warm from her compliment, he felt that everything was already right. He would have asked what she thought was wrong, but she kept speaking.

'I'll look for Sirius, when I'm in the weft,' she said, 'and let you know.'

She turned away from him, and while this often made an involuntary spasm of anxiety in his stomach, that night he returned to the fire perfectly happy. Clarissa went to her bed, and Bellows opened Adam.

Anaximander had questions about the weft, Bellows wanted to know about their destination, but just because a book contains information, that doesn't mean that all it wants to do is share it. It is exhausting to be the source of everyone's knowledge.

'Shall I tell us a story?' Adam said to the others.

The night had taken the fire down to warm ashes, and none of them were near to sleep. The boy and the dog looked at each other, relieved, each having silently worried that the book's consciousness had been somehow erased when Bellows had closed his pages on him.

'By all means,' Anaximander replied. 'There is a soporific quality to the dry drone of your papery voice, and providing the tale is not too compelling, if may well serve to make us sleepy.'

Bellows propped the book open on his knees, stroking his cover calmingly, and the dog came and sat so that he could see its pages.

'Since you can both read, I'll give you the words too.'

The dog looked over to Clarissa, to see if his service-pledge wanted to hear the story, but she had gone inwards.

On the page there became written, and then illuminated, and then illustrated, the title page of a story called 'The Faery Child', and in a shield in the middle there was, painted in watercolours, a mound or tuffet, on which a fat-cheeked child in its late infancy sat cross-legged, dressed in leather armour, carrying a wooden sword. Two faery women, one mostly red, the other mostly blue, with butterflies' wings, flanked him to either side, each hovering by an ear. The child chuckled at whatever it was the faeries were saying to him, but they were both grave.

'I am unfamiliar,' Anaximander said, 'with the spelling of the second word, though I gather from the illustration that it might be a variant of "fairy", which refers to a mythical race of small, mischievous beings that fly like insects. Am I correct?'

With impatient gestures, Bellows assured him that he was, saving his brother the trouble of replying.

'In that case,' the dog went on, ignoring Bellows's impatience, 'may I request a different tale? I find fantastical nonsense of this kind irksome and superfluous. Why populate narratives with things that do not exist when there are so many that do? Moreover, it is easier to hold one's interest in things that are familiar and relevant to the world as one knows it—'

Bellows shushed him, stopping only just from holding his snout shut. Anaximander took the hint, and the magical book went on.

'The Faery Child,' Adam said, and, as if to placate Anaximander, a subtitle appeared below the shield – 'An Instructive Allegory'. The placation seemed to work, because the dog settled back onto his haunches and made no further interruptions.

The light from the guttering coals was very low and uneven and Bellows's knees blocked most of it, but Adam gave the pages magical light of their own, so that the colours shone and the white of the pages gave contrast to the ink of the words. The two for whom he told the story were bathed in its magical aura.

'Once there was a child who was beloved by his mother and father.'

The title page faded away, as if someone had poured water over it to wash the inks off, and as it was erased, a new page was written, the words Adam spoke coming first, and then, drawn by an unseen hand, the child, laughing as he toddled between his parents. They were in a house, in front of a fire, and beneath their feet was a white fur. The child's toes curled into the rug, gripping it, giving him the balance he needed to cross the distance between them without falling. When he reached one parent, he clapped his hands and received a kiss, which he relished, and then, suddenly remembering the other, he turned and made his stiff-legged, smiling walk over to them, his arms held out. 'And their house was full of laughter,' Adam said.

Both Bellows and Anaximander looked at this image with strange and sad expressions, which said, when they glanced at each other, that each knew what it was they were seeing, and knew that it was good, but could not find any memory in their minds that was like it. They turned back to Adam, who sensed their attention and moved on.

Here was a crib, made of wood, which could be rocked. In it was another fur – rabbit, possibly, stitched together, and soft – and the headboard had a heart carved out of it.

The head of a child, when he has exhausted himself with his pleasures, will suddenly become too heavy for his neck, his eyelids closing. A mother will put her hands behind his shoulders and his hips and lift him into his bed, which was what Adam drew next. The child was in his crib, and the mother and the father kissed him gently, so that he smiled but did not waken. 'And their house was full of love.'

Neither Anaximander – who had been raised by Heartless Harold Smyke – nor Bellows, who could only remember the Master's Manse, looked back at the other, but they both knew what the other was thinking. Before they could become uncomfortable in their mutual lack of nurturing, onto the page came an entirely different scene. It was a small mound, the size of an anthill or the eruption a mole makes – they were given scale by the dandelions and daisies which grew like trees beside it – but it was green with a thickness of moss, and on its summit was a castle of high towers, and pennants that fluttered in the breeze.

Adam made the drawings come closer, and closer, so that Bellows and Anaximander could see first that the castle had windows, then in through one of these, where inside the room that the window served there was a faery Queen, minuscule and beautiful, dressed in a gown made of spider thread and gold dust. Then, as Adam had drawn it closer, he drew it further away, until it was once again an anthill with a castle on top.

Below unfurled a flag on which was written 'The Shee of Queen Teelee'.

Anaximander raised his head. 'What is the meaning of the word "Shee"? Also, unless "Teelee" is a name, what is the meaning of that word?'

Bellows, this time, had no answer to save the interruption, so Adam had to turn to a blank page on which he then provided a diagram of a shee, a brief etymology explaining the origins of the term, and a definition which said that a 'shee' was a tumulus within which faeries could dwell, hidden from human eyes unless spells shared the sight of them. 'Teelee' was shown to be a name, and a family tree was provided for the queens that bore it.

Anaximander nodded. 'This is another inferiority that invention has over the real – it becomes necessary to interrupt the story to provide the information necessary to understand invented things, since we cannot know them through familiarity' – Adam fluttered his pages in irritation – 'Do not take offence!' Anaximander pleaded. 'I am happy for you to continue.'

On the other side of the fire Clarissa moaned, as if she was suffering a nightmare, but she soon stopped, and Adam turned the page back to the story. Now he concentrated on the ground in front of the castle, where there were two figures, blue and red, fluttering between flowers.

'These,' Anaximander whispered to Bellows, 'are the pair of faeries the title page depicted whispering to the infant.'

Bellows nodded now, and Anaximander snuggled in closer to him so that they could share each other's warmth, and for the first time either of them could remember, the boy did not move away. 'We might presume,' Bellows said, 'that there will be further contact between them and the child.'

This is how it proved.

In images and words, sounds and sometimes songs, Adam showed his readers the faeries – whose names were Primula and Pomerella – leaving the safety of the shee. He showed them assaulted by faeries from a rival mound, something that caused them to lose their way, and he showed them coming upon the child's crib by accident. In a passage in which a story was told within a story – this one titled 'The Sad and Happy Giant' – Adam made his readers know that Primula and Pomerella saw this infant not as his parents did, which was as an innocent, but like a colossus of their fables – something capable of enormous destruction to the delicate faery places within which they, and their enemies, lived. Between the two of them they hatched a plan, and, enlisting the help of the other faeries of their shee, they carried the child away from its parents in a net made of woven spider legs.

Then they flew with him to their lands and contained him within the hollow of a dead tree.

On one page Adam drew a beguilement in silver and gold blossoms, falling all around inside the black trunk. This spell made the child happy, convincing him that he was amongst the most beautiful toys of his experience, and from then on until the end, the boy was always depicted with two different irises, one of each precious metal blossom, so Bellows and Anaximander could recognise his enchantment.

If the aim had been to make the pair sleep, Adam failed, because now his two readers exerted themselves to remain awake, sitting straight up and holding their eyes wide so as to know how the story resolved itself. They took to nudging and prodding each other if they felt the other was liable to drift off, or if the other's eyes remained shut for a period longer than a blink demands.

What happened in the story next was that the two faeries manipulated the beguilements that the child experienced in the empty trunk, putting him in false worlds, teaching him through scenarios and interactions, through spells and fluences, through dreams and learning by rote the ways of faery warfare, always in the form of games.

On one page Adam drew the child using a hammer to bang a wooden cylinder into a circular hole – this being what the beguiled child saw, delighting in the fun of it – while on the other page there were the faeries, delighting themselves, but this time at the spectacle of the destruction of a fortress by their gigantic champion, this being the true situation.

On the next page the child crammed sweetmeats into his mouth on one side, while the other showed things that Bellows had to look away from. As if it was a helpful thing to do, Anaximander told his friend what he could not see behind the censoring crook of his elbow. 'Look!' he said. 'The faery folk have encouraged the infant, by deceit, to consume their enemies. His gums mash them into pieces. These mythical beings, were they to exist, would make wily foes, don't you think?' He turned to Bellows, but the boy kept his eyes covered, so the dog turned, panting, back to the book, where Adam had now drawn a stylised representation of the passage of a year, with a cross section of the tree surrounded by the weathers typical of the four seasons – snow, rain, sun and overcast – and the leaves budded, grew, browned and fell. The child, though, did not grow. There was a faery hex on him, and instead he became ever better at his games, and Primula and Pomerella ever more pleased with him.

'One day,' Adam told them, 'the faeries were satisfied with their giant, and on this day they opened up the tree with axes.' This he drew, with thousands of ants wielding tiny tools, marshalled like an army, each with a peaked hat of either red or blue, and when the trunk came crashing down, out came the child, one eye gold and one eye silver, and in a cloud above his head Adam drew his thoughts, which the faeries symbolically controlled with puppet strings.

It was the child's birthday, and though he didn't know what a birthday was, having never come into language sufficiently to have heard the word and recognise it, he did recognise the cake prepared for him, which the faeries fluttered towards and indicated with gestures.

He toddled and toppled towards it.

Because his readers might have forgotten it in their excitement, Adam reiterated on the borders of the page by drawing a stylised cartoon in the manner of a decorative illumination the events by which the faeries came to find the child: they were waylaid by the faeries of a rival shee. Perhaps Bellows did not remember that aspect of the story, having drifted briefly into sleep, or perhaps Anaximander's attention was on his thoughts so he missed that detail, or perhaps neither thing was the case, but Adam knew the ways in which stories should be told, having told many of them to Nathan in the Manse. These hints to what must be known he put clearly but inconspicuously on the page, so that they might be used or ignored at his readers' discretions.

He drew, again on two pages in parallel, a high and deliciously iced cake of three levels, topped with lit candles, beside a grassy mound, on top of which was a walled city, on which perched a tower – which also made three levels. These were first what the child saw, and then the shee of the rival queendom of faeries. The cake was red and blue and yellow, with curlicues piped around, and marzipan, all dusted with sugar, while the shee was very similar, except made of minute walls and windows and dusted with the blossoms of their miniature faery trees.

The boy accelerated as he grew closer, the sunlight glinting from his gold and silver irises, his every clumsy footfall heavy as an earthquake, shaking the world of the rival faeries and setting their warriors into defensive flight. To the child these faeries – some who could fly themselves, and others who rode on ladybirds and carried spears – appeared as midges and mosquitoes and fruit wasps, and Primula and Pomerella flew up to a safe distance to avoid being confused with their enemies. From there they cast the spell that allowed a person who was not a faery to pass the borders of a shee, though the child did not notice this at all since his eyes were fixed on the cake, and sometimes on the flies.

No child will allow the annoyance of insects to prevent him from eating his own birthday cake, so he crushed them in his fat-knuckled fists or batted them aside. Some he ate, but only by accident if they went into his mouth, but they did not distract him or delay him by even a moment, and soon he fell onto his knees in front of the shee, his hands flat on the ground either side of it. He peered down into the tower where the rival queen had her chambers, and blew her little tower to pieces, and all the other castle towers, as a boy extinguishes candle flames.

The significance was not lost on either Bellows, or Anaximander, the pair of them now always looking to the right-hand side of the page, where the real world of the faeries was, and only rarely to the left, which was a child eating cake, and while Adam paid equal attention to the depiction of the latter thing, made it more closely work, if anything, to accentuate the difference between the child's innocent joy and the terrible violence he enacted on Primula and Pomerella's enemies, his readers found their interest always tending towards the sublime over the beautiful, to death over pleasure. It may be that these two were unusual in that, but Adam doubted it, knowing through his experience the directions minds drift in, but after a while he faded out the destruction of the tiny city, the accidental gnawing of limbs by hard, toothless gums, the ending of dynasties that stretched back into prehistory, and he showed instead Primula and Pomerella, blood-dizzied and exalted in their victory.

When a person or a dog has been excited, by his real life, or by a story, there is a dip in his energies immediately afterwards, those energies having been expended in a rush the body cannot so quickly replenish, so now Adam made the story match that enervation, drawing away its focus from fantastical horrors, showing familiar things in familiar ways, taking the effort out of any understanding. So it was that the faery pair returned the way they had come, gently urging the cake-encrusted child back to their home, past the dead tree, and up to the borders of their own queendom.

This time they did not cast the spell that allowed him entry because the queen and her entourage were there to greet them, she having heard tell from her spies that her two subjects were seen in the company of a giant, and that they had won a great victory against the queen's sister.

Because, in the tiredness that comes after exhilaration, his readers were showing signs of falling to sleep regardless of his story – wide-mouthed yawns, and tears gathering at the corners of their eyes – Adam transported Primula and Pomerella into their queen's audience so that he could deliver the ending of his tale, the child's face drawn towering, smiling behind them as they spoke.

Primula folded her wings and knelt at her queen's feet. 'Your Majesty,' she said, 'we have ended the war between Teelee Shee and the Mound of Morag!'

Pomerella joined Primula. 'By the Faery Law, we claim our bounty!'

Queen Teelee did not speak – perhaps in a longer telling, to readers not already drifting into sleep, Adam would have told them of the bittersweetness of the victory to the queen, since Teelee and Morag were sisters after all, and a reconciliation where both lived happily had once been possible – but she indicated that her prime minister should bring the allotted treasure for the two.

When they received their rewards, the two faeries danced and sang, which Adam also cut short: Bellows and Anaximander were now very close to dreaming.

'What,' the two faeries said in concert, 'will be our champion's reward?'

Teelee thought, for as long Adam's readers' attention allowed, and then she clicked her fingers. Was this to summon some largesse as his recompense? No. Was this to return him to his proper place, the parental home? No. Instead, a small cut on the child's neck opened like a mouth, and out of it, gushing away to where it could do no harm to the shee, his heart pumped his blood until it was all gone.

As it flowed, the child's eyes faded from silver and gold back to blue and, in the realisation of his pain and degradation, he wailed, once, then fell to the ground, dead.

This, Bellows and Anaximander may not have seen. It might have been that Adam was too slow in the telling of his story, that he missed the right time to deliver his conclusion, or it might have been that Adam was really telling the story to himself and did not require witnesses, which would explain why he went on regardless.

'Why, oh why, did you punish him, he who served you faithfully, though he knew it not?' asked the faeries.

Teelee thought again, this time for as long and in as much detail as Adam liked.

'Well,' she said eventually, picking something from her teeth with her fingernail, 'he seemed like a dangerous sort of thing to have running around, don't you think?'

While this time the allegory was lost on the boy and the dog, now telling themselves their own stories with their eyelids closed, it was not lost on Adam.

XVI

Her Enemy, Part Four

PERHAPS HE HAD started a process too long and cumbersome to be completed to plan, and perhaps he was concussed from too much translation, but when the Master returned to the candidate and pulled him out of the bleach vat, he was much too pale.

First he was too dark, now he was too pale. What next? Soak him in gallons of gravy browning? This thought made the Master laugh, despite himself, but when he opened his eyes to wipe them there was the boy, naked and ominously colourless in front of him.

Now the echoes of laughter were tainted with a memory. It wasn't a memory... it was a story that he had been told when he was a boy, of ladies... old ladies? Old ladies when they were young. Girls? No – 'birds'! When there were no nylon tights, they painted gravy browning on their legs. They had an eye pencil, and they did a seam at the back. Then, in the night, bombs fell, and they were blown all to pieces.

This made the Master sad.

The boy was like Bellows. The Master reached out to him, a tear snaking down one cheek and then down into the creases of his neck. Bellows!

From behind, an alarm – the urgent ringing of a single bell – set off. Sebastian went to attend to it.

It was coming from a table in the corner with a decanter on it, and this decanter forced meaning back into the world. He pulled at his lapels, straightened his cuffs, and marched with a will towards the table, because this table was where the Rescue Remedy was located, and the alarm was his impairment alarm.

For a weft-manipulator, impairment is a very serious business, and common enough to make precautions of this sort worthwhile. Today was a perfect example of why he had, in the templates for all his translated rooms, installed an emergent unit like this. Translation, weft-emanations, inwards exudations, magical vapours, even enemy poisons could all impair a man's thoughts, and while a simple concoction was all that he needed to correct himself, sometimes it was difficult to know that he needed to take it. Hence the bottle, hence the table, hence the alarm.

He took the tumbler that was always there, poured himself a generous helping, and began to feel better the moment its crystalline blueness touched his lips. Translation concussion was no match for the Rescue Remedy, and he downed it in one.

This batch was a little stronger than it might have been – coca wine is hard to manufacture consistently and that was its primary ingredient – but he was glad of that. A certain excitement in the nerves suited work like this, which could otherwise prove tiring.

He went back to the candidate – all thoughts of gravy browning and the backs of Blitz women's legs banished – and the Master bundled him eagerly up the ladder of the next vat.

The sigils on this vat were on the theme of sensitivity and were gnomic in their concision and complexity: *scale, function, self, open*. He licked his teeth and stretched his lips wide. Which vat was this? Which number? It was on the side! And correct! Why doubt himself?

He sat the candidate at the bottom, and the moment the lid clattered shut the sides heated up and he had to get down and off to a comfortable distance.

The clock said three, which was convenient because the rent in the miniature mirror realm was now open.

He knew all the sayings about the watched pot that never boils, but that was exactly what he wanted! If he could watch this pot forever – if that would guarantee it never boiled – then great! He sniffed, gurned a little, clicking his jaw. That would be ideal – remain at a simmer. Simmer forever, for all he cared.

He took from his trouser pocket a folded canvas bag, the kind that could be reused for carrying things from one place to another – say you have several things of different sizes and shapes: five candles, three oranges, a jar, and… it doesn't matter. Sometimes it's useful to have a bag you can put those things in to take them from… wherever – upstairs to downstairs? Wherever…

The impairment alarm rang again, at a lower tone, so he went back to the table, colliding with it this time, rattling the stopper in the decanter. Now there was, emerged, another decanter next to it, with red liquid, and another tumbler.

Clearly, the Master of the past had, when making these preparations, assumed that an impairment that was likely to set off this alarm would be of the sort the red liquid – tincture of mercury – was liable to counteract. But there was the Rescue remedy right next to it. Was he the type of weft-manipulator that would do that by accident, old past-Sebastian? The present one thought not, and with the taste for the coca aspects of the Remedy tingling at the edges of his tongue, numbing his face, he decided it was a lack of this that the impairment bell was indicating, despite the lowness of the tone, in its annoyingly inanimate way.

The glass was filled, then emptied, lips were wiped, and the canvas bag was opened.

It had been folded, so it should have been empty, but instead it was full up to the brim with the lens-entrance to a miniature realm that mirrored exactly, but in miniature – that's what a miniature realm is *for*; that's what it *means* – that part of the world where the Women's Vanguard of the Eighth Atheistic Crusade had their encampment.

He *ignored* their lake disguise with the relevant spell and there they all were, dinky little shrinkages of those terrible murderous harridans, milling about around the relics for their summoning racks – for their *torturing* racks, he should say, since that was the bit that concerned him. Each of them had a cross on their chests – on the clothes they wore on their chests – and their little hairdos were blowing in the wind. Except when they had their crested helmets on. Then the crests blew instead.

279

He put his head further in, so that, if he'd been visible to them, they'd have seen him emerge from between the clouds.

Okay, this was stupid – it was still translation. It was *worse* if anything – his head was very disparate in size across these two realms, and that had an effect on the blood pressure, making everything worse, and exactly at the moment he had that thought, back in the realm that wasn't contained by the bag, he heard the alarm go off. Again!

He took a huge breath through his now conspicuously nerveless mouth hole and, when he'd taken in as much as he could, he blew out a huge raspberry that rained down on the Vanguard's stupid hair and helmets, a heavy, warm, slightly sticky rain, soaking their idiotic relics.

'I'm going to take my locket,' he shouted, 'I'm going to open the Tinderbox. I'm going to burn you lot to ashes! Come on! I'm looking forward to it!'

He had hardly begun to laugh at this, maniacally, when he fell back, entirely and suddenly unconscious.

When he woke, the alarm was still ringing, and his mouth tasted of blood. Above him the Vanguard were settling off to bed, roping down things, laying out things, unknowing of his face peering up at them. Down at them? A few of them were painting their cross on a gigantic crossbow, and the Master felt, from a clenching down in his gut, that he was shortly going to vomit onto them.

Could vomit fall up?

He didn't wait to find out, but instead rolled on his side, pulled the bag away and let the contents of his gut out in gushes onto the floorboards.

The alarm didn't stop going off, not while any of that was going on, so on top of the retching – something he had always particularly hated – his swollen brain vibrated in its meninges.

'Okay!' he said aloud, despite the fact that the alarm wasn't the kind that could be turned off that way.

Roll onto the front, tuck up the knees, forehead on the floor, push with the palms. Rest there for as long as required, then thrust up and hope for the best. This, for millennia, had been the choreography favoured by dancers of this solo ballet, and the Master was no more or less elegant at it than anyone who has found themselves flat out after too much of something.

Unlike them he had the red decanter, so it was after only a minute or two that the worst effects were over. While it tasted like a bicycle inner tube its effects were immediate – cleaning the interior of him until they rang with perfect spotlessness. Never second-guess the Master of the past – this would be his new motto. Though the Rescue Remedy was still there, waiting to be poured…

He went to the vat and found it cool to the touch. It should have been warm. He looked back the way he had come, then at the clocks. How long had he been out?

The copper was very cool. It wasn't cold, precisely, but it wasn't warm. An egg needs to be a certain temperature to hatch it, and a boy in a vat is not very different to that. The vat was definitely not at hatching temperature.

He climbed the ladder, and when he was halfway to the top, he tried not to look over the lip. The lid was glass, and when he eventually got to the top, he had to look down, otherwise what was the point of going up there in the first place?

It wasn't right to say that the candidate was dead – dead things are lacking in their natural Spark and this one had yet to have his returned to him – but he was as close to it as the circumstances allowed. That unmistakeable character that denotes life to a weft-manipulator was not only not present, the possibility of it was gone. He lay there, the candidate, curled in on himself, except at the head, which was craned back so his face was pressed hard against the inner surface of the vat, making crooked the straight blade of his extended nose.

The Master went down the ladder again and over to the cabinet in which the vial containing the candidate's original soul was to be found. 'Soul' is not the right word, any more than it was right to think of the boy as dead, but when you've been brought up to use that word it does tend to override the much more complicated set of concepts that represent the facts more closely. Within the vial was the vibrating tone of the boy's weft-state, represented in the water memory of a second boy's – almost certainly Solomon Peel's – denatured tears, and a drop of it would, when allowed to hit the candidate's skin and during the casting of the appropriate spell, return the boy to a Spark-capable matter/weft coherence.

It glowed a preternatural green, but that was just because the glass was green; nonetheless, sickly and strange shadows filled the room when Sebastian dimmed the lamps so he could provide the candlelight the spell needed. He made the necessary gestures before he lifted the vat lid, and when he pulled out the stopper the inaudible music of the boy's soul flickered the flame, making his body seem to fit and writhe down in the copper bowl. When the Master was sure it had taken, he blew out the candle and returned the lid to the vat.

Inside, the boy would be waking back to his old life, except now his body was proto-Bellowsian and he would, if he lived long enough, be puzzled at the strange bend to his limbs, the expanse of his breath, and the magical sensations he was now cognisant of. That was if he woke up, but from the same cabinet from which the Master had taken the vial he now took a twist of paper wrapped around a pea-sized mass. This was a powder which, when it met the air, diffused through it and soaked up any and all elements of the Spark, and he went back up the ladder and dropped it into the vat. It popped like a firecracker when it met resistance, neutralising the boy's weft-state without entirely removing his weft-presence, and now, Sebastian hoped, he would be sufficiently 'alive' to accept Bellows's vial of tears when the time came.

He went down, turned his back on the suffocation that the barely waking boy would be experiencing, the soft knocking of his head on the copper, and went over to his desk.

On it were his notes for *Pyroclastic Revenance*, now five hundred pages thick and interlaced with almost as many ribbons and bookmarks and ink-marbled insertions. He straightened the edges and moved it into the centre of the desk. Under the title there were various subtitles, crossed out: *An Instructive Memoir*; *How I Inherited the Weftling Tontine, Including Spells*; *Against the Assembly*; *Against God and Man*; *How to Weaponise Your Enemy*; and some so heavily scored through that they were unreadable. Beneath these he had written his name.

About two thirds of the way through the manuscript was a piece of blue felt, and the Master separated the pages there. Across both pages was an illustration of the locket, annotated both in English and in Crusader sigils.

Pyroclastic Revenance was, as some of the discarded subtitles indicated, both an autobiography and a manual, and, looking at the diagram, Sebastian wondered which of these functions he was betraying by not intending to integrate the recent cracking of the locket into the diagram. It was, undeniably, a fact of his life, and while no memoirist includes everything that has ever happened to them, this was not something that he could comfortably overlook. A technical issue with the process, or a weakness to attack both, must be considered essential to any instruction on how to repeat his feats. Why wasn't he willing to take up his stylus and scratch the necessary marks on the parchment?

He took the locket from his pocket, where it bulged out the size of a snooker ball. No, it was more like a piece of coral in glass used for a paperweight. No, it was lighter than that. Like a very solid and unbreakable glass bauble. He dangled it in front of the diagram.

No. It was a failure. It looked like and was a failure. He knew that, and that's why he didn't want to change his book. When the book had been written the locket was a triumph, but now it was a cracked and leaking liability, surrounded by a bodged-up, cack-handed, make-do solution. Ditto the candidate – he was flawed, compromised, a translation-concussed mess of a child. Any Bellows made of this boy would be corrupted, any resistance made with this Tinderbox would be doomed to failure.

The Master was a failure. The book was a failure. The plan would fail. Everything would go for nothing.

He marched over to the Rescue Remedy and, without even considering it, poured himself one, two and then an unprecedented three straight tumblers without water.

From the moment the empty glass hit the table for the third time, events went in a blur that the Master, later, was hard-pressed to piece together with any certainty.

Since there was no day or night in the secondary realm that contained the vat room, and because the decanters on the table were fluenced to be endlessly refilled, he didn't even really know how much time had elapsed, locally, or how much of the remedy and the tincture he had eventually consumed. What he did know – and this coincided with the silent, still images that appeared piecemeal in place of his memories – was that the candidate had advanced through the vats and that the manuscript had been edited in numerous places. This was obvious anyway by the fact the boy was in vat eighteen – its sigils were glowing – and the manuscript was strewn across every available piece of furniture, some of it gathered in mounds, some single sheets isolated and alone.

It is true of all writers, he'd once been told, that the words sometimes came to them in a way they couldn't consciously account for, and this was true of him now, because when he picked up the nearest page there was a screed of crabbed characters, a rhetorically very forceful manifesto that he recognised as being in his own handwriting, and containing his own thoughts, but expressed in a way that gave them an alternately overstated then weaselly and apologetic tone. Also, the ideas were so familiar to him that he had no idea why they needed repeating, particularly in the bombastic then depressive mode this page demonstrated.

The next page was the same, and the next, and with an eye to vat eighteen he returned to the table to find that the diagram that had made him feel oppressed in the first place had now a mess of connections sketched over everything in a variety of different-coloured pencils.

Sebastian sighed, turned his back on *Pyroclastic Revenance* and trod the creaking boards over to the ladder. This he did slowly, and when he put his hands on the middlemost rung, he didn't immediately climb up to see where his forgotten handiwork had left him. A manuscript all scattered about and scrawled on is an upsetting thing to see, for its author, but the Master was not so hard in his heart that to see a boy in a similar state didn't strike him as a worse thing. And this so near to the end of the process when the Bellows-ness of a candidate should be very advanced.

He stood there for quite a while, concentrating on his breathing, consolidating his composure, and while this was partly because his head and stomach were rebelling at their recent rough treatment it was also because he didn't think he could bear to see whatever chaos he'd made of new Bellows. His memories of the old fellow were clear and whole and untarnished, and that was the way he'd like to keep them.

He was just about to become sick of his own procrastination and force himself to do the thing he needed it to do when he remembered something. He remembered going back to the Manse – the real one, the one that he had replaced in the material realm with the intermediate antechamber realm. Why he had done this, he couldn't remember – there was a flurry of activity, an aching need, a nauseating feeling of self-loathing – but he could remember sleeping there. 'Sleeping' was the wrong word – he had entered a kind of coma such as those who have had overmuch of the Rescue Remedy sometimes enter, where the body protectively seizes up and though the mind still races, all that the limbs can manage is to get the person to the nearest reasonable place to lie down. There he lay, sweating, for what could have been any amount of time.

And now, when he thought of that coma state, he remembered rousing himself from it, translating himself back to this vat room. What was worrying, apart from the strange sense that this had happened to someone else – a vastly inferior version of himself – was that he remembered being surprised.

Yes, it was very clear. He had been surprised to see the manuscript all over the place. He was surprised the candidate was in vat eighteen. He had been so surprised that he had come to a conclusion that had made him go back to the table and raise up the decanter of Rescue Remedy like a man drinking a yard of ale. It was that, and the subsequent draining of every remaining drop, that had caused the rest of the lost time.

And now he remembered what it was that he had concluded.

He took the first step up the ladder, and the conclusion became more rounded, the necessary contexts dependent on it becoming clearer, the consequences. The second, third and fourth steps clarified everything, and he took the next few necessary to get him a view inside the vat quickly, all feeling of sickened exhaustion suddenly leaving him. He peered over and then, having seen, for the briefest of possible moments, as he had half-expected, himself crouching inside the vat, peering up, gun in hand, he was shot full in the face with a round from his own revolver, something that entirely removed his head, down to the neck, and which immediately rendered him dead.

XVII

Her Heir, Part Three

WHEN GAM HALLIDAY would wake in the slums – this was before Nathan, before even Prissy, when he was too young to have friends – sometimes there would be horrible things in his mouth. Flukes edged in over his roll mat from the Living Mud. They wanted what was in his head, or down his throat, or up his nose.

Gam might open his eyes in the morning and find a body between his lips, up to its middle, foraging with a spine, claw or tentacle. Or it'd be under his tongue. Or it'd be behind his gums. He'd take a moment to realise what was happening, and then he'd spit, or choke, or clamp down on whatever was there – whichever his panic did first.

That was what took most of his original teeth.

Admittedly, some were knocked out in fights, some pulled out by his sisters to stop his night-time whining from toothache, but the rest were nibbled down to nubs by flukes, or dissolved by fluke secretions, or chipped away on fluke bones when he bit down on them. A couple of wobbly baby teeth were stolen by some blind, idiot thing or other, desirous of them, irrationally, and having enough strength to pull them free while he slept.

Slum boys know there's no replanting a tooth once it's been pulled up, so he didn't waste his resources thinking about them... except in his dreams, since dreams cost nothing. In these, he'd scamper about on all fours, splashing in the Mud, bringing his fists down on crawling blobs, find his teeth in their broken stomachs, bed them back into his head.

He dreamed this now, reaching into the gore of a fluke and pulling out a bright, clean molar. He held it up, wiped it off and put it into the bare gap that was his mouth.

He opened his eyes with a start, and he was grinding his teeth together – the new ones that had grown when Nathan made them in perfect proportion to fill his jaws – and it was as if the dream had come to life.

These new teeth were strong, they didn't ache or wobble, or list dangerously to the side when he bit down on them, and though it's said that people forget pain quickly when it's gone, Gam didn't forget his. He should have been grateful this morning for its absence.

But he was not grateful.

He would have had his old, empty mouth back if he could.

Same for his eye. Padge had pierced the original soon after Gam started working for him, popped it from its socket and snipped it off at the nerve to teach him a lesson. It had ached for years afterwards as his teeth had ached, variably and at a high pitch, even though it was gone. Now Gam didn't want its replacement, radiant though its vision was with varied colours his mind didn't quite understand. It clashed with his natural one. It wasn't that it gave him double vision, or that one was clearer than the other, it was that the new eye showed a more complex world than the other flatter, blander, dimmer eye.

He should have been grateful for this new way of seeing, but he would have cut this new eye out if he'd had the courage.

He looked around with it now, grinding his perfect teeth against each other, and the day was new and clean to his mind. This was counter to how he felt inside, so he put his hand up and looked through the gloomier, greyer eye, which saw everything sad and worn out.

When he blinked the old eye and found both eyes shut, there was Joes, falling, and Gam made himself watch them until they broke their back on the roof ridge below.

'You alright?' Prissy said, speaking from the outside world. 'Something wrong?'

Gam opened both eyes and there at once was his friend – the girl like he was, all torn clothes, no coin and a willingness to do

288

what needed to be done – and another girl, equally pragmatic, but in the necessities of another, higher world, looking exactly like her but making him feel less like himself, as if he should properly be like she was, which was better than before. Reborn.

Only he wasn't.

He shut the new eye and there she was again, the Prissy of old, frowning at him, hands on her hips, just as bad as he was, just as flawed, except that he knew now that she was better than him, and that he'd have to keep lying to himself to see her the old way.

'You deaf?' she said. 'I said, "something wrong?"'

'No,' Gam replied. 'Except the obvious.' He got to his knees, gathered his overcoat and boots, and went outside.

Prissy followed him, and when they were next to each other she put her hand on his shoulder. A good mother, aunt, sister, friend will make this gesture – it means, more or less, 'I care for you' – and when someone who feels they deserve to be cared for feels that hand on their shoulder, if they've been holding in their feelings, they will break down, often, and begin to cry. They'll turn and receive the full embrace the hand was presaging, sobbing in the arms of the other, and they will eventually empty their hearts of the sorrow they have been carrying, placing it in the possession of someone who is sympathetic.

When someone who doesn't feel they deserve to be cared for – someone who hates themselves inside – feels that hand, they'll remove it. They don't want to open up, since what is inside is horrible, they feel. They don't want to break down, since their defences are not for them but for others, protecting their loved ones from the badness inside them.

Gam brushed off Prissy's hand and, without looking back, walked over to where Dashini was standing, Featherhead of old, object of his scorn and doubt. But now when he looked at her, he saw something else, something miraculous and hopeful – the negation of all his negativity, a girl who had faith in magic, faith in her mother, a faith that acted itself out in the world. She made miracles happen, bringing the living back from the dead.

Padge had promised that Nathan would do that, but that was a lie. Dashini made lies true – she took Padge's killers and made life from them, saved Prissy with her magic. Gam, inside, was darkness, so he turned his eyes, both of them, on Dashini, who was light.

She was looking off into the distance, but though her eyes were focussed on the world, her mind was elsewhere.

Where was her mother? Arinne and Sorax would have given the message and she should have been there waiting for them. She should have at least sent someone, done something. Was she dying too? Had she died?

Or was there another reason?

Everything was falling to pieces. Prissy was right. *Secundus est pretium caeli*, that was the bargain, but these weren't heavens.

Something was broken. The patron gods of the first levels were gone and her mother had done nothing to intervene. Why?

Prissy, who was surely dead on the first level of the Mistress's pyramid, suffocated on cattle flesh. How was she here with them now?

Everything was difficult, messy. She thought back to her time in the Manse, the fantasies of home she'd never quite been able to resist.

They weren't like this.

Dashini ran her fingers back and forwards across over the skin of her forearms.

Here came Prissy and Gam.

'Two levels down,' Gam said. He looked at Dashini oddly, in a way she didn't recognise. 'Or is it up? So, what's next?'

'Japalura and her dragons,' Dashini said. 'Thousands of beautiful dragons.'

Gam rubbed his eyes, first the Malarkoi one, then the Mordew one. 'Right,' he said, wearily. 'What are we expected to do? Slay them?'

Dashini sighed. 'Something's beaten you to it. Come and look.'

The entrance Door was inside the cave they'd spent the night in, waiting at Dashini's insistence for her mother to come. When it was clear she wouldn't, Dashini had gone to the mouth of the cave while the other two slept.

It wasn't far, but it opened onto a narrow ledge jutting out from a cliff face, the drop easily enough to kill them.

Prissy had never been very good with heights, and now neither was Gam, so when Dashini showed them out the two pressed back against the cliff and held hands. Whether they thought one would save the other, or they'd both fall and die together, was something neither of them knew.

Down below, when they mustered the courage to look, was flat savannah stretching to the horizon. The sun was high and hot, and heat haze rippled the surfaces of everything, making their vertigo even worse.

'I think I'm going to be sick,' Prissy said.

Dashini went to the edge. Her hands were at her face, and she didn't even watch where she was stepping. 'They're all either dying or dead,' she said. She indicated the world below her, but neither of the other children could look.

Dashini had never considered standing on a six-foot-wide ledge beyond the limit of her abilities and therefore had no fear of falling off one. Seeing this wasn't the case with the other two, she took them separately over to a wider piece of ground, where they acted marginally less petrified. She sat down, indicated that Prissy and Gam should do the same, and waved in the direction she'd pointed in before.

This third level had always been about the sky – flocks of whirling, varicoloured dragons of all sizes – but half a mile down was the ground, and while the sky was empty and blue, silent, the ground was half-covered with bodies: vast bleached bones, tarpaulins of skin, motionless hulks, slowly breathing wrecks of things hundreds of feet long, their long necks heavy in the dry earth, their wings holed and frayed and useless. Up came a low chorus of moans, vibrating like the slow movement of tectonic plates, grating in pain.

The feathered dragons had let fall their plumage, and their discarded down was blown into tornadoes by dusty winds, mockingly, memories of rainbow flight now deprived of mass.

Dashini hadn't cried since she was a little girl. She had learned to use the energy of her sadness to drive her forward, but now tears came without her feeling them, falling like rain on the dry dirt.

Gam nudged Prissy and pointed at Dashini, but neither child could think of anything to say.

Some distance away was the Stone Oak, rising from the earth as if it had been pushed up out of the world's core. It was less like a tree and more like a geological upthrust, high as a mountain, higher, its branches like rivers of rock flowing up into the sky, its leaves like tors.

Clinging to its trunk, almost the size of the tree itself, was a living dragon, a vast, black, green, mottled, heaving, shimmering mass of scales, muscle and sinew. One third of it – the body, with four thick legs and bone spines spearing out of its back – was curled around the trunk. The top third was mostly neck, with a long, pointed, triangular wedge of a head threaded between a fork in a high branch. The lower third was tail, barbed and swaying like a pendulum. Where the tip of the tail met the earth, a valley had been furrowed, the centre of which was new dirt, churned and ploughed up by its swinging.

The dragon's eyes were closed and the rock leaves ahead of its black, flaring nostrils clashed on the branches, those that hadn't been shattered to rubble.

'Japalura,' Dashini said. 'The dragon goddess. At least she's still alive.'

Prissy, whose knee was against Dashini's thigh, edged closer. 'So,' she said, still not having any words of solace, 'where's the way out?'

Dashini nodded off to her left, her gaze not leaving the dragon.

'What, those stairs?' Gam went over to them, bent-kneed and low to the ground. Into the cliff had been carved a rough stair with much winding, perilously steep, sometimes crumbling away. 'Doesn't look like a Door,' he said, 'and it's not much of a stair either.'

Dashini tore her eyes away from the dragon. 'It's the only one we've got, and we're going to have to use it,' she said. 'We've got to get down. Then there's miles to the tree.'

Prissy went over to stand by Gam, and though she didn't like the look of the stairs either, she also didn't feel much like hanging around on the side of a cliff for a gust to wind to blow them off. 'Look, wherever the Door is, let's get over to it, do the business before whatever that thing is wakes up.'

Dashini turned, and now she didn't look as much sad as she looked angry. 'That thing,' she said, her voice cracking, 'is the patron goddess of this realm. She's my friend. She should be flying. She never lands.'

It wasn't that Prissy didn't see that Dashini was upset, but she didn't know what she was supposed to do about it. 'So what?' she said. She looked down the stairs, and though they swam in her vision, she took the first step down. 'It's always something, isn't it? Let's just go.'

Dashini acted like she hadn't heard. 'We need to find out what's wrong.'

Now it was Prissy's turn to be angry. 'Look,' she said, 'when you brought us to Malarkoi you said it was going to be heaven. It's not. It's all horrible, and you need to get us out. So, I know you're cross your dragons are dead, or whatever, but please can you get us out of here?'

Dashini stood up, brushed herself down. 'There are two ways out of this level – death, or the Door. Do you want to chuck yourself off this cliff? No? Then the only way we're getting to the Door out is if she flies us there.'

Prissy licked her teeth. 'And we're going to have to find out what's wrong with her before we can get her to do that?'

Dashini nodded.

'She always gets her way, doesn't she?' Prissy said to Gam.

At ground level, their legs trembling from the nearly endless and perilous stairway down, Dashini, Gam and Prissy eventually stood on solid ground.

There were dragons everywhere – some as small as birds, others too big to see in their entirety, and between these two poles there was every size in between – most were dead, more or less decayed, and those still breathing that Dashini picked up and held seemed to have no will to live.

They looked up at her, stared into her eyes, then fell limp.

'Their Spark is draining,' Dashini said. 'Like they're forcing it out.'

'They've had enough,' Gam said.

Prissy walked between them, picking her feet up high. 'I don't blame them,' she said. 'I'd say we should put what's left out of their misery, but there's so many.'

Dashini turned her face to Japalura and walked forward without looking down, and though Gam and Prissy tried not to tread on anything, they gave up after a while and pretended it all wasn't happening.

The sun never moved in the sky, so it was hard to know how long they walked across that graveyard.

'Is it the same sun in every level?' Prissy asked.

'That's a difficult question to answer,' Dashini replied. 'My mother scryed the weft for every level, and then anchored an accessible volume of them in the Pyramid, using the Doors. The intermediate realms are all derived from the perfect material real, so in one way, yes, that's the same sun. In an equally true way, it's this realm's sun, separate and distinct from the material realm's sun, so no, it's not. In fact—'

Prissy put her hand up. 'Forget I asked.' She looked at Gam, raised her eyebrows and shook her head, at first sharing one of those moments that Dashini felt she would never be part of. But Gam turned away, his face concerned, as if he cared about her.

294

A moment later, Gam caught Dashini looking at him. He shrugged, looked away, and they all walked on.

Dashini showed them which unlikely-looking spiked cactuses contained water, and which of the sparse shrubs had edible roots, but other than that they didn't stop until they couldn't go any further. There was nowhere pleasant to camp; the closer they got to the Stone Oak the more the world buzzed with flies, stank sweetly of rotted flesh. The moaning and the death rattles grew louder and more ever-present. The best they could do was clear the ground around them, close their eyes, put their arms over their ears and their hands over their mouths and hope that their exhaustion took them into sleep.

When they did sleep, they joined Japalura's dream.

It was nothing complicated – dragon minds are very simple – Japalura dreamed of a twilight time, when the sun was setting, when the world was hot but cooling, where her belly was full and there was no need to move. Her people were around her, and their enemies were bested.

This dream, she dreamed with such vividness that it became real for all of those in it.

Gam dreamed it, becoming a dragon in his own mind, and Prissy dreamed it, stretching her dragon wings, swishing her dragon tail.

Even Dashini dreamed it, her memories of the place merging, until Japalura's thoughts turned to death, the food she had eaten poisoning her blood, slowly curdling it in her veins. Then Dashini woke, shook the others, and marched them out of their sleepiness.

The remaining living were mostly lesser dragons, scarcely more than lizards, and they made for the base of the Stone Oak, called by their veneration of Japalura to their goddess.

Now the children were closer they could see the lizards spiralling the trunk, making their way up. Their footholds made steps, their claws scratched grooves, and the slow, cold-blooded, procession of lizards around the tree showed the children the way they needed to follow.

There was a gorge that wound up between the tree and Japalura's ankle, and the three went this way, their left feet and hands on the dragon-goddess's scales, the right on the huge, stone branch.

They climbed, and the lizard procession thinned out, some of Japalura's disciples skittering off to lodge themselves in the crevices of their goddess, others using their claws to take a more direct route up her leg.

Her ankle gave way to her shin, and the climb grew steeper up to her knee. The tree was too smooth now without so many lizards preparing the path, so the three transferred entirely to the dragon and used the irregularities of her scales and the gaps where they interlocked as footrests and handholds.

Hour by hour they ascended into the burning sunlight.

They climbed, and climbed, and climbed in the oppressive heat until their hands and feet were so sore they could hardly use them. As they tired, they slowed until lizards crawled around and over and past them, the sun never letting up in its endless shining.

There was no option but to keep going, no matter how tired they became, and when they thought they must surely die of exhaustion, they got to a broad stretch of membrane that joined Japalura's leg to her body.

They lay there, staring up at the sunlight as it filtered through a temporarily shady expanse of leaves. It was the only thing, the sun, that felt familiar in scale to them, though if it had moved an inch across the sky in the many hours of their climbing they couldn't tell.

Unknown hours passed, but once they were on the dragon's arm, they could walk again.

It was horizontal, perhaps even angled slightly downhill, and they all felt giddy with the pleasure of making up so much ground with so little effort after the endless climbing. It was like flying, running down that goddess's limb, like resting and moving all at once, and the muscles that had protested so earnestly before now delighted in their freedom from strain. The children laughed and whooped, even Gam.

The land stretched unbroken green below, the sky deep blue, and above them the wind rustled the leaves.

But then they came to the dragon's everlasting neck, lacing its way thousands of feet between the branches.

When time isn't measured in days, how do you mark its passage? The sun going down, dark coming, light returning – the human body understands these things. All warm-blooded things know day and night. They need it. The constant, unending sameness of a cold-blooded dragon heaven is not for them; they don't know how to orient themselves in it. Had they been on Japalura's neck for a day? A week?

They couldn't tell.

When could they rest? When they were tired? They were always tired.

If they stopped, they might never start again.

A basilisk walks slowly and steadily. It has eight legs, like a spider, but has a ribbed back broad enough that three people can cling to it.

Basilisks do not have fur to take in a fist and hold on to. They are not thin enough to reach around, but a person can wedge their fingers into gaps between scales and let themselves be dragged upwards.

If their fingers are tightly pinched, they can fall asleep and be pulled past their own ability to move.

They were all past exhaustion, with no end in sight, and Dashini grabbed a basilisk, thrust her hands into gaps in the creature's skin, called for the other two to do the same.

They all three went up, drifting into and out of the dragon goddess's dream of lassitude and death, not knowing her thoughts from reality.

They did, eventually, reach Japalura's head. Prissy and Gam lay where they fell, but Dashini went straight to sit gently on her muzzle. It was broad as the deck of a ship, rising and falling as she breathed like a ship rises and falls on gentle waves.

'What's wrong, old friend?'

She didn't reply.

Dashini reached in front of her, put her hands flat on one oval scale and sang a silent song in her mind. Mothers will sing songs to their infants, some to help them sleep, some to calm them, some to make them play, and though Dashini had forgotten the songs sung to her – if there had been any – in her thoughts she made her own song for Japalura, to let her know only one thing: that she was there.

If she heard Dashini, she made no sign of it. Her eyes remained shut against the world, her breath as shallow and slow as any living thing's breath could be. Why should a goddess recognise a human child? Why should she have sympathy for her, even if she loves her? Love is something a goddess demands: she requires it. She is not obliged to reciprocate.

Dashini sang on silently, even if Japalura didn't hear her. True love does not require reciprocation, it does not expect the reward of recognition, it is a gift, not an exchange. Dashini lay herself flat across the dragon, pressed her cheek on her warmth, her mouth touching her, and the silent words of her song were spoken on her lips.

She lay there for hours while Gam and Prissy slept.

How long should it take to rouse a goddess? Time on the scale that goddesses know it is both infinitely protracted and immediate. To live from the beginning to the end and to know it all perfectly is to be aware of every moment at once, which robs each of sequence, and sequence is how the progress of time is measured.

So, the question is close to meaningless.

Gam and Prissy, waking in the same sunlight they'd fallen asleep under, had long given up on it ever happening, and had decided between themselves that the best thing to do was to return to the ground, where at least they could rest without the threat of falling, but then the dragon's huge eye opened a slit, and she gave a long exhalation that rattled the stone leaves on the tree like a thousand deafening drums.

Dashini opened her eyes too, closed her mouth, and into her mind, until it found a comfortable way to be there, came dragon-goddess-consciousness, all at once filling her with Japalura's knowledge and the dragon's will.

It is impossible to say that a goddess is wrong – it is in the nature of gods that they cannot be judged in this way – but Dashini felt corruption. It was Japalura who had killed the other dragons, draining their Spark into her, and the lesser lizards she was bringing into her stomach so that she could do what she meant to do next.

She wanted to die.

She had been waiting for Dashini to come with the Nathan Knife, sickly sleeping for the millennia that had passed in this realm between Dashini's girlhood and now, waiting out the Master's quarantine so that the girl could kill her.

This all came in a moment, an epiphanic rush, a vision such as those a prophet will experience and spend their life repeating, and then it was gone and all that was left was the sense that the end was coming. In the same moment, Japalura tensed, pushed away from the tree, cracking its trunk down the centre line. She split it entirely and sent both sides collapsing into the corpse-laden plain she had made of her heaven, and forced herself up into the hot sky. Here there was space for the unfurling of her wings, the time she needed to displace all the air below and send her impossible bulk into flight.

The split tree was scoured by the hurricane her launch made, its leaves falling and crushing the ground even as the rockfall of the crumbling trunk destroyed everything below it.

The children clung to her skin, their nails digging into her God-Flesh, hardly able to keep themselves from slipping off.

Below, the Earth was rippled with mountain ranges, over the tops of which the dragon goddess soared, the beat of her wings making avalanches of snow and rock tumble down to splash into lakes, deforesting the lower slopes and sending flocks of birds scattering.

Here was a volcano, and Japalura didn't avoid it, gliding through its sulphurous billowing ash plume, choking Dashini, Gam and Prissy, burning their eyes. Goddesses don't experience the pain of the material world, and rarely remember that others do, but soon they were away from the sulphur and here were the ruins of a city, all overgrown with jungle creepers, its temples fallen in, dragon shrines in pieces.

Japalura turned away and followed the slow meander of a river out to its delta, the land giving way to ocean, the distant white water of breaking waves like lines of tangled cotton thread.

The ocean went on forever, and they flew high over it.

When the thin air became too cold to bear, the three crawled into the mouth of the dragon-goddess and huddled there together. From down inside, there was a rumbling, juddering, irregular beat, her heart, slowing, becoming weaker, more febrile.

'She's exhausted,' Dashini said, but she didn't listen to Gam and Prissy's replies, if there were any. She went back out, risked the wind. The ocean was giving way, and land was approaching.

There was the Door, a henge on a hilltop still miles distant. Japalura made one last beat of her wings, dissipating the clouds, and glided to the land, her eyes glossy and unfocussed, her thoughts quietening in Dashini's mind.

When she hit the earth, she churned the soil down to the bedrock and shattered that too. Her claws stripped chasms that revealed the ancient strata of her land, brought long hidden secrets to its surface, smothered acres with dirt and stone, and drowned those same acres with aquifers brought instantly to the surface. Japalura ignored all this as if it was nothing, slid thoughtlessly up to the Door henge, and the moment her momentum failed, when she was exactly where she wanted to be, she filled Dashini's mind with her will.

The girl did not want to obey – no one wants to kill their friend – but Japalura did not want to be disobeyed, and since she was a goddess, she was not disobeyed.

She turned her head so that Dashini could step to the ground. With her feet in the unspoiled grass, tears in her eyes, Dashini held up the Nathan Knife.

Japalura wasted no time and lowered her head, slowly, gently, perfectly, until Dashini's blade pierced the skin between her scales, cutting an artery she had made to come to the surface.

Because she was a goddess, she made it so that she didn't bleed until she had safely supported her head with one great arm, and with the other she softly urged Dashini to the Door.

Prissy and Gam came, pulled her away from the goddess, up to safety, and when Japalura saw this, she closed her eyes again.

With one last thought to Dashini, she flooded the land with her blood.

The Door opened.

XVIII

Her Champion, Part Five

THE PROGRESS OF GOD'S FACE into the gut of Sirius also marked the progress of the ghosts, now smiling and congratulating themselves, out of the room via the walls, eventually to exceed the range of Sirius's interest. Sirius would have chased them, snapped at their heels, bitten at their hands, but the God-Flesh burned in him and he found it difficult to concentrate on anything else.

With the magical source contained within him, the mystical organ would not be denied, and it blossomed inside Sirius's chest like a flower unfurling in the dawn light. Now, rather than make in the dog a painful inability to contain all, it wished to tell him, in his sensorium, in his consciousness, that there was a congruent growth in his capacities.

Anaximander said, sometimes, that consciousness such as self-aware things exhibit is like height, or width, or depth, or inwardness, or time – it is a dimension that sentient things possess, and this is a function of the way the weft combines the material and immaterial realms. Sirius had only felt the tenor of these communications before – which was a serious and expansive kind of helpfulness in his companion – but now this dimension was extended in his canine thoughts until he could encompass all the things the mystical organ had to communicate.

Into his head came the image of a square, and then one line was erased, and it became the image of a cube, the angles of which were suddenly extroverted, and then forward progress was imposed and everything became a loop like an ouroboros. All of those formerly vague and portentous feelings of what was to come, and the significances of what was to be, came into sharp focus.

We, if we are not Sirius, even if we are Anaximander, are incapable of knowing what it was that the dog experienced in that time, since to comprehend information of that kind is to see behind the veil the material world makes of everything, to become godly, and we do not have the resources required for thinking of that sort. We can only note its effects, and one of these was to send Sirius rigid, and another was to swell him outwards so that he occupied a volume of the room twice that which he had previously occupied, but mostly it was to cause to come over his mien a tranquil yet determined look.

Gods are like this – tranquil – or they are not like this.

Gods who do not turn directly towards death, see and know the run of time, and see and know where they can usefully intervene or remain separate. These gods do not, in their anger, attempt to tear down all that there is. They know that within the architecture of the universe there are structures that should and should not be shored up. Think of a house of cards – some parts of it are out of skew and need to be straightened, some parts are in the process of tumbling and need to be reinforced, some parts have too many cards and weigh down to make a fragile angle. Some cards may be removed entirely with no detriment to the whole. A destructive god will wave its hand through the cards and bring tumbling the whole edifice, but a god like Sirius sets his will to preservation and improvement.

It is not in a person's gift that they can know the will of a god, or the things that influence one to do what it does, but it may be that a god who is a dog by origin takes with him a dog's concerns, and if at this time Sirius came to know how events would play out, and still had within him his pledge to Nathan, then that would explain what he did next.

Sirius bounded up into the ceiling of the room, through into the next room, and then through that, as if the underground den of rooms was nothing but a stair to the surface. In three leaps he was out and onto the steep slope of Mount Mordew. He grew with each jump, so that the creatures that had concerned him beforehand were hardly any concern at all. Gill-men approached him, seeing he was an enemy, and these he destroyed too, shaking them between his now much larger teeth until they came apart at their seams.

To kill the gill-men was to make an act of war against their maker, the Master, and while the integration that would eventually bring together Sirius's mind-as-a-dog with his divine-immaterial-consciousness was scarcely begun, it did not mean that the mystical organ was ignorant of this fact. For demigods to clash implies a competition between their Reals, each attempting to make the material realm reflective of them rather than of their opponent, and the mystical organ, knowing this and working with the God-Flesh, reached inward into the godly future instantiation of Sirius and interrogated its eventual perfect form. This it made, in miniature, into a reflection of things as they might and must become if Sirius was to be the god of this place. Using the power of God-Flesh, it made this condition blossom out through the real, in advance of the Master's future attempt to prevent it, through an inversion that saw the-world-as-it-was tremble in the face of the-world-as-it-should-be.

Sirius, as a type of god, was still very junior, and the Master, far more experienced, had made the mount into which Mordew had been transformed. There was no chance that Sirius's inversion would take hold. Weft-manipulators of the power of the Master cannot simply be wished away by lesser gods, but that is not to say that there are no consequences for the real when an attempt is made. The opposite is true since, even if for a very brief period and incompletely, the world-as-it-is and the world-as-it-might-be come to exist in simultaneity – that is the way it is in the weft, where all things that might be are and always are – it disrupts the fabric of whatever does not have its own defences against powers that alter the real. Most things are powerless against magic of this type, so around Sirius the world buckled and snapped, iterating between the competing Reals, and even when this naturally resolved to the superior power's proper forms, the objects representing these things were weakened, briefly.

This set off in the New Glass Road a piercing racket.

A perfect glass will ring a perfect note when struck with a perfect hammer, but an imperfect one, especially one suffering a magical imperfection, will make a terrible sound, dangerous to the ear. This was heard all over Mount Mordew and its environs, even up to the pinnacle of the Manse, which was high in the clouds. Here the Master was listening, it is to be assumed, because then, after only the briefest period, came a bone juddering re-establishment of Reality that silenced the ringing. Sirius felt this as a punching ache in his mystical organ. It clacked his teeth and made his eyes water and he heard words, though he did not understand them in the vibrations this set up in the sinuses of his skull and these, though they were meaningless to him, had the atmosphere of the Master in them, which he recognised from his previous contact with him.

When he was a pup, this would have been enough to put fear into him, since the Master was an ungentle husband of animals and taught with his fists, but, though it would be wrong to say there was none of this emotion, his courage now, as a dog of experience and a newly made god, answered these words with defiance, though nothing so definite as meaning proper, and this defiance was understood by the mystical organ. Sirius doubled in size, since to a dog size is an indication of power, and his teeth grew in his jaw proportionally larger than this, and sharper, and greater in number, since to a dog the ability to show large and numerous teeth is a way of saying that he is a powerful fighter.

Sirius's great paws crushed across the landscape the Master had made, collapsing the weak slums into pits, pulling down the stretched and deformed fences that had once barred access to the Merchant City but which were now ineffectual and too widely spaced, and there were no slum-dwellers remaining in the slums to bar, only those spiky and multilimbed monsters Sirius had encountered before. In the City the houses were no longer low and regular, but instead stretched precariously up, too thin to hold their own structures, unmoored from their foundations, leaning against each other, falling to the vibration of the dog's passage. In them were, occasionally, children and foolish adults who ran as their structures came apart, but mostly the buildings were empty.

Sirius was so large now that when these buildings fell onto him they barely made him flinch. A dog running though the reeds around a lake would have felt less inconvenience than Sirius felt at these, and a primitive kind of thought, not laid out to him as words, but as images, came from his mind with this exact import, and to himself he gloried in a glad moment of freedom, galloping though the streets, making a tumble of them as an ordinary dog flattens grasses growing on the bank. He crouched and wheeled and lurched like a playing dog does. He mouthed and growled and barked in joy, and all around him the Merchant City fell.

He gambolled in its ruins.

In truth, this was no loss to anyone – the Master's transformation of the city had rendered this place uninhabitable and what still existed of it was a prelude to the Master's refurbishment of his creation, the chaos soon to be magicked away and replaced by new houses and plazas and colonnades, grander than before and more extensive – but loss was not the source of Sirius's pleasure. As has been said, he was already not a god of destruction but of something more positive, and pleasure is a positive thing, even if there are always consequences. One dog's pleasure can be another dog's inconvenience, or worse.

Pleasure to a god of Sirius's sort was not unbounded, though – unlike the way it is to a god whose own desires are all that concerns it – and there came to him in his newly divine state, with his newly divine senses, the smell of Nathan, his service-pledge, which had until then been absent from the world.

'Smell' is not the right word, but there is no word in any human language for the impending feeling that the weft-impression of a person exists – as communicated through an implanted mystical organ amplified by God-Flesh into the blossoming consciousness of a dog made god. Even Sirius had no word for it, but it stopped him in his playing nonetheless. So much was he brought to a halt that, though several buildings collapsed onto him, he remained stock-still, his nostrils flaring, a glow growing in his chest.

He sensed sandalwood, which he felt was Nathan-related.

Knowing the source of the sensation by some directionality that was inherent in it, he turned and looked upwards, to where what had been Mordew stretched precipitously into the clouds. Here, he knew from his memory and from the usual senses, the Manse of the Master was, high and distant, even for a giant dog.

Sirius felt he might grow himself as high as a mountain, stand in opposition to the new Mount Mordew, growl at it, snap at the Manse and thereby secure Nathan's release, but in the same instant that he felt that it would not work, the ripples of the future telling him that any such action would prevent rather than secure his wishes. The trembling of the weft showed that Nathan was not in the physical world represented by this excrescence of stones but was in an offshoot of it, a world separated discretely, the portal to which was in the actuality of the material Manse. Should that building fall into dust – if he were to become huge enough to bark at it so loudly as to shake it into pieces – then he would have to search the rubble for the key, something great size would make very difficult.

This key was the locket – the one that had once held Nathan's father's finger and which the Master had looped around Nathan's neck. The memory of it was clear from the sensation, and Sirius knew where it was, close enough, so he left his frolicking and surged up the steepness of the mountain, his monumental paws dragging rough channels through the foundations of the city, tearing up streets, uprooting deformed trees, destroying parks.

In the sickly geometries of what remained of the colonnades, slum-dwellers cowered in bedraggled mobs. They had, until recently, been making free with the property of the merchants they had driven out, but now they gathered and watched, slack-jawed, awed first by the transformation of the city into a mountain, and then, having run into the streets to avoid the collapsing of the buildings, awed again to see a creature the size of Sirius, who was like no dog had ever been in the history of the world, and not only for his size but also, now, for the divine aura that emanated from him in every direction.

Sirius passed, having no interest in these persons, but where his aura lit the world transformations were made – water into nectar, rubble into manna, new sprouts of green in bare ground. Lame men became hale, the emphysematous breathed, and the eyeless grew eyes, just like Gam Halliday had under the influence of Nathan's Spark. God-Flesh in a sufficient amount, with sufficient material – such as a magically derived creature made by a Master – can make a thing with powers greater than an inhibited boy child first exhibits, even if that boy is destined to be a god himself, and a dog is profligate with his energy, not properly understanding restraint as a person does, so all around he made wonder as he passed.

For reasons no god can be expected to demonstrate, Sirius travelled clockwise around the mountain, and then anticlockwise, and then clockwise again, sometimes returning down, then surging up. In this way, like any dog playing in a garden, he made strange and illogical movements towards his goal, bringing into view the Factoria, which were spluttering with unchecked fires and gouts of water from interrupted plumbing, and the Entrepôt, which was pungent with rotting and charred food decanted from the ruined warehouses and run amok with livestock. Only the Port was relatively unchanged – there is not much transformation that a patch of water can be made to suffer, though the walls that surrounded it were all fallen over, especially the Sea Wall Gate, which no longer closed neatly and magically together but was two huge blocks, listing drunks leaning against each other, singing and shivering in the wind.

Rather like the people in the colonnades, this was not something that impinged on Sirius's consciousness, but it did not need to, since his being-in-the-world was becoming extensive enough that whatever there was to be known was becoming known by him whether he chose to concentrate on it or not. Moreover, the knowledge of the world that passed into him was knowledge, unmediated, of the things of existence in their most fundamental forms, untainted by understanding. While it is true that this purity would have dissolved if he had attempted to interrogate it, Sirius had, in the mental recreation his senses made for him, the effects of all the local material realm, and, held in abeyance and similarly discrete, the immaterial concepts which might be married to them.

This is how the mind is, for gods – a peculiarly extensive though largely passive comprehension that is not suited to specifics – and it was only because Sirius was not yet free of his former existence, and yet untutored, that he thought as he had when he had made Nathan his service-pledge. Despite the meandering route he took, it was still with an aim – to find Nathan.

Perhaps Sirius would be the type of god for whom worldly concerns remained. A god may choose how to make himself, and while all knowledge tends to the universal, it may be that a dog's universal and a man's universal are different things, so god dogs might very well be more interested in the way things are than the way things always have been, just as a dog thinks only of the present moment – the bone that he is chewing, and not in those bones that he has chewed or might come to chew.

In the sky the clouds were thickly gathered again, heavy and grey. With the end of the flocks of firebirds, red birth-death no longer picked out the contours of these clouds, but nonetheless they flickered in that peculiar way particular to the skies over Mordew, this time orange from the fires that raged on every slope. As Sirius ascended, these clouds became a fog which lingered around the trunks of colossal trees stretching into invisibility, becoming diffuse as they rose, soon nothing more than darknesses spotting the uniform mist.

Sirius went always up, the tangle of trees ever denser, the clouds thicker.

His fur was slick with unfallen rain, his breath cold, and the magic of his divinity made rainbows everywhere he looked – perfect circles of colour in reflection of his glory back at him from whatever object was ahead.

The slope steepened.

Imagine you are pulling molten caramel up from the pan preliminary to beginning sugar-work: at the surface the gradient formed as you pull is gentle, then there is an exponential increase in the angle until the liquid solidifies into a flexible spike. This was what had happened when the Master made Mount Mordew. Sirius, in his all-knowingness, could see backwards to the moment this had happened, the world made like toffee. He watched as the Master imposed solidity on his new city, holding it perfectly in place despite its unnaturalness. The New Glass Road circled this vertiginous new spire closely, slicing through the trees which still grasped ever upward, distorted by the same magic that performed the stretching, and Sirius scrabbled between the perfect construction of the Master and the ever more unstable trunks, all the while swallowing and breathing in the cloud air.

When he put paw to the New Glass Road its hexes activated, making him slip, so he would have to leap while his footing held onto into the mess of trees, which would then give way, forcing him up to the road again, which would throw him off, and it was only by virtue of his powers as a god that he could do it at all, slowing the world so that he had time to react, escaping gravity and density by robbing both of their ability to act on him through time.

Then he could go no further, and the Manse appeared.

Sirius made time stop altogether for everyone and everything but him, which is another way of saying that he sped himself up infinitely quickly, and in this state he rested, not breathing and not moving, since the air around him was too slow to be drawn into his lungs and was, in fact, immovable.

His rear legs were on a thicket of tree limbs, crumbling forever beneath him, and his forepaws were on a loop of the New Glass Road, its hexes always beginning to slip him down.

He faced the Manse.

This building was the same as it ever was: the same proportions, the same pennants, the same facades, the same alcoves. Now, unlike the last time he had seen them, Sirius recognised the slender figures in the alcoves: they were the ghosts, his spectral, human wolf pack, each one perfectly represented by a statue of the man they had been. With his god's understanding, he knew that these figures were bound there in stone, material representations of their immaterial presences, the Master's magical proof against them ever taking body again in the city.

Around their ankles, under the sculpted stone robes, were magical anklets, attached by magical chains to a magical steel rod that ran through the walls, securing them in place should anyone ever attempt to resurrect them to the real.

They were ancient, as old as the Manse, lichen-crusted but unweathered. With their outstretched hands they pointed down. The object of their indication was no longer mysterious to Sirius – it was the place where the frozen corpse of Nathan's brother still was, faceless, now toppled from the table on which it had stood.

Some gods can undo magic of the sort that bound the real forms of these ghosts, so long separated from their bodies, but Sirius was not one of them. If the ghosts had meant him to reunite them, they would be disappointed – he left them where they stared, pointing – but it is just as likely that they meant him to destroy the Master and undo the spells that way, something that was still very much possible.

He could sense all this with his mystical organ, knew where their enemy was, but the Manse was too high to reach, even for a hybrid of god and dog, and whenever he slowed his experience down to interact with the world he went away from the peak, down the slope, sending trees toppling, clouds whirling, and making the New Glass Road ring with piercing alarms. Then he would have to speed up again.

Nevertheless, Nathan was in there. Sirius knew it.

A lack of progress is something particularly troublesome to a dog, who is a type of creature that likes to be always gaining on something when it seems just out of reach. Pensiveness, thoughtfulness, planning and logic were all but impossible for him, and Sirius wanted to bound up and reach the Manse. When he tried to do it though, it did not work. So what was he to do?

In the distance, he heard a howl. It was the bitch's call he had heard before – first triumphant and exalting in the destruction of the city, and then encouraging and siren-like as he struggled to remain above the waves – but now it was close at hand.

Into his mystical organ came an apparition of a female dog, perfect, shining white, beautiful, and Sirius knew that she was the one who had spoken.

She howled again, calling out to him from down the slope, and with only one brief look back up towards the inaccessible Manse, one uncertain swallow, he set himself to find this bitch. This was not to deny his original goal, only to supplement it with a new one, and who is to say that a god cannot do two things at once? No one, since gods are potent in that way and have the power to perform many tasks at once.

Sirius made a howl of his own, and with that galloped towards her.

Dogs love to run, no less do god dogs love it, and when they have something to run to, they glory in the movement their limbs make, the wind in their fur that sleekens their faces, that flattens their ears, that makes of them a perfect arrow that curves through streets, between trees, across whatever expanse lies between them and their object. Their paws seem never to be on the ground, yet when they are they thunder it, concuss it like the mallet of a bass drum concusses that instrument, only impossibly quickly, thrumming the earth as they pass.

A lesser animal would have been distracted by birds, or by flukes, or by the tumbling of buildings their footfalls made, but Sirius was focussed on one thing – his movement towards the howling bitch.

She howled again, much louder now, and he tended towards her, the line of his run taking no account of obstacles, since as he digested the God-Flesh of the weftling's face his divinity grew, exceeding the ability of the material real to contain him. Buildings that might have stopped him before were dissolved out of existence at their protruding edges, giving his being priority. People who might have defended themselves against him, his oncoming presence threatening to crush them, became unborn, never existing, Sirius's right to the world erasing them backwards through time, and also their parents, so that neither he nor they were troubled by his coming.

There she was. He skidded to a stop, his claws digging gouges in the cobblestones, spraying up bricks and paving slabs in a heavy cloud that clattered urgently against what remained of the street.

She stood at a distance between two deformed warehouses in what had once been called the Factoria. Huge and sturdy, a match to Sirius, she was in heat, swollen, and though it was her howl that had drawn him here, the vision of her in his mystical organ, it was her scent that now filled the dog's senses. It overwhelmed him, blinded him, deafened him, even silencing the mystical organ. When she presented her rear to Sirius, he mounted her without hesitation and performed his role.

In his mystical organ, now she was close enough, the bitch communed with him. She read his mind, descried in him his recent actions, and understood why it was that he was unable to find entrance to the Manse. Sirius read her mind too and knew her for an avatar of the Mistress of Malarkoi, enemy of Nathan's enemy, and so a friend of his service-pledge by the ancient law of common foes.

The moment Sirius withdrew his member, it diminishing in the knowledge that its work was done, out from her issued seven pups, each both doglike and elemental – one of fire, one of water, one of light, one of darkness, one of wind, one of mountain and one of some indistinguishable essence, but which was fundamental nonetheless – and they did not mewl or gasp for their first breaths, instead they cavorted at the feet of their father, barking the songs proper to their natures.

At first, he raised his huge paws, as if these creatures were vermin, but they did not bite him and their scent was close to his. Soon he knew they were of his pack. He lay down and let them on him, and danced across him and buried their heads in his fur, and because he was a divine dog, their fire did not burn him, nor did their darkness blind him, nor did their mountains crush him – instead they were exactly the right order of thing for him to delight in.

In the Factoria there was a mill wheel, and while the brackish stream that had once turned it had dried up, and the elongation to which Mordew had been subject had made an oval of its circle, Sirius was large enough now to take that wheel from its gears and toss it up into the air. It spun and flew, crashing down whole in the wreckage of the city, and there it rolled down an otherwise forlorn and abandoned avenue.

Six of Sirius's seven new daughters ran for the wheel, their mouths making smiles, open and panting, while the seventh – she of the unidentifiable element – stayed by her father's side. He licked her until the others returned with the wheel, and when he tossed it again, he nudged her forward, urging her to fetch. She denied it again, pressed against him. On the third throw Sirius chased his own wheel, six of his daughters racing with him, but the reluctant daughter remained where he had been, for a moment. Then, as her father and sisters returned, she ran away from them, up the hill.

The white bitch went with her, and the two led the others back up the mountainside, the journey a joyous game of chase, with much circling and leaping, mouthing and barking. If an enemy of the Master of this city had wanted them to make chaos of it, then their play would have done just that – there was not a place that was not flattened by them, and the remaining people were driven in fear of their lives down to the waterside to glumly watch the long retreating ships.

When the dogs reached the place where Sirius had been, as high as he could go, the white bitch made a rift in the fabric of the real, and the reluctant daughter stood by it.

Sirius, though, was too wrapped up in his playing. His life to this point had been one of service – first of the Master, then of Heartless Harold Smyke, then of the merchant, and latterly of Nathan Treeves – and while his companionship of Anaximander was real, it was never as joyous as this, he being a dog of philosophical disposition, unsuited to thoughtless frivolity.

His six gambolling daughters distracted him and for a wonderful time, even for a god, he revelled in their jumping, their snapping, wagging tails and high yaps.

But then, through the rift, a voice called to him. 'Here, Sirius! Here, boy!' it said, and when Sirius heard it, he froze for the briefest moment. It was Nathan's voice, and his summons brought a rush of memory, of obligation, of duty that he was still dog enough to be moved by. He swallowed, looked at the little pups, the white bitch, but he obeyed the call, bounding up and out of the real, into the Manse.

XIX

Boy, Book and Dog, Part Four

'WAS SIRIUS IN THE WEFT?' Anaximander said, the
next morning, as they doused the embers of the fire.
The relaxed Clarissa, the pleased Clarissa, the
Clarissa of the warming compliments of the night before, was
gone. In her place was the tense, irritable, dismissive Clarissa.
'What?' she said. 'I'm busy.'

Anaximander repeated his sentence, his head lower than
before, his eyes averted, but before he could finish, she walked
away from him and went down to a stream to wash.

Why shouldn't she attend to her toilet? He was her service-
pledge, she was not his. She owed him nothing.

The dog returned to the others.

Bellows was reading Adam, the pair of them entirely
engaged in whatever story the book was telling.

If Clarissa had not looked for Sirius, perhaps Anaximander
could do it himself.

Yes, that was better – he should never have given his service-
pledge work to do on his behalf. It was up to him to do that
job, following the lead she had provided.

He shut his eyes and pressed himself flat on the earth.

Immediately he sensed it, much stronger this time, as if
another dog was right below him. Anaximander breathed
deeply, silenced all other sensation, and interrogated that
feeling, seeking information in it.

Direction, extent, depth – none of these things were
clear. The source of sound, because a dog hears it with
both his ears, can be triangulated, its relative softness or
loudness speaks of proximity, and its clarity can indicate
whether there are obstacles in between. The situation is
similar with the other physical senses. Magical senses are

deficient in this way, even while in other ways they are much more precise.

Quality, though, Anaximander could sense. This magic was very similar to his own, almost the same in its – for want of a better metaphor – flavour. So, was it Sirius then? Was he active in a non-material realm which was reverberating somehow within this land?

Anaximander wanted to believe that this was the case, not least because Clarissa had suggested that it was, but a magical dog's character is as much a part of him as the flavour of his magic, and Sirius's was not present in the sensation. There was none of the familiarity that Sirius's presence should have brought. Instead, there was an uncomfortable wrongness.

He tried to feel past this wrongness, to locate Sirius in the feeling, but no matter how he tried, he couldn't do it.

Eventually, when it was clear that he had failed to do the work Clarissa had set him, and the sense of presence was still too strong to ignore, he went to where Bellows and Adam were, and read the story they were engaged in over their shoulders until it was time to leave.

That afternoon, having made good progress, Clarissa stopped their walking.

They made camp early and she busied herself again with secret preparations, gathering roots and husks, digging troughs of various depths and shapes, chipping at and arranging stones in cryptic patterns. Anaximander watched her throughout, determined not to be absent when there was any way he could be of help, but also trying to know what it was that she was doing, matching her actions to the contents of his mind, hoping to give them significance. Bellows, though, mostly paid attention to the pages of his brother, and whatever was written there was known to them alone.

Later, Clarissa asked for privacy, and boy and dog went to hunt for food, taking Adam with them.

It is not easy to satisfy the dietary preferences of a disparate group of individuals. There is always one who will not eat what the others will, and what some people insist on having is often what will disgust another. Bellows would have cheerfully eaten seeds and berries, but these were no use to Anaximander, and Clarissa's tastes ran to difficult to catch red meat, she needing, she said, 'the iron'. Adam did not eat, but he did, within his pages, have instructions as to how to make a snare, and illustrations of the tops of edible roots.

'Let us settle on rabbit,' Anaximander said, 'and supplement its meat with whatever else we can easily forage.'

Bellows agreed, and the two of them opened Adam and lay him on a patch of clean dry ground, where they could consult him easily.

Anaximander's paws were not suited to the tying of knots, and Bellows's fingers were too fragile to dig with, so despite the fact that the boy would have preferred not to eat the rabbit, and the dog could not digest potato, each one did what he was best suited to. Bellows made the rabbit snare, with a stick and a length of fabric from his jacket, and Anaximander excavated the bases of the plants Adam drew on his pages.

When the preparations were made and the roots gathered, the three hid in a secluded place from where they could not be seen but where they could see the snare.

It was getting late. Adam, who knew more about game hunting than the other two, said, 'Make yourselves comfortable, this can take a while.'

No sooner had he said it, though, than a scream tore through the quiet of the woods.

Bellows leapt up, but Anaximander bit at his clothes and pulled him back. 'It is Clarissa,' he said. 'I know that cry – she is at her work in the weft. There is no need to concern yourself; the source of her fear is not of this world.'

Bellows was about to ask him how he could be so sure, and to insist that he removed his teeth from the seat of his trousers, when, seemingly startled by Clarissa's noise, a brace of rabbits came jumping though the undergrowth, directly at where the snare had been placed.

Boy and dog held their breath, but the animals swerved at the last moment, missing the trap.

Bellows nodded to himself, as if this confirmed some suspicion in him that things must never go his way, but then a third rabbit emerged from a bush and seemed to dive head first into the loop of the snare. Anaximander darted out from their hiding place and dispatched the thing with clinical effectiveness, returning with it in his mouth. 'It is quite the specimen!' he said, happily. 'I cannot wait to show Clarissa!'

When they returned, Clarissa, exhausted, slept early without eating, and showed no interest in the catch.

In the twilight, Bellows and Anaximander stared into the fire. The boy suspended the skinned rabbit between cleft sticks, where it could cook. When the fat rendered, it fell onto a log, and, for a moment, a brighter flame flared. Its smoke, redolent of the rodent's flesh, curled up into the sky.

Anaximander, his eyes fixed on the passing of these drippings, turned his head to the side, first one way and then the other. In an unspeaking dog, this is the sign of mute incomprehension, but this dog was not mute. On the contrary. 'What, I wonder, is fire? Clearly, I understand that it is that hot, red, flickering presence above the burning wood. But what is it made from?' he said.

When Bellows didn't answer, but only turned the spit to brown the topside of the rabbit, Anaximander went on. 'The question seems nonsensical – fire, after all, is made from fire. But of what sort of thing is it? Clothes are made of fabric' – he looked over at the ones that contained Clarissa, groaning restlessly in her EYE fugue – 'and fabric is made of threads. Threads come from plants, and plants gain their matter from the soil. Can it not be said, then, that clothes are of the earth, transformed from it by degrees?'

Bellows turned the meat again, though this time it didn't really need turning. He didn't speak.

'What can fire be said to be transformed from?' the dog asked. 'Not earth, certainly. Nor is it of water, which is obvious, since water douses a flame and kills it. Nor is it of the air, since air is invisible and flames can be seen.' Anaximander took a log from the fuel pile with his mouth and threw it onto the blaze, making it burn brightly. 'Is it then light? No, since light gives illumination to an object but is itself invisible, whereas, as we have noted, fire can be seen. Is it then heat? No, for the reasons it is not light. Light and heat are effects on things – everything can be made light or dark, hot or cold – but fire is a thing of itself. Look, Bellows' – he indicated with his muzzle – 'fire dances above the wood. And look' – he blew over it with his breath – 'see how the movement of air directs it. Air cannot direct light, nor heat, it only acts on physical things. So, fire must be physical. Yet it cannot be captured in the mouth and held, and if one tries one receives only pain.'

Since the fire was now much stronger after Anaximander's addition of superfluous wood, Bellows had to take the spit away, and since the meat was cooked – he prodded it with his finger in the way Cook had done many times in the Manse and it gave, but not too much – he passed Anaximander his share. As he did it, putting a portion at the dog's feet, he said, 'The Master taught me many things, but the nature of fire was not one of them. It seems to me that the world is a place where there are things that are acted upon, and things that act upon them. Fire, like lightning, is not a thing in itself but is a sign of an actor, acting upon the acted-upon, transferring its power, in this case destructively. We are acting upon the logs, turning them into heat. Fire is the sign of this, so that we see that it is happening. It is a particular sign of a particular action. Just as tears are the sign of an unhappy action in a man, or thunder is the sky's anger acted out on the air.'

Anaximander had been eating while Bellows delivered his speech, but when he sensed the boy was finished, he swallowed his mouthful quickly. This wasn't because words couldn't leave him if impeded – his magic voice could not be obstructed by a mouthful of meat and bones – it was more that he didn't want his enjoyment of the food to distract him. Anyway, it was a politeness he had learned from Clarissa, who never spoke with her mouth full. 'This may be true,' he said, licking his lips, 'but the question remains – from what is it made?'

As if from the empty space where no one was sitting, Adam spoke. 'Fire,' the book said, 'is a flux of combusting gases. Heat and light combined given off by reactions in the presence of air. It can be moved because the combusting gases that make it can move, it dances because these gases themselves dance invisibly in a breeze.' There on the ground Adam lay open in the dirt, lit by the flames, his two visible pages covered with diagrams, short pieces of text and arrows indicating which words referred to which images.

Anaximander could see the pages from where he sat, but they didn't seem to convince him. 'You say it is a "flux", but I ask again, what type of thing is a flux? Is it a quality of exist-ence that only fire exhibits? I have never seen any other flux of this type, except to recognise it as "fire". To say fire is a flux—'

Adam interrupted him. 'If the word means nothing to you, then that is because you are ignorant and so should turn your attention more assiduously to your studies.'

'You're all wrong,' said a voice, startling the three, who had believed themselves alone in the gathering night. It wasn't Clarissa, waking, Anaximander knew this in a moment, and so he went into an attacking stance. Bellows stood; Adam snapped shut.

The voice, the source of which Bellows and Anaximander strained to see through the flames, was high but strong. She carried confidence, but not arrogance, and had there been a woman of sturdy middle age there, a schoolmistress or a doctor, then they would not have been surprised. But there was no one of that sort.

Instead, there was a tall and beautiful woman, in travelling clothes, with a pretty face and long hair in ringlets. She had almond eyes and glistening lips, and on each finger she wore rings, all different from each other. In one hand she held a sword, thin and stiff as a fencing foil, sharpened to a point. 'I am Sharli,' she said, 'and I'm here on business.'

Anaximander indicated a plan to Bellows with nods, that the pair should circle the fire, each converging on the woman by their closest route, but Bellows remained where he was, rigid with fear.

'Your friend is sensible, dog. Stay where you are.' Sharli indicated with a jerk of her head to where Anaximander's service-pledge was sleeping. 'I'm here with my lover. He is called Deaf Sam.' This 'Deaf Sam' had a handkerchief over Clarissa's face and a knife at her heart. 'He has ether at her mouth, but if you wake the woman up, his blade will do the killing.'

Anaximander set up a low growl, but at whom it was difficult to tell, since he could attack neither of them without risking Clarissa's life.

Sharli put up one hand, the other swishing the sword through the air. 'Fire,' she said, 'is made of death. As am I. If you don't believe me, we can put it to the test.' She didn't wait for them to agree to this, instead she took a step forward, into the flames, standing with one boot in the ash at their fire's centre and the other on the most fiercely burning log. She stood there, seemingly unaffected by heat or flux, and looked directly at Bellows. 'Would any of you like to join me?' she said. The flames licked up her calves, encircled her legs to the knees. 'No?' She smiled and then, in one quick and smooth movement she reached down, speared Adam with the sword and dropped him into the embers.

Bellows, suddenly overcoming his fear, stepped towards her, but Sharli aimed her rapier at the boy's throat.

From over by Clarissa there was a senseless bark that stopped whatever murder she was about to attempt. It was not Anaximander, as anyone familiar with him would know. It was Deaf Sam, attracting Sharli's attention.

She turned to him and read the signs he then made, never moving from the fire, never suffering its effects. 'Theatrics? They've never bothered you before,' she replied to his objection. 'Fine,' she said. 'My lover doesn't see the need for all this... flair. Fair enough. If you're curious, my boots and trews are coated with a paste that's resistant to flame. I, through my many years of training, am resistant to pain.' She smiled. 'I'm still death, though... at least as far as two of you are concerned.' She faced Bellows, who was anxiously stepping forward and backward, staring at Adam.

Anaximander spoke now, creeping forward in the luxury of all the others' attention on Sharli. 'There is no need to fear, Bellows; Adam cannot be destroyed in that way. See, he remains as untouched as this woman appears to be. Her bodily integrity will not last, though, and nor will her gentleman companion's.' Anaximander lowered his head and raised his lips and in the firelight his teeth, sharp and long, glistened. He growled as Heartless Harold Smyke had trained him to, a sound that men and dogs felt in their anxious bowels. 'I will kill you, and then I will kill him, and, if I still live, I will gnaw your bones white.'

This, the dog felt, was a threat that seemed to ignore the couple's own threat – namely to kill Clarissa, his service-pledge – and he made it having considered three aspects of the situation, each of which he had understood with the magical speed he possessed by virtue of his fantastic provenance, and in combination with the information his magical senses gave to him.

Firstly, when he had been to Padge's office to fulfil his debt to the gin-wife and where he had been shot with the poisoned bullet, there had been very many sensations that circumstances dictated he ignore. This is true of all of us – a person must always focus on the business at hand, though that does not seal off the senses to all other input. Whatever you are doing now, pause. Look left, look right – those things do not seem entirely unfamiliar because they were at the periphery of your attention while you were reading, yet they still impacted on your sensorium. So it was with Anaximander back then, in Padge's quarters. He had, he now realised, smelled these two people before, faintly, by virtue of their previous presence there. They had also been in the restaurant outside the office, amongst the sense-signatures of the people who made up the patrons there. He thus knew these two to be particularly dangerous by their association with Mr Padge, who was himself a particularly dangerous man.

Secondly, there was about the persons of these two a conspicuous number of weapons, some of which were visible in the outlines they made in their clothes, some of which had odours associated with them – gunpowder, whetstone, solid smoke, etc. – and some of which had caused reactions on their skin, or which were carried in their sweat, so that Anaximander knew that they had been altered in some way. Some unscrupulous dog men will poison their fighters' claws, so it is not uncommon for others to dose their animals with antidotes, and these poisons and cures have subtle but recognisable scents, and both of these people smelled of these, which made him know that they were the kind of people who felt it was in their interests to do such a thing, something that made them likely to be assassins, or skilled roughs of a similar type.

Thirdly, Anaximander was very familiar with the sleeping breathing of Clarissa, he having laid beside her many nights in her place in the Merchant City, hoping that she was resting, keeping watch over her until the morning. He knew her to have been engaged, before the assassins arrived, with her inward, dreaming activities, and now knew, although she feigned to be unconscious, that in fact she was not unconscious at all but was preparing for some action. The ether, he could smell, was fresh enough to be effective, so it must have been that Clarissa was tolerant to it – perhaps through regular use as a soporific – which is why he could hear micro-muscular movements of her jaw in the clicking of its joints. While he could not decode the words, he guessed, knowing enough of the rhythm of spells, that she was in the process of silently mouthing one.

These three facts, as they were now to him, made him sure that his best course of action was direct attack, this being, as is often asserted, the best defence.

Assassins assassinate, so there is no point in negotiating with them; Clarissa was not under threat, even if the man who threatened to kill her thought she was; and if fighting was in the offing it was better that it occurred on his terms rather than theirs, since it is a rule in combat that the person who strikes first has an advantage. This is why he made the threat to gnaw their bones white, because it would, in order to correct his seeming failure to understand the gravity of the situation and restore their initial strategy to effectiveness – that is to blackmail them to compliance on the threat of the murder of all of them rather than one – require Sharli to make a clarification of some kind, verbally or by action, during which time he could make his first strike.

This is what happened, because the woman in the fire opened her mouth to say something, even as the flames licked up behind her, and this gave the dog the opportunity to attack.

Someone not trained to fight in a dog pit might think that a pounce upward is the best tactic, with the aim, perhaps, of hitting the chest with force, revealing the throat and then biting it out. This is too bold and leaves the attacker vulnerable to any quick counterstrike. It takes time to soar though the air, and to attack the chest is a mid-level attack, meaning that anyone upright on two legs – person, bear, rearing stag – is presented with a dog's most vulnerable parts when it is very easy for them to use whatever weapon they might have – knife, claw or antler – to pierce that creature's heart, and many was the dog that Anaximander had seen defeated that way.

If you have a long memory, you might recall that he had leapt in just that way at Mr Padge – and thus got himself shot. This was at the forefront of Anaximander's mind, so instead he ran directly into the fire a little to the left of the foot that Sharli was resting on the burning log. He flung himself through the flames, clamping his jaws down on her ankle as he passed, then snapping his neck around so that the full weight of him pierced her boot down to the talus and spun her leg out from under her, causing her to fall to her knee in the flames, screaming, entirely unable to riposte with her rapier. Moreover, it meant that the dog himself was not in the burning part of the fire, and anything the man by Clarissa might have attempted was obscured by an upwards billowing cloud of embers and smoke, confusing everyone. This was exactly what Anaximander had hoped and is an object lesson in why it is wiser to strike at non-fatal weak points, and to consider one's next moves rather than always to go for a direct kill in a fight against a skilled opponent.

What he had not considered, and this is because it is hard to know what someone you have never seen fight will do under the circumstances, is what the book, Adam, would do. He hadn't imagined there was anything he *could* do, fighting being a bodily activity, but that was to underestimate what a magical book is capable of.

Any magical book has within it spells, and Adam was made as a catalyst, one, incidentally, entirely immune to burning, as we saw before when he went with Nathan Treeves to kill the Mistress of Malarkoi, so he brought his catalysing powers to bear, burning up everything in the fire that could be burned up in a single moment, causing a deafening and blinding explosion of light and heat that left Anaximander and Bellows singed, and Sharli, who was in the epicentre of the blast, kneeling, scorched and hairless, blistered and furious, where the fire had been.

She dropped her rapier – it had absorbed so much heat that the pommel was burning in her hand – and clawed all over herself with her blackened fingers, pulling everything metal away from her – her throwing knives, her belt buckles, the poison needles in her sleeves, the necklace of steel links Deaf Sam had given her, her bracelets and bangles, her earrings and the rings of her many victims – and they burned the remaining skin from her fingertips.

Even her gold tooth she spat out, burned loose in its socket.

Bellows, not known for anything but the most secondary forms of violence, did not shrink from the fight. Though he was slight, he was cunning, and he took the spit he had earlier used for the rabbit and drove that into Sharli's back. Admittedly, he put it in the least useful place: there are many organs that are easily pierced, and which will end life sooner or later when

326

destroyed, and he missed all of these and hit her spine instead. Regardless, it is harder to fight a battle on multiple fronts than it is on one, and Anaximander had regained his feet, preparing to show this assassin the mercy of a quick death.

All the above was the work of a moment, and Deaf Sam was distracted enough not to even attempt to carry out Sharli's threat against Clarissa, and this gave the woman in question the chance to turn him to stone by uttering the final syllable of the spell she had been preparing.

In her childhood Clarissa had always found pleasure in the legend of a woman so ugly that to look upon her petrified a man. This she liked not for the reason that story was told – to make girls understand that it was their duty to be beautiful, and the perils of failing to attend properly to their looks – but because she thought that it was fitting that men who attempt to steal beauty from a woman should receive more than they bargain for – and so she used a spell which loosened the weft sufficiently to confuse the material realm in the volume of this man's existence with the certainty that instead of being made of flesh he was made of a quantity of granite. This is what Deaf Sam immediately became, ending his life.

When this was done there was a short period in which nothing happened physically, but there was much taking stock, and it was everyone's conclusion that, despite what an observer might have expected, the assassins had been routed easily, and there was nothing for Sharli to do but surrender, if she lived long enough to do that.

Anaximander, always eager to provide service, said, 'I can end this person's life very quickly. While she may not appear dangerous, my assumption is that she is an assassin in the previous employ of Mr Padge, most likely here on a long-standing commitment to revenge his killers – in this case the boy Bellows, who, while he did not provide the finishing blow, did at least distract Padge with his murderous employment of a magical concentrate. I doubt she would recant her ways, even at this late stage, and may well have recourse to small acts of aggression, the biting of a poison gas tooth, for example, or the ability to explode in the proximity of a foe.'

As the dog spoke, Clarissa came closer, staring all the while at the woman, who was on her side in the ash, breathing heavily. 'What are you?' Clarissa said, but it wasn't a question for Sharli as much as it was one for herself.

Sharli backed painfully away, but soon stopped when Anaximander barked a warning at her to stay still.

When Clarissa was within touching distance, the puzzlement left her face. 'She is a weft-replica,' she told Anaximander, although he didn't understand what that meant. 'You are a copy,' she said to Sharli, 'if that's any comfort to you. Your original has already died, or still lives, somewhere. You aren't real.' Clarissa turned her back on her and walked away. 'She won't be any trouble.'

Anaximander, looking back just in case, followed Clarissa. 'She did at last find out what fire is, first-hand,' he called after his service-pledge when he was at a safe distance, but she didn't seem to hear him.

Bellows picked up Adam, blew the ash from him, and followed the others.

Sharli remained to die there of her burns, something that inevitably happened shortly afterwards, watched over by the silent statue of Deaf Sam.

This deathly tableau provided a disturbing sight for another assassin, the Druze, when that neuter person arrived later, their magic paper having changed to indicate that Bellows and Clarissa were now the assigned targets.

No killer blanches much at the sight of death, but the scene that confronted the Druze did certainly influence the tactics they then went on to employ.

The sun rose slowly and in the weak light of the dawn – which for Anaximander was perfectly adequate, his other senses doing most of the work his eyes were spared, but which for Bellows was hardly enough, his arms held pre-emptively out in front of him when they were not trying to grab the dog's tail – Clarissa led them through the Island of White Hills until they came to a strange place.

'What,' Anaximander asked, 'is a weft-replica?' The question had been occupying his mind as he trotted along after Clarissa, down to the submerged forest, and no amount of considering the dictionary definitions of those terms had provided him with an answer.

If he expected Clarissa to satisfy his curiosity, though, he was mistaken. 'We don't have much time,' she said. 'If there's a contract on us, then there'll be others following behind.'

Anaximander cursed himself for not thinking of it. She was right, of course, and now, when he interrogated the sense-memories linked with the two who had attacked them he realised that there were five others like them, all probably in Padge's employ, although he imagined some would have been concentrating on finding the child Gam Halliday, whose knife thrust did the actual work of killing their employer.

They had risen by gentle ascents, but now she drew them down into a bowl between two high granite ridges like the backs of starved grey horses, spaced a mile or more apart. It seemed in the shadows these ridges made as if this bowl was filled with black oil, with thick tar, with congealed and darkened blood, its surface reflective and viscid, a petrified lake perfect in its flatness, except that spears erupted through it everywhere, the silent, stripped tops of dead trees. There had been a forest here, Anaximander guessed, one that was now almost entirely below the surface of a lake.

Clarissa went to the line where the ground met the water – for water it was, not oil, something Clarissa proved when she walked into it, so that it rose above her ankles easily, not struggling, like tar might. She turned to the two following her and said, 'The first time I came here was as a girl. It was called the Arboretum, then. I don't think it has a name now. I remember because that was also the first time I ever smoked. Behind the gift shop.' She frowned, put her hand to her temple, as if the memory gave her a headache. 'Such a long time ago. A different world.'

Anaximander, seeing she was in distress, ran to her side, and Bellows stumbled after him, but in the short period that facilitated their arrival she had pulled herself together, forcing a smile. 'Anyway, that's by the by,' she said. 'There's a cave system, down at the bottom. We need to find our way in.'

Anaximander sat at her feet and looked up at her. He paused, opened his mouth, shut it, then opened it again. 'While I am pledged to your service,' he said, eventually, 'I am not required by that pledge to execute my obligations blindly. You must know that I will do whatever you ask of me, almost without exception, and I ask that you repay this courtesy by taking me into your confidences. I am an intelligent being, and I do not enjoy being in ignorance. With these considerations foremost, I ask: what are you planning by coming here?' This said, he put out his tongue and breathed heavily over it, thereby cooling himself and indicating that he intended no further immediate conversation for his part.

Bellows scoffed, loudly. 'A dog should never place stipulations on his obedience! No! He should do without question what his mistress wishes, knowing that she exceeds him in her intellect, in her wisdom, and, most importantly, in her requirements, she having many where he should have none. Ignore him, madam, he—'

Clarissa interrupted him. 'Bellows,' she said, 'you don't seem to have learned your lesson yet.'

Bellows was chastened, and even went so far as to put his hand over his mouth. Clarissa came over to him and removed it. 'You can say what you like, boy. Just try make sure it's what you want to say, not what you think someone else wants to hear.' She turned away from him. 'The caves lead to a ceremonial chamber, a pocket of air surrounded by a rough sphere of stone, one of those geological quirks people like to come to visit. But I know what it was. What it is.' She paused and Anaximander waited.

Bellows, having thought of some other argument against the dog, began to make it, but Clarissa spoke over him. 'Most objects exist entirely in the material realm, but some powerful things have a dual existence – here and in another place. At the same time, most places are entirely in the material realm, but some powerful places have a dual existence too. If you know the INWARD EYE, if you can see the conditions of the weft, then the combination of a dual object and a dual place is quite distinctive. Like this glacial valley and its forested lake, it stands out.' She walked further out into the water until it was up to her thighs, and then she kneeled.

Reflexively, Anaximander lurched forward, his body thinking she might be in danger. His mind knew that she was not, so he stopped himself the moment he could.

Clarissa stayed there for a while, and then she put her face, slowly and carefully, down into the water, her eyes open and staring. She stayed there for thirty seconds, possibly a minute. Her hair surrounded her head, spreading on the pillow of the water. When bubbles of her breath broke the surface, she pulled herself out again. 'Down there is a magical thing, waiting. A relic from a past.'

At the edge of the lake the sense of another magical dog's presence was very strong to Anaximander. He went to Clarissa, and this time she anticipated his question.

'I looked for Sirius in the weft,' she said. 'I didn't find his presence here. There is something, though, and I am glad you're here.'

Again, Anaximander was filled with the warmth of her approbation. His ears picked up and he became alert to every possible nuance of what she was saying to him.

'I'll need you, where we're going,' she continued, 'My work's very nearly complete. I just need the relic, now, and everything will be fine.'

Again, Anaximander had no understanding of what she meant. 'What will you need me to do?' he said, the answer he requested not a means of deciding whether he'd do it, but more as a way of preparing himself to do the best possible job.

It seemed as if her mouth went dry, and she swallowed, but then she smiled and left the question unanswered.

XX

Her Enemy, Part Five

THE MIRROR MASTER had been suspicious about his
material status for a while.

Knowing himself as well as he did and doing exactly
what the other Master was doing while thinking he was the
prime, he had felt, on occasion, the sense that he was fate's
puppet, or that he was slightly too slow, or that he was not
himself when catching himself in a mirror. Whatever it was,
he had set up a tampering chime on his realm that would
recognise any attempt to synchronise this realm with any
other primary realm, and one day this had shone telltale red.

Both Masters had become lax of late with the oncoming of
the Assembly Crusaders, and had lessened the frequency of
their synchronisation regimens from daily to once every two
days, and the doubt the mirror Master had become infected
by was allowed to flourish into that wayward period when
two synchronised realms diverged by virtue of the nature of
the complexity of realm mirroring. When, by the third day,
the realms had not been synchronised, he had glimpsed the
other Master coming along the corridor through an accidental
transparency of a mirror, and had known, suddenly, that he
was a step behind. That was all it took to know that he was
not the prime. The mirror Sebastian set himself into action
with all their characteristic determination to win against a foe
or competitor.

Realm-mirroring is not entirely unreciprocal, and there are
spells to temporarily invert the mirroring, so first he took an
antidote, activated one of these spells, and then set to work
drinking as much of the Rescue Remedy as possible, the prime
Master mirroring him for a change. Then, he went to what he
thought was the original Manse but was clearly now revealed

332

to be a tertiary realm and lay down on a sofa until the prime Master fell into a Remedy coma, at which point he went to the real secondary vat room and resumed work. Admittedly he did, in a kind of depressive rage, spitefully deface his own manuscript, but one cannot expect to discover one has betrayed oneself without it having some effect on the mood. Once that was out of his system he calmed down, swore off ever using the Remedy again – at least in the same quantities – and from then on it was only a matter of keeping himself busy until the prime Master returned.

This could prove to be several weeks, his subjective time, he eventually realised, so after he'd made some progress with the Bellows work, he went to the same realm the Master was passed out in, into the same room, into dangerous proximity to him, and lit a rousing incense. Quickly back to the vat room, he bundled the almost finished Bellows under a settee, and went up into the vat where he waited, pistol in hand.

The rest has already been recounted, and now the mirror Master was the prime, and all that remained was to tidy up.

In all practical respects it was precisely as if nothing had happened – a prime and his mirror are near enough identical – that is the point, after all – and once the corpse was dissolved and flushed away, the necessary weft-resonances re-established, a re-sync performed on the real Manse, and some of the more egregiously angry edits to the manuscript reverted, business went on as usual. The Master altered the sizes of the decanter and cup for the Rescue Remedy down to a phial and a thimble, pulled the candidate out from under the settee and transferred him to vat nineteen, and soon even he forgot the swap.

There was nothing to remember – one man who already thought himself was still himself, the Crusade was still at his border, and the Tinderbox was still going to defeat them. That same man still pined for his Bellows, and the candidate was still almost finished. Admittedly the Bellows in front of him, blurry through the cold glass lid misted with his breath, was still mirrored in the tertiary vat room, and... Sebastian pursed his lips: that boy would still be in vat eighteen with no Master to move him on through the sequence.

The whole emotional engine behind this vat-work was the sympathy, unusually acute, that the Master felt for Bellows, and wasn't that orphaned replica candidate as much a Bellows-in-waiting as the one under this lid?

Vat nineteen was for annealing, something that could be assumed to be self-monitoring, so as soon as he was down, the Master translated himself back to the secondary realm, from there into the primary Manse, and out of that Manse to the tertiary vat room, each translation like a punch to the back of his head and with the same number of blows awaiting him on his return. When he stepped onto the bottom rung of the vat eighteen ladder, he missed it entirely and lurched forward, striking the vat with his forehead like a gong player strikes the boss, the same sound ringing out.

Whether it was the pain of this, or the translation sickness, is neither here nor there, but he had to pause, hands on his knees, breathing hard through his nose to prevent himself from vomiting. This went on long after the vat had stopped ringing, and even when he stood up straight again and fixed his gaze on the unwavering picture rail, he wasn't able to prevent his vision from swimming. With the antidote in his system, there was no amount of Remedy that could repair this, and as if to underline that thought the impairment alarm went off.

The Master ignored it. He ignored the swimming, and the ringing, and the sense that he was standing on a roundabout as it spun, and went as surely as he could up the ladder.

Inside the vat, the orphan replica candidate had begun to rot. His pale skin was tinged with varicoloured moulds like those that blossom on the skin of a forgotten orange. His fragile outline where it met the shadowed vat depths was – unless it was Sebastian's eyes crossing and uncrossing – losing solidity, wavering between something whole and something inchoate. And there was an odour, definite and uncomfortable, which made the Master turn away.

334

Some spells are very simple, some spells require work, and some spells are repeated so often that they become second nature. It was one of these last spells – *scourge* – that he cast as a reflex, and it filled the insides of the vat with something very like fire but which was made of the same kind of supernatural flux that a will-o'-the-wisp is made from. This emptied the vessel and Sebastian turned his back on it. In fact, he no longer had any use for the entire tertiary realm, so he collapsed it in on itself and found himself, punched again in the back of the head, in the Manse proper. Though it meant another blow, he went directly to the secondary realm, suffering another punch, and then another when he returned to the remaining vat room. These blows he took because he knew how much time would pass there in the annealer, and he couldn't risk another rotting Bellows.

The glowing of the sigils on vat nineteen indicated that there was still a little while left, and so the Master took the brief respite to empty his stomach behind a nest of tables.

Now, whenever he opened his eyes, there were two of everything, circling each other in figures of eight, and his stomach took this as a sign that he had eaten something that needed purging. There was nothing in there, but stomachs do not consider this an obstacle to their work – his squeezed itself into its smallest possible volume with a consistency and commitment that would have been impressive under other circumstances.

Sebastian groaned and clenched through an unpleasant quarter hour, sometimes barely able to catch his breath, mostly on his hands and knees, occasionally on his side. When he had the wherewithal, he made calculations as to when the antidote would wear off. Rescue Remedy had its dangers, but it also had its uses. And in small doses…

What ignominies a Master suffers on behalf of his servants. To go to these lengths on Bellows's behalf made him question who was the master and who was the servant. Surely the purpose of a servant is to relieve the master of his burden of work. What was this then? Wasn't it demeaning?

Sebastian got to his feet. He didn't care if it was demeaning. There was no one there to see, not even some mirror of him, and he went to vat twenty, which was filled past the brim with thousands of sheets of parchment with the life of the previous Bellows transcribed onto them on both sides – all his thoughts, dreams, hopes; all his education, reading, achievements; all his foibles, failings and fears – monitored and recorded by an invisible indentured telepathic homunculus employed for the purpose and sourced from a relatively material intermediate demon realm in the moment the original Bellows stepped from his vat. The Master set fire to these with a common or garden phosphorous match, and once the vat had begun to smoke, he battled his vertiginous nausea into abeyance and pulled the candidate over.

Why even call him the candidate, he thought, as he pushed him into the flames. There had only ever been time for this one. It was this one, or no one, and no sooner had this thought been formed than he remembered that he hadn't protected the candidate from burning. He cursed, knocked himself on the side of the head, as if yet another whack would correct the problems all the others had caused, and quickly made the sounds and gestures that would cause to form on the boy's skin a syrupy kind of wax that hardened on contact with heat into a sort of insulating meringue-like substance.

But it was too late. He knew it would be too late. What on earth was wrong with him? Why was he making so many errors?

Was this grief? He could scarcely remember the true emotions, the ones that predated God's death, but this one was difficult to forget entirely.

This was grief – a sort of repressed, disavowed, stifled grief – and it was affecting everything. The antidote would wear off any time now, and the Rescue Remedy would put pay to these thoughts, but while that was not the case, he remembered what it was like to grieve, and this was very like it.

The smoke puffed out in gasps from under the lid, rattling it quietly. Bellows was inside – his replacement – and even if all the memories, all the traits, all the everythings that Bellows had been were to properly embed in the candidate's sensorium, he would still not be Bellows.

Grief. It blinded you to everything.

The Master went to the table and took his thimble of Rescue Remedy. Then, when that wasn't a match for his thoughts, he took as many thimbles as he required to silence them.

Once the Remedy had taken effect, the Master reminded himself that the twenty-one-vat process was perfectly capable of replicating Bellows, and once the final vat had re-anchored the weft-resonances into the candidate there would be no difference, spiritual, physical or philosophical, between this Bellows and his Bellows. The Remedy, in one last thimbleful, convinced him of that and let him remain convinced as he took the scorched and waxy Bellows, now the size of a juvenile young man, to the final vat.

Sebastian had picked him up with the intention of taking him directly, but as he went the skin sloughed under the candidate's knees. That was how it felt – an odd and unnerving slippage that he couldn't immediately account for and which he needed, desperately, to ignore. Sometimes when a person wants something very badly and has worked very hard to get it, there is almost no lie he will not tell himself in the face of its apparent failure, even if he is otherwise a very sensible sort of person.

The Master told himself a lie like this – that he had felt nothing – and then, because he knew that lie would immediately be revealed if he did what he planned to do next – to mount the ladder and cure the child in Spark energy – he told himself another lie. This second lie – that the new Bellows should be dressed head to foot in the old Bellows's clothes prior to the final part of the process – meant that he put the boy down on the table and translated himself directly to Bellows's former room in the secondary antechamber Manse.

The other translations had felt like a blow to the head, but this one rattled his entire spine, sending waves of pain vibrating along every nerve. Like the ripples made by a pebble

337

in a still pond, these diminished immediately, but they were still there while he went through Bellows's things, selecting from the wardrobe all the necessary garments, though not worrying too much about collars and cuffs and socks, items that Bellows could attend to himself once he had left the final vat.

The ripples made it so that he didn't think too much about what these clothes would cover and didn't then draw a line of causation back to the sloughing, through that and to his own failure to prevent the burns the boy's history made on his skin. They were convenient in that way, and though the pain was worse when he translated back, oscillating his teeth until the pitch of the vibration blinded the place where his pineal eye would have formed, if there had been such a thing, this too made the rationale for the dressing obscure behind a general sense that he had decided to do something and now he was doing it.

He went back to the boy and pulled the underwear over his feet and up, eventually, past his thighs. He put on his string vest, slipped the sleeves of his shirt over his arms. Anyone who has cared for the young or the very old knows that this is a difficult business, but one that a carer can become skilled at, and while the Master couldn't remember for whom he had provided these services, he recognised that he must have done, because the proper ways came easily to him, as if they had been learned by long and wearisome repetition.

When the boy was dressed, he was, repressed knowledge aside, the spit and image of old Bellows. There was no hat, but otherwise all the attributes his manservant had possessed in the visual mode were there in this unconscious child – the proud jut of his nose blade, the recessed pigginess of his eyes, the counter-intuitive bending of his joints, the hedgerow tangle of his limbs, all finished with his expert and precisely tailored suiting. In the dressing, this 'candidate', this vat-boy, was now New Bellows for true. The Master's heart leapt to see it, the disappointments of the process of making him forgotten in this verisimilitude.

The Master swallowed and pre-emptively moved towards the table where the Rescue Remedy waited. It was as if his body knew what his mind was about to think, and if it did it was right. Verisimilitude. That was a quality a derivative thing possessed. Even perfect verisimilitude was derivative. This was a categorical truth, a priori, and to be derived from something was not the same as being it.

But the weft!

The weft. He knew the arguments, he knew the spells, he knew how to convince himself that the weft was what made Reality. Weft-resonance, weft-congruence, weft-bonding – they were all perfectly true and right, so much he had proved a thousand times in a thousand different ways... but a man who was born under God, with one immortal soul, in one mortal body, even if he goes on to see that God killed – it is hard to shake the conviction that the original thing is the real thing.

This Bellows wouldn't be needed if the other Bellows wasn't dead. Only his grief insisted otherwise. That a copy could be made, joined with the weft-state, wasn't this a very convenient truth to believe? And himself, a derivative Master, the original one headless and dissolved, formless and flushed into the nothingness that the pipes entered?

His body was right. It had known that this line of reasoning would emerge, and it had shown him how to counter it. Sebastian completed his body's plan and went to the table and poured and drank thimble after thimble of the Remedy. Mind-body dualism: it was a false division. When the mind was incapable of providing the certainty a man required, it must allow the body to make up the deficit. What is one without the other anyway? There cannot be a separation. To imagine a body without a mind and a mind without a body is a nonsense!

He turned and picked up New Bellows again, walked him to the final vat.

It was as he was doing this, oblivious to anything but the denial of his grief, his rationality and the futility of his own second-hand existence, that the divine creature that Sirius had become – Goddog, as he was sacrilegiously to be known by the Assembly – erupted into the centre of the vat room, biting, scattering the huge copper vessels as if they were bowling pins. He growled a growl so deep that it made the entire realm vibrate, and he bit the first thing that was biteable. This thing was the candidate, the boy, the replica, and because the dog's maw had grown giant it was enough to sever New Bellows in two, tearing through his recently buttoned jacket and waistcoat, shredding his shirt and his string vest, splattering the Master with a terrible spray of gore.

XXI

Her Heir, Part Four

JAPALURA'S LAST THOUGHT wasn't a word; dragons do not use words and so cannot think with them. Dashini was filled instead with shadows, and that was how she began to understand what was happening on the levels.

She, Prissy and Gam arrived through the Door to the fourth level of the Golden Pyramid of Malarkoi just after its sunset. The moon was rising over a dark forest, perhaps five, perhaps ten miles across, a bare-topped mountain at its centre. In the sky the stars were blurred in their firmament, glittering lazily as if they had lost the will to shine consistently.

There was a path down from the Door, into the trees, and Dashini wasted no time following it. 'Ygrayne!' she called. 'Gorlois!' When there was no reply, she ran on further, shouted the words again.

There was still no reply, no sound at all.

Prissy and Gam didn't know what she was saying, but Dashini didn't give them time to find out. 'Come on,' she told them. 'We need to get out of here as soon as we can.'

Prissy galloped after her, Gam trudging behind. 'What happens if we don't?'

Dashini didn't turn back. 'Shadows,' she said.

The path led directly into the forest – verdant, dense, resin-scented – and then, after a few minutes, to a ramshackle village that had been built amongst the trees. It was mostly lean-tos and simple shelters made from sticks and leaves, gathered. In the centre was a firepit surrounded by stones. It smoked quietly to itself, warming a metal stewpot hanging from a tripod.

The moonlight through the branches cast shadows in the near darkness. They swayed strangely in ways not entirely caused by the movement of the wind, and there didn't seem to be anything else around to account for it. Dashini bit her lip and held her breath and waited until she was certain.

Soon she was. 'Gather wood,' she said, 'and stoke up that fire. We need to keep it light.'

Gam and Prissy ignored her. The three of them had eaten nothing but cactus and raw root tubers for days and the other two fell on the stewpot. In it was a ladle and thick broth with cubes of meat. One after the other, they tipped it into their faces, chewed and drank and wiped their cheeks.

'Aren't you going to have anything?' Prissy called to Dashini, between gulps.

Dashini brought branches and twigs back from the shadows and threw them onto the fire. It blazed up, lighting the clearing, carving out some lit space from the darkness.

Gam emptied some of the stew into a carved bowl, circled the fire, and handed it to Dashini. 'What's wrong with it?' he said.

She didn't understand what he meant at first, but he pointed about the place they were in. 'It's a Druid village,' Dashini replied, picking out a piece of meat from the stew with her fingers and making herself eat it.

Prissy went to one of the shelters. 'Empty. Where's all the Druids?'

Dashini chewed for a moment and then spat gristle into the fire. Ash and sparks billowed up. 'Dead,' she replied, 'unless I'm mistaken.'

Prissy and Gam looked at each other. 'Sounds about right,' Prissy said. She wandered off, away from the fire, curious about the rest of the village, but Dashini ran over to her, pulled her back.

'Keep by the fire,' she said.

'Why?'

Before she could answer, through the undergrowth came a slowly rolling skull, its skin seemingly gnawed off, the stump of its spine rustling the fallen leaves. After the skull came a mass of innards, moving like a huge slug, and then a ribcage. 'That's a Druid,' Dashini said. 'Its remains. It won't hurt you.'

Gam froze as part of it oozed over his boot.

Prissy kicked it away from him. 'Why is it moving?'

Dashini didn't answer, but took a burning branch from the fire, held it in front of her, and led the two into the forest.

They walked through the trees, and everywhere they went pieces of things moved through the undergrowth. There was a patch of ground on which intestines were gathering, here was a scalp, matted hair wrapping itself around a bone. Everywhere smelled like a butcher's back room, catching the back of their throats, making them breathe mostly through their noses.

In the light of the burning branch everything danced, and the shadows encroached on them strangely, almost right but not quite, nearly moving under their own will. When they got too close, Dashini waved the fire at them, and they retreated.

Then, there was a wolf.

It was bigger than any dog they'd ever seen, Sirius and Anaximander included, rearing up on its hind legs in an impossible posture, a statue balanced on the tips of its rear paws, completely still. Its fur was white from snout to tail, but wet with blood. This blood was the only thing that moved on it, creeping like treacle down to the ground, where it made its way to a gathering pool.

'Let's get back to the fire,' Dashini said.

'Heaven's gone sour again?' Prissy said, when they were back.

Dashini looked into the fire. 'Gam, get more wood, please. Quickly.'

Prissy expected Gam to object – he wasn't the kind of boy you could boss around like that – but his mind must have been elsewhere, because he did as he was told.

'This is the realm of the Wolf Pack and the White Stag,' Dashini said. 'Day belongs to the wolves – they use it to hunt – and the night belongs to the stag. It bathes in the moonlight. Both should be overseen by the Druids, keeping everything in balance, but something has made the wolves kill them all.

The stag is resurrecting the Druids, slowly, making their parts reincorporate. But until whatever is goading the wolves is removed, they'll just get killed again at daybreak.'

'So, what's goading them?'

'The shadows,' Dashini said. 'I think it's the shadows.'

Between the trees the light from the fire was weak, picking out some surfaces of things but leaving most of them in darkness. Gam turned back and there were the two girls, silhouettes edged in flames.

Beside them, deep and black, were Joes. Their bodies. The fire-light didn't affect them at all; they seemed to suck it in, dousing it with their death. Gam's normal eye couldn't make out their features, but the new one could. Even in the perfect blackness his half vision could discriminate detail in their expressions. They were jealous of the living, their mouths contorted with hunger for life, with anger at the injustice. Both Joes reached, their hands clutching claws, grabbing at the girls' faces.

Gam dropped the wood he had been told to gather, and Joes heard him. They turned away from the fire, saw him in the darkness, came for him, moving as slowly as corpses, judging him as they came, knowing him, understanding his guilt. They were going to bring him to book. Punish him.

You deserve it, the shadows thought.

Die, the shadows whispered silently.

Gam would have done it, if he could have, but Prissy saw him now and she came out from the fire.

'Stop pissing about, Gam, and bring that wood over here!' She waited for him to do it, but he didn't move. She hates you, they thought. We all hate you.

Prissy knelt down and picked up the branches. She stood back up and pushed the wood into his stomach. 'You expect me to do everything.'

Gam nodded, mutely, and walked back to the fire.

Prissy went from hut to hut, a burning log from the fire keep-ing the shadows at bay, and gathered rags, sticks and cooking fat to make proper torches, one each, so they could explore the forest.

Gam took his in silence, but Dashini and Prissy made up for it, talking everything through. They saw five other wolves between them and the mountain, and countless dead things in various states of dismemberment. The closer the mountain got, the more dead things there were, not living but always moving, always coming together, streams of blood lubricating them.

If the children slipped on a liver, or on an eye, or in a puddle of lymph, it left their boots cleanly when they stepped out of it. It wanted to go back to the rest of itself, from wherever it had come.

That's how it seemed.

The girls were similarly unaffected by all this death, its gore leaving their minds as clean as their boots, but even with the torch, even under the moonlight, Joes were always at the corner of Gam's sight.

He patched his new eye with the palm of his hand.

'There he is,' Dashini said.

The mountain was forested until the peak, which was a bald patch of rock. Dashini pointed, and there was the White Stag, pale as chalk, pacing a circle that let him see his whole realm. At the middle of his route was the Door.

'Let me try something,' Dashini said. She handed Prissy her torch. 'He knows me. I should be able to go to him.'

Dashini walked slowly and carefully out from the trees, holding her breath, but the moment her shadow touched the bare outcrop of rock, the Stag's head went up, its ears flicked, and the moon was suddenly back at the horizon.

They were on the path down to the village where Gam and Prissy had eaten the stew, and the skull with a bit of spine had rolled towards them.

'I thought so,' Dashini said, as if suddenly appearing somewhere else was completely normal. 'The shadows have spooked him.'

She led them back down to the firepit, took another carved bowl, ladled herself some stew, and explained it to the other two.

The White Stag was easily startled. It was the same for all deer – their lives depend on it – but for a god in the form of a stag, startling didn't result in him running. Instead it made him revert the realm to a place he was happier with.

Dashini told them about the weft-states and intermediate realms, about the White Stag's particular ability, about his priority of will over the reality of this place, about the re-establishment of former reals. 'If we're ever going to leave here, we need to get to the Door without him noticing us. If he does, he'll startle, and we'll come straight back here.'

Gam wasn't listening – in the forest Joes was waiting in the dark – but Prissy said, 'That doesn't seem so difficult, not compared to the first level, or the third.'

'It shouldn't be difficult at all,' Dashini replied. 'None of this should be.'

'Let's try, then. Perhaps we'll just be able to go straight out.'

Dashini shrugged, and a voice in the back of her head said it wouldn't work.

They reached the clearing again, and the Stag was facing the other way. Prissy turned to Dashini and whispered the beginning of the sentence – 'Shall we make a run for it?' – but she only got as far as making a 'ssh' shape with her mouth when the stag bolted.

Back in the village, everything was the same as it had been – the cubed meat, the empty huts, the body parts moving by themselves, Gam sullen and silent. Prissy made torches again, and set off into the forest again.

The wolves were in different places, in different postures, but otherwise it was all the same. They got to the base of the mountain, Dashini lay the torch gently on the ground, and up at the peak the Stag was circling.

This time everyone agreed not to say anything, but when they weren't even halfway up the mountainside Gam stood on a branch hidden beneath a pile of leaves and it made a crack. This must have set the Stag off because back they were again, on the path down to the village, the smell of stew in the air.

They did all the same things again: torches, stew, the same route to the mountain, the positioning of the wolves the only difference, avoiding the branch this time. They each took off their boots and toed the ground ahead of them so they didn't make a sound – but then they were back on the path to the village for no obvious reason.

It's not possible to get physically tired on the re-establishment of similar weft patterns, since the muscles are mostly returned to the resting state they enjoyed before the change, only the mind, the internal states of which will tend to carry over regardless of the material repetition – it functions through the immaterial concepts that the White Stag did not have the power to affect – eventually becomes exhausted and confused. That brief period of memory that pertains to the previous world before it is removed and becomes something that cannot properly be said to have existed is enervating and depressive of the morale, even when the muscles are as willing as they ever were.

'What happens if we wait until morning?' Gam said, after ten, perhaps twelve attempts.

'You know the body parts?' Dashini replied. 'They're reforming into Druids and animals. To answer your question, Gam, in the morning the wolves will wake up and make anyone and anything in this realm back into body parts again.'

'We've got no choice, then,' he said.

'Not unless you like getting ripped to pieces.'

They made, in various orders, sometimes forgetting the strategies were doomed to failure and so repeating them:

Hundreds of attempts at sneaking to the Door, none of which ever got within fifty feet of success.

Many, many attempts to kill the stag from a distance with weapons. First, they used their knives and whatever clubs and coshes Gam had secreted about him, but when those didn't seem to be any use, they tried others made from the forest: strong bows and arrows tipped with toadstool scrapings, stones flung from slings made from their ripped clothing, ingenious trebuchets constructed from supple trees made to bend enough to launch rocks higher than the stag could see. It always sensed the danger at the last moment, rendering their work of hours entirely redundant.

Several attempts, suggested by Prissy, at digging a tunnel to the Door, under the places where the stag was standing. These were promising at first, but they failed each time; the stag sensed vibrations and startled.

They tried disguises of all sorts – of wolves, of stags, of the prey of wolves, of the animal associates of stags, thinking that, if they only looked sufficiently like animals, the stag would let them pass. But the White Stag could tell the difference and startled again.

They covered themselves with organs and bones and blood and moved as if they were flowing together like the corpses did, and while this got them closer, there always came a time when they needed to break their disguise so they could reach the Door, and when they did, he would startle.

They mimicked the call of another stag, so that the White Stag might be distracted, but the sound of another stag startled him.

They did a hundred other things, a hundred other times, but the White Stag was so easily startled that none of them worked, and they always ended up back on the path.

To say that Prissy and Dashini dealt with the situation well would be wrong – they both suffered as anyone would – but Gam took it the worst. Every day his visions of Joes became more real to him, were more pervasive, more vivid, and because he never slept, he never dreamed, and because dreams are cures for waking anxieties, his guilt and horror became ever worse, until, almost always, he stared at the Nathan Knife, stared at the moving viscera, stared at the wolves, and listened to the voices from the shadows, wishing him dead.

The solution came to Prissy just before dawn. They had arrived, after so many failed tries, at a point where they would sit, unhappily and restlessly thinking, sometimes all night, sometimes right up until the rising of the sun, surrounded with Druids and animals almost raised up from their deaths, until someone mustered the will to startle the stag and take things back to the beginning.

Prissy had been imagining birds pecking worms from the Living Mud and thinking back to her days at the Temple of the Athanasians. There she'd seen many girls startle, and once she'd seen a pigeon startle on a windowsill as it was eating the seed that she'd put out for it.

In a history of Prissy's life, she would have raised a finger and cried out at this point, remembering this pigeon. But she didn't. It took quite a long while for the beginnings of her revelation to cohere in her mind, and even then she wasn't sure she'd found the solution at all.

It would, though, prove to be the way out.

'What do you reckon a pigeon wants?' she said, as much to herself as to the other two.

Gam looked up from his poking of the logs, his face solemn in the light. 'What pigeon?'

Dashini said nothing, but they could tell she was listening because she had developed a nervous tic – fanning out her feathers and then smoothing them down, over and over – and she suddenly stopped doing it.

A log crackled and sputtered in the fire, sending smoke up. Prissy coughed and wiped her eyes and moved over so the wind wasn't blowing the smoke in her face. 'This pigeon at the Temple. It was pecking seed and then it heard a noise, and it flew off. What does it want?'

Gam and Dashini didn't say anything, waiting for Prissy to answer her own question. Time passed though, and she didn't say anything. Gam cleared his throat to ask her what the hell she was going on about, when she said, 'It wants a bit of privacy, that's what it wants. It wants to be left alone to peck its seed without noises startling it. Right?' This time

349

she didn't wait for them to answer and went on, hurriedly, speaking as quickly as she was thinking. 'And maybe that's what the stag wants. Maybe he's shy. He certainly acts shy. We reckon he's up there, looking down on his kingdom, protecting his realm, when perhaps he just feels surrounded by wolves and corpses and shadows and all of them lot. Perhaps he's as timid as the pigeon. Perhaps he'd like a bit of privacy, so he can come down off his peak and do whatever it is he wants to do without anyone interrupting him. Right?'

Now Gam and Dashini were getting it. It would be wrong to say that it excited them, her idea – their thoughts by now were shadow-black – but it was something they hadn't thought of, and now in the light of the fire their faces were turned to her, the endless enervation of repetition, at least, gone from their expressions.

Prissy went on. 'What if we move the wolves away? Because, I don't know much about it, so tell me if I'm wrong, but wolves eat stags, don't they? What if they weren't there? What if we put them far away where he wouldn't see them? I reckon he might come down, peck his seeds or whatever his nature tells him to do. Then we run up behind him while he's otherwise engaged and get to the Door. What about that?'

Gam, whose black thoughts had already seen the conclusion of the plan where Prissy hadn't, said, 'It's got to be worth a go, hasn't it?' and Dashini, whose thoughts were as black as his, said, 'I think it might work,' and so it was that they found their way out.

There was no argument from the shadows.

For the next few nights, they reconnoitred the mountain.

There were never fewer than ten wolves on the mountain-side, sometimes as many as twenty, but most of those were towards the base, with fewer higher up. Dashini suggested a couple of reasons for this, but the most convincing one was that if wolves got too close to the stag it startled, stopping their feeding, so they'd learned not to get too close. This, she said, if it was true, was good. It meant that there was a distance

350

beyond which the stag couldn't sense the wolves. If they could move them past it, then the stag wouldn't startle.

Moving the wolves was more of a problem. They could be tipped over, but they were very heavy and so tended to fall with a thud that startled the stag. If they were on all fours, this wasn't such an issue: then the three of them could push and pull the wolf over to the nearest stream of blood, which acted as a lubricant, allowing them to ease it down the mountainside. The wolves that reared up would always fall when moved, making a noise that startled the stag unless they were supported on the way down. This involved makeshift ropes and cushioning, the raw materials for which could be salvaged from the Druid village – but it was time-consuming, and if there were more than two rearing wolves it proved impossible to do the work before sunrise.

The difficulties were many, but none of them were insurmountable, and one night, they got lucky.

They gathered the materials for the ropes, baffles for wolf impact, and the leathery green leaves that could be used to make an easier surface to drag wolves along, and carried them to the mountainside.

There was the White Stag, silently pacing the mountaintop in the moonlight, as it always did, and when they surveyed the mountain for wolves there were fifteen, which was quite a lot, but all but one of them were on what they'd come to think of as the north side. The other was on its own on the south side.

This kind of distribution had never happened before; the wolves had always been almost evenly spaced. Dashini had said this meant that each wolf had its own territory, but this time they had gathered as if they had been fighting, their faces snarling angrily.

Perhaps the shadows had got to them too, made them fight amongst themselves.

'This is it,' Dashini whispered. 'We move the wolf down the hill as far as we can. The stag, if we're right, will come down the south side, do, as Prissy says, whatever it wants to do, and we'll have time to make it to the Door.'

'What are we waiting for?' Gam said. He was hollow-eyed, as he always was now, haunted-looking, and so the others couldn't see this, he paced away into the forest in the way they had all learned was fast and quiet.

Dashini and Prissy went after him.

There were no cracked branches, no unexpected startlings, even the wolf was easier to drag this time, it being frozen flat to the ground, gnawing something that had since slid away to become alive again.

Once it was done, they circled around to the north side of the mountain, made their way as close to the clearing as they dared, slowly as they dared, expecting to see the stag and for it to see them.

It wasn't there.

It must have, as they'd hoped, left the mountaintop, left the vicinity of the Door, gone down the wolf-less south side, just as Prissy had said it would, like a pigeon that needed its privacy.

After so many failures, Prissy couldn't believe it. Tears pricked at her eyes, and she turned to the others to confirm that what she was seeing was real.

They were looking at each other, these two, darkly. They had sad and serious faces and before she could ask them what was wrong, they grabbed hands and ran for the Door.

At first Prissy didn't understand. She thought perhaps they were trying to leave her behind, that they'd had enough of her, but then Dashini took the Nathan Knife from her belt as she ran, and Prissy realised what they were doing.

She should have known it all along. It was obvious. Completely and utterly obvious. She was an idiot! She'd come up with the plan that had killed her friend.

Prissy ran after them, saw Gam pull up by the Door, sink to his knees.

The sacrifice – they needed a sacrifice to open the Door – and Gam was it. Happy to be it, trusting Dashini's mother to make up for Joes, to stop his guilt.

352

Dashini pulled Gam's head back by the hair and Prissy screamed.

She screamed and screamed loud enough that she should have startled the stag. She ran screaming for Gam, hoping the god would make it moonrise again, and put them all back on the path to the village.

But the stag didn't hear her – it was too far down the mountain, too involved with its business so endlessly frustrated – and while Prissy screamed Dashini muttered and gestured and slit Gam's throat, freeing his Spark, opening the Door to the fifth level.

353

XXII

A Description of a Fight from Two Perspectives, Part One

THE MASTER, for all his repressed grief, was not the kind of man who was slow to realise when a fight had started.

When he was a boy, another boy came up to him when he was bicycling home from school. This boy, whose name was Dean, would bully the other children out of their dinner money and now he intended to steal Sebastian's satchel, or so it seemed to the young Master. Dean dragged the bag by its strap from Sebastian's shoulder as he innocently pedalled by, causing him to skid over and to scrape his bare right knee.

A slower child might have stopped to look at this new wound, might have cried to see the gravel embedded in it, the blood prickling up, but Sebastian knew that there was a wrong to be righted first. Though this Dean was several inches both taller and wider than his victim, he soon found himself with the Master's satchel strap around his neck. The bully's eyes bulged, his capillaries ruptured, and though little Sebastian stopped short of throttling the other child entirely to death, he did leave a very marked impression on Dean, particularly on the skin around his neck.

The boy never bullied him again.

Later, when the Master was an adolescent, similar things happened – fisticuffs over a debt, revenge over a slight, a slapped face over a twisted arm – then later still, as an adult, a knife drawn to punish a rival suitor, the shoving of a man into a canal, a headbutt that knocked someone's front teeth out. Before none of these actions was there any undue pause, nor when, eventually, Sebastian Cope graduated to murder did he hesitate. All this was before he learned about the weft and how it might be manipulated to adjust the progress of time.

Too late, of course, was his spell – the inappropriately named, but nonetheless useful, *Languorous Extension of a Pleasant Afternoon* – to save New Bellows, who now lay in two pieces on the floor in front of them, but it did give the Master a moment to prepare his counterattack.

The dog he recognised. It was one of a pair, made for the purpose of reading the future. This dog was constructed around a mystical organ of the Master's own devising that saw potential outcomes in the material realm from interventions in the other realms. This dog couldn't understand what it saw, nor communicate it, so it was paired with another dog who could understand and could also speak. That way, the Master's thinking had been, neither dog was overly powerful, since a creature who could divine, understand and communicate the future would be dangerous, whereas one that could only do half of those things was more manageable.

In any case, there was only so much one could achieve with a dog's natural being, and to cram it full of both a mystical organ and a man's brain was to stretch it beyond its capabilities. Also, mystical visions and reason are hard to reconcile, reason having the tendency to overwrite everything with logic and mysticism tending to cause the disease of irrationality.

Unfortunately, the experiment had been a failure. The one dog – was its name Snap? – couldn't be made to concentrate on the things the Master wanted it to concentrate on – so he had put them both to other uses. Now here was the mystical half of the pair, returned huge and vibrating with divine power. How exactly it had found its way into the vat realm was a mystery, but here it was.

The Master watched the languorously extended enthusiasm with which the huge dog crunched down on half of what remained of New Bellows. The candidate's skull popped slowly between the intruder's rear teeth like a shelled pea, and his ribs and spine, glossy and red, dropped their slow journey to the floor.

While, as has been established, he was not a man who waited to join a fight, nor was he one of those people who wasted his effort needlessly. Some people, when attacked, will go entirely crackers, risking their own safety in intemperate action, flailing their fists and kicking out when a slap would do, and end up hitting a brick wall and fracturing their wrist – the Master was not a person like that. He got the measure of a situation instead and used the bare minimum energy to get what he wanted. This was a kind of rule for him, a principle, and it was based, he knew, on a kind of narcissism – it is only those who have a very low opinion of their own abilities who expend themselves entirely at every slight, and Sebastian knew the extent of his abilities very well. So, he decided he would use his gun – the one he had used to destroy the head of his predecessor Master – on the dog, as he had seen Heartless Harold Smyke do with other dogs on several occasions, and thereby put this thing down.

He drew the gun, cocked it, fired it, and the bullet shot slowly towards a spot on the bridge of the dog's snout, between its eyes.

A little while earlier, Nathan had seemed to call, 'Here, Sirius! Here, boy!' to Sirius through a rift in the real. This the white bitch, avatar of the Mistress of Malarkoi, had made, and had so given Sirius access to the intermediate realm to which the Master had translated himself, where he was hid and worked on his new Bellows. Sirius had bounded through the rift, looking for Nathan, but there instead was a man. In Sirius's confusion, he'd bitten it, at first feeling it must be his enemy.

Before he could register that it was not, Sirius was struck with enormous force directly above the nasoincisive notch by the Master's bullet.

Sirius reeled back, rising onto his hind legs like a dog begging for a treat, his paws held out in front of him, a gurgling and plaintive whine arising from his throat.

This should have been, as anyone who has watched a dog shot that way will know, the end of him, and even someone who has never seen a creature dispatched by firearm will guess that nothing shot in the head can thrive. Even a chicken, who can live for a while in a state of decapitation, and who can run around the farmyard to the amusement of onlookers, eventually falls on its side and will never again regain its feet.

Sirius, though, by virtue of his consumption of God-Flesh, was not like a mundane animal. Just as a piece of a holy relic is the same as the whole relic because it is divine in whole and in part, he was himself existent in this way. His brain, into which the bullet had passed, was not the host of his undying soul. Rather, the material representation of him was now an impingement of his immaterial concept into this intermediate realm facilitated by his weft-form, so while a normal dog would have died from the shot, Sirius did not, since the divine Sirius, in its conception, was not a god in the form of a huge dog with a bullet in its brain but was, instead, a god in the form of the particular incidence of Sirius at the moment of his consumption of sufficient God-Flesh to render him divine – a state in which no bullet was present at all. Where the bullet now was, and along the path it had made through the dog's face, there came into existence the concept of his flesh made light. This was done by a process like that which had made a spectral limb of Nathan's wounded arm, and like that which had made Nathan become insubstantial through unrestrained use of his Spark energy. But, where Nathan was not a god, only the material instance of an albeit unprecedented Spark Inheritance, Sirius was divine, which is qualitatively and quantitatively different. He, not enjoying the presence of the bullet in his brain, also willed instinctively that it was no longer there, and because what a god wills can come to pass, his head returned to the way it was before, albeit dizzied by the process.

When his eyes uncrossed, and he looked around him, there was the Master – a man he knew from his previous experience of him. He was moving in a blur, doing something at a speed Sirius found irritating, and so he barked with such volume that it deafened the entire realm, even those senseless things like objects. A dog's bark is also an expression of his will – a

357

dog will bark because he wishes to be let out, or because he wishes to be paid attention to, or because he wishes an unwelcome intruder to leave – and Sirius's will was that the Master should not move with such irritating speed, and because he was a god, his will came to pass, so the Master slowed down to a less troubling tempo. This was sufficient for Sirius to lunge for him, seize him in his jaws, and clamp down hard on him.

When the dog did not die as he'd expected and hoped, the Master, still under the effects of the languorous extension, knew that other tactics would need to be employed. It was clear, from the defensive evolutionary dematerialisation of the thing's head, that he was dealing with an opponent with weft defences, possibly a god. Narcissistic as he might have been, Sebastian knew when he was under-equipped, so he turned to defensive measures.

The vat realm's function was to facilitate the making of New Bellows. He hadn't thought it necessary to provide it with any other function than that. A realm has certain qualities – the passage of its time relative to the material realm being an obvious one – but there are other things a realm can possess too. This one was very porous to the ingress of Spark energy, as was the antechamber realm his quarters in the Manse occupied. But the opposite could also be the case. As a weft-manipulator, Spark-resistant realms were extremely useful – powerful but capricious objects could be placed in them safely, for example – and where better to put a divine dog than in one of these? Once in there he could, at the absolute last resort, retrieve the locket, remove the quarantine, and use the Tinderbox to dissolve the creature into nothingness.

Extreme, but effective.

With this knowledge in place, in the confidence of his eventual victory, the Master could consider other less definite solutions to the problem which weren't so expensive, but the first step was to relocate this thing to a more appropriate realm. He took the chime that allowed the translation to the vat realm and began retuning it to the realm in which he stored the most Spark-sensitive artefacts – the *White Book* of Ibn Ghazi, jars containing six of the nine surviving Delphic nymphs, a Pontificus sanglor, that type of thing – when he realised he needed to use a tool he had on the bench.

The dog was up on its haunches still, its head scarcely half solidified, stretching the extent of the realm up, dragging the angles of the room's walls, and because he was looking at it, and still feeling the worse for wear, the Master tripped over part of a shattered vat base and fell forward, the chime skittering over the tiles then under a pile of tumbled equipment and furniture that itself was becoming stretched by the deformations this thing was making to the very limited extents of everything.

The Master cursed – there was a long rip from the knee of his left trouser leg down to the hem, and below that a graze on his shin. He sat down, licked a finger, and cleaned out some dark grit that had gathered in a patch of now raw skin, forgetting in a haze of Rescue Remedy, recent memories, and exhausting new events exactly what he was supposed to be doing. The grit was deep at one edge, forced below some otherwise undamaged skin, so he tried to edge it out with a thumbnail. That only made it go in deeper. Did he have a penknife? Probably. On the bench?

In answering this question, he was reminded of the chime, and then of the fact that he didn't have it. Wearily, he forced himself up, the leg of his trousers flapping, and went as quickly as his protesting body would allow over to where the chime must have gone.

Behind him – he could feel the thing's breath gathering on the back of his neck – the dog's head was coming back. There was the chime, over in the corner. No real problem to get, but as he manoeuvred himself into a position where he could lean over and reach it, his ripped trousers caught on something – a loose plank, half a chaise longue, a nest of tables, there was no telling in the mess the damned dog had made – and he managed to trap himself in the corner of the room, which was no longer at the proper ninety-degree angles that make up a cube but was more like the shape a jelly makes when it's out of its mould, wobbling on a plate.

He picked up the chime and turned back and now, languorous extension or not, he was going to have to get a move on, because the dog was shaking its almost reconstituted head, saliva and blood spraying in leisurely arcs in every direction.

New Bellows was at its feet.

The Master bit his lip, ran for the table and applied the electric fork to the chime base, tuning it in like his father had tuned in the wireless radio, looking for the right frequency in the sea of static.

Like that radio – probably not accidentally – the Master's fork had numbers, and while the number for the realm he was looking for was constant, the Master's memory could never encompass it. Numbers – there's no content to them. You can't remember them. 107.4? 102.9? 275? What's the difference?

The dog's eyes were clearing and now he knew he had no choice but to take the chime, take the tuning fork, and run for the ring binder that he kept the list of realms in. Then he'd have to look up the right one's page in the index and check its frequency. So that's what he did.

Except the filing cabinet wasn't where it was supposed to be, and now, as the dog took a huge breath inward, he ran about looking for the bloody thing.

He found it just as the dog barked so loudly that his ears almost burst and, in the sudden end of the languor, its jaws came rushing down at him like a hideously fast, hideously silent mantrap, so he dialled a random number and went with that.

A dog, biting down on something, closes his eyes and expects it to crush between his teeth. If it does not crush, he expects it to squelch, or perhaps to clang. He prefers for it to crush, will be pleased if it squelches, does not enjoy it if it clangs – because the thing is made of something too hard to bite – but what he will not accept is if his teeth clack together around nothing. This means he has missed his target, and because the target is likely to remain nearby it makes him bite again and again until he feels the crush, squelch or clang he is expecting. Sirius felt his teeth clack and so he bit and bit and bit again.

None of his bites met resistance of any kind.

He opened his eyes and now he was in a dark and dingy place into which so little light came he was unable to make out anything much, certainly not the place where the Master was. He turned, in case the world was different in a different direction, but it wasn't – everywhere was the same – dark and close, stuffy and quiet, black in his mystical organ, futureless and plain.

He circled first one way, and then the other. He ran to the extent of the place in one direction, and then in the other. There was nothing to see, nothing to smell, nothing to know.

Dogs left alone will keen, and this is what Sirius did. They will miss the dogs of their acquaintance, since they are pack-dwelling animals, and this Sirius did too. They will long for the things they desire, and Sirius was no different, despite his divinity. Indeed, his divinity made him do these things to the absolute limit of their ability to be done, since he was the god of dogs, possessed of the maximum extent of all their traits.

His keening was at a pitch so high and heart-rending, his loneliness so profound, his longing so precise, and all these things divinely charged, that the realm itself could not contain them, since it was not designed for these things, and no god can exist in a place that cannot contain it because a god is a type of being who determines what a place is, not the other way round. It is not that there is a heaven, and that makes a god, or that there is a hell, and that makes a devil. Gods and devils make places they like to live by the power of their wills, places being mostly neutral, and so it was that Sirius collapsed the realm that he was in, tearing it to pieces with the force of his loneliness.

XXIII

Boy, Book and Dog, Part Five

CLARISSA EXPLAINED that she couldn't replace the lake water with air using her weft-magic because that would require a great deal of Spark energy and a more thorough knowledge of the conditions of the weft as it related directly to the extent of the water's existence in the material realm than she could possess without scrying, which she'd never been any good at. None of the three had any real understanding of what she meant by this, but why would they? She was one of the very few in the world still alive who knew how weft-magic worked, and they shouldn't expect to know, should they?

So, what was her solution? She had a perfectly workable plan. It required Anaximander to swim down under the water and drag her behind. She would then replace the exhausted air in their lungs with fresh air from the weft, which was much less Spark-intensive and would use fewer Sparklines because the volume was so small, and because she was always within the necessary anchor radius she could remain in her trance and repeat the spell ad infinitum.

Bellows could come or stay as he wished, and Adam too. After the recent fireside events both decided to go with her. Even though the process seemed dangerous and worrisome, the idea of being at the mercy of further assassins without the protection of friends seemed more dangerous and worrisome still.

The two people who wore clothes stripped down to their underwear, and Clarissa made whispered instructions to Anaximander about where he should swim. He, having absolute faith in his service-pledge, was very calm, but Bellows and Adam shared their own whispers, which were considerably more anxious.

There was no need to wait, so they all waded out into the moonlit water, Clarissa holding Anaximander's tail, Bellows holding her free hand and Adam clutched at his waist. They would have seemed vulnerable, this unprotected chain, shivering, reflected in the still lake surface, had there been anyone there to see them. There was not, yet, since the names and places on the Druze's paper had only very recently changed and the assassin was still some miles distant.

Anaximander reached a place where he could no longer continue without submerging. He looked back and Clarissa nodded for him to proceed, so he dived without pausing, Clarissa following. Bellows was more reluctant than he wanted to be, but he was only a boy and Clarissa had him in her grip, so reluctant or not his head was underwater before he was prepared for it, which made him exhale in shock.

When a person empties their lungs like that the reflex is to open the mouth and breathe in, which is why so many inexperienced swimmers drown when they are out of their depth, but Clarissa had identified that portion of the weft that corresponded with the totality of possible states of the interior surfaces of Bellows's lungs – she had done the same for hers and Anaximander's – and when she knew that they were empty, she located the certainty in the weft that the material realm was filled here with air, and she dissolved the membrane that separated that instance of things from the one they all experienced as real. A small sacrifice of a redundant Sparkline of a middling and unremarkable merchant family was sufficient to provide the energy necessary for the transfer, and she said the words in her head. Rather than breathing in choking water, Bellows found air in his lungs without effort. This he held there and knew no more about it, Clarissa replenishing the life-giving elements of his lungful so that it never occurred to his body to request new breath.

For Bellows it was dark all around, because his eyes were entirely closed, as were Clarissa's – she needed a lack of material distraction to remain anchored in the weft – but Anaximander's eyes were open.

The insufficient light that penetrated this water he supplemented with his other senses, though these were mostly subdued by all the liquid around. There was enough to give an impression regardless.

Anaximander was not a squeamish dog, by any means, but the scene was a troubling and grotesque one, even for him. It was not simply that this was a forest, drowned by a rising sea – though it was certainly that, with a gradually thickening density of branches as they descended, which were stripped of their leaves, stripped of bark, like skeletons of trees, beribboned by trails of seaweed like their putrefying flesh, swaying in the gentle currents the party's swimming made.

It was not simply that it had succumbed to an invasion of sea creatures, flying surreally like birds: rays and small sharks and jellyfish where magpies and starlings and pigeons should be.

It was not simply a place of eerie and uncomfortably stagnant silence, all voices stopped by drowning and filled with brine.

It was all of these things and also a mausoleum of the land, everything that should have been above laid to rest here – the ground, the forest, the grass, but also the bones of the creatures tangled where they could be tangled, trapped by an ankle bone in a clump of roots – this a weasel – wedged by the horns between a rock and a branch – a bull – trapped beneath a fallen limb – a man, his eye sockets home to urchins, one black and one white.

Anaximander swam between all these things, shaking others loose from his person and his mind when he needed to, and the mood was grim and portentous. What, he thought, could Clarissa need from down here. In this still and funereal place, what was worth coming for?

Here was a carriage of rusted metal, pulled by the bones of four horses still bridled and reined. Inside was a colony of crabs who startled when Anaximander went by, scuttling away to reveal clothes but no bodies, sitting calmly where they ought to be, their owners spirited away, seemingly, to escape whatever fate had stopped them there.

Further on was a small shop – part of a sign over the door read 'Confectioners to Royalty', but the rest was rotted away. In its window were shelves and arranged on these were jars, all empty. Perhaps, Anaximander thought as he swam, this Royalty had exhausted the shop's supply of confections before the flood. Or perhaps confections were also prized by fish, who now swam between the shop's displays in carefree shoals.

Clarissa had told him to look out for an archway in wood, and now here it was, and along a path picked out in gravel there was an entrance to a cave, the mouth of it too dark for even Anaximander to see into. As if she knew it – perhaps she could see it too, from in the weft – Clarissa spoke to him in his mind and gave him directions so clearly that he no longer needed to look where he was going. She didn't say 'go here' or 'go there', instead she told him which leg to paddle with and how hard, and they made slow but gradual progress where she led them, Bellows and Adam pulled behind.

After what seemed like an inordinate period of blind twistings and turnings through tunnels in the rock, they came to the surface of a subterranean pool, from which each, except for Adam, emerged spluttering and coughing and wiping their eyes.

The space was roughly spherical, perhaps fifty feet in diameter, the pool surrounded by dry ground all around, and although Clarissa had led them to expect a natural formation, this was anything but. The stone floor and walls had been scraped, or chiselled crudely, to make them flat, and there were bas relief columns spaced at intervals throughout, straight and true but irregularly finished, as if the mason had chosen an off-putting, naïve style, or had died before they could complete their work after crudely sketching the beginnings. Between the columns were alcoves, gashes clawed into the rock into which equally primitive vases had been placed, and where vases often contain flowers, in these were seaweed and fish heads, shells and pebbles.

Where the light by which the party could see was coming from was not at first clear, but then, when Anaximander turned to find it, he saw something that puzzled him. Between two of the columns there was no alcove but instead a huge crystal, like a wall of glass, gently glowing. At first, he thought that one of its surfaces was a mirror, and that Clarissa had emerged from the pool to stand behind him so that she was reflected in it – he turned to see if this was the case, but she was sitting beside Bellows on the pool edge, wringing the water from her hair. He turned back, and now he saw that he had not seen a reflection at all, but that, within the crystal there was a woman exactly like Clarissa, only perfectly frozen.

'What—' he began to say, but then from the pool behind emerged a dog, fish in its mouth, and Anaximander suddenly had other concerns.

This dog, dripping, dropped the fish and, without even shaking himself dry, advanced on Anaximander. 'This temple accepts no pilgrims,' it said in a low, growling voice, crackled with years but vibrating with menace. He was as broad as Anaximander, as scaffolded with strong bones and muscles under the skin, as suggestive of violence in his posture, only he was grey, half-bleached, seemingly, through centuries of existing in the darkness. 'Return the way you came.'

Anaximander took him in instantaneously, sensing all the attributes of him, but it was the voice he focussed on. 'How is it you speak, dog, when that is a privilege I uniquely own?'

Both lowered their heads – they were about ten feet apart and the ground between them was as sound and clear as any fighting ring needed to be. Like negatives of each other – opposites of the same thing – each bared their fangs.

'I am Scrap, who is called Thales, and my voice is a gift from an enemy, as is my reason. You are in the shrine to my service-pledge, carved from the rock by my own claws. Leave, now, or I will force you to leave.'

The two circled each other, slowly, each going first towards and then away from the other until a rough arena was outlined, a line made from paw prints and the scraping of claws.

'I am Bones, who is called Anaximander,' he said, but before he could say anything else, Thales was at him, launched low through the air, snapping as he flew, narrowly missing his opponent's leg, then skidding through the dirt, already poised to attack again. Anaximander retaliated, pouncing, so that his whole weight collided with the other dog's shoulder, knocking him to the ground, though only briefly – if he was old, this dog, then that had not made him frail; he was stiff as an oak, and sturdy.

These first, testing moves made, the two took to circling again. Never closing his mouth on his snarl, Anaximander spoke directly from his throat. 'My service-pledge is Clarissa Delacroix, whom you see with me. She has led me here for a purpose, and I will not leave until it is complete.'

For the first time, Thales spared the others a glance where they were now gathered against the cave wall, flickering in the candlelight. 'You are mistaken,' he said. 'That is not Clarissa Delacroix, for the woman of that name and appearance is my service-pledge, entombed in the wall of crystal I have been charged to protect.'

Anaximander stopped his circling. There was a moment – scarcely half a second – in which he did nothing, but this was not a pause made through doubt, or confusion, but was a determination to invoke a ritual known to dogs that would result in the death of one or other of them. For a dog to claim another dog's service-pledge was the worst type of crime, an insult to all dogs, and once done it could not be undone.

Anaximander looked back at Clarissa. She didn't have to speak – the dog could see what it was that she wanted. A thought occurred to Anaximander that would never have troubled a less intelligent dog: was this why she had brought him here? Had she planned for a dogfight all along?

'Kill him,' she said.

Regardless of his doubts, Anaximander would have started fighting immediately, but Bellows strode between the two. He put his frail hands out, one at each dog. 'You must not kill,' Bellows said. 'It is necessarily wrong.' He looked first at Clarissa, apologetically, then at Anaximander. 'Learn my lesson,' he said. 'No matter how much you venerate your mistress, there are decisions you must make for yourself. I was the Master of Mordew's scion, and I committed terrible crimes in my love for him. I bitterly regret those crimes.'

The boy Bellows edged towards Anaximander, turning a little to face him, determined that his friend should understand. 'I have facilitated the deaths of hundreds, perhaps thousands, and the weight of their murders is like a millstone around my neck.'

There were tears welling in Bellows's eyes, memories visible in them. He wiped them away. 'If this does not move you, then think of the allegory my brother told us.' He held Adam up in front of him, like a shield. 'Are you not like the Faery Child? Are you not bemused by the magic of others into violence? Will you not, when you have outlived their purposes for you, meet his fate?' Bellows held Adam out to the dog, symbolically offering him his wisdom.

Bellows was about to conclude his argument, make some last rhetorical flourish to complete his plea, when Thales, leaping on him from behind, bore him to the ground, cracking his head against a rock. 'The child's words are irrelevant. If you do not kill me, then I will kill you.'

Without looking back to his service-pledge, Anaximander walked directly up to Thales, who allowed him to do it. Neither made any feint or ruse, and Anaximander clamped his jaws tight on the shoulder of the grey dog, thereby leaving his own shoulder vulnerable. 'I bear you no ill will,' Anaximander said, anchoring his teeth in flesh and feeling teeth anchoring in his. 'I have sensed your presence these last few days, and am eager to know who you are.'

Thales bit down until he could feel bone, and then, with his four feet planted firmly, began to wrench whatever parts of Anaximander he had contained within his jaws away from their fixings. 'I felt your coming,' he said as he did it, 'but one of us will not live to know the other, and it is hard to be friends with a corpse.'

Forcefully, the two began to pull and tug and chew at each other. They formed in a clench dogmen call 'German kissing' because the animals remain so close to each other throughout, and because of the violence with which that now forgotten nationality were supposed to make love.

Against the rough-hewn shrine that Thales had scraped with his nails over centuries the diamond threw insubstantial shadows, ragged at the edges, and the pool rippled.

As the dogs fought, Clarissa took Adam from where he had fallen, and that mystical place in which the four of them had previously communed opened again.

Adam was there, in his form as a handsome young man wearing a uniform, and Clarissa was as she always was. In the cave, the others were motionless, interrupted in their progress while these two met. She walked over to him, but he backed away.

'I did ask myself,' Adam said, 'why a woman of your power, weft-manipulator, spell caster, would take a boy, a book and a dog with you.'

Clarissa smiled. 'What was your conclusion?'

He shrugged. 'My brother? I don't think you needed him, except it was easier for him to bring me than it was for you to take me.'

She nodded. 'Go on.'

'You need Anaximander to kill the other dog.'

She nodded again. 'So why do I need you?'

It was Adam's turn to smile. 'There's a lot of information in me,' he said. 'I'm filled with all sorts of lore. That woman in the crystal. That's you – at least another instance of you. Your husband quarantined her. It's not a great quarantine, a little primitive by the Master's standards. You need me because I have a spell that can dissolve it.'

Clarissa came over to him. She put her hand on his shoulder, affectionately at first, but then with her other hand she grabbed him by the hair and pulled it. 'If you know all this, what are you waiting for? Do it.'

Adam became like mist. He stepped back, leaving Clarissa holding nothing. 'I don't know what you've been doing in the weft,' he said, 'but I know you're out of sacrifices.'

Clarissa stepped away from him now. 'You don't know anything.'

'But I do. I'm full of stories, Clarissa Delacroix, and one of them is about you. The other you, I should say. She cuckolded her husband with every man she could find, fertilised all her eggs, kept them in her womb, and sacrificed them, unborn, to power her magic. Correct?'

Clarissa said nothing.

'It's a very clever idea, to maximise the Spark release by making sacrifices of people who haven't used their lives. Your husband found out and quarantined you here, full of power waiting to be unleashed. Whatever you've been doing in the weft, you've exhausted your supply of sacrifices, and now you've come to get more.'

'Do you expect me to be ashamed?' Clarissa said.

'You misunderstand me,' Adam said. 'Your body is yours to do with as you will. I know this better than anyone. I don't want to stand in your way. I want to help you.'

In the air between them, the spell that would dissolve the ice was written in gold, sigils, letters, vibrating with power. 'The Mistress of Malarkoi tortured me to make this book, the Master of Mordew used me as a killing machine. You are their enemy, or at least you were. I'll give you whatever you want, providing you punish them.'

'Deal,' Clarissa said, and the bargain was made.

As Clarissa and Adam communed, Anaximander and Thales pulled and chewed, standing across Bellows's unconscious body. Throughout, they exchanged words magically, even though they growled and whined while they did it, and never once released their grips.

'How do you exist?' Anaximander said.

'Your Clarissa is a secondary Clarissa, derived from mine,' Thales replied, his voice betraying none of the pain his guttural moans suggested he was experiencing. 'I was made in the past of the original Clarissa, by her enemy, and I have pledged myself to her through her kindness.'

Now Anaximander lost his footing, trampling Bellows, allowing Thales to gain purchase. The old dog used this as a platform from which to drag, powerfully, until he pulled the flesh away from Anaximander's muscle, ripping an artery.

Anaximander whimpered, but continued talking. 'You consider her kind? Still? After your long isolation?'

Thales pulled, and then pulled again, and his bite did all that a fighting dog could hope for – it took out a chunk the size of a fist, leaving a grim and bloody absence where Anaximander's shoulder should have been. The wound leaked Anaximander's life blood onto the arena.

This was both a victory and a disaster, though, because in the tearing away of the meat, Thales fell back, allowing Anaximander, wounded though he now was, to leap, landing with his huge paws on the older dog's head, pushing his face across the dusty and congealing stone floor. There was one crack, and then another one, and Thales screamed; his teeth had met rock and split, two shearing in half.

There are few pains as acute as those caused by the nerves of the teeth, which require the armour of enamel to prevent them, but more problematic was that these were Thales's main weapons, and a wound to the shoulder is not comparable, in a dogfight, to a wound to the mouth, since a dog who cannot attack can never win a bout.

Anaximander pressed his advantage, attacking without fear of counterattack, biting and snapping wherever he pleased. 'My Clarissa is the true owner of the name since she is the one that most deserves it, regardless of who used it once. Your service-pledge is entombed in a crystal and cannot therefore be said to be at large in the world. Proper names are things used to identify people who require identification; her ownership of it, down here, is redundant. In short, she has given up life and so has given up the right to her name. She is no longer Clarissa Delacroix, if she ever was, whereas the woman behind me still is.'

Thales was not finished. He had not lived for centuries beneath the earth without learning how to counteract pain – the pain of hunger, of loneliness, of fear – and so he used his teeth, ringing with agony though they were, without reference to it, and dragged them through Anaximander's vulnerable underside. 'Sophistry,' he said. 'A name belongs to she who is so named, and naming carries on indefinitely. How else would we continue to reference the dead? Also, an identity is not simply dependent on the bearing of a name, otherwise two men named identically would be the same man, and we know this not to be true.'

Anaximander yelped as he was bitten. When he looked down, he saw the source of the pain – Thales's broken teeth had torn a ragged gash in his belly. He paused, appalled, for what might have been a fatally long time. It is not easy to see the body in pieces, and there is no adequate preparation for doing so, not even the horrible education Heartless Harold Smyke provided. 'The final answer to the question is this,' he said, when he had recovered his composure. 'Whoever says a name only does so while living, so let whichever of us survives decide on the accuracy of its use.'

Thales, if he had attacked earlier instead of speaking, could have bitten out Anaximander's innards. He could have plunged his jaws into the wound and grabbed for the liver, the lungs, the heart, and torn them until they no longer functioned. Thales should have done these things – that was his duty, the same as Anaximander's was – but he was ancient, and slow, and too committed to defending his service-pledge's honour in words, so he could only bite down on Anaximander's forelegs instead.

This is why Thales died: if the old dog had been able to make the *coup de grâce* he would have been the victor, but he argued verbally instead, and in that indulgence the fight was lost and won.

Anaximander lunged, clumsily but effectively gripping Thales's head in his mouth, anchoring at the grey-haired lower jaw. His tongue pressed over the shredded and lifeless leather of Thales's ear, and with his upper teeth he clamped down into the groove that ran along the centre of the old dog's skull. Without pausing a moment, Anaximander bit with all the force that remained in him. His teeth slipped, tore through the skin, but eventually found enough purchase so that Thales's skull bones beneath splintered.

Thales went immediately limp, his head compromised and with it the brain it contained – but the dog spoke magically from the cadaver he was now becoming. 'You make of me a failure and put the life of my service-pledge in jeopardy. Also, we will never now know each other as friends. We are the same, you and I, in every important way. We have the same voice, the same mind, the same duties. It is bitter to meet one's brother, only then to die.'

Anaximander listened, panting. He spared Clarissa a glance – she was occupied with the book.

'Look at me!' Thales said. 'Know your fate. You will have a life of service and an unhappy death. I have no other words to give you, Anaximander, and no more wisdom to impart except this: life is loveless for dogs such as we, bred for service, and to know that with minds like ours is a curse. Never look down on those of our kin who cannot speak or think, for these skills are a mixed blessing at best, and a corruption of our proper nature at worst.'

Anaximander waited for more, suddenly feeling an urgent need for that brief commonality of feeling the old dog brought him. He nudged at Thales's white-whiskered snout, gory with blood. He licked the surface of his eye, which was far-staring and rheumy. He even pawed his chest, hoping to make the heart within it return to beating.

It didn't.

When Anaximander turned to find help from Clarissa, she was looking at herself, suspended in the crystal.

Though he had never done it before, Anaximander began to cry. He had not believed that dogs could do such a thing, his species tending to howl, but now that strange water came, even though pain made him suppress the sobs inside his chest.

In his heart was a great, lonely sadness, and as the tears dripped from his snout he looked at Thales and let them fall, their unusualness seeming to him a fitting monument for the other talking dog, unique in his experience.

His bargain made, Adam cast the spell that destroyed the quarantine, and the impregnable crystal that had once contained the other Clarissa became nothing but simple glass.

Clarissa searched the ground for a moment until she found a handy rock. She hefted it a couple of times and then threw it overarm at her double. When the glass did not shatter, the rock leaving only a dirty scuff in the otherwise pristine transparency of it, she closed her eyes and reached down into her womb, where she held in place the fertilised eggs, the Sparklines of Mordew. She took the least of these remaining and sacrificed it, releasing its life energy, and this she forced through her palm into the weft-representation of the glass, making it oscillate just enough so that it cracked and fell into pieces, leaving her past self where it stood, its eyelids flickering as if it was about to wake.

She didn't falter, wasn't unnerved by facing herself, as a lesser woman might have been. She took a blade of splintered glass instead and she opened the double's abdomen. Anaximander barked a warning, but Clarissa reached inside without hesitation, pulling out first one, and then two fistfuls of flesh, pale like veal and bloodless, which she put in her pockets. Then she drove the shard into the heart of the other Clarissa, and what signs of life in her died in a moment.

When she turned, her work done, and met the face of her dog, she frowned.

'It's my body,' she said. 'I can do what I like with it.'

Exactly what she meant by those words, Anaximander couldn't tell.

There was no need to swim back to the surface; Clarissa burned a path up through the rock with a tiny fraction of the power she had harvested from her corpse.

'I cannot walk,' Anaximander said, panting, to the retreating back of his service-pledge.

Clarissa stopped in the still-molten entrance of the tunnel, and the dog thought happily that she had remembered him, but instead she cast another spell, this time of coldness, solidifying the rock and cooling it so that she did not burn her feet when she left.

Summoning all the strength he had in his body, Anaximander barked loudly, twice.

Clarissa stopped. She sighed, then turned back to face him. 'I'm sorry, I've got to go,' she said. 'There's somewhere I have to be.'

Anaximander stared at her, his thoughts and emotions a blur he could not express in words.

Clarissa went over to where he was. In one hand she carried Adam, but with the other she stroked the dog's face, wiping away his tears.

'I really am sorry,' she said. 'If it helps, you did an excellent job.'

When she was gone, Bellows, dizzy, eyes bloodshot, came and knelt beside him.

Boy and dog looked each other in the face.

'My forelegs are snapped from Thales's biting,' Anaximander said. 'One rear leg is dislocated. The wound to my belly will kill me through the loss of blood, and if I live long enough it will fester until I rot to death.' He heard himself saying these things, dispassionately, and now he couldn't understand why.

Bellows didn't reply. When he had been with the Master, he had performed minor medical procedures on the staff, when necessary, but the dog was beyond his skill to save.

Anaximander didn't speak again, whether because his heart was broken by Thales's death and Clarissa's leaving or because his body's natural desire to save its mind from pain had rendered him unconscious, but Bellows did what he could for him.

It was very little, and not enough.

The exit Clarissa had made to the surface was done by magic, and so the surfaces were all unnaturally smooth, unnaturally even, unnaturally frictionless, and though Anaximander was heavy and left behind him a thick trail of blood, he wasn't impossible to move, even for a boy as weak and frail as Bellows.

It was hard, slow work, and the bang on Bellows's head made his eyes swim, but he never felt as if he wouldn't be able to do it; the daylight from outside encouraged him all the way.

It was not so far, so Bellows turned the dog over onto his back and lifted him under his shoulders so that he might carry him more gently out into the world again. Anaximander was a much bigger dog than Bellows was a boy, but when you don't have to lift something completely, you can manage it.

Bellows set his back to the effort, counted a rhythm to his steps, and before he knew it, they were out in the sunshine again.

Unlike Sharli and Deaf Sam, who were younger and more concerned with themselves and their affairs because they hadn't been jaded by long decades of repetition in that area, the Druze had few distractions from business. This degree of focus was how the assassin managed to hit Clarissa when she came out, and then killed Bellows without any fuss once he'd laid Anaximander on the ground.

It might also be that the Druze was better at the work than Deaf Sam and Sharli. Some people are naturally more suited to their jobs, or care more about them, or go the extra mile.

Assassins are no different in this respect from anyone else.

The Druze had been lying flat about thirty feet from the exit Clarissa had burned through the ground. One form of camouflage is to lay under a blanket of turf, cut with a special blade useful for that kind of work, and while it doesn't hold up to close inspection, it is certainly enough to hide one's presence long enough to let off a crossbow bolt.

The Druze's hit Clarissa in the face.

It was luck, certainly, that she had come out where she did, since the assassin hadn't the first clue where the party had got

376

to. The map showed the exact spot, but Padge hadn't considered it necessary to make it sensitive to depth, so when the target emerged from a hole in the ground, the Druze offered a brief prayer to the Mother of Mordew and let loose the bolt.

It was skill that guided the shot, though, and any luck soon ran out when the target, having received the bolt and put her hand to it with a frown, snapped out of existence entirely, like a popped balloon. This is not the kind of thing people tend to do, and it was, to say the least, surprising. The assassin checked Padge's magic paper: Clarissa's name was still on it, and the map showed her back in Mordew.

The Druze cursed: bolts to the face make for very dramatic injuries, but they aren't necessarily fatal. A woman can live without most of her face if her brain and neck remain intact – the dark corners of gin-houses were full of people like that, fearsome to look at, and not great conversationalists if they'd lost their tongues, but capable of drowning their sorrows as effectively as anyone else. Quite how Clarissa had returned to Mordew was a mystery, but it was a mystery for another time.

The paper still showed Bellows nearby, so the assassin returned to a prone position, under the turf.

The error with Clarissa was made up for by getting a clean shot on Bellows, hitting him right in the chest as he emerged dragging a big dog. The boy remained where he was and watched the spreading patch of red at his chest, his face a picture of shock, the white linen of his shirt darkening. Without speaking, he fell to his knees and listed off to one side.

After a brief check that the work was done – which it was, thankfully, since the dog was on its last legs and no threat to anyone – the Druze went to high ground. There they set a fire to smoke-signal the other assassins – those that remained – that all should gather together in preparation for the murder of Clarissa, whose powers clearly exceeded one assassin's capabilities.

In Anaximander's dreams, as he lay there bleeding out, Bellows dead as a stone beside him, he made a list.

He dreamed that he would one day:

- Recover from his wounds;
- Learn the magic that makes talking dogs happen in the world;
- Use that magic to make another talking dog;
- Discuss with this dog whether or not a talking dog's service-pledge can be considered to be ended if said dog finds himself betrayed; and
- If the answer to the above question was 'yes', renege his service and punish any and all betrayals against him.

It is not a rule in the world that a dog's dreams will come true, but neither is it a rule that they won't. We can say for certain, though, that the dreams of the dead are nothing in the material realm, and Anaximander was very close to death.

XXIV

A Description of a Fight
from Two Perspectives, Part Two

NO SOONER had the Master got rid of the bloody creature and begun dripping Rescue Remedy into his ear canals, than it was back again, whining and howling. He put down the jug, clenched his fists and started the spell that would shut this thing up once and for all.

Some spells you need a book for, some need an object, some need sigils, some need tools. Some need a bit of everything. This spell, though, was one the Master didn't need anything for. People who've grown up in fear always have something, hidden away, that they can use to fight back with, in a pinch. They might carry a penknife, or something they can spray in someone's eyes. People who've grown up in fear, and then gone on to have those fears realised, have not only got something they can fight back with, in a pinch, but also that they've honed and perfected and made better through experience and use. They might have an actual knife, or a knuckleduster, or an acid spray. People who have a lot of experience of fighting back, in a pinch, get sick of living in fear, so they kit themselves out with weapons they can use whenever they like, and make people fear them instead. The Master was one of this latter type of person. He had, under the clothes he rarely removed in front of people, his entire body scarified with sigils made of uncountable tiny dots. These sigils, when voiced, performed a transformation which the Master used infrequently but which had never failed.

The spell wasn't short, but he knew it perfectly and could say it quickly. The first time he'd used it he'd needed the scroll, but once he'd struck on the idea of scars that had simplified things, and beneath the fabric of his shirt, the marks he'd branded on himself began to Itch.

The dog stopped its howling when it realised where it was and lowered its head, bringing the height of the ceiling down with it. It saw the Master and drew its lips back.

Teeth, even very sharp ones, even divine ones, are just teeth. The Master chanted louder, faster, and across his shoulders, left to right and around, under his armpits and over his ribs, the Itch spread until it met in his solar plexus.

The dog took a step forward, rumbling in its throat, its nostrils flaring, but Sebastian was on the last stanza, drawing into this Spark-sensitive realm the power Nathan had found it so difficult to control until it connected beneath his skin.

As the dog leapt at the Master, the Spark flared out, making of him a man entirely of white energy who leapt himself, determined and unstoppable, directly into the creature's huge mouth.

Sirius swallowed, puzzled, failing to understand, again, where his prey had gone. He didn't understand, either, when from inside his throat he began to burn. There was something hot, something sharp, crawling down his throat, setting fire to the back of his tongue, then to his voice box, so that his barks of agony were dry chokes. Then it went between his lungs, so he couldn't breathe. He tried to bring it up, whatever this appalling obstruction was that was turning him to fire inside, but though he coughed and retched until he felt he would turn himself inside out, the thing gripped inside him and wouldn't be removed.

Then it went deeper, into his stomach, where it kicked and thrashed, making Sirius kick and thrash too, his eyes dry, his nose dry, the silent screams he couldn't scream hot and dry and frantic.

He fell onto his side, unable to hold himself upright, and from where he lay, he could see the thrashing on his skin, lighting him from within.

The Master burnt out whatever he could burn out – the liver, the kidneys, the stomach, the lungs. His eyes were blind with

Spark light and his ears deafened, but he felt for masses and destroyed them. Then, when this was done, he paused, only for a moment, until he sensed the power of the mystical organ he had built the dog around, integrated as a central nexus to the being of this thing, and he made for that. God or no god, he knew how this creature worked, so he set out to destroy the basis of its existence, the heart that was not a heart, lodged in its chest.

It was there, ahead, and though he could only see whiteness, the whiteness fell into this organ, was drawn into it, and all the Master needed to do was follow it down, be drawn with it, Spark energy himself now, until the spell died.

It drew him forward and he let it, helped it, pulling himself through the dog's flesh, pulling at arteries, at veins, dragging himself across bones until here it was, a perfect cube of light pulled into itself. He had created it and he knew how to destroy it: he butted at the centre, at its strongest and weakest part – strong in the immaterial realm, weak in the material realm, fragile to anything but concepts, even grown huge like this – and it began to crack.

It was a flaw in the Master that, once he thought a thing was done, he tended to relax, to allow his mind to wander to the next stage of a plan before the first stage was properly finished, and this he did now, waiting a moment, taking a breath when he could have delivered another blow, and as he breathed the dog's teeth clamped around him and dragged him out into the air, the cracked and flawed organ left behind, not yet destroyed.

It is said, by farmers, that a fox when caught in a trap will gnaw off its own leg rather than remain there to die. Sirius was no less than a fox, since a fox is a type of dog and Sirius was the god of dogs.

As he lay on his side, he saw the light of the Master in his belly, and though he was driven mad by the pain, he still had the cunning a fox has, knew the light to be his enemy, and attacked it without holding back, tearing his own fur away, making a hole in himself, chewing his body to pieces. Since

he did it himself, by his own will, the wounds did not immediately heal, because the actions of a god are not undone so
easily, not even by themselves. 'Thy will be done,' goes the
prayer, and this is true even when it is counter to a god's own
seeming good. As a mother will sometimes pull a pup into the
world when it is born, so did Sirius pull the Master back out,
but not gently, the pain in him causing so much rage that he
ground the man between his front teeth and then his back
teeth until his light went out.

Then, not wanting to swallow him, he spat him onto the
floor, where he scraped at him as if he was digging up a rabbit
in a field, barking all the while, the fur on the scruff of his neck
bristling, his hindquarters pressed hard against the extent of
the realm to give him purchase.

Then he picked up the man again, who was now as limp as
that field rabbit, and shook him from side to side, over and over.

When Sirius had done all he could, he dropped his prey
again, but there was nothing to drop – the Master was gone,
and his mouth was empty.

Sebastian dragged himself through the Manse, the lower half
of him tattered and immovable, the top half only tattered. No
man expects to be bested by a dog, particularly when he has
weapons, but the Master least of all. And by one of his own
making! Heartless Harold Smyke would be laughing at him.
If he wasn't already dead.

These corridors, museums of the faithful, archives of family
and retainers, had become increasingly long over the centuries, and he had recently felt they were too long. Never more
so than now.

The runner that Bellows had Caretaker fit down the middle
of this one would be ruined; inside a man there is blood and
bile and lymph and mucus and who knows what else, and the
Master was leaving distractingly large volumes of it behind
him as he pulled his ragged self to his study.

There was a good chance he wouldn't make it. He had at
his fingertips techniques that could fix minor injuries, but

they wouldn't work for this. He was in a bad way. Worse than he could ever remember.

Up there, hanging from a picture frame, was Sanjeet Cope, dead for what must have been five hundred years. On the other side, his wife Rekha. Would he die between these two? Would anyone remember what they did?

He left a black slug trail behind him, making a mess of everything, his family looking on, unmoved.

Far too long, these corridors.

In his study, on the desk because he'd considered using it only recently, was Deborah Grahame's *Unusual Architectures*. If, instead of being there, that book was here, he'd be fine. Page two hundred and seventy-three? Something like that. Probably not, but in there somewhere was a means of shortening a corridor without reducing its wall space. She'd got it so that the walls only registered length when you paid attention to them, meaning that you could walk briskly through a short gallery when you weren't interested in the paintings, then luxuriate through a long one when you were, the corridor being the same both times. And all points in between.

Why hadn't he done that? Too busy? And that was going to cost him his life, after all this time?

He'd do it straight away, once that damned dog was seen to.

Bellows. If only he still had Bellows. If only the New Bellows had been installed. He'd be here now, scooping the Master up, taking him to his bed, making him better.

Even Caretaker would do. Or Cook. One or two good gill-men.

These were his own mistakes. He shouldn't have sent all the gill-men to repair the God-chamber breach. He should have promoted someone from the material Manse. He was an idiot!

He dragged himself angrily along the unending corridor, his own self-hatred fuel for his possible salvation.

Blood dripping from his self-inflicted, god-given wounds, Sirius turned his mystical organ to the question of to where

383

the Master had fled. Doing it hurt now, as using a broken limb hurts, but that's not to say it didn't work. A dog can limp for miles. He can see through a swollen eye. He can take a beating and still leap up for work, and this is what Sirius did.

The organ showed him his futures, and because he was a god these futures were definite and clear. The moment he saw the Master in one of them, he ran into it. He did not wait, as a man would do, to see how this future played out. He didn't have Anaximander to turn to for reason and sense; he used the organ as he would use his eyes – it showed him his prey, so he went down the path that led to it.

This path was not one Sirius understood – there was no ground to tread, no scent to trail, no distant sound he recognised, no network of physical sensation at all. All those things were taken up with his wounds, which wept to him of their seriousness and their sadness, but he ignored them all and when he did not know what to do, he willed that the things he wanted came to pass, and therefore they did, since that is natural for a god.

Self-hatred will only take you so far, and now, scarcely three or four generations of relatives away from where he had spurred himself into action with it, the Master woke up in a pool of gore. He was dying, there was no getting away from that fact. He had the chime, but he'd dropped the fork, and there was no way he'd survive a translation in this state. He had spells, but nothing useful. He tapped his pockets. Nothing.

He stared up at the ceiling. A spider's web was gathering dust above the picture rail.

He missed Bellows.

Because Sirius had not waited, because dogs do not wait – except one – and he had not thought, because dogs cannot think – except one – he had not chosen the most direct route after his prey. Some of his futures must have led directly to the Master, since there is nothing standing in the way of a god translating himself from one realm to another, since Reals are, to gods, like the rooms of a house are to a person – easily moved between – but he did not take one of these. Instead, Sirius went first into the Manse as it existed in the material realm. There is sense in this because he knew of that place, and knew the Master was associated with it, he having stood outside it when Nathan went there to confront him, but that was not where the Master was. This Sirius discovered by charging through corridors unsuited to his size, destroying that which Rekka had not destroyed and sending people running in fear of their lives.

Nowhere was his prey to be found.

In the corridor, as he lay his back, the Master felt nudges – first at one cheek, and then at the other. He was close to death now, with hardly any blood in his body and a sense of the fading away of all things about him. Consequently, nudges to the cheek meant very little to him. He saw instead the events of his life, many of which he did not recognise, playing out in his mind.

But then there were the nudges again and a man, even on his deathbed, will not be nudged indefinitely without at some point turning his head to see what is nudging him. This the Master did.

Mr Sours was there on one side, and Mrs Sours was on the other, the husband-and-wife pair of mice who did the work of cleaning the playroom. Their tiny red eyes were entirely inanimate, but Sebastian thought to see a glitter of sympathy in them. Perhaps dying men are prone to sentimentality of that type, but the fact remains regardless.

He thought for a moment about the sadness inherent in married mechanical mice, but this moment passed quickly when he understood what it was he needed to do.

Through cracked lips and teeth stained with his blood, he whispered, spluttering his instructions to them, in the manner of a man delivering his final words to a battlefield companion.

Sirius's mystical organ led him to the corridor where the Master was, except only in the material realm, and by virtue of his divine power he translated himself, still bleeding, the hole in his belly unrepaired, into the antechamber realm the Master occupied. He did not know how he did it, or what it was that he did, but does a dog know any more when he travels in a cart, or by train? He does not.

Now he did not need the mystical organ: the Master's scent filled his nostrils, the iron of his blood, the taint of his faeces, the savour of his fear.

Beneath his paws a tiny mouse skittered, no more than a mote in Sirius's eye. It circled once and then darted away to the skirting board, disappearing.

The instructions the Master had given to the Sours couple were these: that Mr Sours should go to the allotment, find one of the green spiders there and gather it up; that Mrs Sours should go to the tallest of the plants, one that was in blossom, shake it until its pollen fell, and then gather the pollen in the dust trap that was her belly; that they should both return; that on their return Mr Sours should let the spider loose, and that Mrs Sours should gather it up with the pollen.

He didn't point out to either of them what the consequences of these actions would be, and neither of them asked or could ask, but when they'd followed his instructions the green spider expanded enormously in size – by virtue of its contact with the magical pollen the Master used for increasing the size of things in spells – splitting Mrs Sours in two so that she lay in pieces on the carpet. Mr Sours went to her immediately and wheeled around her pieces, conflicted by contradictory emotions – his inbuilt desire to clean the remains of her away, and his marital love for his wife.

This was of little interest to the Master – though he did notice it – because the now man-sized spider was attending to him. Its job, magically given to all the green spiders in his gardens, was to dispatch aphids and to repair any little damage they might have done to his plants, and now this one was repairing its Master, or attempting to, it knowing how to fix the systems of living things through the possession of part of a trained human mind, derived from a slum boy suited to the task, stripped and then shrunken down.

The Master was very injured though, and with divine wounds which are hard to heal, so the spider stung the master with an analgesic and wrapped the lower half of him in a cocoon of silk, rapidly spun, which prevented any further loss of blood and began knitting the torn flesh together, its idea being to take its patient to a place where it might receive more intensive care.

When the cocoon was done to its satisfaction the spider dragged the Master along the corridor to the door to his study, leaving Mr Sours to both tidy away and grieve for his partner of centuries, the now defunct Mrs Sours, until a huge dog appeared which frightened the mouse away.

XXV

Her Heir, Part Five

T HE FIFTH LEVEL of the Golden Pyramid of Malarkoi was the realm of the King of the Shadows. What was proper to him? Intuition says it should have been night there, since he was dark. It suggests that his should have been a diaphanous place, since he was as thin as fine silk. It should have been regal, as he was.

None of these things were right.

The intermediate nested Pyramid realm made by the Mistress of Malarkoi for the patron god, Le Roi de l'Ombre, was always in the brightest daylight – indeed there were four suns, and they lived in the sky at each other's hips, like four unmarried sisters. These suns shone down the colours red, blue, green and yellow, and they never set.

It is light that makes shadows, and without any there can be none.

This god's realm was of the utmost solidity, the landscape of it being composed of the primary geometric forms, punctuated by cylinders, spheres, cones and cubes, each as dense and undivided as the last. In the sunlight every object gave four shadows of a different hue, some of them intersecting to make deeper shadows. A shadow needs an object to block light for it to be made, and in the deepest shadows were the king's subjects, since without them a king has no one to rule.

His people were of the lowest type, hardly more than a shape, so that his kingliness should be the more pronounced in comparison with their low station.

He appeared cast on the sky opposite the suns, where he might best observe his world, and was the only shadow that needed no object to make him. He was the only shadow solid enough to bear teeth in his mouth, claws on his fingers and a golden crown on his head.

To the shadows over which he ruled, he uttered soundless proclamations that made the air tremble and haze, speaking directly into their minds. What he ordered them to do no one knew, since no person who heard them understood the import of his words, but shadows did his bidding, leaking into the other realms. Perhaps they returned to him with information, perhaps they performed assassinations for him, perhaps they interfered with business that did not concern them. Whatever it is they did, they did it silently, and there was no sound anywhere in that place, since what does a shadow know of sounds?

No one heard Prissy screaming as she came through the Door.

The image of Gam, gushing blood from his throat, eyes wide, fingers in the gurgling slit Dashini had made, was there – she could see it like the after-image of a bolt of lightning after its brightness shuts your eyes.

'He'll be alive again by morning,' Dashini said. The blood that had splashed over her was gone and she was standing, still holding the knife. She slipped it back into her belt.

Prissy ran over to the other girl and slapped her, hard, across the face.

Dashini didn't block the blow, and she didn't retaliate. She didn't say 'It was your idea.' She could have done all those things, but she didn't.

'We have to go back,' Prissy urged. She ran back to the Door. 'Open it!'

Dashini came over to her and put her arms around her. 'It doesn't work like that.'

Prissy shrugged her off, pushed her away. 'Make it work like that!' She grabbed Dashini's hand, took her fingers, made them move. 'Cast a spell. You're magic, aren't you?'

Dashini let her do all of it, whatever she wanted, and when Prissy fell to her knees and started sobbing, she knelt

389

next to her. 'You can go back for him, I promise. There's just one more Door, and you're there. One more and my mother will fix all this. For you. One more Door. It's easy, this one.'

Prissy looked up. 'Do you promise?'

Dashini nodded, took Prissy's face in her hands. 'I promise. Look! Those up there are the Suns and those down there are the Forms, and in the shadows live the shadow-serfs. Back there, on the sky, is the Shadow King. I think he's the one who has been ruining the realms, sending his shadows, thinking bad thoughts, making everything evil. There must be a rift, somewhere. My mother can repair it.'

Prissy looked around for the first time, but nothing made sense to her. Everywhere was colour and shape and in the sky was a cut-out thing, like a dressmaker's pattern, huge but inconsequential, a child's drawing of a bad king.

Dashini pulled her face back, made Prissy look into her eyes. 'He's going to think thoughts with your mind – shadow-thinking – thoughts of murder, but the Door is about a mile's easy walk away.'

'And that's it?'

'That's it. Keep your eyes down, try not to think, walk. You can do it.'

'And who are you going to sacrifice this time?'

An expression passed over Dashini's face that Prissy couldn't read, but then she smiled. 'Let's not worry about that now.'

No, Prissy thought, you wouldn't want me to worry about that, would you?

Prissy wiped her tears and put out her hand. 'Come on then, let's get it over with.'

Dashini took Prissy's hand as she had taken Gam's, and she walked her only friend to the final Door.

They kept to the light, sometimes blue, sometimes red, sometimes a combination of colours, but they avoided the shadows, where flat things were hiding.

Dashini. Clever, proud Dashini. Terrible, powerful Dashini. Bad Dashini.

The walk was just like she said – easy. One foot in front of the other, skirting the shadows, looking down to avoid seeing the Shadow King in the sky.

Does she think she can get away it? How many has she killed? And now Gam?

Thoughts are silent. They do not make a sound. You can hear them in your head, but they do not make a sound.

Dashini with blood on her hands.

Prissy kept her eyes on the ground, its surface unnaturally flat, unnaturally clear, the line between light and dark unnaturally defined. Blood requires blood. The blood in Dashini's veins, in her heart, on the blade of her knife.

'It's this way,' Dashini said, and the words came to Prissy's ears as if through water – dull and flat.

It's this way. The way of the knife.

Prissy looked up at the King. He was impassive in the sky. She stopped. His teeth were white, and his crown glistened and glinted. The law of death must be reciprocated.

Dashini took her by the hand. 'Come on!'

Come on. Can you feel it in her hand? That pulse? What is it for, but to pump the blood? Out onto the knife. Reciprocate her murders. Gam's killing requires her killing.

'It's only a little way further.'

Thoughts make no noise. You do not have to listen to them. Listen to him by knowing him. She longs for death. She makes death and you must make death. Her talk of sacrifice. Make the sacrifice.

The blood Door.

Now they were in front of the Door. Its frame was perfect, the King's blackness was behind it.

Prissy knew Dashini for who she was: her sacrifice.

She went up to her, close, just like Dashini had with Gam. Reciprocation was a law. Prissy knew what to do. Dashini had taught her. The King had taught her.

Make her your blood sacrifice.

Prissy took the fraction of a step forward towards Dashini that was left.

Dashini tensed, but she didn't move away. 'It's okay,' she said. 'I think this is what my mother wants.' She traced the sigils of the Door-opening spell in the air with her hands.

Beneath the shadow in the sky, Prissy glared hatred at Dashini, but Dashini didn't push her away. 'It's okay,' she said. 'She saved you for this.' Face to face, Dashini made soundless powerful chants.

Now Prissy pulled Dashini close, knotted her arms behind her back.

'It's okay,' Dashini said.

She is your sacrifice. Reciprocate murder.

Prissy took the Nathan Knife from its sheath on Dashini's belt. It was heavy in her hand, shaking with the power the Door spell Dashini had provoked in it.

She trembled. The knife was urgent at her fingertips, knowing better than its wielder did what it must do, what needed to be done, seeming to grow in Prissy's hand in size and potency.

It burned with the black fire, under the black shadow, au pays du Roi de l'Ombre.

'It's okay.'

Dashini flinched, a little, when Prissy slid the blade straight between her ribs where they met her spine. That is the best way to reach a girl's heart, the Shadow King thought, with Prissy's mind.

She held Dashini there until she died, and the Door came to life, then she left her to slump to the ground unregarded.

'Okay,' Prissy said as she left, making her way through the last Door without looking back.

The word floated lonely in the air.

XXVI

A Description of a Fight from Two Perspectives, Part Three

THE MOMENT the Master was in his study he clapped his hands – the spider had not bound them – weakly, and in various rhythms. This activated some of the many fluences placed on his rooms. The first one almost stopped the progress of time – clap, clap, clap-clap, clap. The second one – clap-clap, pause, clap-clap – infused the air with a mind-body stimulant. The third was a single loud clap that caused the door to take on the maximum possible weight and solidity, thereby barring any unwanted ingress from an enemy. There was a final fluence that was activated on his arrival but that was automatically provoked by his injuries – for the obvious reason that the requirement for its use might well prevent any clapping or other active prompts – which was the drawing in from the immaterial realm of a vast amount of the concept 'good health'.

Usually this was something that would immediately make the Master feel better, but so serious were his wounds that it was a good while before he no longer needed the ministrations of the green spider. With its numerous and dextrous limbs it performed every technique it knew to knit together flesh and staunch bleeding, but because the circulatory systems of plants and men are largely unalike, it performed no miracles.

When the Master eventually felt enough 'good health', he tore the remaining silk from his legs and immediately tottered on tingling limbs to his desk. Here he found the necessary charm and returned the spider to its previous small size.

He took a deep breath, assessing the state of his body as he did it. Adequate, though just barely.

It was all well and good to slow time, to stimulate himself, to bar the door, to repair his injuries, but none of these things were insurmountable defences against attack from a god. A demon, probably. An angel, possibly. A man, definitely. Gods, though, were a different matter entirely. Even stupid gods with the minds of dogs would only be slowed by his efforts.

Still, he had seen them killed. Knew it could be done. The Assembly did it every crusade. But they had the racks. What did he have?

In the corridor outside, the pre-materialisation alarm rang. First things first: the Master ran to *Unusual Architectures* and grabbed it as the alarm rose to a pitch indicating the arrival of something into the antechamber realm. Time was slow, but these things could be done in a flash, so he turned to the page that dealt with scaling and performed the necessary adjustments to the door and his rooms.

Almost as soon as he had done it, there was an almighty concussion on the door, as if someone was knocking with a battering ram, and his recently healed ears ached again from the pounding.

Was he going to have to use the Tinderbox? After all the work? He couldn't immediately think of an alternative and now the door was rattling in its frame, regardless of whether it had the maximum possible solidity.

Where had he put it? He went to the desk, looking for the telltale shine of the quarantine shell, picked up every book, shuffled every pile of papers, upturned every magical object. It wasn't there.

Now the door was splintering. Holding, but splintering.

He went to the drawers – nothing.

He went to the safe – nothing.

He went...

Across the carpet, a key huge in his tiny mouth, raced Mr Sours, a fixed and concentrated look on his murine face. At first, the Master was too surprised to understand what he was seeing, but then, with a rush of speed, the traitorous little machine accelerated towards a ramp that it had made from a book – *Practical*

Superpositions of Old-World Totems – propped against the draught excluder, and he knew what it was trying to do.

He leapt over the desk, struggling even in the excess of 'good health' fluenced into the room and not nimble enough to reach Mr Sours before he flew in a perfectly calculated arc that allowed him to both insert and then twist the study key in the door lock, which flew open at the external force of the dog's banging.

The Master turned as he landed, forcing himself back, barely seeing Mr Sours fall, tumbling triumphantly to crash against an ornamental weight that kept the coat rack from toppling over and breaking into pieces, as his wife recently had, but cursing him regardless.

The dog forced his muzzle through the doorway. The walls tore and shook until the plaster came off in chunks and the Master's precious sanctum was violated.

Some dogs are bred primarily to point, some are bred primarily to retrieve, other dogs are bred primarily to dig, but all dogs, because of their common ancestry, are inclined to do all these things, even just for fun. Sirius, though he was not of the digging breed made to dig up warrens and setts and holts to reveal rabbits, badgers and foxes, still knew how to do it. As he pushed his face into the small hole, he forced one claw of one forepaw into the gap, and this he scraped back, making the hole a fraction wider, and into the fraction he pushed harder, and with his other claw he did the same on the other side. This, when he could, he did harder and harder, and when there was enough room, he did it faster and faster, and soon the hole was big enough for his head, and then his shoulder, and he forced and clawed and bit his way into the space ahead of him, just like a terrier does in the earth, revealing a nest of leverets or whatever it is he has been sent to root out.

Sirius's prey was the Master, and he was running from place to place, looking for something and failing to find it, up to the point where the dog was filling almost the entire room and could get his teeth around desks and shelves, could pull up floorboards and rupture the pipework beneath, could bring down the ceiling in clouds of dust that iced the little man and made him blink.

As Sirius pulled himself further into the place he yelped, the bloody gap below his ribs catching on the shattered timber. He turned to lick the place that hurt, as a dog will, and from the corner of his eye he saw the Master hold up something – the quarantined locket – heard him cry out in triumph, then saw him disappear.

If he was going to do use the Tinderbox, the Master needed space. Pyroclastic revenance of this type, untested, unpredictable, would make the destruction a god dog could produce seem like nothing, and he wasn't going to destroy everything he'd done, all the progress he'd made towards winning the Tontine, close to a millennium of work. He left the protected realm and returned to the real, to the material realm, a place where destruction was not his problem, and he manifested himself in what was left of the Zoological Gardens.

The buildings of that place were warped and corrupted, stretched and pulled against their physical tolerances into perversions of matter, held together against complete disintegration by remnants of the magic that had performed the Mount Mordew deformation. The animals were gone, fleeing their previous captivity, and the Master stood now where the tiger enclosure had been, the railings as thin as hair, stretching up into the night, as if a child had drawn something in pencil and it had become as solid as the previous iron had been, contradicting their thinness.

Sebastian knelt in the sawdust, the paw prints of the previous occupant deformed but still recognisable. He put the locket on the ground, stood with it between his feet, addressed it with his posture, letting the material realm know that the magic he was about to perform was to undo its quarantine.

His lips formed the first syllable of a spell that was difficult but not impossible, but the sound which came next did not come from his lips.

Instead, the white bitch growled, she having sensed him the moment he resolved back into Mordew. 'How wonderful to see you again, Sebastian,' she said.

Into the Master's study, Sirius's seven daughters came.

When the owner of a house is out, it is easier to enter his home, and now the Master was gone the puppies came in easily.

They spoke to Sirius as dogs speak to each other, in sniffs and circlings and the adoptions of postures. When he lay down, they came to him and licked his wounds – the daughter of fire cauterised where the flesh was torn, staunching the flow of his divine blood, and the daughter of water cooled the burning, setting the skin into scars. The mountain daughter filled the space the Master had made inside him, and the wind daughter filled his lungs. The daughter of light showed him where he should go, and the daughter of darkness told him what he must do when he got there.

The daughter of the indistinguishable element did nothing.

The six who had helped him stood and came to where his head was, each licking his teeth and sniffing him closely. One by one they made their way into his mouth and across his tongue, and down his throat, just as the Master had, except that where he had sought to kill, they joined with him, not consumed but in partnership, existing in the safety of his healed belly, lending him their strength.

As each one entered him, he grew in power, fire making him burn, water giving him the force of a tidal wave, mountain the power to crush, wind to be a hurricane, light and darkness to blind and scour.

When this was done, the seventh daughter pulled at his tail. When Sirius turned around, she showed him where to go, which was out the way they had come, back to Mount Mordew.

The Master knelt, took the locket, and backed away from the white dog. He didn't recognise this avatar, but he knew its voice. Portia, the Mistress of Malarkoi.

When he moved back, she growled. 'There's nowhere for you to go, Sebastian, except one place. That's where I want you to go.'

Behind his back, he toyed with the Tinderbox, as if he might be able to remove the quarantine without speaking the charm.

'There's no point,' she said. 'You've already lost. You must see that.'

He was used to hearing this kind of thing from her. They'd once played chess, back in their schooldays, and she was always telling people that mate would be in three, or four. Sometimes six. He'd listen, as he was doing now, because she was the kind of person who would go on until she got the response she wanted. Which was for everyone to tell her how great she was. How clever. But he wasn't a child now, and chess is just a game.

'One mistake,' she continued, 'was to quarantine that locket you have behind your back. Now you won't have time to free it before the dog gets you.'

The Master didn't nod, didn't shake his head, didn't smile, didn't frown. He didn't do anything.

'The other mistake was to get attached. You've always been so good at avoiding that. Until now. And to Bellows, of all people. You've been bereaved, Sebastian, and bereavement weakens a person. You know that, right? You can think it doesn't, but it puts death in you.' She trotted up to him, tapped him on the chest with her paw, on his sternum, where he'd put the mystical organ in the dog that she had now sent to kill him. 'And when death is inside you, Master, part of you yearns for it.' She turned her back on him, took a step away, took a breath, as if she was going to say something else, but he brought the quarantined locket down hard, hoping to smash her brains in.

A glass paperweight, a fist-sized rock, a ball of something heavy – a pétanque ball, something like that – can do some damage, but this dog was an avatar of the Mistress of Malarkoi. Portia had made herself a goddess in her own city, nested in realms so deep that nothing from the material realm could touch her. She was immortal there, omnipotent, the creator of heavens unnumbered. Rather than smash in her brains, the locket bounced and away, and she continued walking away from the Master.

She said what she was going to say as if he had done nothing, which was, essentially, what he had done. 'And when you yearn for death, Sebastian,' she said, turning back to face him, 'you'd better have a heaven waiting for you.'

She stepped to one side and, galloping down the mountainside, came Sirius, bolstered by his daughters, blurry with the power of every element, divine Goddog.

The Master ran.

XXVII

The Mistress of Malarkoi

THE MISTRESS'S LEVEL, Malarkoi proper, was full of pyramids.

Some were on the ground and the right way up – with the big end downwards going up in steps to the top – some were in the air, upside down, almost interlocking with the ones on the ground, except never quite neatly and never touching. Some were huge, some were smaller, some were made of dark stone, some were made of light stone. There were even tiny ones the size of a bird that just hovered there in the air in front of Prissy's eyes, so she had to change focus to make sense of their scale and move her head to the side so as not to bump into them.

It was hot and bright, and the air shimmered in the gaps between the pyramids and there was a humming sound that came from nowhere, as if there were steam engines or something inside them.

She turned back, but the Door was dark.

With no obvious path forward, she went for the easiest route between the pyramids. The one to her left was gigantic and made from porcelain, bright white and smooth, where the one that hung down from above was sandstone, rough and red. A clump of smaller ones was to the right, the bottoms of them all facing each other in a circle so they looked a bit like a flower. Because they only almost interlocked, all these pyramids, there was enough space, but only just, for her to go by the porcelain one, and squeeze past the sandstone one, doing a limbo-type bend, while avoiding the points of the flowery ones.

She had to squint when she did it because the light that was coming from somewhere was bouncing brightly off the white pyramid and it made it difficult to see whether there were other floating ones in the air. She banged her head a couple of times and had to clamber up and down the steps where she could find gaps to squeeze through. When she did this her ears got close to the stone and that was when she could hear what the humming was. It wasn't a steam engine, it was the noise of talking, hissing sometimes, or mooing, which was how she guessed what must have been inside these things.

They were worlds, like the bad ones she had come through to get here – places full of people and stuff – all making noise that she could hear if she listened closely enough. She didn't do it, but she reckoned if she could slip a brick out from one of these pyramids – that's what they were made of, loads of bricks all piled up – and look in through the brick-hole she'd see them all up to their weird business in there.

There were more pyramids than she could count, hundreds and hundreds of them. In fact, there wasn't anywhere where there wasn't a bleeding pyramid, except for the gaps, so God knows how many people must have been in there. Cow-heads and snakes and dragons and Druids and wolves and stags and shadows and... well, who knew?

Could be anything in there.

Prissy leaned against a block of sandstone that was coming down from the sky.

How many people lived in Mordew? She'd been around the city a few times, on errands, scoping out jobs, that kind of thing. She reckoned there were more people there than she'd seen cow-heads, but not nearly as many as there were snake people. And if each of these pyramids had that many in? There must have been millions inside there. More even than that, probably.

It made the Master look stupid – him fancying himself such a big deal when the Mistress was hiding all this stuff.

And how far did it all go on for? Prissy hadn't spent much time contemplating the nature of infinity because she'd grown up in a very finite, cloudy kind of place where you couldn't often see the stars, or the dead, black expanses between, but she looked around and started to contemplate it now – the endless cram of these pyramids, each endlessly filled with worlds, all packed tight with people living their lives and getting up to whatnot.

It was mind-boggling, especially after all that had gone on to get here. It didn't make much sense, so she stopped thinking about it.

Where was the Mistress, anyway?

Prissy climbed up, squeezed down, turned corner after corner.

It occurred to her that if pyramids were such a big deal in this place that perhaps all these ones were stacked up into a big one, like the hill that Mordew was made on. The more she thought about it, the more right that seemed, and because she was down at the bottom – she could mostly see the ground between the lowest stones – if she went up as high as she could, she might see the top of it, if there was one.

It was certainly worth a try.

One pyramid nearby was very irregular. Most of them were smooth, but this one was made of cut-up bits of mountain, with handholds and ledges, and cracks that Prissy thought she might be able to slide herself into. She went over to that one and started to climb it.

It was hard going, and she kept banging her knees and scraping her elbows. Sometimes she had to reach out and hold onto one of the small floating pyramids, trusting it wouldn't move, though it looked like it was going to, but she eventually got high above ground level.

Just as she thought, she started to see sky between some of the gaps. Pyramids are much less broad across the tops than they are at the bottom, and as she got higher, she realised there was an edge nearby, up and to the left, because she saw a cloud moving across it.

She had to do some complicated gymnastics and contortions to get up there, stretching her legs so her back was wedged in just the right way to let her reach up to a handhold and swing herself up, but eventually she was perched on a medium-sized floating block of stone up high in the air with nothing above it, sitting halfway up a slope.

Below was a sunlit plain, and while there hadn't been much grass in Mordew – not where she lived, anyway – there was loads here, except not green, a kind of vibrant yellow, like the picture of the lemon in the cocktail glass on the poster behind the bar in the Athanasians – artificial, but somehow still enticing.

Up in the sky there were firebirds in big flocks. Out of habit, Prissy flinched and started back into the gap she'd just come out of, but when she got over that she realised this lot weren't going to dive-bomb her. They were swarming all over the sky, cheerfully soaring up, and then following each other, swooping about. None of them were exploding, or screaming, or dropping feathers that burst into flames when they hit your hovel. They were in very good condition, from what Prissy could see. Not mangy at all.

They were having a great time.

There were smaller birds too, sparrows and swifts and all that lot, and while they weren't in flocks or anything, they were flying about everywhere too. In the far distance there was something that must have been a dragon it was so big, and this one was alive and flapping its wings. There was a lot to see, up in the sky, and none of it seemed to have its sights on Prissy, so she looked down.

There in the grass were herds of cattle-headed people, pulling up handfuls of grass and chewing on it, so that it stuck out of either side of their mouths. Some of them were sitting down, some wandering around, and here and there were cattle-headed children feeding from their cattle-headed mums' tits.

There were person-headed snakes, slithering through the grass, talking to each other, just like in the place she and the others were all summoned to, except these were more happy-looking and relaxed.

Prissy started to get the idea that this place was going to have all of the stuff she'd already seen if she looked long enough, and that this was the right place for them.

There were other creatures that she didn't recognise and because she didn't recognise them, they were hard to give names to. She thought of them as thin pigs, tall dogs, wasp-women and wobblers. None of them looked like they would kill her, so she decided to get down to where they were, because even in a place like this she might come a cropper just from falling.

When she got to the ground she went forward for a bit, then looked back, and there, just like she'd cleverly worked out, was a pyramid of pyramids, huge as could be, like a mountain climbing up into the sky, made of a patchwork of stones of different sorts, cracked all over with the gaps she'd climbed through.

Why it was like that she didn't know, and it looked so weird she didn't blame herself for not being able to guess, but weirder was that above it all there was another pyramid, just as big, balanced by its tip on the tip of the first pyramid. It was black stone – jet, or onyx, or coal – and it blocked out most of the sky behind. The way it hung up there, solid, as if it had the right to balance like that, was very eerie and odd, but by now Prissy was used to seeing eerie and odd things, and to ignoring them, so she turned her back on it and left it there to hang heavily where it oughtn't to have been.

She walked down into the field, which at least had the good grace to be under her feet where the ground usually was.

The wind blew soft and warm, making slow, wide waves of the grass stalks, perfect yellow ripples that marked the contours of the ground below them and hugged the hills.

People walked through the grass, outdoorsy and sun-kissed, with nice skin and good posture. They were tall, and though they didn't look like her in the face, Prissy thought they carried themselves like Dashini.

Haughty? She didn't know if that was the right word, but it meant the right thing to her as she thought it. Snooty, except they probably deserved it.

They weren't poshly dressed, this haughty crowd; they all had barely anything on, slips and dresses and short trousers like it never rained in this place or got cold.

They weren't angry, either.

What were they, then?

Prissy couldn't tell.

The closer they came, the higher they emerged out of the grass. There were children with them – all sorts of beautiful, little children, all about the same age: fat, thin, short, tall, fair, dark, noisy, shy – all sorts. Around their necks these kids wore chokers in silver, which glinted in the sunlight.

There must have been at least a hundred of them, and in the grass behind there were more. Some had their shoulders out of the grass, some just the tops of their heads. She could see the faces of some of them – serene and graceful – and lots of the time the glinting of their silver chokers made the grass look like a field of stars, only if the night sky happened to be yellow.

When they got closer, Prissy saw that they were looking above her head, off to the left of her, ignoring her completely. She was part of the foreground of a scene, and they were only interested in the background.

Prissy turned to see what they were looking at.

Some people are surprised by a lot of pyramids hanging about. Some people are surprised that those pyramids all make one big pyramid. Some people are surprised that, in the sky above the one big pyramid there's an upside-down big, black pyramid, and some others are surprised when they see a whole bunch of stuff they'd already seen before and had thought they'd left behind. All those surprised people would have been even more surprised by what surprised Prissy when she saw it, and so was the girl herself.

There, off to the left of her, was a gigantic Mistress.

Gigantic wasn't really the word, because Prissy had thought the dragons were gigantic. The pyramid of pyramids had been gigantic, and the pyramid upside down and on top of that was gigantic too. This Mistress was *gargantuan*. Prissy wasn't absolutely sure whether 'gargantuan' was bigger than 'gigantic', but she meant it to be when she thought it to herself.

The Mistress was absolutely massive: hundreds of miles across and hundreds of miles high, even though she was sat on the ground with her legs crossed.

Her feet were higher than the great big pyramid, her knees higher than that, her waist, her chest, her arms, her shoulders – all of it really, *really* high. Her head was so high up it was hard to imagine she could breathe all the way up there, where the air was known to be thinner.

She was also stark naked, though the way she was sat preserved her enormous modesty, her skin etched in blue with symbols and pictograms and hieroglyphs, and she was holding her arms so that both were on the one side, one hiding her vast bosom. These arms were like the hands of a clock reading about a quarter to ten, with the hour hand the left one and the minute hand the right.

If it hadn't been for the Mistress's face – which was just like an older version of Dashini's except with spines around it instead of feathers, said spines radiating out like rays of light – Prissy wouldn't have recognised her, because most people you recognise don't tower up into the sky, awe-inspiring in their monumentality. Prissy would have taken her for some stupidly enormous statue, but she was breathing in and out and her eyes were open.

In one hand – the hour hand – she held the sun, and the other one she clenched in a fist, but Prissy reckoned there was a good chance the moon was in it. It was that kind of thing: like the cuckoo clock which told the weather above the bar at the Temple of the Athanasians, a place that suddenly seemed a very long way away.

The people and their silver-necklace-wearing kids went past where Prissy was stood staring, goggle-eyed, up at the Mistress, and walked slowly and seriously down the hill towards her. There must have been a good fifty miles to go, Prissy thought, and not much of a path down there. They sang as they went, under their breaths.

There was a good game that you could play in the slums – kabaddi, it was called, though no one knew what that meant – which was like a kind of tag, or tig, or it, but where you held your breath when it was your turn to be it and had to give up when you breathed in. When you played you had to say 'kabaddi' under your breath, over and over, to prove you weren't breathing in. That's what these people were doing as they walked, except it wasn't 'kabaddi' they were saying, it was something else which Prissy couldn't catch.

Anyway, they were saying it as they walked, and it looked for all the world as if the Mistress was listening and smiling at them, which gave Prissy the fear because you can't go around killing people's daughters without them getting arsey about it, and if she could see these haughty followers, she could probably see Prissy too.

Then, like the clockwork head of a clockwork cuckoo on a clockwork cuckoo clock, the Mistress's head spun round, suddenly, and there was a new face, the same but with the eyes closed and the mouth unsmiling. Prissy would have been lying if she said this didn't disconcert her somewhat, as Gam might have put it, but not so much as the idea that the Mistress was staring right at her.

The people and the kids didn't seem to mind: they stopped, flattened the grass out below them and sat around in groups, chatting and passing each other flasks of water and packets of sandwiches, or whatever they ate – waiting it out until the other face was back?

They beckoned Prissy over, these picnickers, and for want of anything better to do, she went and sat with them. When one of the kids came across – all big smile, silver choker and dimples – and offered her half of a juicy round something, she realised that she was a bit hungry, as it happened, so she took it, and said thanks.

They were speaking in a language with words that she didn't recognise, but somehow Prissy could understand what they meant. When she said her words in reply they could understand her, which was weird, but only until you got used to it.

'Firebird daughter,' one of them said – an old lady who nonetheless looked like she could pick Prissy up and spin her over her head if she fancied it, because she was very chunky about the arms and shoulders – 'your pallor speaks of a life under the clouds of Mordew. Do not fear, your paleness will dissolve in time.'

The others sat around, nodded seriously. Now they mentioned it, Prissy realised she was a bit pasty compared to this lot. 'I've never caught much of a tan before,' she said, 'so I doubt it.' She rolled up her sleeves and twisted her forearms so they could see both sides.

This made the others laugh, but Prissy didn't know why.

Another one – a man this time, with a long nose and a serious look in his eyes – said, 'Did it hurt, to be unprepared for death by fire?'

The others stopped laughing about her arms when he said it, which Prissy was grateful for, but now they were all staring at her, waiting for the answer, which she didn't have to hand because she didn't know what he was going on about. 'What fire?' she said.

The man put down his food on his plate – he had been holding a rolled-up bread thing, with salad poking out – and brushed the crumbs off his knees. 'How did you die, sister?'

Prissy said, 'I'm not dead, am I? Look at me!' but the face she pulled when he asked the question – puzzled and dismissive – communicated something to them before she even got the words out, and while she was talking, the people gathered their kids in and put their arms around them as if she was going to drag them away.

The serious-faced man stood up and walked away to a patch of grass where no one was sitting, gesturing for Prissy to follow him, which she did.

'What's the problem?' she said when she got there.

'Did you come by the Door?' he said.

Prissy nodded, because she had come by the Door, and couldn't see what difference it would make lying about it. The man took a step back and did one of those whistles you can do by putting your fingers in your mouth and blowing.

A loud, long, piercing note sounded, splitting the quietness and making everyone in a mile radius spin round to look where they were.

Once the whistle had stopped echoing across the plains, the man bowed and walked back away from her to where his lot were sitting, though none of them were laughing, eating or doing anything else but staring straight at her.

Now, Prissy had had the coppers called on her a great many times in her life, so she guessed correctly that this was what was going on now – the man had summoned the constables and she was about to be delivered into the hands of the law. In the past, she had always had a place she could run to, knowing Mordew like the back of her proverbial, and though she looked around just in case, she knew she had no means of egress: no sewer, no backstreet, no safe house, no loft into which to abscond. So, philosophically, calmly, she waited to be nicked, knife in hand hidden beneath the folds of her skirt.

She didn't have to wait long, though rather than some unsavoury blokes in dirty uniforms and clutching hands rushing her, she was apprehended from above by a team of firebirds.

There were four of them, much sleeker, neater and less motley-looking than the ones she'd seen in Mordew. She'd got up close to a few, back then – everyone had – but most of them were on their last legs, wounded, in the process of being killed, half-exploded or already dead. They were raggedy things, those Mordew firebirds, with their feathers pulled out. They looked like plucked chickens and their eyes were dulled by an opaque mist of suffering. These four, though – one taking each arm and lifting her up, one flying underneath so she could sit on its back, the last one flapping in place off to one side and supervising proceedings – were perfect specimens with elegant demeanours, sensitive eyes and a lithe turn to their limbs, of which they had all four, none of them broken or dangling.

They were a little bit alight – puffs of smoke came from between their feathers when they ascended skywards, little candle flames came from the corners of their eyes – but they weren't hot to the touch, so Prissy didn't burn her thighs even though there was no saddle on the one on which she was sat.

Their feathers were cool and soft and, all in all, it wasn't a bad way to get handed over to the authorities.

The supervising firebird was leading the way, by the most direct of routes, to the Mistress's head. Even though the huge woman was facing the other way still, there was no doubting their destination because it was slap bang right in front of them, the long spines of her hair trailing down her back, ending about halfway.

It was still a long way to go – they were only just above the end of the Mistress's arse crack and some miles back – so Prissy made the best of it and looked down at this weird place.

The slums had a border with the Southfields, back in Mordew, and if her sister ever ran out of weed – which was rarely, because she had a strong taste for it and worked in just the right place to lay hands on it more easily – she'd send Prissy to pick fresh, and the Fields were where it grew. Obviously, it was fenced off, but no fence can tell a plant where to grow since plants don't give a monkey's about any of that – and fences can't talk anyway – so there were usually a few bushes here and there that people hadn't stripped.

Anyway, when she was there gathering it, pulling off sticky buds and wrapping them in wax paper to keep them fresh, avoiding the plants that grew out of the Living Mud, she could look into the Fields. It was a bit of a relief from the shitty places she spent most of her time in, so she'd stand on the lowest rail and put her face between the bars so that most of her head was out of the slums. She'd pretend she lived there, in the Fields, in the countryside.

It was pretty.

Had she seen then what she was seeing now – the whole of this world was like fields, yellow and rippling, hills and mountains, divided sometimes, crazily overgrown other times, dotted with groups of people and herds of weird animals, lakes and rivers, forests and all that kind of thing – she'd have known that the Fields weren't that pretty after all, because this place was much prettier.

The wings of the firebirds beat in her ears, their smoke gentle in her nose like sandalwood incense. She wanted to pull her jacket across her chest because it was a little bit chilly the higher they went up, but the two firebirds that had her arms were still holding her. She looked one of them in the eye and it opened its beak a bit, as if it understood. It let go of her arm and so did the other one. They both swooped down – to catch her if she fell off, probably – and now she closed her jacket and kind of cuddled the one who was carrying her around the neck, which made her much warmer.

It was so nice, she felt a bit bad for thinking, when it crossed her mind out of nowhere, that she could cut this thing's head off with the Nathan Knife if she fancied it. Shadow King thoughts, she reckoned, not quite gotten rid of. She swallowed them back, along with a lot of recent memories.

If you've ever climbed up to the top of Mordew – or a mountain, if you've never been there – you'll know that even when you can see the top and think to yourself, 'Good, I'm almost at the top,' you're always wrong because there's still miles to go. This was what happened to Prissy: she could see the Mistress's shoulder and the firebirds were looping round so that they were coming in more to the front, where her face was, and Prissy thought that it was getting time to pay the piper or whatever, making her sit up straight and get herself prepared, but the last bit took ages – so long that she got a bit fed up with waiting.

That last part when you're climbing is the most tiring and dispiriting part because you delude yourself that you're almost there, and then when you realise you aren't it makes you feel like an idiot, and your legs act like they might not make it. Prissy wasn't tired, because the firebirds were doing all the flying, but she still got the pip because the last part was never-ending. She'd geed herself up for answering to the Mistress, whose daughter she'd just sacrificed, and was expecting to get, at the very least, an earful about it, even if it wasn't her fault. If people's daughters don't want to get sacrificed, then perhaps people's daughters shouldn't give other people no choice in the matter, really, when you think about it. And if people raise their daughters so they do things like that, then do people really have anyone to blame but themselves?

Prissy had all these arguments in her head, but it was quite stressful going over them repeatedly. The longer it took to arrive, the more knackered Prissy kept on feeling, and the more nervous. The firebirds flapped gracefully around her, their faces maintaining an implacable expression that spoke of an internal self-confidence that Prissy would have loved to have felt, but that she wasn't feeling in the slightest.

That's also the kind of thing that brasses a person off – when they have less poise and equanimity than a bleeding bird does, even if it is a great big fiery one.

Eventually, the profile of the Mistress was completely side-on, demonstrating that she had two faces – one awake, staring into the distance, and one asleep, eyes shut. Despite this, there was only one ear per side and only one earhole in the middle of an 'S' shape the pinna made, it serving for both faces.

Whether it was because the firebird sped up as it swooped into land, the other three swerving off to leave the one she was sat on, or because it was a trick of the perspective, the ear came forward with what seemed like a dangerous rapidity. Prissy was deposited in the black tunnel of the Mistress's external auditory meatus, unceremoniously dumped there by the firebird as it spun off to join its mates.

To Prissy's relief there was no earwax to speak of, just a smooth, marble-like surface, as if the Mistress was made of rock. It gave a bit, though, and was warm against her palm – which Prissy put flat on the floor – and against which a slow, heavy heartbeat pounded.

She started to wonder how huge that heart must be, given that this earhole was about fifty feet high, give or take, when the loudest sound she'd ever heard made her put her hands over her own tiny ears.

It was a voice, but God knows what it said because it was so loud it made Prissy's eyes water and any words it said distorted so she couldn't make them out.

'Sorry!' the voice said, much more quietly now. 'Any better?'

Prissy nodded, but the Mistress's eyes were round the front, so she called 'yes' down into that cavernous earhole.

'Great,' the Mistress said. 'Apologies for my enormous size – it's a side effect of being worshipped. Realms like this are very flexible, and my people have as much say over how I appear as I do. Anyway, welcome to the sixth level of the Great Golden Pyramid. Sorry it was such a slog to get here. I've been watching your progress keenly.'

Prissy, thinking there was no point messing about, started in with the apologies straight off the bat. 'I'm sorry about killing Dashini. I didn't have much choice.'

There was a pause, but people pause for all sorts of reasons, not necessarily related to whether they're going to turn their wrath upon another person.

'No problem at all. That Shadow King is a pain,' the Mistress said. 'He loves to have people kill each other. If it hadn't been you killing Dashini, it'd probably have been Dashini killing you. That's why I keep him in a realm with no people in it.'

Prissy didn't feel that quite covered it, so she said sorry again anyway.

'Never mind. Hadn't you wondered why she took you with her in the first place? I think you and the boy might have been earmarked for the chop, one way or another.'

It was so high up there that even the clouds passing below were tiny things, like cotton wool balls held at arm's length.

'It's all gone to shit back there,' Prissy said. 'All your heavens have turned to hells.'

413

It was strange, talking to this goddess, standing in her ear, waiting for her to reply.

'Sorry again,' the Mistress said. 'My fault, I suppose. I haven't been doing my maintenance much of late. I'm getting on a war footing, what with the approaching Crusade. Makes heavens a little inconsequential, I'm afraid.'

'I don't know what you're going on about,' Prissy said, because she didn't.

The Mistress laughed, which sounded odd. 'I guess not.'

There was no way down from where she was standing. Prissy would have broken every bone in her body just jumping down onto the Mistress's shoulder, but she was strongly of the opinion that if she could have gone, she would have. 'Can you do me a favour?' she said. 'I don't know what all this is supposed to be about, and I don't care. Dashini said you could rescue my friend Gam. She killed him and left him in the Wolf and Stag place.'

The great head twisted on its neck, spinning Prissy round and making her fall. She thought she was going to slip out of the tunnel, slide down the earlobe and die, but one of the firebirds came and caught her before she did. It put her back where she had been and then sat down in front of her to stop it happening again.

'Of course,' the Mistress said, ignoring what had happened, the direction of her face seemingly changing without her noticing it. In her hand the sun rose another notch in its progress, shining out from between her fingers. 'Work of a moment. But can I make a suggestion? I need an heir, and you killed mine. I don't have the time to make a new one, so why don't you do it?'

'Do what?'

'Become the new Mistress of Malarkoi. Dashini was next in line when Nathan killed me, and she only needed to Inherit. Why don't you Inherit instead? You're eminently qualified, which is why I brought you back after you suffocated.'

Prissy didn't understand this either, but in front of her a slightly larger than girl-sized pyramid resolved in the air, and in this was a girl-sized door. The door opened, and inside that there was a room filled with things. Prissy couldn't be any clearer than that because she didn't recognise any of them, except perhaps a table and chair.

'I'm afraid I can't leave here,' the Mistress said. 'I'd be too vulnerable to Assembly racking. You can, though, once you Inherit the position of Mistress. You'd get my material realm magics; you'd get the Golden Pyramid. You'd get all sorts of things.'

Without thinking it over, Prissy said, 'Not worth the trouble.' She'd never make it through those realms again. Not on her own.

'It wouldn't be any trouble,' the Mistress said, reading her mind. 'You're in the Pyramid now. Rescuing Gam would just be a matter of going down a couple of flights of stairs, putting your hand through the Door and pulling him out. Easy.'

'And then what? We live in a pyramid forever?'

The Mistress paused again, while, possibly, a puzzled frown crossed the expanse of her waking face. 'Oh, you mean the quarantine! Not a problem. Easily cracked if you know how. Just unleash a flock of firebirds – they'll have the job done in moments.'

Prissy took a step towards the new pyramid, peeked around inside the doorway. 'I'd get to do that, would I? Unleash flocks of stuff? What's the catch?'

The Mistress could have laughed at this point too, but she didn't. 'Malarkoi is at war, Prissy. Remember? You have to take that over too.'

Prissy thought that she might take the powers and forget about the war.

'You think that now,' the Mistress said, 'but just you wait. It's not that easy to ignore. The Assembly are on their way. They want to destroy all of this, dissolve all these realms back into nothing, take you all back to a re-education facility and make you live in their real world. That's something which would not be, I'm going to tell you now, much fun at all.'

While the Mistress was saying her piece, Prissy had already decided what she was going to do. A slum girl like Prissy, offered something valuable, takes it, even if there are strings attached. Why? Because she's never had anything of her own. Things, as far as she's concerned, can't ever get much worse, so there wasn't much point in looking gift horses in the mouth. That said, she still had a few questions. 'Does Dashini get to come here, to your heaven, now she's dead?'

The Mistress might have smiled at this, it was impossible for Prissy to see. She sounded like she was smiling. 'You're very bright, aren't you, for a slum girl? Yes, Prissy, Dashini gets to come here. And, to answer your next question, she's not going to be pleased to find I've given you her city, and to answer the question after that, she might try to get it back. But then again...'

The Mistress carried on talking, but Prissy was tired of listening to her, so she walked forward into the girl-sized door in the slightly larger than girl-sized pyramid. Dashini might do this, Dashini might do that, Dashini needed a friend. Blah, blah, blah, something, something, something. There's a type of person who likes to yap on and on about everything, and the Mistress was definitely one of those.

Prissy closed the girl-sized door behind her, and the gargantuan woman's voice faded away.

'I'm the Mistress of Malarkoi now,' Prissy said to herself, 'and my first order is that everyone give me some peace. I'm sick to death of the lot of you.'

XXVIII

A Description of a Fight from Two Perspectives, Part Four

THE LOCKET WOULD NOT be caught up with. Every time the Master thought he was going to – when the angle of the bounce went directly up and he felt he might be able to get under it, catch it like a cricket ball – it would be dragged away from him by some invisible force.

The locket was being drawn to the God chamber! All magic things went there if they did not have the will to go elsewhere. He had seen this for himself, on nights spent on the balconies of the Manse, the magical pollutions of the engines in the Underneath drifting down like fog to where the weftling's corpse was, and now the locket was pulled there too, its magic attracted as material things were repelled.

The Master stopped.

It was not simply that his body was incapable of endless running, or that he did not have the speed. It was that he was thinking. He had become reactive, doing what Portia wanted him to do, failing to approach the world on his own terms. That is what an animal does – acts without thinking, provoked by stimuli. Had he fallen that far? It had been a bad day, certainly, but not sufficient to degrade him entirely.

As he thought, a distorted fluke raised a tentacle to him, feeling him out from its lair in a tumble of rocks. He muttered the *basic defensive response* at it, and it shrivelled like a dead leaf.

Keep it simple, he told himself.

He made the signs and said the words and put himself at the works where the gill-men were shoring up the breach to the God chamber. Very easy. Child's play.

Here came the locket – still some way off, but shining brightly, illuminating the greasy skin of the gill-men as it came.

It was bouncing directly at him. Behind it was the divine dog, but perhaps far enough away.

Panic, he thought, was the enemy. Calmness was the key.

Panic was what Portia had wanted to provoke with her mate-in-two proclamations. Then and now, what she wanted to do was to unsettle him enough so that he made mistakes. Sitting on the other side of the board, her hands clasped, a superior look on her face, riling him up, taunting him into making tactical errors. And he had made them – there was no doubting that.

But he didn't have to continue to make them.

The quarantine ball was coming nearer now, in range for the dissolution spell, so he began that. Another thing he could do, providing that he didn't panic.

The ball bounced, he said the words, he made the signs, and, by degrees, it became less bright, and less bright, and less bright until it disappeared above a scaffolding on which gill-men were working, shoring up the containment walls that would prevent the Assembly accessing the weftling's corpse.

He ran off up the hill to where the locket would be – a hundred yards, perhaps two. Very simple. Climb a ladder, get the locket, destroy the dog.

Even though he kept telling himself not to panic, he couldn't quite help it – the dog was almost on him. He could see the locket – it was wedged in a gap between two planks, six feet away at most, but the ladder was shaking, the shoddy workmanship of these gill-men was no match for his weight. He put his foot up another rung, but the ladder listed over to the side when the platform above collapsed. The dog was right there, its breath ruffling his hair.

The Master leapt over to where the locket still was, grasping as he flew through the air.

Why hadn't he translated himself there, he thought, as he felt the pull of the ground on his body, tugging him away from where he wanted to be. Panic. Stupidity. He reached past the possible extension of his limbs to where the locket had been, but it wasn't there.

If it had been there, he wouldn't have reached it, but, by chance, when the dog collided with the structure which the Master was climbing, it dislodged the locket precisely to the place where his hand was waiting to grasp it, and now the chain was looped over one fingertip.

That was the good news, but the force of the dog's collision sent him careening away, to the very edge of the still unsealed breach of the God chamber, which glowed with the putrid orange glow he had so hated on his visits to the corpse. Worse, the locket was pulled towards it, even though he was stuck at the edge, and worse still, a link of the chain from which the locket depended was now coming loose, gold being a relatively flexible material, particularly in a piece of delicate jewellery such as Clarissa's heirloom.

Now, as he held the chain, the locket strained to be with the weftling, and the link was losing its integrity, becoming not a link but a straight piece of metal, unconnecting of the links either side of it.

The Master grabbed at the locket, but the dog slammed into the ground beside him, knocking him dizzy, its breath hot on the back of his neck. When he opened his hand, it was empty, and all that lay by the edge of the breach was the chain, flat and limp and broken.

The Master turned onto his back. Above him the dog stared down, jaws slavering. There was no time for anything else, and no solution he could think of, but before he could decide to do anything – perhaps he would have turned back over and dived into the God chamber by his own volition – he was seized by a fluke, glowing blue, the exact size and shape of Nathan Treeves. As the dog lunged, moments before the Master would be bitten in the face, the Nathan fluke threw the Master down after the locket.

Sirius dived for the Master through the breach as if he was chasing the escaping scut of a jackrabbit entering its burrow, his momentum taking him into the God chamber.

His teeth he'd bared, in preparation for biting, but the inside made him immediately frightened. It was bathed in sick light, humming low and constant, and all around was the sweet smell of rot, like meat on the turn.

There was the Master, screaming as he fell, tumbling through the horrible nothing, and Sirius fell behind him, clawing the air, down into the putrid orange-blueness of this place.

The Master had lost sight of the locket, not because he had turned to see if the dog was still after him – he'd assumed that was the case – but because it was too small to make out, and there was no light to glint off it.

He knew this place, though, had been here a thousand times – more – and knew where the locket would land. It was drawn to the weftling corpse, it would land on its chest, and now, because it had been cracked – because Portia had cracked it, something he had known all along but had never admitted – Nathan's Spark would connect with the weftling's corpse. Because the Spark was the energy of God's nerves, the weftling would begin to resurrect.

There is something calming about falling that is like the opposite of panic. The body knows and tells the mind that there is nothing one can do as one plummets through the air, so fretting might as well cease. In the calmness that situation brought, the Master considered that, no matter how serious he thought a situation was, how perilous, it was always, in actuality, even worse.

He had thought, in his stupidity, that his main problem was being chased by a divine dog, determined to bite him to pieces, but now he saw that his main problem was the weftling.

This was what she had meant, the avatar of Portia, when she had said he had already lost. He had thought, because he was too dim to play this game, that she had meant he was going to die. She had said his error had been to quarantine the locket, and this, just as she had intended, had made him even more determined to remove its quarantine, but that had been another move on her part, because now, when the unquarantined locket met the flesh, he'd have to turn his attentions from one foe to another, much worse one.

The closer he fell to the weftling corpse, the brighter its invisible light became.

She was very good, the Mistress. He could admit that to himself, at least. But...

The vagaries of his bodily motion turned him over on his back so that, as he spun, he could briefly make out the silhouette of the dog, picked out in the light of the breach it had widened out. He continued spinning on some axis he was unaware of, and then down below was the first indication of the corpse – a darkness at a distance.

But... she couldn't want him dead.

If the Master was dead, what would stop the weftling's return? It would mean the end of the Tontine and, worse possibly, God's retribution. Was the dog a match for it? Absolutely not. So she must have intended that he prevent the resurrection. And this was a comfort.

Could the Tinderbox do it?

No.

Was that the locket, that impossibly minute thing there? No, it was more like a mote in his eye.

All other matter the Tinderbox would burn from the world, but not the weftling. If anything, it would wake him up more quickly.

What did that leave?

There was only one thing.

Even a man beaten can see the skill with which his opponent bests him. If he is a sportsman about his game, he will shake his opponent's hand and tell her 'well played'. If Portia had been there, he would have done just that, if she'd have let him.

The Master turned himself in the air, made himself as much like an arrow as he could, and prepared for his next move.

Sirius barked and snapped and flailed with his legs, not knowing to where he was falling or to what, but this was a short-lived concern, because soon he was enveloped in a painful light that seemed to lessen him, compressing his godly self, shaking the mystical organ within him until he was again a dog that would not raise eyebrows – large, certainly, formidable, certainly, but not a god. He wouldn't have looked out of place in Smykes's pit.

Here was the Master, right below him. He was up to his elbows in a man's body and the light that had diminished Sirius was coming straight from the Master's eyes, as if he was directing it with his gaze.

Which was exactly what the Master was doing, drawing power directly from the weftling's pure God-Flesh, tapping the perfect material Real, returning the dog to his proper concept regardless of any other perversion of the weft that had caused him to diverge from God's will. Sebastian could see everything now, knew everything, took it in an instant. There were the six daughters that had merged with Sirius, themselves daughters of the Mistress. He dissolved these back into non-existence and pulled the dog's divinity out of him, leaving a mass of God-Flesh in his belly, potent and undigested, the remnant of power, which the dog vomited up.

Sirius could feel the loss of his children. They had lived inside him, and he looked around for the last, nameless one, but she was gone. Without them, he remembered his service-pledge to Nathan and howled that he should have forgotten it so long, its obligations suddenly felt more strongly, since they had been ignored.

Then, seeing Nathan's enemy, smelling Nathan in the air, he locked the man with his eyes in the way that a dog will when he announces his intention to fight, and growled.

The Master found the locket – that's what Portia had meant for him to do. If he left it any longer, then the weftling would have awoken here and then, and he needed the Tinderbox to finish the dog. The moment he pulled the locket out from where it lodged in the weftling's chest, the light left his eyes and he replaced it with the flame of the Tinderbox, which snicked open very easily, as he had designed it to.

Sirius was burned down to his ghost in a torrent of ignited weft-stuff as he collided with the corpse. The Master had to pull the stream of Tinderbox power away so that it did not reanimate the weftling, but as both these things happened, Sirius's seventh daughter, whose name was Treachery, that unknown and final element of the world as it is, snapped from the locket with her long and graceful mouth the pellet that the Master had made of Nathan, and leapt away.

The Master had expected this, had thought that was the end of it, that he knew know the Mistress's final mating move, the destruction of the Tinderbox that might have destroyed his enemies and won him the Tontine, but then, as he looked down at the weftling's corpse, expecting to see nothing more than its familiar inanimacy, instead he witnessed the thing's featureless face transform, the skin replaced by the flesh that had been removed and which Sirius had vomited up.

The Master scrabbled at the place where the dog had collided with the corpse, trying to drag the reunited parts of God-Flesh apart, but it was too late. *This* had been her plan, then: to end it all, to bring the weftling back to life, to upturn everything, and for a new game to begin, her preparations already in place.

The Master grabbed the weftling by the face, but there was no murder he could do to it, no damage, and there formed a nose and mouth, eyes.

But it was not the face he expected.

It was not the face the Mistress would have expected either.

In the place of the solid and familiar face of the weftling – that bearded god of iconography – instead there came another's.

It was Clarissa there, as if sleeping. Nathan's mother, her manipulation of the weft-state complete enough that the weft had accreted around her form, was now God, albeit separated from her Spark. Bizarrely, incongruously, from her cheek jutted the flight of a crossbow bolt.

The Master fell back, appalled, scarcely able to understand what he was seeing.

Then she opened her eyes, which, for Sebastian, was the final straw.

XXIX

What Treachery Did Next

THE SURFACE OF THE SEA is protean in its variability. To an etymologist this is a tautologous statement, and any experienced sailor knows that it's a truism, not worth saying. But to sailors who have found a new love? Though they will not quite admit it, everything seems fresh, even useless and overfamiliar things.

To Captain Penthenny, the sea that day seemed protean in its variability, new and exciting.

So was the wind. So was the flotsam of Mordew that so recently had been nothing more than a tedious obstacle to steer around.

When Penthenny reached down, she found, where the extent of her arms reached, a warm hand – Niamh's – which she held, and then, in the middle distance, she saw a blot of blackness amongst the bobbing and charred beams of collapsed houses.

The blot was steady in the uncertain and changeable blue.

If it had been Oisin at her side – she would not have touched his hand, let alone held it, but if, by some coincidence, it had been him – the captain of the *Muirchú* would have taken the blot for a floating plank, or a dead shark, or some other marine commonplace. She would have turned aside, gone to her cabin, uncorked a bottle of whatever remained to be uncorked and would have drunk herself to sleep.

But it was not Oisin at her side.

People newly in love – perhaps it is better to say people whose love is newly reciprocated – are always alert, though they might not know it, for situations that, while they do not test their love object – that would be too negative – do at least have the opportunity to demonstrate the truth of the feelings that surge in their blood.

424

It is not that the loving heart does not believe itself, but more that it desires events though which new love might be expressed, so it can enjoy them. This was the case with Penthenny, though she didn't know it consciously, and so, when she saw the blot, she sought out that loving agreement that a kindred spirit will demonstrate on the shared experience of something unusual.

Penthenny said: 'What's that?' and though she didn't expect an answer that gelled with her own feeling, her heart longed in its desire for it, since it would be as good as proof to it that its burning was not unjustified.

Fortunately for the captain, heart, mind and all, Niamh said, 'Looks like a dog, I think.'

The smallest things: these are what love is made of, in the beginning. As time passes, the life of lovers gains gravity and import – it gathers life and death, joy and sadness – but right at the beginning, the shared sight of a dog, at a distance, when someone else might have said 'What are you going on about?', these almost nothings are enough to solidify the world around something that otherwise might not come properly into being.

They will be forgotten, certainly, in the passing decades, but that makes them no less true, no less vital when they happen.

Penthenny had her idea confirmed, and this was what saved the seventh daughter of Sirius – whose name was Treachery – because who could not, at the risk of undermining their new love, let a shared vision of a dog at sea falter through lack of interest, or lack of action?

No one loving, is the answer.

And the fish, who was recently made aware of a future mate? It too invested in the rescue, looping through the waves back the way it had come, back towards Mordew, a place it now held fondly in its heart where once it had been only the source of a strong, but troubling, magnetism.

The *Muirchú*, without any orders being given, made the adjustment to its course that brought Treachery into its orbit.

Niamh, waving away her captain's insistence that she need not do it herself and that one of the sailors should be called, took a boathook from the rack, and placed it in the water, thinking that, since a dog will grab a thing with its jaws, this dog, all grey and wet and sleek as a seal, would do that, and so allow her to draw it in.

She did not know, Niamh, that the dog had its mouth filled with the pellet Nathan Treeves had become – how could she? – but she was disappointed when the dog did not seize the wood that would have saved its life.

She, like Penthenny, had her happiness invested in its saving.

She had long harboured an irritable type of desire for her captain, one day attraction, the next day fury, and this was solidifying in favour of attraction now, so she could not brook this lack of will on the part of the dog to be saved, because what woman will prefer a continuation of irritation to the satisfaction of her longing? Who would prefer to see a dog drown to saving its life? Very few who are not disposed to those odd types of pleasure, which Niamh was not.

Consequently, by a rational resolution of an internally written equation, such as Niamh was wont to draw up for herself, she stripped down to her underclothes – something she was now glad to do in front of her superior, rather than appalled by the prospect of – and dived over the side, entering the water like a cormorant does, perpendicularly, surfacing as the same bird will surface, fish in mouth, before forcing itself into the sky and away.

Niamh did not fly up, but crawled through the waves towards the dog instead, who was very near now, and grabbed her under the forelegs.

Treachery rested her head on the sailor's shoulder, to breathe more easily through her nose and the corners of her mouth, and both of them were hoisted up onto the deck of the ship by Penthenny, who had sent Oisin away back to his cabin when he had tried to help. There he attended to whatever it was he occupied himself with – the imagined details of which were the source of much amused and belittling gossip at the mess tables at mealtime.

Was it his fault that he was to be the focus of a new couple's separation of themselves from the loveless of the world? No, it was not, but then he was to perform a similar unkindness on the people of his acquaintance years later when, his brass nose shining, he attracted the delighted attention of a partner suited to him, the particulars of whom this tale does not provide, and which you can therefore choose for yourself.

Treachery – once she had been dried with towels, fed, watered and combed – by standing at the prow and indicating with her nose where it was that she wished to be taken, made use of the captain's almost infinite intention to see this dog's story end positively to have the ship take her to the waters above the sunken city, Waterblack. These Irish-derived sailors knew it better by the name 'Dublinn', which was like 'Black Pool' in their ancestral language, and there Treachery dropped over the side the Nathan pellet, as her mother, the Great White Bitch, avatar of the old Mistress of Malarkoi, had bid her to do.

It sank down and landed on the Ha'penny Bridge, now rusted and barnacled.

Her job done, Treachery allowed herself to become the pet of Penthenny and Niamh, who named her *Perdida*, the lost one, which from that time overwrote her given name and thereby provided her an entirely different fate – a story for another time.

XXX

The Thousand Million Flames

NATHAN HADN'T FELT PAIN as the Master killed him – the remains of his nerves in the material realm were communicating with a mind that was already disconnected from agonies of that kind – but that's not to say that he didn't suffer.

Suffering takes many forms, and ones the body provides are not the most acute, even though that's sometimes difficult to remember. Crushing, breaking, rupturing are all sensations that have an immediate effect on the attention, but there's a limit to them: eventually the body will be overwhelmed, and the sensations will disappear, even if their causes continue. Spiritual pain, though – that can be unlimited, since the immaterial realm, where it dwells, and where Nathan's spirit now suddenly and entirely dwelled, itself is unlimited.

When the Master did what he did to Nathan – compacted his physical form into weft-stuff that contained, in a seed, a great part of the boy's Spark so that the Master could store this energy in the perfectly destructive occult artefact known as the Tinderbox, intending to use it later as a defence against his enemies in the Assembly's Eighth Atheistic Crusade – the boy knew it, but it was another type of suffering that occupied him, and this was much worse than the pain his body had wanted to express.

He felt, overwhelmingly, that he was not where he ought to be, and that the place where he was didn't wish him to be there.

This sounds like a lesser thing than pain, but when a person puts their hand over a candle flame it should not be there if it is to remain in consonance with the negotiations bodies have made with the world over countless generations. If a person steps into a bonfire, they should not be there either, and the pain is even greater, a bonfire being to a candle flame as agony is to a scorch. So much should that person not be there, that there is a threat to their existence that this pain announces, that they jump out of the fire and extinguish themself to the best of their ability.

The same for the molten rock in the cauldron of a volcano, pooled molten metal, even boiling water. The physical nerves announce to the mind as pain the fact that the body is where it should not be.

When Nathan's concept, conscious in a way only his enormous infusion of Spark energy made possible, suddenly became manifest in the immaterial realm with no means of jumping out of its fire, this was represented as the worst of these burnings, akin to the hellfire of scripture. While it's possible that this burning was the source of the images of a burning hell used to frighten sinners into repentance, it was only Nathan and a very few others that had ever experienced them first-hand, since the concept of a man is usually unconscious to any experience in the immaterial realm, a function of the realm's sempiternality, its abstractness, and its timelessness.

The moment the Master succeeded in bringing Nathan to a state of null material presence vis-à-vis his body, his concept experienced an infinite blossoming of immaterial sensation, if there can sensibly be said to be such a contradictory thing. Though the immaterial realm does not have any interest in the affairs of the material realm, since it does not know time, which material affairs rely on, Nathan, by virtue of the weft as binding the material and immaterial realms through the Spark, brought with him his own pre-existing material interests. These were difficult to reconcile with the existence he now found himself experiencing, poorly anchored in anything except the overwhelming burning.

There is no way of providing a sense of how long Nathan suffered like this, since the passage of time, as has been said, is alien to the immaterial realm, all things existing there in a solid state, unchanging, but we can understand that there existed a state of Nathan's concept that was typified not only by a 'suffering Nathan-ness' but also, and to a greater degree, an 'unsuffering Nathan-ness' which, to the material realm, would seem like a development, a passage from one state to the other, a gradualness and change that, while not actually present in any demonstrable sense in the immaterial realm, can be understood, no matter how fallaciously, as Nathan coming into an awareness of something other than hellfire.

Within these concepts were notional 'knowings' of the things of his attention as they were represented in the immaterial realm. That is to say Nathan, inasmuch as he had retained that sense of himself that we, as people, understand ourselves to have, knew immediately all the things that had, were, and might be happening in the material and intermediate realms by virtue of their presence as immaterial concepts in the immaterial realm, since that is where the concepts for all things reside.

This is where the omniscience of gods comes from – facilitated by the Spark and the weft – and Nathan, immaterial as he now was, was party to this 'all-knowingness'. That said, it is an effort to contain this within a consciousness in the immaterial realm. A direction of attention is required, and this is not easy, since 'direction' is non-commensurate with a realm that has no natural spatial dimension. Nor is there any 'consciousness', since that is quality mostly possessed by material things. Nathan only achieved a semblance of direction and consciousness by virtue of his weft-infusion and his recent material presence, and neither of these in sufficient quantity to make thought easy for him.

Also, Nathan was prone to the immediate lessening of interest in particular things following the omnipresent realisation that they are only instances of general things.

The same can be said for that thing that we call time.

Nathan's previous existence in the material realm had trained him to know progression and development, entropy and disordering, pattern and meaning, so that events flowed in one direction in a causal arc, each thing logically determined by the last and in its turn logically determining the next. So, he was used to expecting and wanting these things from matters to which he turned his attention. Like the reader of a story, he wanted to know what happened next, but the realm he found himself now in was more like the glossary of a book – all information was contained within it, but in no chronological order and without the necessary linkages between one entry and another that a narrative gives.

But much better was this arrangement of a glossary suited to the mind that he now possessed, if such a thing as a mind can be said to exist in the immaterial realm. He could follow the references to the other concepts that each concept held without first having to wait for this or that event to occur, placed into existence by this or that actor under this or that influence.

Instead, he need only to-have-wanted-to-know, and he knew it in its entirety.

This, we might think, gave him the answers to all questions that might ever have been posed about 'Nathan Treeves' and the life he had lived, was living and would live. This is certainly true, in that all the information was immanent and present to him. Such immanence and presence, though, also makes very trivial the concerns of a simple iteration in the material realm of the infinite immaterial concepts. The turning of the attention to general ideas robs the mind of its sense that there is value in the limited material realm. It also reduces the desire to know, since 'value' and 'desire' are both effects of a poorer sort of relationship with knowledge than a weft-instantiated mind – a god's mind – possesses.

He did know, immediately, what it was that his mother had been doing in the slums and why.

He knew and could have replayed, if he'd had the urge to do that, what now seemed an almost non-existent and irrelevant event: the moment when his mother finally removed his father from the material realm.

He could have seen what only she could see with the magical INWARD EYE – her manipulations of the structure of the weft in an attempt to reform it in her own image and thereby achieve prime godhood and to create the material realm entirely consonant with her will.

Yet just because he knew it, that did not mean he paid it any mind.

Similarly, he knew how she would behave, and how others would react, and how, in the end, the matter of whether she achieved the role of the new weftling was resolved, but that is not to say that he chose to direct his attention to that, since there was also the knowledge of how that would turn out, and why, and how the warpling would react, and all the influences and ramifications of all the events his mother had a hand in.

In knowing, and in seeing the concepts of all things, he knew all of that to have been part of a much wider state of things that, in its ultimate wideness, was an unmoving, undifferentiated mass of matter and concept and energy. He knew that at the distances his mind could now know, all things were unmoving in their infinite complexity. They were omnipresent across the weft in themselves and in all the things that were not and could have been. From such a distance who did what and when in an instance of the material real was a very small thing, perhaps even nothing, just as a string that makes up a thread of a tapestry with a repeating pattern is only minutely relevant to that pattern, though essential in its way – if it was not there and neither were the other strings and threads there would be no pattern – but not in a particular way, only in a general way.

Which is to say that he knew what his mother did, but did not care enough to know that he knew.

And still there was the agonising pain that meant he was not for this place.

And if he was not for this place, then where was he for?

And how could he reach that place?

And what was his role there?

He also knew, immediately, the fate of Sirius, his dog. He knew his ascension into a dog-god hybrid by virtue of his consumption of the God-Flesh remains of the weftling's face. He knew his ascent through Mount Mordew to launch an attack on the Master in defence of Nathan's remains, used in the making of the Tinderbox. The concepts, joined in the will to form a chain of causation, were available to him as passive knowledge, and in any form his mind now chose, so he could have watched Sirius cavort through the Merchant City. That part of Nathan that retained an interest did just that, and delighted in the sight, but that was a tiny aspect of the larger knowledge-knowing that was Nathan's mind.

'Here, Sirius! Here, boy!' that part cried, but in the immaterial realm there is no cause and effect; instead there was a tendency for Nathan to lose his character, to lose the anchor he had once felt with a material instance of 'Nathan'. Increasingly, 'Nathan' tended to be the entirety of the immaterial realm. This is the fate of almost all spirits as they exist after death. In the material realm everything is limited, subjective and distinct, in the immaterial realm it is all unlimited, objective and diffuse. For the self, this is a dangerous thing, since, like a cordial dispersed in too much water, the flavour is lost after only a minor dilution. Nathan knew things, but only part of him was conscious of them – the whole of him approached a knowledge of everything and was conscious instead of that.

And still there was the agonising sense that he was not where he should be, manifested to him as pain, and that there was somewhere else that he ought to be.

Perhaps he was being drawn to where he ought to be, as oil is drawn to the surface of vinegar with which it is commingled since it is a lighter stuff and thus thereby floats up and separates, even if some agitation, in Nathan's case his Spark infusion and weft-coherence, might make a temporary heterogeneous mixture, in the same way that oil and vinegar make an emulsion when shaken or beaten with a whisk.

Where would Nathan separate off to, and under what influence?

Here were the perfect forms of the ghosts, their weft patterns manifest as concepts, and if Nathan had wanted to know what motivated those clubhouse shades who recognised him during his life in Mordew, who urged him to actions he could not understand, he could have interrogated their instances here.

He did not.

There was only one such instance that held his attention against the general tendency to fog and become general, and that was the character of his father, who appeared to him as a musical motif comes to the listener of an opera, as a pattern that can be discerned in other things, a sequence that is noticeable in the appearance of notes and is developed and mutable but still recognisable in part or whole and in different moods or keys.

His father was always there in the places to where Nathan directed his attention, or as contour in the deformation of the landscape that Nathan made representative of the immaterial realm, or in the path of a body of water as it travels seaward, or in any of number of metaphorical senses that had no exact immaterial corollary but which a material mind can picture. Always there, his father was, always altering the world or being altered.

He was there in the idea of Nathan's mother as she ate her husband's flesh to power her spells, and though Nathan knew that horror was associated with this concept he did not experience it, the body being now a thing of almost laughable particularity and the concerns of proper digestion and consumption an almost inconceivable aspect of universal patterns, free from the moral concerns a material mind fixates on.

Here were the assassins that Padge had hired to kill his friends, and here was the Mother of Mordew, her troglodytes, her pet, the cattle-headed people, the person-headed snakes, le Roi de L'Ombres. Here were Prissy and Gam, Joes, in their heaven, Dashini, dragons, and wolves and the White Stag. Here were Bellows and Adam, Anaximander and Thales. Here was the Master, drunk on Rescue Remedy and grief, and Penthenny and her crew, their ships made of fish and oysters and squid.

All these things and more – all things – were there.

But there was only one thing that Nathan cared about, one thing that Nathan's broad and focusless mind would focus on:

his father's finger, that interdicting digit always forbidding, wagging in his face until it became the only thing he thought about, except the pain of the wrongness, and the feeling of separating off, of being drawn away.

The finger, severed and scabbed, his dead father filled with pain, now further and further away.

This complex of concepts, the matter of thought, the diffuse totality of everything-at-once was a state of timeless being in which Nathan was inherent.

Then there was the pressure of air against his skin, moist air in his nostrils, a sufficiency of air inhaled into his chest. There was the sky, paler than a duck egg, a shimmering line of distant mountains, no clouds to obscure anything. There was the closeness of a person, a woman, her arms around his waist, embracing him from behind, hands clasped in front of both of them, across his breastbone.

'Hello,' she said, and though he recognised the voice he also recognised the feeling of his weight, and the feeling of his knees, and the feeling of his bare toes spreading on cold polished stone.

He was on an altar, around him a menagerie of creatures, all with their throats slit, and below them a hill, patchily covered in heat-browned grass and low thorn bushes. He looked over his shoulder and there was the Mistress, Dashini's mother, whom he'd killed with the Nathan Knife. Except now she was alive, and in her clasped hands red to the wrists she held her own knife.

In the air was the smell of incense, thick and sweet, cinnamon and sandalwood. The Mistress stepped back, smiled apologetically and carefully put the knife down at her feet. 'Sorry!' she said. 'You're perfectly safe.'

Nathan had never been a boy who was quick to understand what was going on around him. Gam had an instinctual understanding of any situation, so that he could do whatever needed to be done. Prissy knew instantly where danger was coming from, so that she could avoid it.

Nathan could be in a situation indefinitely and not under-stand any of it.

Now though, with the immaterial realm so recently gone, he knew who this woman was and where they were, and why. 'I know,' he said, and he did.

The bodies of the animals around him were sacrifices she'd made, having rolled up her sleeves and the hems of her loose trousers, having put on a butcher's apron and clogs, having pulled back the spines of her hair and tied them with a ribbon. These offerings had come to her, knowing wordlessly that she meant them no harm, so that she could take their lives.

Nathan could see them as if it was a painting. They gathered around her in a circle, each sacrifice coming after the other in a calm procession, their choir of gentle purrs and bleats suggested by the swaying of the tree branches nearby. She opened her arms to them, gathered them up onto the altar and killed them. She made her spells with their life energy and by this method he was summoned away from the immaterial realm to be here, with her.

'It's my turn now, Nathan.'

He knew what this meant too.

Unlike the Master, she would not delegate her work to a Bellows. She liked to get her hands dirty – that's the kind of thing she'd said in the past, in the long-distant years of her youth.

Nathan knew this as if it was obvious, carried over from the immaterial realm. If he tried to think how or why he knew, it was too broad for the mind he was now materially constrained to be. Almost like reaching to hold the smoke that comes from a recently snuffed-out candle, as Nathan reached out to capture the thoughts they spread out at his touch, lost their shape and dissolved into nothing.

But the sense of the familiarity of the truth remained with him. That is something a person can have to an infinite extent, unlike knowledge, which fills the conscious mind very quickly.

He didn't wait for her hand, but held his out to her, and she led him through the Spark-drained flesh that surrounded him, off the altar, and down onto the grass.

She was tall and slender and moved with the easy, fluid unselfconsciousness of a dancer. Where the Master's confidence was stiff across his shoulders, tense in the line of his jaw, grey in the impassivity of his eyes, hers came from balance, solid in the flatness of her feet, symmetrical in the placement of her hands, slow in her breathing. She smiled where the Master gave nothing away. When she swept her arm off across the landscape, he was not anxious as he turned his attention to where she indicated.

She showed him the world: low hills, vegetation short-cropped and neat, here and there cairns of the same stone from which the altar was constructed – a kind of smooth, pinkish quartzite – dotted at random, between the cairns, following the contours of the earth, drystone walls that stitched the land into a patchwork quilt of enclosures. Within these were herds and flocks of animals, some white, some brown, chewing methodically through the greenery overseen sometimes by dogs, sometimes by eagles.

There was a curve to the horizon – not too tight, but unusually obvious – where the green land met the blue sky, and in that sky there was no sun. It was not hidden behind a cloud – the sky was entirely clear – it simply wasn't present.

'This is a waypoint,' the Mistress said. She took a few steps to stand at his shoulder. She made a gesture – surreptitiously, Nathan felt – that made nothing of the altar corpses and dissolved away the blood on her hands. 'It didn't seem necessary to kit it out with anything much beside the basics.'

An eagle lifted off from a nearby cairn, heavy in the air for a moment, dropping close to the ground before a single beat of its wings lifted it up and forward until it was gliding in a circle over the enclosure it was charged to observe.

The Mistress saw Nathan looking at it. 'Would you like to be an eagle, Nathan? It can be arranged.'

In the distance a dog barked – two quick yaps – and on the breeze there was the scent of sheep dung, sweet and fresh.

'They are embodied spirits of the dead of the past, living out their dreams, waiting to be transitioned into their heavens.

If you want to be a dog, or an eagle, or a goat, or a firebird, you can come here and serve out that time. When I use you for magic, I can pay you back.' She put her hand on his shoulder. 'I know you won't take me up on the offer, Nathan, but it's a genuine one. I can embody you in whatever way you wish and then, when you've shown that you can serve me, I can find a world for you.'

She took her hand away from him, weightlessly, because she had not allowed even the pressure of her material form to disturb him, and she went down from the hill they were standing on. 'I can find a place that even you would be happy in. I can fill it with friends. With love. With adventure. Whatever it is you want.'

When she looked at him it there was nothing but a guileless wish to give in her face, but Nathan saw something else. He saw her motives. He saw her desire to punish him for his destruction of her city.

She knew what he was thinking, and Nathan knew she could hear his thoughts: this was a realm she had chosen, and if she chose to know what took place in it, even inside a mind, then it was only right that she could. 'Of course, I have my own interests to serve. In other realms. Threatened realms. But not here.' She danced away, simultaneously above and within the earth, simultaneously beneath the heavens and constituting them, and when she winked, her eye was the absent sun eclipsing and returning to beam on him. 'Here we can relax.'

When she said this, it was like a commandment, and Nathan slumped where he stood, his head strange and heavy in his hands, to sit cross-legged on the dry grass, helpless in her primacy of this place. His mind knew the vibration of her pitch, and everywhere was the strong smell of sandalwood.

'Nathan, do you want to be an eagle?'

His gaze was fixed on the rock in front of him.

One of the smallest spiders is a little red mite, and one of these was running in undisciplined circles on a rock between his thighs. It dodged, in its redness, between patches of green moss and yellow lichen. It ascended pale, crystal extrusions, salt-like against the grey. Nathan reached out, not really trying to touch it with the tip of his finger, more to divert its course, expecting it to avoid this new obstacle.

But it didn't.

A small red spider mite has feathered limbs, and the moment a frond touched Nathan's skin he became that mite, leaving his body, which then towered infinitely high ahead. For a moment he saw the colossal mass he made in this creature's eyes, knew himself suddenly as a more gigantic and complex thing than any other being in its world, understood the awesome extent of his own presence in the realm. Then, he thought instead as a mite thinks – entirely coldly and empty of any doubt. There was an obstacle, and this he avoided. There was light, and this he tended away from. There was hunger, and now he sought to eat.

No pause, no consequences, no thought.

With his mouth he made something move, took it down into his gut. It was lichen, but it filled him with the scent of sandalwood, and he was back in Nathan's body, the mite a tiny dot of blood red that he could choose to crush away to nothing in a moment.

'Would you like to be a spider mite?'

She was a diaphanous presence now, half matter, half wind.

Nathan stood up. 'No,' he said, and he looked the Mistress in her face, solidifying her back to a human woman, defining the edges of her being with his thoughts. 'I want you to answer some questions.'

The Mistress smiled – her name was Portia, this fact Nathan now knew – and she gestured to another hill, where a pavilion had been standing, unregarded, with a table and chairs beneath its canopy. 'Let's talk over a drink. I have *anisette* on ice for occasions like this.'

'What,' she said, 'is your first question?' There was a jug on the table – blue and white porcelain with a crackled glaze – and she picked it up and filled their glasses.

'Why aren't I dead?'

The Mistress frowned. 'Well,' she said, 'you are dead. Sorry, I should have made that clear. You're dead, and your remains belong to the Master of Mordew, as does your Spark. I've summoned you from the immaterial realm, because I think I've got a way to bring you back to life.'

The Mistress took a sip of her drink.

Nathan opened his mouth to speak, but she shook her head.

'I haven't finished. I was just wetting my whistle.' She stood up abruptly, making the glasses on the table rattle, and Nathan instinctively drew back. She took two fingers and whistled, and from a distant field a sheepdog, lithe and eager to serve, raced to her side, bounding over the drystone walls, and startling the flocks.

'I'm not going to do it, because I know you can understand an abstract, but I could, very easily, take my dog's head off.' It was panting happily, now it was in her presence, and she scratched it under the chin. 'If I wanted, because he's mine, I could separate his head, where the little fellow's mind is, and hold it in this hand.' She put one hand out, palm up, and mimed holding a melon in it, or a small pumpkin. 'If I let it, this separated head would die – I can stop that happening just as easily, by the way. I'm not going to do it, because I know you don't need to see something happening to understand that it can happen. Once it was dead, and its body was dead, and even after both had rotted down to compost, I could, with a finger click, bring it all back, stick his head back on his shoulders, and he'd be none the wiser. He wouldn't even know he'd died. I'd take his immaterial concept and marry it to his material presence, and he'd be good as new. That's manipulation of the weft for you – anything that was, anything that could have been, anything that will be, can be brought into being. If you know how and no one stops you, that is.'

The Mistress ordered the dog to sit. He did, so she gave him a treat.

'What if this was someone else's dog? What if that person killed this dog and he didn't want it brought back? Then it gets tricky. If I kill a dog, then I'm part of that dog's existence, right? Birth, death, they're defining moments, and just like your parents own you, because they're associated with your birth and are part of you, then your killer, if you have one, owns you too, because their weft-presence and your weft-presence are bound together. There's no avoiding that.'

Nathan put his glass down. 'Are you saying the Master owns me?'

The Mistress nodded. 'That's exactly what I'm saying. If I own this dog, kill it, let it rot down, then it's relatively easy to bring it back because its conceptual presence in the immaterial realm ended when it no longer made sense to identify it with any existing material presence. When the Master killed you, he condensed your material presence into weft-stuff, effectively removing your existence from the material realm but tying it to a new object. Which means that not only does he own you, but you also can't be brought back into the material realm by anybody else because you're already there. In the locket.'

Nathan went to get up, but the Mistress put her hand on his shoulder.

'Don't panic.' She sat back down, took a stalk of celery, used it to stir her drink, dipped it in salt, and said, through the crunching as she ate it: 'I think we can fix it. That's why you're here. We just need enough Spark to revise the weft so that he doesn't own you, and then we can free your material presence from the locket. Before I tell you how I'm going to do that, I'm going to show you why.'

Before Nathan could say anything, she put down the celery, took the sheepdog's head and, muttering under her breath, slit his throat. 'Razor blade on the underside of the ring – in case I forget the knife,' she said, as if this was the cause of Nathan's frown. When that didn't cure it, she went on. 'Don't feel sorry for him; he goes now to the realm I have prepared for him, where he'll live an infinity exactly to his wishes and desires. He's already there. Always has been there, really, if you think about it. Always will be. Infinity courtesy of the weft. And he wasn't a dog – he was one of my faithful high priests, living out his purgatory, awaiting his release. Anyway!

441

No time to waste or we'll need to do another one. Take my hand!' She held it out.

Perhaps it was because this was her realm, and she, ultimately, determined what occurred in it, or perhaps it was his own will, but he took her hand, and they were suddenly on a concrete plain, divided into hundreds of bland, functional corrugated iron-roofed units about ten feet cubed.

The sky overhead was grey and overcast, the countryside behind spoiled and largely featureless, but the people who milled about amid this gloom were of an incredible variety and colourfulness. It was almost as if there was a rule against any two of them being the same.

The Mistress was beside him, the dog's corpse gone. 'This is one of the places that the Assembly learn their Hailey-Beth specialisms, deep in what they call the real. Those buildings are the entranceways to subsurface halls where they study their disciplines.' The way she said 'study' and 'disciplines' suggested she didn't think much of them.

She wheeled the realm around until they disappeared behind the units.

Now in their place was a mountain-sized block, shimmering with heat, a black wedge tens of miles across, tens of miles distant, from which bands of rippling light emanated like the colours on a puddle of oil, tinting the ground, painting the overcast.

'And that is the source of their energy – a weft-state reactor. In the material realm – this is just an observational duplicate – that facility is wired, using some technology that I haven't been able to reproduce, or even really understand, directly into the weft, and it draws on it somehow – the mathematics is baffling – to manufacture everything they use. Long story short, they don't like people interfering with the weft.'

Now the two of them ascended into the air and the ground below them went blurring past without any sense of motion at all. Nathan felt it in his inner ear, the dizziness of things not being the way they ought to be, and he was about to be sick when the movement shuddered to a stop.

'And this,' the Mistress said, as if not nauseated in the slightest, 'is what the Assembly intend to do about it.'

They were stood amongst hundreds of women beneath a huge tarpaulin. Everyone wore a cross somewhere on their clothes, but otherwise they were like the people from before: all completely different. Some were unloading things, others were putting things together, others were directing people to where still more people were working. None of these people saw Nathan or the Mistress, and when they looked like they'd collide with them, they went straight through.

'The Women's Vanguard of the Eight Atheistic Crusade. Malarkoi is about a hundred miles from here. Mordew just over the horizon. We've been interfering with their weft, and now they've come to put a stop to it.' She turned Nathan to face her. 'I can't let them do that, Nathan. It would mean the end of everything I've built. The war with Mordew? Nothing in comparison. That was a distraction, to keep the Master busy. If truth be known, we need him, if only to divide the Assembly's efforts.'

'What do you expect me to do?'

The Mistress smiled, and now they were back at the table, the porcelain jug in front of them, the ice cubes in their glasses unmelted and everything as it was.

'I expect you to stop them, Nathan. I can't do it because I'm mostly in these intermediate realms where the Assembly don't come. The Master can't do it because he's stupid. Your father won't do it. Your mother – who knows what she's doing? No, it's down to you, Nathan.'

'How?'

'Well, you aren't going to like it.'

This realm had no ground, sky or distance – this was a space with no landscape, no geography, hardly any light.

In it were second-borns, extending off in every direction.

They were neatly arranged, precisely ordered, columns and rows and stacks, all suspended in the air, none touching, perfectly clean and healthy and naked and sleeping.

They were mostly the children of people, but there were also those of animals, of insects, of people-animal hybrids, of dragons, of firebirds, newborns all of them.

Some types of magnet in the material realm repel each other, and when ball bearings are made of them and then placed on a flat tray, once that tray is shaken the bearings arrange themselves regularly a set distance apart in a grid. These children were like that, and this realm separated each from the other by a set distance in a grid in three directions and seemingly extending forever.

Nathan and Portia were in the middle of the realm, and everything diverged from them uniformly, off in perfect lines of suspended infants up, down, left, right, all perfectly the same.

The realm was silent, but there was in the air the smell that babies have, an entirely pleasant and soporific, milky, tranquillising miasma that fills every aspect of the mind and prompts thoughts of quietude and rest. The infants did not move, they did not pass water, they did not seem to breathe, but they were alive.

The Mistress smiled, swallowed, then started to speak, only to stop before she'd made a word.

The nearest infant to them – a human child no more than an arm's length away – was pudgy and creased, her forehead curved and covered with a light brown gauzy down. Her eyes were closed, her lips parted so that her toothless gums could be seen, matt and pink, like solid xanthan. Her hands made relaxed fists either side of her umbilical scar, which was newly healed.

The Mistress tried again, but Nathan interrupted her dry-mouthed pause. 'Why...' he began, but the words were so loud in his ears that he stopped before he woke them all, his hand automatically covering his mouth.

Portia put herself between him and the endless realm of still children, at least in one direction. 'Electricity,' she said, 'can be thought of as consisting of a vast number of sparks.' She waited for some reaction from Nathan, but the words to him were almost meaningless. 'Fire, then. A fire – a campfire – is

444

like a collection of candle flames, each merging together to make one big thing...' She bit her lip. 'A wave...'

She stopped and, perhaps for the first time, Nathan saw emotion on her face. She felt guilty. He didn't know how he could tell – perhaps it was the lingering influence of the immaterial realm – but he saw it. She had made a plan, started a process of which this was the result and now, when it came to pulling the trigger, she didn't know if she could do it.

'When you make a sacrifice,' she said, 'it lets out the remaining life force. That can be used to deform the weft. The Spark is God's will, and most spells don't need much of it. What we're talking about, Nathan, needs a lot.' She made a gesture that indicated with a sweep of her arm the babies. 'It needs a lot,' she repeated.

Nathan nodded. It wasn't that he understood, or that, in understanding he could see her logic, or that, in seeing her logic, he endorsed what the Mistress was telling him, tacitly recognising its necessity. His nod meant none of those things. His reaction was a simple response to the words, and the fact that they made sense. His mind was filled with questions, none of which his shock would allow his mouth to utter.

'They're not procedurally generated, if that's what you're thinking. I take them at birth, with the full consent of the parents, and warehouse them here. *Secundus est pretium caeli*, that is the deal. I give them heavens, their second-borns are the price. I take them before they leach their Spark back into the weft. That's what mortal life is – the gradual return of Spark to the weft.' She looked at Nathan, not so much to see if he understood but more, it seemed to Nathan, to gauge whether he thought this was a reasonable thing to do. Whether it was something he might have done.

Nathan made no expression at all.

Not finding what she wanted, Portia went on. 'I've found heavens for each of them, don't worry. They have a direct path to their perfect realm – sometimes that's their parents' realm. Bespoke realms of their own, or a direct translation to the realms of their loved ones.'

Nathan looked at each of the babies he could see. There weren't that many – the volume had so little light he couldn't see more than twenty feet in any direction – but still it seemed like a terrible, awe-inspiring thing.

'Where I couldn't determine the best possible life for them,' she said, 'I worked through the weft, one strand at a time, and made a judgement. Admittedly, this was subjective – I understand that – but when I release their Spark it will be wonderful for them regardless. Heaven.'

One of the babies had the body of a snake. Another the head of a cow.

'I've done my homework, spent lifetimes, subjectively speaking, making sure I do this right. There's a thousand million of them. All tiny flames that will make one huge fire. With this fire I think I can retrieve you and break the locket from the inside – which would otherwise be impossible.'

The baby next to the snake-bodied one had a face that was scrunched and creased like a bulldog's. There had been a dog-faced girl in the slums, Nathan thought, but her face had had a muzzle, long, spiked with irregular teeth. This one was the other way – it hardly had any nose, and it seemed as if the absence was drawing the rest of its features in to fill the gap. It had red skin, almost purple, almost mottled, almost blue, and on its skin was thick white mucus. Its cord was still attached, the end frayed.

'Do you realise how much Spark energy is required to retrieve a pattern from the weft when another manipulator has claimed it? Do you know how much energy it is going to take to shatter the locket from the inside?'

Nathan didn't realise, but it was some multiple, he knew, of whatever Spark was contained in these second-borns, whatever Spark could be released. 'And you need me to say yes,' Nathan said. 'You need my blessing?'

She didn't seem to answer him. 'To make someone from his immaterial concepts and put him in a new realm – that's easy. The immaterial realm is where the intermediate realms come from. I can bring you into one of those, move you around

446

between ones I've already made, show you the world. It's easy – I'm doing it now. But to wrench you back from the Master? To purge you from the weft, re-establish you, instantiate you back in the material realm? Your father thought only God could do it.' There was a twitch in her cheek, and she blinked. She twitched again and blinked again, and then she rubbed her face with her hands. 'Do you understand, Nathan?'

He did understand. He understood that, if he agreed, she could return him to the world, regardless of the Master, regardless of anything. 'But what if I don't want to?'

She relaxed at this, as if she was relieved at his resistance, as if it solved everything. 'I don't have the power to force you,' she said. 'It would take ten times this number if you weren't willing. There isn't enough Spark in all the people of all the realms.' She looked away from him, and if she was seeing into the souls of every one of those children then Nathan didn't know it.

He was thinking other thoughts.

In his mind was that day, back in the slums, when he had forced the Spark silverfish into his father's body, to cure him of the lungworms. He had made them, those worms, with his Spark, conjured them up from the Living Mud. This is what he had seen in the immaterial realm. His father's lungworm infestation was the physical expression of his hatred for his father's weakness, hidden by his desperate and miserable obedience.

Nathan had tried to fix it then, but he hadn't had the skill, hadn't had power. He had lost the battle and his father had died.

He hadn't had the power to make his father live again. Hadn't known how to bring him back.

But now he did.

Portia had shown him.

'Do it,' Nathan said.

Without pausing a moment, without waiting to ask if he was sure, she clapped her hands together and as one every infant woke, screaming, spluttering, bawling as only newborns can, with a fearsome and horrifying needfulness.

'They have to be awake,' she said.

Nathan closed his eyes and ears to the terrible noise. 'Do it!' he cried.

The Mistress of Malarkoi sighed, but before he could change his mind, she clapped her hands again.

To the last the babies fell silent, leaving the entire realm echoing.

EPILOGUE

The Death of Sirius

WHAT IS THE DEATH of a dog in the run of things? In a world where people live out their lives in pain, where they are less than objects, burdens when they are not playthings, why should anyone shed tears over the fate of a dog?

Do not concern yourself – no one does shed those tears.

Innumerable dogs die every day. They are dying now, in their thousands, unregarded, unmourned: dogs starving, dogs drowned, dogs beaten, dogs euthanised.

You do not mourn even your own species who die in the same way – infants starving, children drowned, adults beaten, the elderly euthanised – it would be obscene for you to mourn Sirius in his death, since you do not grieve for your own people.

But poor Sirius did not deserve to die. He did nothing but faithfully serve his pledge. He looked up at the world, clear-eyed and panting, tail wagging, in all good faith, in expectation of love, and he received only violence.

Imagine a child who runs to you, open-armed and smiling. He laughs to see you. He loves you, and here he comes in his delight. He is a step away, jumping a little so that you might take him up in your arms and hug him to your chest, whirl him around so that he will throw his head back in joy.

You do not pick him up, though. Instead, you bring your open hand down across his face. You slap him.

There is, on this child's face, even before he feels the pain of the blow, a brief and all-encompassing failure to understand what has happened. He cannot believe that you have done it. Then he bursts into tears.

This is the first time that you hit him.

Once you have gathered him up, convinced him that he has misunderstood, told him that it was an accident, you send him off to play. He goes, unsurely and gradually, back to the world he knew before, the one of security and pleasure that he had lived in before you hit him.

Eventually, he forgets that the blow happened. Perhaps a year goes by, so that when he comes to you one day, laughing with his arms outstretched, he isn't expecting you to do it again.

Now you do it harder, punching him in the stomach, but before he can properly register what has happened you pick him up and hug him to you, which was what he wanted. You hug him tight and turn him round and round, and you laugh, as he should be laughing, and when you eventually put him down, you pat him on the head, affectionately, and send him off.

He is in pain, but he cannot reconcile that with your behaviour. His is only little, he doesn't understand the depths of your cruelty.

Even you don't understand it.

When you next see him, you are loving. You are loving for days and weeks and months so that the punch must not have happened. It is not something that can have happened when you are so loving.

There he his. His back is turned. He is enjoying something that is nothing to do with you – perhaps he is watching his puppy play. You walk up to him and kick him hard in the back, sending him sprawling. Before he can turn to see what has happened, you walk away. He must be four or five.

When you keep doing this to him, over years, he becomes a sad child, who finds it difficult to love the world. Why should he, when it has this horrible aspect to it? Unpredictable, irreconcilable violence is corroding of the spirit.

He becomes an unhappy adult, who others find difficult, but because a person is a type of thing that adapts well to its environment, he finds a way to be in his world, albeit joylessly.

Imagine a puppy now, raised to the same plan. He is strong, lively, large for his age, and so the dog man places him to one side of the crate in which his litter has been delivered. One by one his littermates are examined. This one is a runt, and with a twist it is dead, laid beside our puppy. This one is female and so she is reserved to another crate. This one is strong, but yet not as strong as our puppy, so it is twisted again, its mewling silenced. Three, four littermates are put beside him. He snuffles at them, wondering where their playfulness has gone, waiting on the time when the dog man's assistant will gather up his brothers and grind them for feed.

You must show kindness to a dog when it is tiny. Just as no boy will willingly come running, arms outstretched, to a man who hits him, at first a bond of love must be established, though this is false. He must love you, trust you, come bounding to you. Once he does this, his training can begin.

You know how this works, by now, having imagined the poor treatment of a boy. Spare me this, you will think, since you find it easier to hear of a child mistreated than a dog. You have learned, through your own mistreatment, not to care for people in the main – they are, after all, the source of all pain. Dogs, though, these you can still love, and you do not wish to be subjected to descriptions of their suffering.

Sirius suffered many cruelties in the pits of Heartless Harold Smyke. He was like that boy – wide-eyed, curious of spirit, delighting in the world – and he was shown cruelty.

Yet Sirius was different to that boy.

Where dogs differ from people is that they never find a way to be in their world. They never learn. They are less likely to lose their capacity for joy. They maintain their faith. Every slap is like the first one, every punch a mystifying shock, every kick a betrayal. The child, as he becomes a man, learns to anticipate random acts of terror. He prepares his defences against them. Dogs are stupid, defenceless. Slap a dog and he will cower and then come back for more. Punch him and he will let you do it again. You can kick a dog half to death, and he will come back to you, tail wagging.

He will flinch, eventually, there is no doubt of that, but he will come back to take his punishment. That is the type of thing he is. If he has his own cruelty to act out – and of that there is no guarantee – he will do it on others. Drop in a bait dog and issue the command and those dogs suited to violence will be as cruel to it as you were to them. This is why cruelty is necessary in the training of fighting dogs – it is a behaviour you model to them with your own, so that they can use it to kill in the pits.

They suffer their own pain, they take it inside, and while they may snarl and snap, if you are slow enough, patient, they will allow you to pat them, to stroke them, to ruffle their fur. They will lick your face. They will roll over onto their backs for you to tickle their stomachs. You use this trust to hurt them again, and then laugh about it.

Poor Sirius.

The Master turned the Tinderbox onto him in self-defence, the weft-stuff within it excising the dog from existence, taking him from the material realm. And was this not a mercy?

He was a good dog, taking joy where he could, bearing his pains. He was used with no thought for his feelings. The Master made him as a tool, raised him in dogfighting pits, sold him into servitude. He went from one owner to another, used for one purpose and then the next. Since that was the world that he knew, as soon as he was free, he bound himself to Nathan Treeves, a boy who had received as many slaps and punches and kicks as Sirius had.

They didn't deserve to be killed. Nathan didn't deserve to be made into the Tinderbox, and Sirius didn't deserve to be killed by it. Boys and dogs don't deserve cruel treatment like this.

But who receives what they deserve in a godless world? Do you?

What of the dead? What is their fate?

That depends on to whom they are bound. The Master of Mordew's dead go where they will, some becoming ghosts, some becoming ideas of themselves, others becoming nothing at all. The Master has no need of the dead, and they are free of him. The Mistress of Malarkoi's dead live with her in her heavens. She takes them, and at the price of their second-born children, makes halcyon places for them. Here they live with her forever, whether they want to or not.

What of Nathan's dead? He is to be the Master of Waterblack, the so-called City of Death. Those who have received cruelty in life go to this drowned place, and there they petition its Master for revenge.

The gates of Waterblack will soon open. Its citizens will gather in its streets, shoulder to shoulder. Under the command of its Master, they will return to the world and redress their wrongs.

Sirius will be at Nathan's side, at the head of this army, and who knows what he will do next?

APPENDICES

Photostats of a Notebook Taken by an Assembly Intelligencer (with annotations from Prose)

8.7912.22 – Transcription from Assembly Doc.Store B; cat. item 8.1345.23; (with annotations); intelligencer artefact; *auth.* Hailey-Beth Ambreen Prose; [*8.7912.20 permissions] *in progress.*

[cover and pages missing]… she always was. [l/b] Still, even without her undeniable facility with it, I am making progress – it won't be quick enough for either of them, but that was always true. [l/b] ***[1] [l/b] It's the look on their faces that makes me laugh – like they're despoilers. It almost makes me feel guilty. That might be overstating it. [l/b] Sparklines [?] of a sign painter from up on the Roche [l/b] Useful – an area of town you don't get much. [l/b] Hundreds of firebirds in the background. [see table][2] [overleaf][3]The boy is watching me. I'm sure he knows what's next. He can't do. Can he? [l/b] The atmosphere over the past few days has been intolerable. His father creaks and whistles and coughs until it makes my fists clench, and Nathan just stares up at me. His huge eyes – I'm sure he knows. [l/b] I've sent him out to the Circus. [l/b] just time? [l/b] ***[4] [l/b] There was time, but there's so much to note: much clearer today and the reifications more solid – not quite

---

1 [Desc] There's an image – like an eye, but squiggly. Isn't an intelligencer error; I've flicked through – I was careful! Don't have a heart attack – and it appears throughout. No idea what it is. Hereafter: *eye*
2 [Note] She keeps very accurate accounts. There's what looks like a double-entry grid.
3 [Note] New ink; tidier hand.
4 [Desc] A different image – semi-random cross-hatches – throughout, like the eye. Hereafter: #hatch#

sight, but very close. Whether this is because that's the way it is, or whether I've just stumbled on an area of unusual susceptibility, I can't tell yet. It may even be an effect of the Sparkline – this one was very strong. Regardless, it was possible to lay a marker! I can't quite believe it, even as I write it down. I was, before the energy waned, able to come and go, all the time tied to that anchor. So much easier. Impossible to describe the relief. I think it can work, now. I'm certain. With a known location, it's just a matter of effort. Time. Sacrifice. I have all those things. So I'm perfectly certain – I can do it. Everything will be worth it. Everything. All the way back. I feel sick at the thought. Everything I've done. Everything I'm doing. Everything I will do – it's all going to be alright again. Better than alright. Even for him. I drew out a pinprick from a darker patch, pulled it into a thread. I lay down the first vein, made twists into and out of its time. It held. I half expect to see these words fade when I write them. It held. As if the page knows that this is wrong. It held. [l/b] it held [l/b]5

[page discoloured recto, verso, damp, mildew spots, various incomplete strokes of the pen where the ink hasn't flowed properly, no legible marks visible (or made?)]

How am I supposed to work like this? I think all the time of the Merchant City house – at least there it would be dry. His coughing. The smell. The boy cries for him. His eyes brighten when he thinks of a plan to save him; his lips spell it all out – where he's going to go, what he's going to do. To save his father. [l/b] I'm going to have to end it soon. [l/b] Of the remaining options only one saves him, and his precious father won't lower himself to that. I had the woman in, but he wasn't having any of it. If he doesn't do it, what choice is there? To hide the boy brings Seb out looking, to run makes him chase: either way Nathan suffers sooner. His one chance is to give himself time. That means going directly to the Manse. Put him off his guard. Make him overconfident. Keep

---

5 [Desc] In large, scratchy letters.

Nat there long enough for me to do my work. If only I can get some [indecipherable: **ace: *poss.* 'peace', *poss.* 'space'].
I need quiet, at least. Thankfully the waves drown it all out.
[l/b] I can feel a storm. [l/b] *eye*

8.7912.23 – Transcription from Assembly Doc.Store B; cat. item 8.1345.23; (with annotations); intelligencer artefact; *auth.* Hailey-Beth Heather Prose; [*8.7912.20 permissions] *in progress.*

[page has passages heavily amended, passages around edges, palimpsestic diagrams, etc. Only interpretative rectification of text possible.][6] The working assumption is that the presence of God's corpse HERE has left an absence in the structure of THERE and that the HERE as it exists THERE is accessible from HERE (specifically Mordew, specifically the slums, the lower the better) by a *tying-together* or a *puncture-between* (neither metaphor works – there's a slackening and a loosening in the boundaries that neither phrase contains) is caused by the God-Flesh. Simply, God's body is here HERE and here THERE, and that loosening is what allows for the marker (that I have come to think of now more as an *anchor*) that performs the linking. More Sparklines than I have ever used are needed – I think that bringing something through from elsewhere is EASIER than keeping a route open (think of fishing – easy to pull fish out of water, very hard to dig tunnel in pool and keep open). Very exciting, though. Will need to switch focus from gathering lineage to promoting strength. Need more to work with. In some ways easier though, as he fades. Before it was as if he was always dragging IT down into himself. Now it's a little tug. Nathan, I can't feel yet. Hopefully won't have to. Weather – constant rain. No link possible with the Merchant City – even a few feet, just to the Wall, and the distance THERE... not distance... CONSISTENCY! Even

---

6 [Note] Sorry if I disturb your delicate sensibilities! Joking – there was no other way. Tricky piece of work this.

that is too much. Will have to put up with it. For how much longer? [along the right margin: equations] Soon? Or years? One day, certainly.[7] [along the top margin: a sequence of stylised frogs drawn to suggest a single frog hopping across the page – on top of this in a different, lighter ink: words written, then scribbled out] [along the bottom margin: scorch marks.] [overleaf] #hatch#[8] [l/b] Very busy, several valuable, The Regular,[9] few purged to Mud. Nathan hovering outside throughout. The father – silent. It has worked before. REMEMBER. It might always work. THE HOLY CUCKOLD Any time. Like snapping his fingers. REMEMBER THAT TIME!!! [l/b] It's so difficult. Painful. [l/b] Better to forget. [l/b] Plenty to work with. Can foresee an end. Everything is acceptable with that end in mind. [l/b] I remember the aurorae that would light the night snow at the Winter Palace. At the House they tried the same thing with coloured glass and shredded paper, but it was nothing in comparison. Some days I'd have a headache. From nowhere: behind my eyes and into my teeth. I'd need to lie down, but then the good thing was I'd sleep in the afternoon and wake up after midnight; the headaches went when the lights broke, so it didn't hurt. They were beautiful, up there, moving to the silent music. [l/b] Here the Mud does something similar. HE waxes and wanes, in his chamber, and the Mud reacts. Today I have a headache, and tonight it will be strong. [l/b] [with different ink] *eye*[10]

8.7912.25 – Transcription from Assembly Doc.Store B; cat. item 8.1345.23; (with annotations); intelligencer artefact;

---

7 [Note] I've made this read more clearly than I should. There's a lot of interpretation. If you're happy to go back and check my work, I'd really appreciate that. I think it keeps to the spirit though – I hope you'll agree. I'm no hermeneut, but is there any real need at this point? I know you'll say yes. You're right. I'll try harder.
8 [Note] Happy to use this.
9 [Desc] This is underlined in the text. She's done it several times, each line harder pressed than the last. The mimeo only lets me add one underline.
10 [Note] This too.

auth. Hailey-Beth Ambreen Prose; [*8.7912.20 permissions]
in progress.
<HIERATIC ISOLATION PROTOCOL MANDATED –
contact archivist for access>

[11][insertion – torn – between pps. 9/10 and pps. 11/12 of parent
cat. item, heavily folded into eighths, frayed – recto advertise-
ment {text: 'Beaumont's Bacon' w. image: stylised pig, standing on hind legs, holding strip of meat in each hand/trotter,
smiling, straw hat with ribbon around, w. slogan: obscured
by tearing – *poss*: Try Me, I'm Delicious!} verso: list/passages,
graphite, different hand] THE INWARD EYE [l/b] [sigil: the
ox] [sigil: dawn] [sigil: the fallen queen] [l/b] Leviathan Lens
blooded[12] [l/b] down into, closer, down into, closer, down into,
closer (on-the-lips-repeated) [l/b] zeige, ring, mittel; zeige, ring,
mittel THUMBED [l/b] ZRMZRMZRMZRM[13] [repeated
until the edge and over] [l/b] at peak – ABORT [scored
through] Sparkline [beneath, in notebook hand] [l/b] [sigil:
the crossed arms] [sigil: moonrise] [sigil: blackbirds in flight]
[l/b] USELESS [l/b] [116 in tally marks over several lines, final
mark interrupted and nib-trail] [l/b] the idiot had the wrong
sigil [notebook hand] [sigil: three-armed] [arrow joining to
sigil: the crossed arms] [l/b] ZRMZRMZRMZRMZRM
[l/b] [bottom edge torn and singed]

8.7912.26 – Transcription from Assembly Doc.Store B; cat.
item 8.1345.23; (with annotations); intelligencer artefact;
auth. Hailey-Beth Heather Prose; [*8.7912.20 permissions]
in progress.

---

11 [Note] I've prewarned Hailey-Beth Pavel Catalogues re. HIP – he's
expecting a knock. Actually, you won't read this until… never mind!
12 [Note] The Palaeologue Cathedral macula? It would make sense. Will
request a closer look.
13 [Note] If this is an occult attempt at the intrascope – frankly, what else
could it be? – there's a lot of mucking about. Impressive amendment,
though, given she's working from first principles – do you think she could
be convinced to Hailey-Beth? It might be worth a try?

[one unbroken passage in smaller letters written with a fine point] This morning I went for a walk outside. Nathan left early and I followed him. I don't know why. I kept my distance. The bloody bell was ringing, the rain was falling. I think he heard me because he stopped. I turned away so he wouldn't see my face. Above the Wall a pair of firebirds rose in a spiral, sparks trailing from their beating wings, necks stretching to the clouds. They stopped high, as if they had died in mid-air, twisted and turned, locked around each other, still. They fell together. Before they hit the Wall, I turned back, and Nathan had walked on. There's a corner at the end of the Mews and he was there, looking off. He didn't move. In my heart I wanted him to come back – I don't know why. It must be done, but the heart doesn't understand that sort of reasoning. It's for the best, you tell it. It's the only way, you tell it. But the heart is like a fool – it doesn't understand. Doesn't listen. It just aches. Up into the neck. In the hands. In the eyes. I took two steps towards him, went to pick him up. When a baby cries, you pick him up – it doesn't matter what you think. You pick him up. That's what I wanted to do, but after my two stupid steps he went forward. There's a pile of trash that used to be something but now is nothing[14] and he went behind that, so I couldn't see him. That stopped my feet. There was the urge to run, in them, so that my eyes could see him again. But I'm not a creature of hearts and eyes and feet – I am a thinking thing. Primarily. I look inward. A mind. So that's why, I suppose, I can let him go. That's why, I suppose, I can do my work. That's why, I suppose, I'll be able to do what I need to do – with Nathaniel – when the time comes. Because I <u>know</u> what it is that needs to be done. Tearing off the plaster. Breaking the neck of a chicken. Cauterising a wound. Pulling the trigger.

---

14 [Note] One of the Vanguard Hailey-Beths (I'm not sure you know them: Hammurabi?) reports this as the intelligencer nest. It's possible that it made a record? Might be useful as a cross-ref? Worth a Catalogues's time in any case. If you agree, would you make a req.? Pavel knows where the forms are.

The heart objects, the nerves falter, you go weak at the knees. But you do it anyway. Because what's the alternative? Worse things. Endless cycles of suffering. Infections and gangrene. Nathan will go to Sebastian and Sebastian will train him and while his back's turned, I'll pull the rug out from under their idiotic feet – all of them – and then I'll make it all better. It's always raining. Firebirds die. I am in the slums. The men come. My love rots. Nathan. In my chest there is a pain like a hollowing-out. Hunger made from tears and choking. But I look inward and here there is everything – all possibilities. Inward there is the world. Inward there is the future. Inward is where I am, and when it is finished, I will scour out all the putrid flesh. I will clean the wound. I will dress it, and all these fools… It will be ended. They will be repaired. [l/b] When I came back there was a queue – I'm making them wait.[15]

8.7912.42 – Transcription from Assembly Doc.Store B; cat. item 8.1345.23; (with annotations); intelligencer artefact; *auth.* Hailey-Beth Ambreen Prose; [*8.7912.20 permissions] *in progress.*

---

15 [Desc] One of the few pages with no Mud damage. This may be a coincidence, but it may indicate that this was a page she considered particularly important and therefore kept clean. There's bleed-through on the paper stock throughout, but she doesn't usually care. The other side of this is blank, though. Because she doesn't want to obscure the text? It's one of the more human passages – perhaps she realises this? I don't suppose she was imagining a trial by peripatetic committee (though she might have had some access to the future from the weft?). More to remind herself? Either way it's evidence anti? All the more important that there's a cross-ref in case challenged. Please do put in that req., Ambreen. I'd do it, but I hit my quota already and they're working to rule. You can give them one of your smiles? Right? Pretty please, etc. If the veracity of the above is questioned on the stand her advocate will want to know we belt-and-braced it in her interests. Could equally be a concocted piece of evidence before the fact – 'look at me, all sad and justified.' Both sides benefit from backup.

[preceding page left blank, cryptic bleed-through analysis beyond the skills of this transcriber, expertise sought from Codes] [17]I'd hardly finished gathering the Sparklines and there he was. It's obvious now what the plan is – to force my hand – but I didn't understand it when I saw Nathan's face. A lesson in taking things for granted. If Seb didn't take Nathan in now, while he's weak enough to slave – the long game – then he wants him strong for something, sooner. Has she taunted him into something rash? Is he trying for a decisive strike against the odds? A Nathan alight? That means education, means inhibition, means an Interdictor, means Nathaniel dead, which means Nathan stronger. Burning. [l/b] I need Nathaniel. I need and want him alive, but I can't risk Seb killing him because that would give him Nathan. I can't rely on Nathaniel to defend himself. So I'll have to do it. Use the God-Flesh instead. But how long does that leave me? It was all coming together! Why now? [l/b] BECAUSE it was all coming together. BECAUSE of the anchor. BECAUSE of the vein. [l/b] I should have waited. Or sent the boy earlier.

---

16 [Note] If that was supposed to be flattery you'll have to put more effort into it! Also, given the number of forms (included preceding here for your information) it takes. Anyway, I gave one of 'my smiles' and requisitioned the intelligencer query, but no amount of pretty pleases is going to make anything happen on the ground. Hopefully it'll do some good, but it's field practice to wipe IT records before setting a new target to minimise overwrite corruption. It probably dumped anything that wasn't this notebook when we hard set it as the focus. Unless Hammurabi thought to RAID, I guess. Anyway – I agree: .12.16 looks like a key section, legally speaking. You can't both be a deranged demigod and a potential Hailey-Beth simultaneously (unless you know the future). Might get her off/on the rack.

Don't kill me, but I put in a request for a posting to the peripatetic court of the Vanguard. For both of us. I'm going to leave that hanging. Last thing – will you, for pity's sake, make your notes in a [Note] field and not as an addendum to a description? When I filter by notes, looking for your messages, they don't all come up because you're scattering them where they don't belong. This all typed with exasperated fingers. I have asked before.

17 [Note] More paperwork. There's no paperwork in the field... Just kidding! You know I hate confrontation – just trying to defuse tension in advance.

I gave him exactly enough time to react. Or perhaps that's the weftling – allowing me the breakthrough, knowing I would take it, goading me to show my hand. And I allowed myself to be goaded. I sicken myself. Yet there was always going to be the counterattack, and now it is my turn. Reformulate, reorganise. Resist. And Portia – who knows what she is planning? If she is still in the game. Is it a game now? It seemed like it once. There was pleasure in it! And camaraderie. Now there is no one except the CORPSE-IN-WAITING. And a game that cannot be put aside, the stakes are so high.

8.7912.44 – Transcription from Assembly Doc.Store B; cat. item 8.1345.23; (with annotations and condition scan); intelligencer artefact; *auth.* Hailey-Beth Heather Prose; [*8.7912.20 permissions] *in progress.*

[18][condition: see scan] Frustrating night's work. The progress made in the past week re. manipulation all undone. INWARD EYE lacked focus and I thought this was the issue, but now feel external influence to blame. Looked where the anchor directed to find complete reversion to weftling state. First assumption: anchor failure, overconfidence in the method, but secondary markers still in prime formation. Second assumption: tidal drift in approach, but no indication of that on distant samples. Third assumption: natural weft reversion, but such reversion uneven across marked range. Fourth assumption: weftling interference. Think he is sensing the infringement of his body space. Counter-intuitive since he is dead, but that fails to consider the incomplete synchronisation of the weft and the material realm. All my expenditures have relied on a neutral experimental environment. If fourth assumption correct, will need to reinforce BLINDNESS at *every* intervention.

---

18 [Note] This better? You know that if we're posting we need to get a clip on? I'm reducing the descriptive level and relying on the scans – makes me quota-neurotic, but I don't suppose it'll be an issue if we're cycling at the front. Don't appreciate the press-ganging, but it will be nice to have some flesh-time. Expect you to bring gifts of apology.

Significant Sparkline resourcing and sourcing implications. Wish hadn't purged so much to the Mud – could have burned through the lesser lines daily and saved work. Will now need to waste generations on spells that don't require them. Or source multiple low-grade lines to prevent redundancy. Probably light relief, all this accountancy.[19] [overleaf]All this effort to conserve such little things. Keeping my temperature down shouldn't be as difficult as this, given the draughts. If I had half Portia's skill, or even a tenth, I could make a place to store them, but as it is I have to waste valuable EYE time moving the fertile ones and dumping the dreck, and even more on stratification. It's worth it, of course. Even taking into account wastage there is room for a year, maybe two, at the previous rate, and six months even if there's resistance from the weftling. I can't spare the time to gather any more than I am gathering, but word of mouth brings me new sources, so if I'm clever with it I can minimise returns. I know what I said, but the anchor was such a breakthrough. I think it was THE breakthrough. Better for the weftling to move against me than for the anchor to have been a false hope. I feel closer. When I'm there it feels righter, and the weft knows. I'm learning to read it. He'd say it was mysticism, wishful thinking, but I'm in there, not him. What did he ever achieve anyway? Nothing off his own bat. One lucky... Never mind. I know as well as he does that if he'd just stand up and shuck off all the misery I'd never stop smiling. If you can read this from deep down wherever you're hiding: I LOVE YOU, YOU IDIOT. Why are you making me do this? I have to empty the worms; I have to listen to you. Don't you know what it does? Can't you feel the shame. Remember the Balcony of Appearances? The Bower? The Ha'penny Bridge? Come back to me and we'll take the

---

19 [Desc] Can't help it – the hand here is much neater than in the foregoing. The strokes are even, the word choice relatively free of aggression, and what smears are on the surface are thin and orderly. She says she's frustrated, but the documents don't lie. And is this line a joke? I think that's the first reported. If so. Might I suggest that she's happy the demigod didn't take her son? Or is that reading into it too much?

boy – raise it all up from the water.[20] Please, N.? Please? He won't read this. I'll find a way in from the weft and make him. I'll let you win! Promise.

8.7912.45 – Transcription from Assembly Doc.Store B; cat. item 8.1345.23; (with annotations); intelligencer artefact; *auth*. Hailey-Beth Ambreen Prose; [*8.7912.20 permissions] *in progress*. [user locked, ref. HBAP/NIX, retrospective]

[portfolio of fragments transcribed here as one block on the grounds of possible timeline reconstruction][21]

[torn from notebook, made into taper, lit, then stubbed out. Left edge charred, ash stains throughout, numerous visible fingerprints {original sent to organicist in Archives}] I can tell the medicine won't work. Even if he wasn't blocking it, there's no medicine that can stop it. Poor Nathan. If he knew the source of those worms. He will get to know, one day. Which way will it send him? Maggots – they're horrible things, of course. But how else does one dispose of a corpse? HOW ELSE DO YOU DISPOSE OF A CORPSE, CORPSE? We used to laugh together. Didn't we? What I wouldn't give to hear you laugh now. Please laugh, Nathaniel. It was a very funny joke. Wasn't it? You used to think so.

[written vertically on the paper left on the left margin after page torn out, then torn out] ...turned the INWARD EYE outward, last night. The boy went into Seb's place. It's nice there. He always kept things nice. There was a time when we

---

20 [Note] I think that seals it? Either option accelerates the TRS timeline. I had my bags packed, so to speak, but I think I'd better tell the juniors that rec. cycles are cancelled for the foreseeable.

21 [Note] Peripatetic court nixed the req! Wants to upchain it and demote us to consult! Needless to say, I nixed the nixing. Do you still have sway with Sascha? Can feel your ire, but no time for avoiding sore points. Did at least give me time to arrange these pieces into something useful. Feel they might cover the lost pages? Partially.

all had such a nice time, before all this. He was the only one of us who'd managed to keep hold of money. Always such good food – shrimp, lobster, beef – everything so expensive. Take good care of my boy, Seb. We all need him.

[found in bundle tied in string hidden in rear flap – intelligencer image on request] I was inside when he came back, and his presence kicked me out. It was all going bad anyway. It wasn't working. Everything reverts – he makes it revert. I wonder if it isn't Nathaniel. Are you blocking me? Have you left your patterns in there, knowing what I'll do? IT'S YOU, ISN'T IT? I shouldn't take it out on the boy. He feeds you, but it will never make what he wants happen – not when you're blocking everything. You're leaving me with no choice. Or is that your game? To push me to do the things you won't do? If you leave me these traps, one day I'm going to fall into them. When...

[found in bundle tied in string hidden in rear flap – intelligencer image on request] you're gone. What am I going to do then? Is it that you think I'm too good to do it? I don't think I am, Nathaniel. When Nathan comes in, I want to use him. If you think I'm too good to do it, YOU'RE WRONG. Can you hear me? PLEASE. You're making me do it, and when you're gone there'll be nothing else. Is there part of this I'm missing? I don't think there is. After Nathan went, I almost did it then. I came in and I had the cooking pot. Your eyes were shut, and I was so angry. I brought it down, but I couldn't do it. I pulled back at the last minute and the thing slipped out of my fingers. It was comic – even I could see it was comic. It bounced about between my fingers and then when it fell it bashed my knee. You know, when it makes that...

[found in bundle tied in string hidden in rear flap – intelligencer image on request] reflex, giggling sort of pain. I cry a lot, you know that, but this time I couldn't help it. Sometimes you make yourself cry, to show to yourself that you're sad – not

468

completely, but a little bit, deep behind it all. Not this time. I started crying and then I kept on crying. I was shaking when the next one came and had to make him wait while I blacked my eyes back. I'm not going to talk to you any more. You never reply.[22, 23]

8.7912.46 – Transcription from Assembly Doc.Store B; cat. item 8.1345.23; (with annotations and condition scan); intelligencer artefact; *auth.* Hailey-Beth Heather Prose; [*8.7912.20 permissions] *in progress.* [user locked, ref. HBAP/NIX, *pwp]

[very neat page, bound to spine, hardly any Mud] I thought Nathan had done it, today. [l/b] There was a moment when I thought he'd brought him back and I was SO happy I'd never killed him. [l/b] It filled me with happiness. I haven't felt like that for as long as I can remember. Perhaps I've never felt happiness like it. [l/b] I thought it was all going to be over, it was all going to begin. I think it's one of things we get from stories – the endless delayed gratification, the grinding into the dust that is the prelude to the glorious resurrection. The legendary comeback. Just when it looked like everything was lost. I fell for it. All those living sparks – not even ~~you~~ – HE – made so many, so vital. [l/b] I thought Nathan had lit the flame and ~~you~~ HE was going to rise. In my stomach I felt the excitement. [l/b] But no. [l/b] On the other side of that, what are the choices? The expectations, the fantasies, the joy of a moment, when that moment has passed: what are

---

22 [Desc] Realised I'd put part of the last note in the wrong field, but the mimeo won't let me delete with the lock on and I'm not taking it off until the Vanguard see sense. Also realise that this is now a note, and it's in the description field. What I had meant to put was that if we insert these fragments here they do at least have a home, and from a cursory vis-match analysis they are consistent, materially speaking, with the artefact. Unless dating has come on since I HB cycled, that's as good as we're going to get. Will defer to your superior experience, obviously, but not anticipating the need.

23 Leviathan Lens scans came back – looks a lot like the macula. Kept in water on crate top by bedside in a glass jar! Have alerted HBs in Conservation.

they? [l/b] They're ridiculous, that's what they are. [l/b] And I was ridiculous to feel them. [l/b] It's time to become stern. Disciplined. I thought that's what I was, but that was just stern and disciplined INSIDE. About me. It's time to be stern and disciplined with everything else. Everyone. Ridiculousness can be turned aside. Hope and love and joy – all these things can be turned aside. IRON DISCIPLINE, then, FOR EVERYONE and everything.[24]

8.7912.48 – Transcription from Assembly Doc.Store B; cat. item 8.1345.23; (with annotations); intelligencer artefact; *auth.* Hailey-Beth Ambreen Prose; [*8.7912.20 permissions] *in progress.* [user locked, ref. HBAP/NIX, *pwp]<SUPERVISOR LOCKOUT PENDING EMERGENCY MARTIAL TRANSFER>

If he won't wake, I'll have to kill him. His flesh will be mine. Of course, I don't want to do it. I DON'T. He's making me. What else can I do? Knocking. [l/b] What else? Knocking. [l/b] What else? There is a crowd at the door. They're laughing. They wouldn't laugh if they understood what they were gifting me with their custom. All their Spark. All their lines. Backwards and forwards, for me to own, to use, to make into dust. Let me black my eyes and I'll open. [l/b] Even I can tell the

---

24 [Note] Gulp. Yes, I do still have sway with Sascha by virtue of local chapter X-social. By (no) coincidence, meet was called by quorate (anon) vote – took some organising and at the last min. – and YT contrived a bumping-into. Long S cut S, conv. eventually turned to real possibility of unremarked archaic demigod in North-western Peninsula achieving or causing theus and only sensible solution was to send the most intelligenced HBs to the Vanguard. Not sure they understood I meant us, but thumb-stamping of the next relevant reqs to cross the desk looks likely. Nice password BTW – only took me three guesses, and one of those was capitalisation. Iron discipline for everyone/thing? Red flagging like a maniac, here. What's the timeline? Intelligencer got this back pronto, and there's not so many pages remaining. Tried to skip the process, but by the time the hack-validation comes back from Archives we can have it done without. Candles burning double-ended from now on. Will shunt this into your feed with override prejudice ASAP. Would appreciate the same lack of politeness your side.

difference between a beautiful man and an ugly one. I know that's nonsensical – they're all ugly, and besides, it makes no difference – but it's an objective fact – sometimes they are BEAUTIFUL. [l/b] This one was. [l/b] He wasn't diligent in his pleasure-taking. Sometimes they're nervous, the new ones, but it wasn't that. He wasn't really interested – it was perfunctory. Then I knew why – it was a front. He wasn't here for that. If pressed, I'd say he was an assassin. [l/b] They're a lot like actors – perhaps that's why he was beautiful, or his beauty made it easier for him to get his job – they have a superficial performance they're obliged to make their audiences buy. His was 'client', and he'd convinced himself he needed me to buy it so he could do his real work. [l/b] He needn't have bothered – I'm no match for a trained killer, and neither is Nathaniel – but I took his Sparkline. PROVED VERY INTERESTING! Anyway. Why not? [l/b] After, I pretended to tend to my eyes, and he went into Nathaniel's side. He was very good – he kept talking, speaking just louder enough to make me think he hadn't moved, clinked coins onto the bed as he did it, as if he'd dropped them. [l/b] This was to hide the fact that he muffled Nathaniel with ether and snipped off his finger with a cigar cutter. [l/b] He used some magical sort of styptic paste to staunch the blood. A trick of his trade no doubt. [l/b] And then he was dressed, immaculately, and out before someone who wasn't me would have noticed. I let him go, of course, but I could see what he'd done the moment I pulled the sheet across. [l/b] He harvested Nathaniel's interdicting finger. Since he wasn't a fish boy, it must be some plan of Portia's. They're forcing my hand with this. [l/b] Even if it's a trap, I must fall into it. [l/b]

You want me to do it. SPEAK! I know you want me to do it. [l/b] How then? I'll do it. With this pen! I'll write it up in your divine blood! Nathan needs it, if this is going to be the way. That's my excuse. But it's because I hate you. Do you understand? Lying there! I HATE you. FIGHT ME OR I KILL YOU. [l/b] He didn't fight. [in brown/red]

8.7912.53 – Transcription from Assembly Doc.Store B; cat. item 8.1345.23; (with annotations and condition scan); intelligencer artefact; *auth.* Hailey-Beth Heather Prose; [*8.7912.20 permissions] *in progress.* [user locked, ref. HBAP/NIX, *pwp]
<SUPERVISOR LOCKOUT PENDING EMERGENCY MARTIAL TRANSFER>

I didn't think I could do it. Perhaps I couldn't. Perhaps this is where I change into something else so I can do the things that need to be done. It happened to Nathaniel, it happened to Seb, it happens to the kids. Now it's happened to me? Her? He was right – I feel that now. Don't use it. To do what has to be done you have to make yourself into someone else. Something else. But I HAVE made myself into that. I am that, now. She is dead, and now I'm in her place. And I CAN do it. I WILL do it.

8.7912.54 – Transcription from Assembly Doc.Store B; cat. item 8.1345.23; (with annotations); intelligencer artefact; *auth.* Hailey-Beth Ambreen Prose; [*8.7912.20 permissions] *in progress.* [user locked, ref. HBAP/NIX, *pwp]
<SUPERVISOR LOCKOUT PENDING EMERGENCY MARTIAL TRANSFER>

I cut a strip off his back – an inch by two inches, something like that. It had hairs on it – all God-Flesh, but I put it in the fire to burn them off. To dry it out. Not cooking, just making it possible. [l/b] It was just a piece of meat – an inch by two inches. A piece of bacon – Beaumont's like the flyer. That's what she thought – Clarissa. That's what she had to think to make it possible. It made it possible. [l/b] She performed the INWARD EYE with the bacon under her tongue and the results were – to her – INCREDIBLE. [l/b] She had a box once, when she was little – it was made of mahogany and there was a special way of opening it, a puzzle. She had to pull the sides apart with her middle finger and thumb [l/b] MITTEL AND **** [l/b] and then push the two parts of the top back ninety

472

degrees with her index finger and when she did everything slid neatly into place and the compartment came open on a spring. It was wonderful, the smoothness of it, the secretness revealed of it, so beautifully constructed, so right. Only she knew how to do it, the girl Clarissa. A rich child's toy. [l/b] That's what the weft was like with the strip of God-Flesh, an inch by two inches, dissolving under her tongue as she cast the INWARD EYE. [l/b] The structure conformed to her wishes. It conforms to my wishes. When you've done something once, and seen what happens and it's so perfect, so beautiful, it doesn't matter what you have to do to make it happen again. [l/b] When she was older, Clarissa a young woman, she'd got in with a crowd who were interested in drugs, and there was one drug – it was called BLISS, or DREAM, something like that, depended on who was selling it – which only the most fearless had the courage to take. There were users of it around, and they were emaciated and filthy, their faces collapsed on collapsing skulls, so you needed courage to take the first dose. She did, and it was so perfect, so beautiful, that it didn't matter about anything else. She'd have died from it, if it wasn't for Nathaniel. She'd have done ANYTHING for it. [l/b] That was what it was like in the weft. That is what it is like, for me. Now, he's down to the bone all down the left side of his back and I'm starting tonight on the right. [l/b] I'll take ten pieces, an inch by two inches. Now my mouth knows how to process the God-Flesh, it's even better. [l/b] When you touch the stuff, it changes you. My fingers, my hands, my wrists, my elbows are powerful now, sharp, cutting, crushing, precise – I don't need a knife. [l/b] My mouth dissolves whatever I put in it – I don't need a stomach. I don't need water – whatever I need comes from the weft and from the God-Flesh. It is taking form. [l/b] If the weftling resists, I resist him, and I win. It is taking my form. As soon as it is done, there will be one perfect material realm and it will coalesce around me. If I was Clarissa, still, it might occur to me that I am the thing that is changing – I am becoming the weftling, becoming him. That's the kind of thought that she would have had – she was self-doubting, self-loathing. [l/b] But not always, and I feel no doubts of that kind. [l/b] You have a will, and that will find expression, under the God-Flesh, and that expression is made concrete through manipulation of the weft. [l/b] Tontine logic, proven over generations. [l/b] And now I have solved the puzzle and the box will slide open, perfectly, the rush will come, perfectly, and then it will be within my power to do anything and everything that needs to be done. Even back to the beginning – I will make it so it has always been me. Tonight, I start on his right side.

8.7912.55 – Transcription from Assembly Doc.Store B; cat. item 8.1345.23; (with annotations and condition scan); intelligencer artefact; *auth.* Hailey-Beth Heather Prose; [*8.7912.20 permissions] *in progress*. [user locked, ref. HBAP/NIX, *pwp] <SUPERVISOR LOCKOUT PENDING EMERGENCY MARTIAL TRANSFER>

When you've been bullied for years and then you get your chance to get your own back. God knows he deserves it. But it turns on a sixpence. [l/b] One minute you can feel yourself justified. Justice. The little people getting what's owed to them. Of course, it's exciting. Of course, it's intoxicating. [l/b] It's incredible. [l/b] Last night, I felt it slip into my form. More mine than his. You're running up this steep slope, you aren't going to make it. You're going to give out before you get there and then you're over the summit and it's downhill – that vertigo, the wobbliness in your legs, freedom and flying, and the SPEED. Harder to stop than to get what you've always wanted. [l/b] Can a person show restraint in that kind of situation? [l/b] Thinking of all those men, queueing at my door, Nathaniel choking. Now every time I'm in there... it feels sadistic. [l/b] But I like it. [l/b] I see that I like it, while I'm liking it, and I know what it makes me, what I'd have thought of the kind of person that wants to hurt another thing in the way that I want to hurt him, and I don't care. It has to be done – that's the bare fact of it. [l/b] He has to be purged from the weft – every moment of him through the ages. [l/b]

So I understand that. But I can't help but feel that's an excuse, to myself. Necessity for violence, necessity for pitilessness, cruelty: they are beautifully convenient excuses. [l/b] I go further. I justify that I have to be a thing that likes to be cruel to do the cruelties that need to be done. I make of myself a tool for the way things must be, and thereby allow myself to feel the pleasure in his pain, because if I don't, and I falter, or I show restraint, then it opens the door to him, and I'm under the yoke again, we all are, and everything good that I want to do will be made impossible. [l/b] Only, what if I can't do the good things because of the evil I've made of myself? The tables have turned. Nathaniel told me not to do it. He told Nathan. But I've done it. I've done it. Not yet, but soon, it will all be me. Regardless of what anyone or anything chooses to do about it. Seb loses. Portia loses. Nathaniel loses. The Tontine is mine. But what am I?

8.7912.62 – Transcription from Assembly Doc.Store B; cat. item 8.1345.23; (with annotations); intelligencer arte-fact; *auth.* Hailey-Beth Ambreen Prose; [*8.7912.20 per-missions] *in progress.* [user locked, ref. HBAP/NIX, *pwp] <SUPERVISOR LOCKOUT PENDING EMERGENCY MARTIAL TRANSFER>

The Master's butler came today, so perhaps I had no choice after all. [l/b] I could smell the fish-boys a mile off and then there was this gangly big-nosed monster peeking politely through the sheet. [l/b] I don't think I know him, but I know the type – Seb's always got at least one convert to be guru for, and this one had all the signs. Completely unaware of his role. Fawning. He saw that Nathaniel was gone, bowed, and left. [l/b] Then Nathan came in, sweating and Sparking. He put two and two together and I didn't correct him. I suppose it's shame. I don't feel it, but what else could it be? I'm not proud of it, and that's a kind of shame. Isn't it? God knows! [l/b] I shouldn't laugh, but I can't help it.

8.7912.63 – Transcription from Assembly Doc.Store B; cat. item 8.1345.23; (with annotations and condition scan); intelligencer artefact; *auth.* Hailey-Beth Heather Prose; [*8.7912.20 permissions] *in progress.* [user locked, ref. HBAP/NIX, *pwp]
<SUPERVISOR LOCKOUT PENDING EMERGENCY MARTIAL TRANSFER>

Ha! I spoke too soon. I wasn't cruel enough. He's so wily. There are no words for this, but it was a bait-and-switch, and when I noticed he launched his counter. The work is undone, and now there isn't enough God-Flesh to get back to where I was. I've used it all up – his plan all along. Nathaniel is down to the bones and offal. It will take it all now – the heart, the liver, the bowel – put it in jars and squirrel it away for the future. I can take the brain and use it for a tiny realm, unreachable in its smallness. It will take all the sparklines to maintain the anchor. If the anchor is in place I can do it again – crueller this time, knowing his tricks. I hadn't considered the possibilities of making an intermediate weft – it shouldn't be possible, but then what is the weftling unless he's the one that makes impossible things possible? But the anchor – that goes through, and the techniques – they are all refined. He made it too convincing. He doesn't know what it is that I know and don't know, what I'd be convinced by, so I've learned everything. All of it. It's etched in me – these notes are IRRELEVANT. The only option is Clarissa. If you want a job done properly, you'd better do it yourself.

476

More on Mr Padge's Assassins

FOR SHARLI, the Mother of Mordew's translation of her to the Island of the White Hills was even more fraught than it was for the others, since she – and 'she' she most definitely was, having taken the pledge to be a woman to the exclusion of all other ways of being – was not Sharli as the other assassins knew her, but was an imposter.

The Sharli the others knew was in an Assembly re-education facility in Shemsouth, coming to terms with the ideas her new life would rely on, whereas this Sharli was Hailey-Beth-Martial Clementina Roads, cycling in the Women's Vanguard of the Eighth Atheistic Crusade, living undercover as an observer-in-general in Mordew with responsibility for monitoring possible Theistic Resurrection Scenarios. As such, she knew, as all Assembly members knew, that to be translated through the weft, and in this instance the warp, was the same as dying, and she only did it because she knew that if she didn't, Deaf Sam would kill her anyway.

She had been thinking, this Clementina – who we shall continue to call Sharli because that is the name she had taught herself to think of as her own – of ways to leave the company of the other assassins since before the meal at which Padge had laid his contract on the table, but had come up with nothing suitable.

She turned the rings of Sharli's victims one after the other, on that afternoon already described, this being a mannerism the previous Sharli possessed. She sucked at the pipe clenched between her teeth, to the opium of which she was rendered immune by Assembly pulmonary engineering, and, as the conversation continued, ran various scenarios through her mind.

To be translated through the weft or the warp was to be destroyed utterly in the real and then remade anew in either the real, or in a false realm. It was a theistic nonsense to imagine that consciousness continued across this process, it only appearing that way because the replica created to replace the original person was in every way convincing to those who remained, as perfect replicas always are. These replicas always claimed that they felt as if nothing had happened and that they were fine, and that, please, would everybody stop fussing over them. By doing this, they unknowingly convinced the gullible that they were the same person that had existed before the translation.

But this was what the Hailey-Beths in Prose named 'the propaganda of the immaterial soul' and was a technique weft-parasites used so that they could dangle the fantasy of heavens in front of their believers and thereby distract them from the value of their one true life as part of the human Assembly. It is no compensation for an early death to know that someone exactly like you, but not you, lives on in your place.

Sharli needed to avoid this fate, but how?

If she had claimed she had business elsewhere, this would have given her away – there could be no more pressing business than this for an assassin in Padge's employ – and the moment even one of them suspected her of being an imposter she would have been as good as dead. Assassins, after all, are excellent at killing – certainly better at it than she was at self-defence, despite her Vanguard training.

If she had called for help by signalling any nearby intelligencers then she'd risk her sisters' lives, forcing them to come to her rescue, jeopardising their own missions, and quite probably she'd still be killed. So there was no point in doing that.

If she had left the table and never returned, they would hunt her down, very quickly, and anyway, it was her pledge to investigate weft anomalies like the Mother of Mordew and to report about them to her sisters, so while this would save her own life it might endanger the work of the Crusade, something she would never risk doing.

She took her glass from the table, licked the tannin from around the rim of it, and downed whatever remained. Knowing that Sharli could not leave a stemmed glass unsinging, she held the base tight against the table and ran a fingertip around the recently wetted rim. The tone it gave was light and jolly, entirely unlike how she felt inside. Fortunately, Deaf Sam lowered the note by filling the glass with wine. The surface of the liquid rippled and danced, and Sharli smiled at Sam, who could see the vibration even if he couldn't hear the sound.

He smiled back at her.

When Sharli was a woman, Deaf Sam and she were lovers, regardless of who he, she or they were on those days, and since Clementina had replaced the original, she had honoured this obligation. Now she gazed at Sam with a demure and simultaneously coquettish fluttering of her eyelashes, something that the Vanguard surgeons had made semi-reflexive by building the nerve paths into Clementina's own muscles during the process of altering her to mimic her cover.

If she tried to take them all by surprise, Deaf Sam included, by, for example, breaking the bladder of poison gas she had taped to her inner thigh, there would be significant collateral damage. Sharli had seen the effects of this poison in the field during the co-option of Judea, though, granted, used on a much greater scale. Half the restaurant would be blue-faced, bulge-eyed corpses before the agent dissipated, and, more likely than not, at least one of the assassins – the Druze, or Montalban, probably – would have immunity. Both had spent time outside Mordew, and they were paranoid enough to spend their commissions on wide-spectrum defences against poison.

Could she defeat them hand to hand? She imagined an attempt, visualising each move at speed in the battle notation that assassins knew – a kind of algebra of violence by which the outcome of a fight could be predicted through the playing of a complex tactical game – and there was a very low chance of success. In fact, in none of the elaborations of any known line of play did she manage to kill four of them before she herself was killed, and this was most likely by Deaf Sam, which added the taint of betrayal to the outcomes.

Often, when assassins have taken more opium than is sensible over lunch, minutes pass in which each quietly communes with their thoughts, the world given clarity and significance by their smoking. Such a period passed now, and Sharli adopted a face that told of the fascinations of a passing bluebottle, or of finding patterns in the rattling of pots in the restaurant kitchens, or of how exquisite a cool breeze feels on the flushed skin of a wine drinker's cheek. In fact, she was thinking no such things, and to hide that fact she looked down so that no one could see her real thoughts playing out inside her eyes.

Could she turn down the call to the Mother of Mordew for religious reasons? Not at all. Though religious people seem to an observer to have entirely lost their senses in the obvious falsity of their beliefs, and thereby appear like madmen, unlike madmen, whose thoughts tend towards the unanchored and variable, the faithful are attached to their delusions like limpets are to rocks – that is, very tenaciously. This was particularly true of these assassins, the last people in the city of their gestalt and thereby by definition the most attached to it. If she recanted now, they would kill her on the spot as an imposter, or a heretic, or as someone who had developed an incurable illness.

She decided to bide her time and keep an eye out for opportunities.

One of these came almost immediately when Montalban and the Druze left to prepare for the visit to the Mother of Mordew, so Sharli pretended to do the same, but instead went by the most direct route to the mines, keeping to the shadows, head down all the way.

Montalban had never liked Mordew, but he couldn't deny that it was a profitable place to live for one of his skills. His childhood home – a city that did not have a name pronounceable in his adopted tongue and which consequently he had now forgotten – was under transition to Assembly option and his father's training was no longer sanctioned. There was no use for them, and with neither father or son willing to retrain they packed up their things and made their way north across the floodplains.

Wet, cold and the consumption of algae have hardening effects on those who can withstand them, as do hunger, illness and grief, and those who cannot bear them will often die. Montalban's father did the latter, while Montalban experienced the former, the only visible effect on him the leaching of all colour from his hair. One day, he turned his back on his sire's body, leaving it semi-submerged in a marsh since he had no way of burying him and lacked the strength to pull him a hundred miles to drier ground. He took the old man's knives and his blowpipes and the few coins he had kept back for emergencies, and trudged away without once looking back. What was there to look at? A puffy and mouldering cadaver? The soul was gone, and what was one more pile of tainted meat to the living? This he told himself, but the following morning his hair was white as a ghost's.

When he came to a port, reclaimed from the brine swamp, and made passage to Mordew by murdering a ticket holder of a trader berth, he found in that city employment sufficient to allow him eating and drinking rights in a brothel. He was very grateful for the fact, even if the city itself was rainy and cheerless. His joy was in the things of the past – in coloured yurts and whooping horse riders, women with spirits as lively as the bells on their silks – but the past is always gone, and one must find happiness where one may.

His father had always taught him the value of money, the prospect of it being a useful lubricant when a job seemed stiff and dry, so when Padge made his speech, now, many years after Montalban's arrival, and laid the contract before them all, his mood had risen. Before that there was only the possibility of the world as it already was. But this? To take all that Padge had? That might be enough to buy a new life.

How much was a ship? How much was a crew? How much were provisions sufficient to sail to a place that was neither present nor past but which might contain all the pleasures Montalban had once imagined were waiting for a man like him, but of which he had lost sight through the drudgery of life? Possibly one seventh of Padge's fortune, an amount he

481

might now come to possess. Even more, should one or more of them die.

Sharli he could see, turning her rings as she always did, sitting across from him. She was off her game – they all knew it – and some of them suspected she had lost faith in her path. She was always staring away somewhere, her eyes naturally focussing on the far distance, and thinking thoughts that were closed to him. This his father had called 'the traitor's gaze', since a true friend found sufficient interest in whomever they were friends with, and had no need to look away to the true source of their duties and obligations, which was somewhere else. She, then, might well not live to claim her share – even if her gaze lied, her distraction would prove just as fatal. An assassin cannot afford to be thinking about anything other than the immediate here and now.

Montalban took a sugared almond from a dish near the contract, white as his hair, and watched to see whose attention flickered over to examine what his hands were doing. Deaf Sam, as he had expected, saw him, as did Simon, but the Druze seemed not to notice at all, which was suspicious since an assassin's hands are dangerous things which must always be watched.

'You have an uncommonly sweet tooth today, Montalban,' said Mick the Greek, thereby letting both Montalban and the Druze know that *he* had seen it, and knew that it was odd that the Druze was pretending they hadn't.

Simon sniffed at this, and there was exchanged across the table that subtle and exhausting complex of interactions that assassins exchange when gathered. This, incidentally, was why most people of their trade worked alone – to do otherwise was too much effort for a mind to take. But once Simon had made his recognition clear, everyone knew it, with one exception, Sharli, who did not reply in any of the accepted ways, and who they all knew now was a traitor to their group, though they did not know why.

Montalban, who had stood to indicate that they should all visit the Mother of Mordew, now suggested, verbally, that they should make what preparations they needed to make prior to that journey.

After they all secured the contract and paper, Montalban left to go to his residence and the Druze went to theirs, and they met on the road, where the Druze had something to say.

The Druze got their name from an ancient sect that was famed for its willingness to dissemble, and this the assassin used only because they were good at bluffing at cards, and not because of any supposed hereditary link to the Druzes of the past, or any of their surviving relatives in the present. It was only coincidental that this assassin had some of that sect's features, facially and in skin tone, and only whimsically that they adopted a Druze's supposed mode of dress – which was a conical headdress known as a *tantour* and so-called Ottoman-trousers, which were baggy and jewelled in costume rubies, diamonds and emeralds.

They lived in that part of Mordew known as the Forest, which was uphill, so there was no reason they should not have gone along with Montalban when he left, since they both went the same way.

Once the two had checked for spies and telltales, they spoke quickly as they walked.

The Druze said, 'The time comes, and we are prepared. What are your ideas?'

Montalban replied, 'That seven will be two, that there is a traitor, that the others are pairs.'

To which the Druze replied in turn, 'This is also my reading. Sharli is an imposter, I think. Deaf Sam is faithful to her, Mick the Greek will go with Anatole.'

The Druze went on to say that Padge's bequest was unexpected but was as good as any of the group-breaking possibilities previously discussed, both assassins having tired of their associates.

They said all this between the street known as Indigo Approach – for the colour the Glass Road gave to the alabaster that clad the buildings there – and an area that was demolished to make way for the preliminary foundations of a new townhouse. The architect of this residence had boasted, in the queue for a local purveyor of delicacies, in this case cheese, that 'it would be the highest and most needle-like structure in the Pleasaunce – so I can bill the client double – yet cheap to build, maximising my profits.'

From the waste ground there scuttled a rare beetle, which was entirely transparent and productive of a sleeping venom prized by poisoners. Both the Druze and Montalban went to scoop it up, but the Druze got there first. They agreed between them that Montalban should have third share of the beetle's milkings, since now they were partners by conspiracy and should act mostly in concert.

The Druze said, 'The major obstacles are the contract terms and the invigilation the Mother will enforce.'

To which Montalban replied, 'Then we will need to get to her first.'

And the Druze asked, 'What if the attempt fails? There is a possibility she will punish us.'

The 'need to get to her first', and 'the attempt' were references to a plan these two had drawn up to come to an agreement with the Mother of Mordew to their advantage at the expense of the other assassins by convincing her that the other five were heretics, a fact they would introduce by exposing Sharli to her, so that she might have an empirically definite example of the possibility of such a thing, before tarring the others with the brush with which Sharli had been tarred. The 'failure' worried about was the small chance that their god would 'punish' them for their subterfuge, though since she was a god of assassins, they posited that such a position on her part would be contradictory and that she would be just as likely to reward them.

The Druze stroked the length of their nose while this was being said and swished the fabric of their tantour in gentle swirls that released a pleasant odour of lavender. The gems on their trousers glistened and shone.

Montalban reconsidered, as he had many times before, whether his rule against attachments with other assassins

484

was as necessary as it once was, given the Druze's significant charms. This was a little way away from Indigo Approach, on the road outside The Five Carnelians which was a hostelry frequented by Mordew's more wealthy grain and nut merchants.

Montalban said, 'We must do what assassins do.'

The Druze replied, 'Then let us go there now, without delay, and bargain for our plan.'

These two then went not to their residences, as they had said they would to the others, but straight to the mines. In doing so, they met Sharli on the way and, shortly after, Deaf Sam. This made their subterfuge redundant, and simultaneously put paid to any of her own that Sharli might have had to save her life, as she saw it.

Anatole, he of the obscenely tight clothes, pondered, with half the remaining company only at the table, not including himself, what exactly he thought he was playing at, sitting here while others left.

He had come late to assassinhood, having first ruled out other careers by a process of what seemed, to those around him, unnecessary comprehensiveness.

He had been, in order: a milker of cows, a carrier of letters, a clearer of glasses, a clerk, an architect's assistant, a washer of pots, a chef, a dealer of drugs to chefs, a collector of debts from chefs, a moneylender to chefs, a moneylender in general, a gambler with other people's money, a singer of songs, a writer of songs for other people to sing, a bare-knuckle boxer, an enforcer, and then a singer of songs (again). None of these jobs had stuck, most of them being forced on him by circumstances, though he did find himself both writing and singing songs, even when he was not paid for it.

One day, a childhood colleague who had worked with him in the dairy, and who had become the owner of a delicatessen high in the Merchant City, had come upon him during a trip to the slums. He was visiting, this childhood friend, a woman who blacked her eyes in the hovel where Anatole was sometimes wont to collapse under the influence of strong drink. He had said to Anatole, 'Pull yourself together and apply yourself to a trade!'

These words made an impression on Anatole, as did the fact that they had come from someone like this former associate, a person whom Anatole had considered not only an idiot of the weakest water, but a tedious one. From that moment he had vowed to do as this dolt had bid him, but not in the way that might have been expected.

He followed him – his name was, if Anatole remembered correctly, Farelle, or Lafette, or something with a similar proportion of vowels and consonants – singing songs softly to himself. He tracked him for days, finding out about his life, tracing his movements, familiarising himself with his confidantes and housemates.

When he knew all that he needed to know about him, Anatole pierced one of his arteries when he was at his slum business. He spilled his blood in gushes, to the tune of some self-penned doggerel, across the bare breasts of that black-eyed woman. She objected, of course, and Anatole agreed to return with enough money to compensate her if she agreed to quieten down and dispose of Lafette, or Farelle, or Rafael, or whatever the now exsanguinated fool had been called.

She didn't want to agree to any such thing, of course, but then he sang her a song and showed her his blade until she changed her mind.

To close this part of the story and remove the requirement for us to return to it later, Anatole did come back, and he did compensate her, very generously, for her trouble, and she became a friend to Anatole to this very day. He found enough work for her, in various ways, that she rarely, if ever, blacked her eyes any more.

Leaving the corpse to the woman to burn, or sell, or portion up, he went to where Rafael – let us settle on that name, for want of a better one – had lived, and slipped from room to room, smothering those who lay abed, sticking any others in their ribs, and generally making the place his own.

Whistling, he took the keys to the delicatessen and found the safe, the combination of which was left at the default setting, and so he helped himself to the sum remaining in it. He reserved a portion to compensate the slum woman, and with some of the rest he hired a drayman, his cart, and a boy. He had them empty the shop of all the comestibles that would survive a night, since he intended to go to the trade market in the morning and sell these to the chefs sourcing goods for that day's specials.

Finding the cart only half full, he went back to the house, and, paying the drayman and his boy a silver to ignore the corpses, had them load up with whatever valuable things they could see. While they did this, Anatole let his eye drift from here to there around Rafael's former home. He found himself not in the least bit guilty for what he had done, and noted this of himself. It profits a man greatly to know who he is, and it is not everyone who can butcher a family without it impacting on his emotions.

This realisation was quickly to prove useful to Anatole, since the next day, when he tried to sell the goods he had acquired, he, the drayman and the boy were quickly recognised as murderers, and while a crowd of Rafael's former associates beat the other two with staves until they were dead, Anatole managed to slip away to a secluded place where he then determined to become an assassin, since the killings had caused him no issue and it was only the selling of the stolen goods that was a problem. Anatole reasoned that if he could be paid for killings in advance there would be no problem at all, and he'd be spared the trouble of fencing contraband.

Here he was, wondering, years later, whether he should be coming up with a plan to make the greater part of Padge's fortune his. The thing that stopped him, and he would admit this to anyone, if asked, was that he was perfectly happy as he was, suited to his work, and very much enjoying every aspect of it. Unlike the others, he was sad to hear that Padge felt he needed their insurance, because his employer paid him a good wage, the work was not onerous, and who else would he work for once Padge was gone?

In his mind he composed a lament to Mr Padge, and though the man had no funeral, it would have been very fitting had Anatole performed it there.

Of Mick the Greek nothing is known, but what of Deaf Sam and Simon? Those two remain to be discussed, though both have been covered in part, and so we must return to the table at The Commodious Hour because if we did not do so it would be inequitable, and all assassins are equal in the eyes of the Mother of Mordew, and so in our eyes, which are subsidiary to hers, since this story is hers, whether we know it yet or not.

Of Deaf Sam it is necessary to speak without reference to sound, for reasons which are obvious. We should not say that we speak of him at all, which is an aural metaphor, instead we shall say that we deal with him, or treat of him, or put him front and centre, since those things do not make noise.

Which is not to assert that Sam – who was Deaf Sam to the others but Sam alone to himself – lived in utter silence. He heard many things, except that these sounds were not related to events in the world but were things his mind made of the truncated paths that did not reach the organs of hearing that the others had. He heard swooshings and ringings, high tones and low, tak-tak-tak and mah-mah-mah, and any number of meaningless noises so that he ignored them, mostly, unless they were useful for lulling him to sleep, or waking him up.

In his mind he did not think in words, since he had never heard any, nor had he troubled to learn to read, but he was fluent in a visual language that made distinctions of the most minute kind and attributed meaning to them, and other people's meaning he derived from the movement of their lips, or the wrinkles at the corners of their eyes, and these he loved in Sharli to the point at which he cared about little else.

A clarification is required. The Sharli of old he did not love – she was a hard creature, her features rigid and unkind, and though they made the motions of loving together, the feeling never grew in his heart. He loved her substitute, the new Sharli, there being an ineffable something in the way that she was now that provoked in him the loving sensation, which he felt deeply whether he was clothed or unclothed, during the day or night, asleep or awake.

There she was at the table, hiding her true thoughts by gazing at her knees, framed by empty bottles and the high backs of their chairs, in the foreground of a scene he had seen a hundred times: the restaurant lazily full, drinking off the richness of expensive lunches.

We have learned the pasts of some of these assassins, but Sam's present was what typified him, because he had never loved before, and here was Sharli, so perfect in even her imperfections, the slight drift of her left eye, the kink in the line of her nose, all of which combined with her other attributes – strength matched to intelligence, thoughtfulness matched to action, doing matched to being – and the otherwise obviousness of her beauty, that he could scarcely look away from her, even when the contract was laid on the table and Padge made his speech.

Money, this was no small thing, certainly, but only if it could be shared with her, this imposter who had improved on her original in ways that Deaf Sam could not understand.

If he had known that Clementina's liquid engineers had over-tuned her pheromonal balance, and that much of the source of his new love was a slight flaw in the mimicry of the odour the Assembly had made as camouflage, then he would have killed her on the spot, knowing himself to have been played for a fool. But he did not know this. He luxuriated instead in the delusion of his love for this not-Sharli. He didn't play in his mind battle scenarios, but the wooings and seductions that might take their mere physical bonding to another level entirely.

Until Padge's arrival, and for an hour or so afterwards, these internal love plans had all taken a similar path – an intense intimation of his authentic yearning for her that would overcome her natural assassin's suspicions – but now that the Padge information had sunk in, he turned his mind to a demonstration of his devotion. He would secure the eventual bounty from Padge's death by killing all the others, leaving him and Sharli alone to claim it, and then he would give his share to her. He would, at that moment, make it clear that he had known that she was an imposter all along and thus, by his efforts and his openness, win her heart where now he only possessed her body.

Granted, this plan overshadowed the one sticking point in the whole business – if she was an imposter, for whom was she working? – but Sam allowed himself to ignore this issue, love being like that, turning the eyes of even the deaf to inconvenient facts that they would prefer not to consider.

It is not easy to stare at an assassin – they have an ability to determine whether they are being observed, honed by years in the field – but Sam was used to taking pleasure from his other senses to supplement what he could not get from sight alone. He could smell her skin, which was redolent of the leather wax she used on the sheath of her dagger and the uppers of her boots. He could feel in his fingertips the slight rasp of her breath that too much smoking had made, the air forced between narrowed bronchioles. These were enough to add to his sight – her lips were contained in the reflection of a butter knife, one clavicle was in the bowl of a polished vase – and he could have watched her for hours, forever even, if only that was possible.

Then she stood, and he realised that Montalban was gone, along with the Druze, and she went after them, brushing her fingers over his shoulder as she left, and now he cursed his lack of hearing. In truth, though, if he had not been mooning over Sharli he would have read the progress of the conversation on the others' lips and would have known more surely what it was he needed to do.

That considered, he did what he would have done anyway, and followed Sharli shortly after, relying on his relationship – carefully cultivated over years – with all the doormen of all the establishments in a mile's radius to allow him to follow Sharli to where she was going, something he did without alerting her, despite her being on her guard throughout.

Simon only remains, and we know that he went to the mines and met the others there, since we said he went to call on the Mother of Mordew, so we only now need to know why. Perhaps we also need to have information about who he was. We have intelligence on the others – except the mysterious Mick the Greek – so why would we exclude Simon?

But why do we have intelligence on the others? Why have we returned to this gang of miscreants when we could equally have left them well alone and dedicated our time to more obviously important matters? Because those things that seem to not be relevant, those marginal things, those unspoken voices, are the very essence of some cities, are the source of its energies, are the important parts, even when this seems not to be so at all.

Mordew – that was a place that suited the concentration on one person very well, with all the others ignored or relegated to a subsidiary place, but Malarkoi – which was the place to where all these assassins would be sent – that was a place of many levels, of many centres, of many disparate and minority opinions, all coming together under the aegis of its Mistress into a unity. What is a unity, if not a unity of parts?

It should be said, despite the above, that Simon was the least interesting of the group. He mostly kept himself to himself, conserved his wealth by buying dividend-bearing interests in going concerns in the city, ate crackers and meat paste alone most nights, and slept on a straw mattress in a single cheap room. During the day he practised his slices and punches, and kneeings and knife-throwings, put targets of paper on distant trees and made his best efforts to hit them with thrown knives, caring as if they were living things and not circles and outlines.

When addressed, he had nothing much to say, parroting the last thing that had been said to him in a gin-house, or at a cockfight, and that in a solemn monotone, so that people were reluctant to continue conversing with him.

Like all the assassins he was, or had been until recently, a very beautiful person to look at, and therefore he was never wanting for company, even if that was of a very vacuous and tiresome sort. He performed his sexual role with whomever seemed to want him to, taking some pleasure in it, but he had tired even of this, preferring to spend the time he wasted on intercourse in repetitive and soothing calculations of returns on investment, and the possibility of retirement, and his eventual flight to some place where the standard of living was high while associated costs were low.

This preference was why he had decided to make himself plain-looking, even ugly. Then he would not attract other beautiful people, who were confident in their looks enough to bowl in on his privacy and force him out of it with their wiles and attractions. He sought, by transforming himself by turns into a ratlike creature, to relegate himself out of any category of superficial handsomeness. He would then be in a league with other people generally unconfident enough in their looks that they would not approach others but would always wait to be approached. Though he did not make himself so ugly that he would be ranked amongst the desperate, who, in their desperation, will do almost anything to attain a mate, and force themselves on another's attention in ways very much like the beautiful do in their entitlement, though for the opposite reason.

Some of the work he did himself, by dressing poorly, stooping his posture, and by wearing unpleasant colognes, but other things he went to a costumier for, and to a person talented in the cutting of hair, and to people who performed bonework on the face.

Those ignorant of cosmetic facial reconstruction would say that if someone needed to break the bone of the nose, or of the cheek, then surely there are ways of doing it very cheaply – entry into a boxing tournament in a rougher part of town, or picking a fight with a drunk and then failing to block their flailing blows – but this is not to know the sophistication with which bonework could be done, or the extent that this work could be more or less permanent.

He decided to hire a woman called Eleanor who, though expensive, could, with tools, enlarge or reduce any part of the face to order and within stated parameters. He went to her back room, which she kept soundproofed with pillows and blankets on the walls.

At first, she would not do it, seeing his face and knowing it to be something she could not labour over without spoiling. She was a beautiful person herself, with olive skin and pale brown eyes and a face so perfectly symmetrical that it was sometimes difficult to believe that such an object could exist in the world, so she felt a kinship with him, and an attraction too. When she told him this, and put her hand on his wrist, and drew him to her, he made her understand that this was precisely why he had come to her, to prevent what was happening now from happening ever again.

He said it with an angry curl on his lip.

This she found insulting, since no beautiful person likes to be rejected, and so she began the work for which he had sought to commission her on the instant, and certainly before her analgesic creams had had time to kick in.

First, she took a chisel to his chin, chipping away enough bone so that what had once been a firm jut was now a ratlike recession into the neck. She did not trim the excess skin, as she might have, so that the effect was accentuated by a stepped series of wrinkles that went from Simon's lower lip down to his Adam's apple.

Then she applied a depilatory to the same area, and prised wide the follicles of his top lip so the hair there grew thicker and more wiry.

She applied a restrictive cage to his teeth and by turning a cog she altered the angles of his incisors, mostly, but all the others too, so that they sloped back in the manner of a rodent.

She glued a prosthetic beneath the skin of his nose, to change its angle, and put drops in his eyes that made them redder than they should be.

493

Lastly, she plucked out the hair from his hairline, so it made his forehead sweep back. In every way she did what she was asked, which was to make him seem like a rat.

The effect he could not see immediately when she held the mirror up for him, defiant and irritated at the end of the procedures, because she had bandaged him up, but when he moved to seduce her in a way with which he had salved many irritated and defiant women in the past, he was pleased to see her flinch and step back, taking this as a sign of her newly found repulsion for him.

He paid her his coins, with extra for more bandages and eye drops, and returned to his straw cot. Here he waited through a fortnight, as she had suggested.

His landlady brought him soup and emptied his pot, and for the next two weeks he was very content with his own company. The only thing that disturbed his equanimity was the excitement and anticipation he felt at the prospect of returning to the world and seeing how it reacted to him. The other assassins would not blink, since they never did, but he was curious to see how the patrons at The Commodious Hour would regard him, since they had, until that day, to a man and woman, made him feel by their glances that they knew him to be a beautiful thing, and a proportion of them felt the need to attract his attention, or waylay him on the way to the facilities, or in some other manner alter the course of his life in ways he did not appreciate.

When eventually the day came for the bandages to be removed, he looked upon himself in the mirror with a kind of awed bemusement, seeing not his own face there but the face of an ugly man who had features very murine, and on whom, if he had seen him in the street, he would not have allowed his gaze to linger, feeling that there was nothing pleasurable there to enjoy.

Without waiting, Simon put on his waxed coat and his pointiest shoes and made his back crooked and held his arms in front of him, bent at the elbows. His moustaches, unmatched by any beard below since Eleanor's depilation, he pulled out long and straight, and he sidled into the street, where no one then spared him a second glance if they completed even a first.

This was like joy to him, to walk unregarded along the streets, and he took a long route and many detours to his meeting with Mr Padge, up and down the hill, from the Pleasaunce to the slums, in unfamiliar streets and places where he was well known. He excited no attention anywhere, and, because this was more than a temporary disguise, he felt from himself a great weight lifted off, permanently, of other people's expectations, so that when he took his place at the lunch table, the others the only people recognising him the whole way, he had never been happier in his life.

So unlike himself was he now that he went to the Mother of Mordew to re-register himself with her, fearing she would not recognise him when the time came to keep the contract. He need not have worried – her comprehension of the world went beyond superficial things, and she knew him immediately.

The consideration of Mr Padge's assassins is complete, except for one important thing: what these disloyal and untruthful scoundrels did not realise was that the Mother of Mordew, to whom they had all gone, was an avatar of the Mistress of Malarkoi. It was in this mode that she had communicated to Mr Padge, the very man whose contract each was trying to both fulfil and cheat on, in her successful attempts to make Nathan Treeves come to fruition. She had no interest in any of their betrayals, having her own plan to kill Clarissa Delacroix and resurrect Nathan Treeves so that he might take his throne in Waterblack, City of Death. He would, at the end, wreak such havoc that the warpling would intervene to end it, giving the Mistress the chance to do what she had always planned to do, which was to kill that god and take her place.

An account of what happened when Sharli and Deaf Sam arrived on the Island of the White Hills

ASSASSINS – even those who have recently been translated through the weft and the warp by their patron goddess, even those who find something missing inside themselves that they cannot define, even those who look at their partner and wonder at the force of their love for them – keep out of sight of the people they have come to kill. It is much of their work in fact, almost all the rest being to wait for a suitable time to strike with their favourite weapon.

So it was that the woman, the dog, the boy and his book, despite their various sensory particularities and magical proclivities, did not notice Sharli and Deaf Sam, who slunk through the sparse undergrowth and made no more noise than a grouse, or a fox, or an adder.

Sharli, who had left The Commodious Hour with the intention of going directly to the Mother of Mordew, had not been able to do it, Deaf Sam coming to her a short distance up the road to the mines. He took her by the arm and earnestly communicated with her in signs, only some of which she understood – he delivered them in an excited rush, and she was distracted by a worry, an anxiety, some problem, the details of which she couldn't now remember.

She could remember other things – Deaf Sam had marched her to the Mother, smiling, and she'd gone, thinking that that was what she'd have to do if she was going to behave like herself. This memory confused her now. Why did she have to behave like herself?

She was herself.

Sharli shook her head, blinked, then focussed on her work when that didn't help.

Their contracted targets – Clarissa and Bellows – were little more than specks, chatting and gesturing with the other two, trotting through the low, flower-covered hills in the distance.

There was a tightness in Sharli's chest. It was like in a dream, or from a repression, a heavy, pervasive constriction, for no reason. When she was a girl, sometimes she woke in the night and couldn't move. Paralysis pinned her down to the mattress, made her eyes stay open, made a silent scream with her mouth. There was nothing to see, no phantom that would account for it, but she felt an all-invasive fear, lying there in the darkness. Now she felt a waking version of that, a kind of choking need to say something, or to call out for help, but she didn't know why or how to do it.

Deaf Sam turned her face to his and made the shapes with his lips that she made when she said, 'What's the matter?' Sharli could read them, the shapes of her own words mirrored back to her, but she didn't know how to answer him.

She turned away and tried again to let her work rescue her. She signed that they should follow their targets, and then left Deaf Sam where he crouched, expecting him to come with her, which he did, eventually.

For the rest of the day, they tracked the party ahead, and by sundown the horrible feeling was gone and Sharli couldn't quite remember what the problem had been.

An account of what happened as Sharli and Deaf Sam watched their targets at camp

NIGHT FELL and Deaf Sam's sense that all was not right with the new Sharli had gone from a puzzlement, to an anxiety, to a certainty, to a plan. He was quick like that, his thoughts never needing to achieve a verbal definitiveness before his intuitions told him all he needed to know. This was a useful thing in an assassin, this efficiency of mind, and as he watched the moon coming from behind a wind-sped cloud to light the curves of Sharli's nose, and then the pinna of her ear, he knew that he would have to kill her.

We are not, probably, assassins, and we are assuredly not Deaf Sam, so we will need our hands held if we are to understand how he came to this conclusion.

He knew, earlier in the day, when they hit the earth of this new place, that there was something wrong with her. He was very attuned to her expressions, Deaf Sam, finding something so beautiful in their perfectly formed confidence and then, sometimes, their heart-rending lack of confidence, two sides of her that, combined, he had come to love. These expressions had come along when whoever was masquerading as the Sharli he had not loved in the past had arrived. He knew this as a less sensitive man would know if his friend was wearing a false nose; it was very plain to him, as it would be to us in that latter situation. The thing that he knew was wrong, was that, though he watched her closely all day, it was only the confident expression that he could see, even though there had been something bothering her, and never the other one.

It is difficult to understand this, so imagine Sharli, to him, was wearing a false nose.

He had been signing his love to her on the road up to the Cave of the Matriarch, and he had determined that he would tell her that he knew she was an imposter, that they should win Padge's fortune, and then that they should leave Mordew together and never return, to follow whatever life was authentic to her. He was not ignorant of the Assembly – he could think of no other organisation that would employ Sharli as a spy – and he wanted to tell her that he would gladly join her in the life she lived there, if she would have him. Perhaps he was overexcited, perhaps she was distracted, but she seemed not to understand him. Eventually, he stopped trying to explain and did what he often did, which was to substitute action for communication, taking her to the Mother so that they might both leave Mordew and then have more time to converse.

Sharli had seemed reluctant then, but that is often the case when a person is attempting to make you do something without first explaining why, so Deaf Sam had let himself be more assertive than he might otherwise allow, and they eventually came the Mother, who took them both and made them do as she wished, as is the way with gods.

During this whole time, she had been the Sharli he loved. He knew this very simply, but once they arrived in the Island of the White Hills, she was different.

Still, he did not immediately want to believe this fact, since he loved her. He told himself, at first, that he was mistaken, but by mid-afternoon he was sure of it. This was not the replacement of Sharli, that he loved, this was the original Sharli, for whom he had no feeling.

Why did he plan to kill her? Partially it was because she represented the loss of his love to him, but mostly for a man who is used to killing as a solution to his problems, then it is often the easiest way to resolve a difficult situation.

Then there was the matter of Padge's fortune, and the natural increase in his share if she was dead.

He watched her, making sure of his certainty, for the rest of that day.

Now, in the moonlight, his hand rested on the pommel of his dagger, and he wondered if it was time to do the deed that needed to be done.

An account of why Sharli became angry before launching her attack

SHARLI WATCHED from a distance through an extensible eyeglass Deaf Sam had bought her from a seller of useful instruments he'd met. The wise assassin only used it at night because otherwise the glint of sunlight on the lens had a habit of giving you away to a careful target. This lot weren't careful, and it was dark, so she made a comprehensive survey of their camp while the opportunity presented itself. They were, as far as she could see, largely unarmed if you didn't count the dog.

She was interrupted when Deaf Sam came and sat himself down in front of her, getting right in the way. She sat up, and tried to push him aside, but he caught her wrist and made signs at her.

He'd been like this the whole time, and it was getting on her nerves now.

'Look,' she said, pulling her arm away, 'I haven't got any secret to tell you.' She backed up her sign replies by talking out loud. In the moonlight he'd just about see her mouthing the words with her lips, but it wasn't about that – she wasn't not speaking just because he couldn't hear her. She wasn't the deaf one. 'Why do you keep going on?'

Deaf Sam started a complicated sentence, full of motions he was rushing in his now overfamiliar, irritated way, so that she couldn't work out what he meant.

'Forget it!' she said, not signing at all now and turning her back on him.

He stomped round to where she'd turned and made a new set of signs, but they didn't make any sense. 'Are you an imposter', is what she thought he'd signed, but that can't have been what he meant.

'Am I an imposter? Is that what you're asking?'

Deaf Sam, after a while in which strange emotions that Sharli couldn't understand played across his face, nodded.

She didn't reply, but instead slammed the eyeglass shut, took his hand, and slapped the bronze tube into it.

He took it, and Sharli stormed off into the darkness.

She thought to herself, as she left, that the sooner this job was over, the better, and that these next two targets were really going to get it.

On the Religion of the
Hollow Hill at Malvern

IMAGINE A HILL only a little shorter than a mountain, something that is steep enough to tire the legs quickly when walked up, but never so steep that it needs to be scaled with ropes. Firm resolve and good shoes are enough, occasionally some clambering and reaching, but never is there any sense that a walker will fall back down the way they have come if they happen to stumble. Two terranes, joined, of hard rock. A mile in length, this hill is, perhaps more, rising just under a thousand feet.

If you cannot imagine a hill without imagining the surface of it then picture grass and trees, ancient footpaths worn on convenient routes to the summit, small buildings at the lower levels, wells and springs. Do not waste too much effort on this, since it is the inside of the hill which is of concern, since this hill is hollow, the combination of those words making its name – the Hollow Hill.

It was made hollow, the Hollow Hill, through the efforts of the patron god of the cattle-headed people, who itself was cattle-headed. Entering through a cave in the lowest part of the hill, it smashed the material with its horns, scraped it out with its hoofed feet, scooped it out with its hands, lubricated its workings with the milk of its udders, which was as transparent as water and which still trickles through the standpipes the people of the outside of the hill use.

This is not plausible, some might say, and they would be right if they thought that a man was doing it, but Vigornia – the name this god gave itself – was a god, and for gods many things that are implausible for a man are, while taxing, while time-consuming, not impossible. Also, it had made the cattle-headed people in its own image – though some were bulls and some were cows, while it was neither – and these people helped in the work of their god, through the natural and overwhelming gratefulness a child feels towards its parents, since without them, where would that child be?

Nowhere.

Vigornia was a craven thing – just like cattle are. When roused, it would fight, making in the violence of its terrible fear intemperate fits of destruction, but its first instinct was always to run and then to hide, and the Hollow Hill was for this purpose. Gods are often made in pairs – one of light and one of dark, though which is which is a matter of argument – and the pair to Vigornia was Cren, the snake with the head of a person. It saw Vigornia and was appalled. Instantaneously, it vowed to undo any work that this thing did, because it was an abomination in its eyes that anything should live without a human head, since where, then, was that thing's reason?

Cren hated all things that had no reason, but Vigornia and its people more than anything, because it was of the same order of being as Cren itself, and had the power of grace and creation, which Cren knew was only properly given to it. The enmity between cattle and snake continues to this day – a cow will trample any snake that it sees, and that snake will poison the cow in its turn by biting its leg – and this is the source of it, this ancient pairing, and the resistance to it one felt from the other.

A snake is a brave creature, knowing that without bravery it can never live, since it must strike at its foes and kill them in order to eat, whereas a cow can live by grazing. Cren roamed the land, looking for prey, and with the cleverness and ambition of his person's head he filled every crack and dark place with his own kind, and made them slither beneath the surface of the seas of grass that cattle feed on.

So, what was the choice for Vigornia but to hide away? Except that its people's food was only to be found under the sun, and this was grass and some digestible plants like heather and gorse as, though its people had human stomachs, they could still eat plant fibre by virtue of Vigornia's grace, which was the gift to be able to do all those things that cattle do.

A coward's fear is always the most characteristic thing about him – if it was not, he would be known by a different name, like 'glutton', or 'miser' – so Vigornia and his people hid themselves pusillanimously inside their Hollow Hill even though they starved through hungering. When the lowest parts of the cavern were filled, still more cattle-headed people came in their herds and trampled upon the others. Anyone who has husbanded kine will know that a herd in movement will stop for nothing, and the herds went into the doorway of the Hollow Hill until their numbers were exhausted to nothing and so many of them were they there that they filled the whole place up to the top and blocked up the entranceway.

Outside was the slithering of snake bodies and the voices Cren and its people used to reason the cattle-headed men out of their hiding place. When this failed, they wrote sweet songs that might recall to their prey's cattle-headed minds the green grass of the plains, and the cool rains, and the wide open vistas.

Vigornia's people were always too fearful to come out, and Vigornia itself, surrounded on all sides and above and below, made its own songs, which it lowed to them as a mother cow lows to her calves and a father bull barks to make them feel that they are in the presence of strength against their foes, both at the same time. In the absence of food, it let leak from its udders the clear milk; in this way did the god tend its flock and soothe them from their agonies.

Soon Vigornia's milk dried up and the people began to starve in earnest, and the snake sounds from without grew in volume as they gathered, and it was clear that all was lost, even the life of the god itself.

Into that place, then, came the Mistress of Malarkoi in the form of a woman with a woman's head, and she made the space inside the Hollow Hill one of her Realms. This Realm she made bigger to accommodate them all, and its air was like food and drink to the cattle-headed people. She lifted from them the burden of their weight so that they might all hover comfortably and no longer crush those beneath them. Their waste was consumed by innumerable insects, too tiny to see, and these tiny things excreted into the air the food the cattle-headed people ate, once it was clotted enough together.

She taught them a rough sort of speech, favoured to their large tongues and full of long vowels like their lowings, so that they might communicate with each other and make stories.

In short, she made of her Realm a place perfect for Vigornia and the cattle-headed people, safe from predation, with endless food and water and always near each other and their god.

All she took from them in payment for this gift was whatever little light came in through the cracks in the earth above them, and with it their eyes, for which they had no more need, and the second-born of all their children she had them send to her at birth, so that she could use their life energies in her magics, and so that those children should join with her and sing the songs of their people in her Heaven, which they all might attain and so be reunited should they tire of their own blissful place.

If she ever called upon them for soldiers, she made them vow that they would come, and then she left them.

Her tribute was to be made each year at a henge the cattle-headed people built for her where the entranceway had been, and another she had them build just the same, though the purpose of this second henge was hidden and both were rickety structures, always needing shoring up because it is hard for a blind person with a cattle head to do masonry, and with no weight a stone will not long remain where it is put.

So, when they were not living their blissful lives of commune and storytelling, Vigornia's people tended their henges and kept them in good order and waited for the day when they might be called upon, and this was the only fear that people felt, because Cren and his people could not come to this new Realm, which the Mistress had nested within her own Heaven. She had hidden the Door with spells so that, with time, the snakes were forgotten except only as figures in stories. Such figures cannot be said to be real, no matter how real the things the stories referred to were, since there is some disjunction between the telling of tales in words and the world as it is, and neither can a word *be* a thing, nor can it *summon* a thing, and so were the calves of the cattle-headed people soothed, even when they learned of the bite of fangs, venom, the narrow-slit pupils of their former foes, and the hissing dart of cloven tongues through their being in their lullabies.

On the Religion of the Realm
of the Wolf Pack and the White Stag

THE ISLAND of the White Hills, like all places, has a particular variety of flora and fauna, a unique network of watercourses and lakes, hot and cold winds, irregular lattices of paths and boundaries, loam and peat and humus and mushrooms and trees. We gather these things together, know them for what they are in their difference to other places.

This melange, rather than the people who populate an area and make their culture there, can be synonymous with the place, in certain religions.

One type of religion – let us use the shorthand 'Druid' – takes the mixture of a place as suitable for worship. It is as if things of demonstrable and universal value – pleasure, love, work, struggle, solidarity – are all to be substituted for flora and fauna, even if those things are vermin and weeds and stagnant water and runnels and mud. For a Druid of the fourth level of the Golden Pyramid of Malarkoi, the human things of the world were discarded and inhuman things put in their place, and these then worshipped above all others.

The Druids there offered up their lives to the preservation of 'nature', to the exclusion of all other considerations.

One of them might have gone to a distant place and communed with a curlew, listened to its calls, bowed down to it, made a curlew-headed offering to it from spittle and reeds, and sung it songs in a curlew voice. If the curlew paid them no heed, then why should it? It didn't share the concerns of a Druid, since it was unaware what one was. It was unaware even that it was a curlew. The Druid's careful worship was not a favour that would be returned, since a curlew would drink the blood of that Druid's firstborn child if it did it the least good, and it was only the fact that blood-meals were indigestible to birds of this kind that such an event never happened.

Druids did not take this as any obstacle to their worship, though, since reciprocity was not a requirement in their religion. Indeed, there was a masochistic streak in them, feeling that their own tendency to self-interest – one that was shared amongst the organisms they venerated – was something of which they were ashamed, since they saw themselves as very powerful, but inclined to evil, and were therefore both arrogant and punishable at the same time. Was there not something inherently self-regarding in making sacrifices of their time to a world which was otherwise so venal? Wasn't it something only the strongest and most powerful could hope to do without dying?

Ask a weasel or an otter what sacrifices it would make for a duckling. They would not name any.

A Druid would see a falcon in the air and kneel, finding it to be a perfect thing, and they would prohibit the gathering of its eggs, or the laying of poisoned bait, even if that creature fed on the leverets on which their neighbours' children relied. They thought that they were exempt from the great struggle for life, and that their Island of the White Hills was free of the dreadful and endless warfare that one species performed on another, down through the scales of size from the man-sized, to the mole-sized, to the worm-sized, to the amoeba, down and down until even one protein sought to supplant another and the very conditions of existence were predicated on violence.

The Druids also held rivers and streams in high esteem and named them. They named hills and bushes, caves and cliffs, and the Island of the White Hills was made of these. Some lands are deserts, and others are jungles, but this land was made of what Druids named, and on it they built henges and circles of stones, and sang poems and lays, and wrote paeans to it.

In its waters they swam naked, on its hills they walked, into its caves they inserted themselves, and while a modest person may have done this, they did it with their arrogance, thinking that their doing of it, which was no more than a stoat or a vole did when it lived where it lived, was somehow worthy of note. A stoat did not praise himself when he dashed low through the undergrowth, and nor did a vole weep when he caused the riverbank to fall in and muddy the water. If he suffocated a dragonfly nymph, he did not lose sleep over it – he did not know it at all.

Creatures live brief lives and are predated upon by anything that predates – it is not theirs to waste energy on sadness and guilt. Even if the otter drives the frog, whose tadpoles and spawn it eats with glee, into non-existence, it does not cause in it the flickering of a whisker. Nor does the frog grieve, since it is only an individual and an ignorant one at that. It was the Druid that saw the weft-spark and knew it as a shape – all other things understood themselves to be a thread in the world-tapestry, the pattern of which is meaningless light infinitely repeating.

The Island of the White Hills is the Mistress of Malarkoi's land, and she knows everything and every place and every-one in it. She knows that there are differences of opinion, differences of belief, and that everyone is ontologically and epistemologically distinct, even within their species. Therefore, she does what she does, which is to make heavens for all those who believe things which are compatible with each other and, for those who cannot believe things that others believe, she makes solitary heavens suitable for them, exacting only her requirements of second-born children to aid in her magic, which everyone is willing to give.

For the Druids, who wished always for themselves to be debased in the name of the lesser things – a ladybird or an adder, a rivulet or a puddle, three wasps circling a decaying plum – she made room for them in the realm of the Wolf Pack and the White Stag, those gods who share a place, since their interests are closely linked.

In this way the other realms were spared the presence of the Druids, and their love of nature was no longer such a tiresome presence in her lands, where they would always be trampling those things, in their ignorance, that they believed to be incorrect, not understanding that all that happened was redeemable in the Mistress's eyes, and that to leave things as they were was the perfect way.

If all the bees died, and all the waters were poisoned, and every frog struggled through its life with five legs where four was the desirable number, then this just hastened the end for bees and rivers and frogs of their redundant labours. She would take them directly to their heavens, where they could live endlessly in delight, since she had found for them inside the weft that iteration of time and matter that suited them most and was able to send them there where all was always perfect for them, asking only for their second-born.

The Wolf Pack live in their realm with the White Stag, and in an inversion of the natural order, the day belongs to the wolves and the night to the Stag, this because the Stag is the superior, and it is his wish to have the night for himself, since he prefers to bathe in moonlight, and the night is where this substance is found. The wolves, though they have no choice in the matter, are happy with the day since the Mistress makes this a time of slaughter, which is what a pack delights in.

Wolves snarl and jump, snap and bite, claw and growl to the exclusion of all else, and the realm is full of things to which their aggression can be directed, because the Pack has made a bargain with the Mistress that their realm shall be stocked by the Druids as a good game warden stocks hunting land, filling it with the best sport in vast quantities, she taking for herself the Spark remaining of each thing killed, and every second-born pup.

The realm is in the image of the Island of White Hills – a large part of it – and so is rolling grasslands and forest, mountains and plains, lakes and streams and rivers, all of a sort familiar to the Wolf Pack and challenging enough to make hunting enjoyable. Into this land the Mistress makes to exist mice and rats, rabbits and hares, roosters and chickens, pheasants and quail, lambs, and a hundred other delicious types of beast – newts, toads, fledglings of all types of birds, fox cubs, spineless hedgehogs, young boar – and in numbers so great that with the turn of a head a wolf can devour a mouthful like a horse feeds from its nosebag. There are wild horses too, though these only come as evening falls, and five of the pack take one, four to the legs and one at the throat.

Up into the air are sent mauled leverets, rabbit tails and heads, the entrails of the larger creatures, and the punctured corpses of anything too small to divide into pieces. Mortal wolves have very strong neck muscles, and wolves who are part of a god exceed the strength of these by many orders of magnitude, so up this gory by-product of their killing goes, and across the land it rains down blood and flesh, bones and organs. The wolves leap up and snap the air when they are not killing, making a joyous noise and bathing themselves wherever they can in blood rain.

How many wolves are there?

Some gods are singular, some are twofold, making a unity of opposites, others are trinities, but the Wolf Pack is variable in number, never fewer than ten but in this realm often many hundreds, as the food allows. The ranks of a pack of wolves swell and diminish with the available prey, but, thanks to the Mistress of Malarkoi, there is always enough food. The only limiting factor is the White Stag, who returns the realm to his preferred state before each dawn.

Stags do not revel in killing, even if, in kemmer, they will butt heads with rivals and rear and charge. When night falls, then, and the cold and still precision which the monotone light from the moon gives to the world makes sharp edges of things, all delineated in shadows, the Stag makes the wolves still, so that they became like statues of themselves, one half of them lit, the other half cast in darkness, and though they are splashed in blood and of disparate colours of pelt they all become grey and black.

There is a monumental quality to perfect stillness, a universal sense that takes over the specific, so the snarling of their lips and the frenzied disposition of their limbs speak not of what they have been doing before the White Stag freezes them, but instead of some inherent quality of the world, which is violence and destruction, only rendered abstract.

In opposition to this, the White Stag breathes and its heartbeat throbs, and the great tangle of its antler rack cuts the air with every shake of its head. It bellows and all the rent and wounded creatures move again, down to the parts of them, so that an otter whose side had been split open so that its guts are dragged out, those guts snake back into the grateful maw teeth made, make warm homes beneath the fur and skin which stitches itself back together seamlessly. Eyes that glazed become bright and clear again, and if they are not in their sockets, they roll back perfectly to find them, the gravity of the world not acting, in the White Stag's presence, towards 'down' but towards 'alive', and all things and parts of things obey that rule as everything in the material realm will always fall when dropped.

The White Stag trots through the viscera which everywhere springs up, hooves making flesh dance, blood turning from splashed drops to rivulets, to streams that run back in time to plump empty veins and give hearts liquid to beat around. Screams become inhalations, fear replaced with cold, fresh air, and from silent mouths come chitterings and chirpings, high calls and chirrups.

All the silenced animals find their voices again.

This continues past midnight, the single god undoing the work the god-in-many have done. This is the triumph of the White Stag, to undo the death its counterparts do, and since one thing that can undo what many can do this makes it better, but not by such a margin as might be supposed – the night passes in its work, but what follows night? Morning, and sunrise is the end of the White Stag's dominion over the world. What is the purpose of its work unless it is to make whole the world for a new ravening when the wolves wake again?

As the light comes new over the horizon, and colour returns to the Island of the White Hills, the White Stag turns and gallops away, startled by the brightness, and the spell it has cast on the wolves is undone by its absence.

When the Stag departs it returns the wolves to motion. They fall on four paws, those who leapt to snap, or they stand up from their crouching, and there is no taste in their mouths of blood, nor is their weight in their bellies, nor still the fall of down and fluff, the splatter of ichor, since all those things are back where they were, in the bodies of the prey animals. Hunger is returned to the Wolf Pack.

What of the animals the White Stag resurrects by the returning of the place to the preferred weft-state? They are given life only for them to be killed anew.

Except not quite.

When the realm represents a state of the perfect weft, as the stag achieves each morning, that is not to say that all such states are the same, or that they progress the same way. There is no saying which number will appear on the face of a die, rolled in a realm from one state of the weft – its motion is uncontrollable and the number it shows is determined by the possibilities open to it, each realm limited to those possibilities, but not within them. The weft contains all possible Reals, the gods only controlling outcomes under the aegis of the existence of the weftling, who allows for such manipulations. But he is dead, and his will cannot be enforced as it once was.

Each Wolf moves in ways possible but not preordained, and its will is always expressed, particularly since it is part of a god itself, and it may also do the impossible, in part, as its godhood allows. On each day it is not necessary that the same creature will be killed in the same way, and so they are not forced into an endless cycle of killing and rebirth. Instead, the Mistress of Malarkoi takes those who have tired of dying and she makes another heaven for them to live in, insisting only that their second-borns should be given to her.

Those she removes to a higher heaven, she replaces with new creatures who have souls eager to do her bidding, knowing that she serves their best interests.

A creature of the Realm of the Wolf Pack and White Stag becomes first prey for the Wolf Pack and then beneficiary of the grace of the White Stag before they pass to their true state, which is the endless bliss the Mistress makes for them – to live as they prefer and to give tribute to their Mistress so that she might continue her magics.

So it is, then, that innumerable souls of small mammals are gathered by the Mistress, and birds and amphibians and reptiles and even insects, and taken to the realm suited to them, which she has found through her descryments, and all these places are anchored on the sixth level of the Golden Pyramid of Malarkoi, which contains all the realms the Mistress supervises.

If you go to that place and find it empty then that is because you have not made the proper sacrifices to enter the realm, or have approached the portal in the wrong order, or on the wrong day, or because you are impure of heart or intention, or because you have given your pledge to the Assembly, whom the Mistress has barred from ever entering, to their eternal dismay.

A Note from Portia to Prissy

HI PRISSY,

Thanks for agreeing to take on the Mistress-ship (if that's a word!) of Malarkoi. It's a confusing place – a few things to help you get oriented.

The part you get to run is in the 'perfect material real'. It's where you were born and where you've been living until now. It's 'perfect' because it's (supposed to be) perfectly aligned with the form of the weftling – more on that in a moment. It's 'material' because there's also a perfect immaterial real, and this one has matter in it, where the other one only has ideas. It's 'real' because reality is something your mind makes when it combines material and immaterial things.

You could call it the material realm for short.

The material realm exists because of a thing called the weft. What's that? Well, the weft is everything that's ever happened and could ever happen, to matter and ideas, solidified into… let's say a ball? It's a ball the size of everything, and everything that happens, or could ever have happened, is in it. There's no time there – at least in the way we think of it – so everything is kind of still. Don't worry if this is hard to imagine, just go with it. It'll sort of make sense eventually.

In this ball are spaces where nothing happened and nothing could have happened. These spaces are filled with the weftling, or God. All the spaces joined together make up his body and his nervous system, all that kind of thing. I imagine a chick inside an egg – the chick is the weftling, the yolk and the white are the possible things in the material realm.

Now, which came first, the chicken or the egg? Some people believe the weftling came first, and that's what decided what could and couldn't happen in the material real. The weft is

515

a solid egg, the weftling is the impossible, if the weftling was shaped differently, different things could be possible or not possible, right? This is why people call the weftling God, because he makes possible things possible.

Because of that, you can think of the weftling's form as being the same as his will. If he changed his shape a bit, he could change the possible. The perfect material real is perfect because the form/will of the weftling made it that way. He could have made it another way by being different, right?

When he was alive, he did do that. He'd change his form, and then some things that were previously possible would become impossible, and some impossible things would become possible. Because he was the weftling, these newly possible things happened. People called them miracles.

No doubt you have some objections. What about time? How can something that lives in a timeless state do things? Well, the answer is to do with the immaterial realm, but don't think about it too much – it's too confusing. Just remember this is a metaphor that kind of works for people working in three physical dimensions. Actually, don't worry about dimensions either. Or metaphor.

Just breathe through it.

Anyway, the weftling, for one reason or another – blame Nathan's dad, if you want – is dead, and his presence in the weft is decaying, forming all sorts of perversions of his form and his will around the edges of the possible and the impossible. The Master uses this fact for his magic, the Assembly use it to power their machines, Clarissa's up to something, not sure what. I've been using it here in Malarkoi to manipulate the intermediate realms, which was something the weftling previously prevented.

Intermediate realms:

The perfect material real inherits from its perfect fit with the weftling the perfect balance between the material and the immaterial. Think of the material and the immaterial as stuff and ideas. Stuff you can see, touch, breathe, interact with, ideas you can think, understand. You can't have one without the other – matter is entirely undifferentiated until concepts are applied to it, and concepts are meaningless until applied to objects. What about concepts without physical referents? All concepts need a material brain to conceive them, or understand them, otherwise they aren't concepts.

Anyway, don't get bogged down.

In the real, stuff and ideas, the material and immaterial, are balanced, and the weftling holds that balance in place. Remember that ball? Well, you can think of the perfect material real as being on the outside of it, and in the middle of the ball is the immaterial realm of ideas, which is all the thoughts and concepts that make up understanding, but without any material instance. We live on the outside of the ball, but if you were to peel back the surface...

Think of an onion!

The material realm is the outermost layer of that onion, but peel it back and underneath there's a very similar 'intermediate' realm that's mostly of the material realm, but with a slightly higher immaterial component. And because the weftling's edges are rotting, in these intermediate realms the boundaries between the possible and the impossible are a bit more flexible. On the outside of the onion, things are pretty similar to the material real, but when you peel down deeper, when the concepts start to diverge from the real the weftling made, there are all sorts of different reals, nothing like the place you live, where impossible things are real.

The further in you go, the stranger it gets, and there are places that you can't live in, but what I've been doing is what's called 'scrying' into the intermediate realms for places that people might like to live in. Some of my earliest scrying found places that were useful for bringing up Dashini – I anchored these with 'spells' to the levels inside the Pyramid, and I kind of worked my way up to the top until I ran out of levels. At the top I made the biggest realm, and then I made more pyramids inside that one, and into those pyramids I anchored what people think of as their heavens.

517

I say 'I' – it turned out to be a lot of work, so I made versions of myself to live inside some of the levels, and let them do as they and I wanted. Some of them, I sent back into the material realm to make sure nothing too much interferes with what goes on in here.

Beware of that, by the way. I'm not telling you what to do, but when there's more than one of you running around it kind of undermines the reality of everything and makes it harder to take yourself seriously. Ditto re. the intermediate realms – go too far in, or nest too many realms inside other realms, and things start to break down. The weftling wasn't a complete fool – he knew how to keep things on the straight and narrow – one real, one heaven, one hell – very easy to manage.

I can't say I haven't made mistakes in this department – I definitely have.

Anyway, part of being the Mistress of Malarkoi, in the material realm, is that you get to scry into the realms. You can use this in all sorts of ways – summoning firebirds requires you to scry into their demonic realm and bring them into this one. Magic, spells, all that, is a similar process. Taking things from other realms, or from the immaterial realm, or the weft, and bringing it into the material realm. And vice versa.

Now we come to the downside.

The weftling could do all of what he did because he was made of Spark. Nathan inherited most of that, and thankfully he doesn't have the first idea what he's doing with it, but living things all have the Spark too. Unfortunately, for those of us who aren't murderous psychopaths, you'll need to release Spark to scry and use magic. The more material the realm is where you want impossible things to happen, the more Spark you'll have to release. There are various tricks you can use to enhance the Spark, but there's no getting round the fact that sacrifices are required. Unless you have God-Flesh, of course, but Sebastian's got a monopoly on that...

Hence, you know, the war.

My strategy? Sacrifice material world people – they give off the most energy – and use that to do work in the intermediate

518

realms. Because those are more conceptual, they don't need as much Spark to manipulate. Think of it like the difference between imagining a bird – the immaterial realm – and making one – the material realm. Birds are easy to imagine, but very difficult to make.

I balance up my sacrifices with heaven-making. I think my people are happy with the bargain. They say they are, but I do realise there's a power imbalance – they probably wouldn't feel comfortable telling me they weren't happy...

Try not to think about it too much.

At least I didn't go unrepentant, like Nathan's father did, and leave the sacrifices hanging... I suppose he planned to instantiate them into the real later. Waterblack and all that.

Anyway, I'm going off-topic. This is just a note to let you know some of the basics. Sorry if it doesn't make much sense. I've left you some books, some artefacts, and the realm you're in is a very slow one, so take your time, find your way around, and help yourself to the food and drink.

I look forward to seeing how you get on.

Don't worry about Dashini – I'll make it up to her.

Oh yes! Why is it called Malarkoi? Well, I like to think it's because of all of the 'malarkey' that goes on here!

Honestly, though, Sebastian named it. He said it meant weak, soft, effeminate, that kind of thing, in ancient Greek. There was something about wanking, too. I think he meant it as an insult. Whatever, we all ran with it, and it stuck. The spellings went out of whack in the early days, so not sure what happened there. Change it if you want.

Best of luck,
Portia
The (former!) Mistress of Malarkoi